Nigel Colborn is a succes̶~~...~~ journalist.
He appears regularly on BBC Radio 4's *Gardener's Question
Time* and contributes widely to the rural press. He is a fellow
of the Royal Society of Arts and a member of the Royal
Horticultural Society's Committee 'A' judging at major
flower shows including Chelsea.

Nigel Colborn has written numerous books on gardening and
country living as well as short stories. *The Congregation* is his
second novel. He travels extensively and lives in Lincolnshire
with his wife and two sets of twins.

THE
CONGREGATION

Nigel Colborn

WARNER BOOKS

A *Warner* Book

First published in Great Britain
by Warner Books in 1996

Copyright © Nigel Colborn 1996

The moral right of the author has been asserted.

A CIP catalogue record for this book
is available from the British Library.

ISBN 0 7515 1461 6

Typeset by Palimpsest Book Production Limited,
Polmont, Stirlingshire
Printed and bound in Great Britain by
Clays Ltd, St Ives plc.

Warner Books
A Division of
Little, Brown and Company (UK)
Brettenham House
Lancaster Place
London WC2E 7EN

For Rosamund

Acknowledgements

Thanks to Juliet Burton, for her helpful advice at the outset of this project, and to Yette Goulden whose original advice on the meshing of the two stories was more valuable than either of us knew when we were working together. Thanks, also, to Alice Wood, my editor at Little, Brown – not only for correcting my glaring errors, but also for listening so carefully. And above all, deep appreciation to my family for tolerating the moods and frustrations that beset aspiring novelists and particularly thanks to Ros, whose criticisms are so constructive.

PART ONE

STIR UP SUNDAY

Chapter One

———

'"Stir up, we beseech thee, O Lord, the wills of thy faithful people;"' intoned the Reverend Jerome Daniels, Rector of Wychgate Saint Peters, '"that they, plenteously bringing forth the fruit of good works . . ."'

Dear God, just look at them, he thought. Sunday Next Before Advent and what have we? Twelve rather grey souls, including me. And, dear God, just look at me! Fifty-six on Wednesday and what great mark have I made on the pages of history? Don't ask! Don't even ask! He glanced down, past the convexity amidships, where his belly fractionally altered the outline of his robes, to the toes of his Dunlop wellingtons, poking out from underneath his not quite white alb. He had discovered that such unclerical footwear enabled him to wear extra socks to fight the cold that crept up from the damp floor of Saint Peter's Church. At least they're black, he thought. He had developed a loathing for green wellies after what he privately called the Kensington Coup – wealthy Londoners buying all the best houses and going 'country'.

So far, though, Wychgate had attracted few of what Jerome's *Independent* called the 'chattering classes'. It was such a small village and not very pretty, with its single main street running downhill past the sinister Pyson Wood to the narrow, twisting basin of the river Dene. The few good houses were dotted about among more humble stone cottages but the period feel was spoilt by a cluster of brick bungalows and six council houses plumb in the centre. The church was inconveniently far from the rest of the buildings and there was no shop, no post office and no village green.

Jerome raised his head – rather a fine one with high cheek bones, an aquiline nose, kindly grey eyes that crinkled at their corners and a clerical shock of silvery grey hair – from the *Book of Common Prayer* and surveyed his flock.

The front eight pews were empty. Further back, in ones and twos, the congregation half knelt and half sat in that embarrassed stoop that, among Anglicans, passes for praying. Next to the iron stove that had not been lit since the Suez Crisis, the Pilkington family pew held but one occupant. Back near the door, on a bench not usually resorted to unless every other seat was taken – because it was so draughty and so removed from the rest of the nave – sat the newest inhabitant of Wychgate Saint Peters. Jerome wondered who she was at first, in the poor lighting down near the vestry, but then recognised her from the chance meeting they had had in early November, when he had seen her opening the front gate of Weir House.

Nobody knew why it was called Weir House, when it was so far from the river, but most agreed that it was the second finest house in Wychgate and Jerome loved its eighteenth-century brick elevations and curved Flemish gables. Set but a few yards back from the village street, with a neat walled front garden and wrought-iron gate, it was more like a small but elegant town house than a country dwelling.

'I'm afraid you're out of luck,' he had said. 'There's no one there. In fact, the place has been unoccupied for months.' Because she was so pallid and so starved-looking, in a dreadful old herringbone tweed coat – tailored for a man as far as he could tell – he had assumed that she was some kind of vagrant. She had turned from the gate to stare at him with blank eyes, and then had shivered and pulled the coat – surely it *was* a man's; in fact Gieves and Hawkes circa 1950 if he wasn't mistaken – more closely round her shoulders. She had seemed about to say something and then to have forgotten exactly what. Probably the dog collar, he had thought. It often had that effect on people. 'I'm afraid there's no one there,' he had repeated and then, 'can *I* do anything to help?'

'Actually I, ahm . . .' the voice was hoarse and sleepy but the intonation distinctly upper-crust. She had seemed not to know what to say next when the front door of Weir House had suddenly been flung open and a large woman had emerged. The girl had gasped, a look of fright replacing the blankness on her face for the briefest instant.

'Are you coming in, *dear*, or what?' The words of the question may have been solicitous but the large woman's tone was too strident for it to be anything but an order.

'Good afternoon!' Jerome had raised his wide-brimmed trilby – a rather flashy number he'd bought in a moment of extravagance at Bates's in Jermyn Street. He'd wanted brown but that would have made him look too much like a racehorse trainer so he'd settled for deep navy. Anything but clerical black, he'd decided. 'Daniels is the name, though I like people to call me Jerry.' No one did. Apart from close friends, people in Wychgate called him 'Mr Daniels', or 'Rector', but there had been an occasion when he tried to calm down an aggressively drunken parishioner who had called him a 'hypocritical fucker', and had been shocked to instant sobriety when Jerome had replied that he had better behave or he'd have his fucking ears boxed. 'Nice to meet you,' he had then said, beginning to feel awkward. By her mien, it was clear that the large woman had every right to be striding in and out of Weir House. 'I didn't know there was anybody here.'

'Well there is.' She had seemed unwilling to elaborate.

The young woman found her tongue at last. 'We, ahm, we plan to move in here. In, er . . .' and lost it again.

'Then, welcome to Wychgate Saint Peters,' Jerome had said. Part of the Kensington Coup? He dismissed the idea. No all-terrain vehicle, no cow-dung coloured shooting jackets and no green wellies.

'You'd better come in, my lady!' the large woman had said. 'You're getting cold.'

'I'm, ahm, Imogen Fitzgerald,' the girl had said, and then reiterated: 'We're moving in here . . . soon.' She took off a thick, sheepskin glove and held out a hand that was translucent white, in the dying winter daylight, with a touch of blue – a bit like sour milk, Jerome thought. He took it gently, thinking that one of his usual hearty handshakes would crush her bones like chalk. It was a cold hand, in spite of the glove, but the skin had felt surprisingly smooth and the fingers had clung for a moment, not with steady pressure, but with an anxious flutter.

'Your friend is right,' Jerome had said after a moment, letting go her hand so that she could replace the glove. 'You do look rather cold. I'll call one day soon, when you're settled in. If you like.'

'Not my friend,' Imogen had replied, 'that's Mrs Crowe.' And with that she had, quite suddenly, emitted an odd little laugh – a sort of giggle followed by a sharp intake of breath. A sob? And had scarpered up the front path to the closing door. Rich, Jerome had judged, in spite of being dressed like a scarecrow; but clearly a raving loony. And that minder! Almost immediately, he had been smitten with guilt for jumping to such conclusions about the girl and for being so uncharitable about the large woman.

He had paused over the Collect for too long. In the tiny congregation heads were being raised, prayerful hands removed from foreheads, eyebrows cocked. He recovered himself quickly: '"May" . . . Aaah – hm! . . . "May of thee be, plenteously rewarded."'

Alone in the family pew, enclosed by a low, carved oak door which swung on brass hinges once regularly oiled and polished, now squeaky and crusted with verdigris, Michael Pilkington was neither kneeling nor leaning forward. A minor leg wound, sustained during a madcap raid twenty-three miles from Tripoli in 1943, had left him with slight stiffness in the knee. Over the years, as all his joints had grown more creaky, the knee became increasingly difficult to bend and nowadays he had difficulty walking without a stick. Sitting suited him better anyway and, since his seventy-fifth birthday last July, he had also decided to stop standing up for the hymns. Jerome, he knew, would be sympathetic. Michael had no friends but Jerome was the nearest thing. The unscheduled silence from the altar made him glance up. The rector's lapses were getting more frequent lately and he wondered how the man could keep forgetting his lines. After all, he had the prayerbook open in front of him.

As Jerome finished the Collect, Michael shifted his position slightly, sitting at an angle to the pew so that he could stretch out his bad leg. In ragged response to the cue from the front, the congregation settled more comfortably to listen to the Epistle. Michael tried to attend at first. A chunk of Old Testament. Good! There was always more drama and excitement among the goings on of the Israelites and that vengeful, spiteful Being they worshipped than all those improving words from Saint Paul. But his mind wandered after the first sentence. The greenish stain of algae, down the north wall had got bigger, he was sure, and the leak just above the altar must be getting worse too. Why else would the Rector be wearing wellingtons? Heaven knew where the village would find the money to patch up the damage. There were so few churchgoers these days and Jerome didn't seem to help much. Not that it needed an evangelical firebrand to harangue the masses – that would be awful – but if only he could be, well, unequivocal about something once in a while.

Saint Peter's wasn't a pretty church but it was old and, Michael felt, needed more looking after than it was getting. The Romanesque tower dated back to before 1300 and had some of the finest rounded arch windows he had ever seen. There were remnants of quite a pretty rood screen and one fifteenth-century tomb which always delighted visitors because it depicted a mediaeval lord and his lady in bed. Side by side they lay, snug under the cold limestone sheets, gazing chastely upwards, their palms together in silent prayer and, on their faces, a serene expression that, to Michael, told of a lifetime of loving companionship.

Whenever he glanced at that tomb or, for that matter, whenever he saw families doing things together or couples linking their arms, he wondered what it might have been like, not to have led a solitary life. Not that he wanted for company. He could look back on a lifetime of Mess Dinners, shoots in the autumn, trout fishing trips in spring and summer garden parties – all occasions where voices rang and merriment sparkled. In the army, especially during the War, and later, around the county he had made acquaintances in droves and, in summer, there were visitors to his magnificent garden almost every day. But love – a deep, loving companionship that was quite another thing. In all his seventy-five years, Michael had experienced that but once. Before it could drift into painful territory, he forced his mind back to the present.

'" . . . and they shall dwell in their own land."' Jerome finished reading the Epistle and the congregation, except for Michael, shuffled to their feet to hear the Gospel. The story of the five loaves and fishes followed, stirring more sediment at the bottom of the old man's memory. Cricket teas, summer picnics on the banks of the Dene, when it was clean enough to swim in, during heatwaves. Not long after the Great War, the village boys used a secret spot for bathing. It could be reached only by crossing the field behind Pyson Wood and then tunnelling your way through a blackthorn hedge that had overgrown to become a huge thicket, armed with vicious thorns. The leafy tunnel was difficult to spot and had an entrance too dark and small to admit an adult. Once they were safely through, the gang of swimmers could shed clothes, unobserved, and jump into the cool, clear waters. Someone had fixed a length of rope to the branch of an ash tree that overhung the water so that the boys could swing from this into the river. In normal life, nakedness would have caused mortifying embarrassment but here, it was acceptable, indeed, proper for the gang whose eldest member had yet to pass his thirteenth birthday, to scamper about squealing like pink piglets. Because of the proximity of the Dene, every boy in Wychgate could swim from an early age.

Michael knew about the bathing place but was not allowed to go, or to associate with the village children. His father forbade it.

'It is not your station in life to consort with such people,' he had said one Christmas holidays, when he had found out that Michael was in the habit of playing football with the sons of farm workers who lived in tied cottages in the village. 'You have your prep school chums,' he had added.

'Yes, Father, but—' The small boy wanted to say that there was so little to do, rattling about the Manor House with no brothers or sisters, no mother and only one old housekeeper living in. His father, who spent most of his time in his study or away in London, held up his hand to prevent any remonstrations.

'In a couple of years, you will be starting at Barleythorpe and can make plenty of new friends there. Friends of your own kind.'

'Yes, Father.'

'Meanwhile, you'll just have to amuse yourself as best you can.'

And that had, pretty well, been that. At his prep school, he was liked by almost everyone; had dozens of invitations to visit other boys' homes, in the holidays, and had invited plenty to stay with him at Wychgate. But without a mother, it was less easy. His father seemed unable to put them at their ease, and few boys ever came back for a second stay.

Girls hardly existed in those days, of course, and they absolutely never swam. Until Violet . . . but these thoughts were getting dangerous again. You're here to worship, he told himself, and flexed his injured leg as hard as he could, so that the resulting pain would snap him to his senses.

Jerome had finished the Gospel and was well into his address. Something about Advent and preparing for death. Michael usually enjoyed the rector's style and settled himself to listen. He wasn't disappointed.

In the front of the congregation, Ernest Busby, Marketing Manager of Bamber Hydraulics, Churchwarden, Clerk of the Parish Meeting, Chair of the Residents Association, Co-ordinator of the Wychgate-with-Wyckhamby Village in Bloom Competition, Neighbourhood Watch Representative and Deputy Editor of the parish magazine was deeply disappointed. What was the old fool going on about death for? No wonder his church was getting emptier each week, if he kept spouting such depressing drivel. Didn't he know about the Enterprise Culture? Customers, that was what the church needed, and Daniels seemed hell-bent on losing the few he had left. Sometimes, Busby wondered whether the rector really cared about the things that mattered. Now that Maggie Thatcher had been in power for half a decade, standards were coming up and up. But Daniels still seemed more bothered about riots in Brixton and single mothers in Stoneford than he did about his own parish. All that money they'd raised last year, for instance, what had happened to it? Daniels had insisted that at least thirty percent be handed over to some Third World charity. When the bloody roof wasn't even water tight! It didn't make sense. And then, when Busby had queried the decision at the Parochial Church Council, he'd been told that the building wasn't as important as the work; and that anyway, the congregation, nowadays, would fit comfortably into someone's front room, or even a shed! What sort of attitude might that be, he wanted to know. It stood to reason, if you let the church fall into disrepair, you'd lose your customers. Besides, all your other standards would slip. That's why he came to worship every Sunday. You had to keep your respectability. If you didn't – well, just look at what was happening in the world: crime on the up, able-bodied people scrounging off the state, this new gay plague – well, there's an example of where God *has* done something about sinners, Busby thought. Serve the buggers right! He smiled at his joke.

'And now, Hymn number seven, "Lo, He comes with clouds descending."'

As the organist began, with difficulty, to pick out the tune, he eased his considerable bulk out of the pew, buttoned the jacket of his new wool and Terylene grey double-breasted and carried the collection plate to the back of the church, where he stood and waited until the beginning of the second verse. He pounced, first on Imogen, holding the plate under her nose. The movement had startled her and now she stared stupidly at the wood and brass object, absently shaking her head and then, reaching into the pocket of her ill-fitting and enormous trench coat and finding a handful of change that included some coppers, a ten-franc piece and a pre-decimal sixpence.

She sorted out three two-penny pieces and placed them on to the plate. Ernest sniffed and moved to the Pilkington pew, where Michael had a pound coin ready. 'Thank you, Colonel,' he uttered, in a stage whisper, as if the gift were to him personally. He moved on to the Jacques sisters, who both fumbled for fifty-pence pieces; to Mrs Maidwall who made her contribution by sleight of hand, so that you couldn't see what she was contributing, except that after the swift movement, palm down, like a game of 'Up Jenkins', there was a twenty-pence piece in the plate that hadn't been there before. He was through the congregation and up to the altar before the last words, 'Alleluya! Come, Lord, come!' were croaked out in unison, the men singing an octave lower than the women, to an excruciating *rallentando* by the organist whose arthritis had got the better of a fragile musical skill.

At last, as the cold in the church was beginning to defeat the feeble glow of the two Calor gas heaters, Jerome concluded the Eucharist and proceeded to the vestry. The tiny congregation began to shuffle to the back of the church, ready to leave. Imogen was already struggling with the catch on the heavy door when Jerome emerged, having shed alb and chasuble, buttoning an overcoat over his cassock. 'Here, let me,' he said, advancing to the door, then, 'Oh, but first, do let me introduce you to everyone.' By now, the Christians were looking anxious, forming into small groups with their backs to the newcomer. They wanted to get home, one or two to baste Sunday joints but most to catch the farming programmes on telly before driving out to a pub for lunch. Michael walked stiffly out of his pew, closing its little door with a squeak. Less eminent parishioners parted to let him through.

'This is Colonel Pilkington.'

'We've met,' Michael said. 'Good Morning, Mrs, er Miss . . .'

'Fitzgerald,' Jerome added, trying to help, and hating himself for not having let her escape in the first place.

'*Lady* Imogen,' Ernest Busby thrust out a plump paw. 'It's a privilege to meet you.'

'Ahm, actually, no. Just Imogen,' she said. 'I don't,

ahm . . .' At the word 'lady', several heads had turned. Now, she seemed desperate to get out of the building but Busby was in the way. She turned a pair of widened eyes to Jerome who felt helpless. 'It's just Imogen. I don't—'

'Busby's the name, Lady Imogen. Clerk to the Parish Meeting for my sins. Marketing Manager of Bamber Hydraulics for my wages, if you get my meaning. I've been trying to call on you ever since you moved in – Neighbourhood Watch, you know. I keep trying but no one answers the door. No doubt you're busy getting settled but there's so much you need to know about and we all want to welcome you and make you feel part of this village. It may not be the biggest but we think it's the best and we're very proud of what we've got here, Lady Imogen, and—'

'—Haah – Hm!' Michael cleared his throat loudly and fixed Busby with a look to shut him up. Imogen seemed dazed. Jerome stopped wringing his hands, seized the hiatus and swung open the heavy door. Fixing himself between Busby and the porch, he gestured Imogen through. Michael took the hint and said, 'Mr Busby, a word, if you would be so kind.'

'Shall I walk up with you?' Jerome said. She shook her head, but hesitated. 'I won't if you don't want.' He thrust his hands into his coat pocket. 'I don't mean you to be pestered.' She said nothing but seemed not to object as he walked through the churchyard by her side. After a few moments, the rest of the churchgoers began to leave and there was a revving of car engines in the lane.

Back in the church, Busby, the pink dome of his head sweating slightly, in spite of the chill, began to collect up the few prayerbooks that had been used. By the time he had walked a dozen paces, he was breathing quite heavily with the exertion. His rounded face, inflated by a surfeit of strong, imported lager, turned an angry red as he banged the books down a little too hard, on the shelf at the back, next to the Series Three leaflets.

'We're not supposed to use these old prayerbooks now, you know,' he said to Michael, the only other person left in the church. 'I've told him but it's no good. He just won't listen.'

'We only use them once in a while,' Michael said. 'I rather

like the words. They have, I don't know, a sort of poetry. "Plenteously bringing forth fruit" – all that sort of thing.'

'Poetry! You've got to move with the times, Colonel. Plain English, that's what's needed now. This is the Enterprise Culture.'

'Is it? Don't you think we follow the devices and desires of our own hearts a bit too much, these days?'

'Negative! This is the age of initiative.' Busby fussed over the pile of prayerbooks, patting them into a straight-sided stack. 'Tell you what, though, Colonel. What you just said? Now that *is* plain English. If the old prayerbooks were written like that, they'd be in a longer lasting situation instead of approaching an obsolescence scenario.'

'I see. Tell me, what do you know about our newcomers?'

'Bought the old Smith place – Weir 'ouse? The rumour is she paid a hundred gees for it. Needs a hell of a lot doing to it, apparently, otherwise it would've cost more. Still, 'er family's loaded.'

'Clearly, you know her family.'

'Don't you? Her old man's the Earl of Methwold. Remember, all that scandal with Fitzgerald. The suicide? The papers were full of it a few years back.'

'Yes, but I don't suppose it will do to gossip about it.' Michael made sure they had eye contact. 'Will it?'

'Oh, er, no. Of course not.' Busby may have been thick, but he was able to read the message.

'Do you happen to know whether the other land was sold?'

'Other land?'

'Pyson Wood and the field behind. The Smiths owned that as well. My father's executors sold it to their predecessors, after he, um . . .' Michael shifted a little uncomfortably. 'Has she bought that too, do you know?'

'Wouldn't know about that, Colonel.' He switched off the lights and held the heavy church door open for Michael. 'I shouldn't have thought so, though. There's plenty of garden goes with the house. I can't think what a woman like *that* would want with a field and a wood.'

'A woman, like that?' Michael disliked Busby's scorn, particularly when he had tried so much to ingratiate himself with her. She was no more than a girl really. Couldn't have been more than twenty-five. Thirty, at the most.

'You know, a junkie.' He mimed the action of injecting himself – a quick stylised movement, one arm out straight, the other hand aimed at crook of elbow, imaginary hypodermic held between first and second finger, thumb pressing home the plunger. It was clear that neither of them had ever seen anyone 'shooting up'.

'Ah!' Michael passed through the door and walked briskly towards Wychgate Manor.

Jerome and Imogen walked more slowly up the sloping lane. At first they were silent, then he said, 'I don't suppose you know your way around yet?' There was no reply. The lane passed along the southern edge of Pyson Wood. Twenty-five acres of spruce trees, planted so densely that it was too dark for anything to grow beneath them, crowded right up to the edge of the road at this point, blocking out daylight. In the sharp, easterly breeze, their branches sighed and sobbed with almost human breaths. 'We're not the prettiest of villages,' he went on, 'and we're rather small and isolated. Nothing happens here. Nothing at all.'

'That's why I came,' she said.

'Yes, I can understand that.' She stopped and turned to him. The eyes, with dilated pupils, looked almost black in the gloomy shade of the spruce trees, but he knew that they were blue. The question in them was 'Why? Why should you understand that?' Her lips were parted, just enough for him to see her front teeth – fine, white and even. If only she weren't so painfully thin and so hunted-looking, she'd be a pretty girl, he thought.

'You can, ahm, understand that, can you?'

'I do know.'

'Do you? *Do you*?' The reproach in the voice made him think again, carefully, to backtrack. He may have been a lousy cleric but he knew how to get people to talk about themselves. It was the first route to ladling

out help – or at least, to getting them to help themselves.

'Not really, no. I suppose not.' Only what I've read in the
gossip columns, he thought. He shivered. 'It's a bit parky
here.' He wasn't actually cold at all, in spite of the east wind,
but Pyson Wood always gave him the creeps. 'Shall we walk
a bit more?' They strolled on past the end of the wood to
the first of the houses. 'That's the old rectory,' he pointed.
'I don't live there. Mine is that red brick thing there, in the
old orchard. Up the hill is Wychgate Manor – that's where
old Pilkington lives. He's a bit of a gruff old stick, but his
heart's in the right place. You'll get on all right with him.
That converted barn, further up, is where Ernest Busby hangs
out with his wife and five kids.'

'What about the shop?'

'Ah, a sad case. Shut down years ago – back in the Sixties.
They built a new supermarket in the middle of Stoneford and
the village shop lost trade. Most people had cars, eventually,
you see. The laugh's on them now. Tesco have built a ruddy
great hypermarket out of town, on the Redburn Road and
that has ruined the one in the town centre. The same family
own the village shop premises, though. Name of Ball. The
grandson of the original shop owner, that is. He's something
in Television – Graham Ball. You may have heard of him.'

'Ahm, I don't think so.' She could never remember names
anyway. Eventually, they arrived at the gates of Weir House.
'Ahm, would you like to come in? Have some, ahm, coffee
or something?'

'Thank you.' He opened the gate for her. 'Pyson Wood
looks less forbidding from up here, don't you think? You can
just glimpse the Dene, there, over the tree tops.' He pointed,
laying a light hand on her shoulder to guide her sight line.
'That land down there used to belong with the manor. The
Smiths have it now. Those firs ought to be felled, by rights,
or at least thinned. I'm sure some of the trees near the road
are getting dangerous.'

'Why dangerous?'

'Branches overhanging the street. And some of the trunks
are beginning to lean. It is, after all, a crop, just like wheat or

barley, except that it takes a bit longer to mature – and these are past being mature by several decades. I've mentioned it to Michael Pilkington but he won't have a single one of them touched. His father planted them all, you see, back in the Twenties.'

'Actually, you're, ahm, not quite right on that one.'

'Oh believe me, he did. In fact he owned most of the village.'

'No, no. I mean about the, er, the Smiths. You see, we, that is, I own the wood. It was bought with this house.' They reached the front door. It seemed natural for Jerome to keep his hand on her shoulder – after all, he was a quarter of a century older – but it was a surprise when the door was snatched open by Mrs Crowe.

'Thank you, vicar. I'll take over from here,' she said, and manhandled Imogen over the threshold. Then she was gone, and the door slammed in his astonished face.

'Well actually, it's rector,' he murmured, as he turned towards the gate and closed it quietly behind him. He walked back to the church, slowly, wondering whether to call on Pilkington on his way. He would have liked a chat, perhaps over a glass of Michael's excellent malt Scotch, but decided not to call, in case he was intruding.

In the kitchen of Wychgate Manor, Michael was about to prepare his own lunch. His daily woman stayed away at weekends but he was quite capable of looking after himself. Today he had a packeted curry, which he would jazz up a bit with extra Tabasco sauce, and some instant rice. There was a shop-bought apple pie to follow. He had seen Jerome walking this skinny new girl up the hill and had a gut feeling that he would drop in on his way back down. He rather hoped that he would. He even thought of popping out into the lane to intercept him but felt that might be a little too forward. He set out a second glass and water jug near the whisky decanter, and quickly fluffed up the cushions in the drawing-room, just in case.

By one-thirty, it was obvious that Jerome wouldn't be coming and it seemed too late to mess about with the curry thing. Instead, he found a crust of bread and a piece of cheddar in the refrigerator and ate these with a slice of raw onion. Then he made himself a cup of tea, dunking a single bag in the cup of hot water, and took it into the drawing-room. A long, dull afternoon stretched out before him. He put a couple of logs on to the sulking fire, wondered whether to draw the curtains to shut out the gloomy daylight, but thought better of it and sat with the *Sunday Times* on his knee while the trees dripped moisture outside. Soon he was dozing. In that moment of limbo, between sleep and wakefulness, he muttered a single word. A word which briefly stimulated his tear ducts so that just before he shifted into what scientists had chosen to call 'rapid eye movement', he felt his eyes prick. 'Violet,' he said. Just once.

Chapter Two

'Violet! Violet Ball, what *do* you think you're doing?'

'Just watching.' Violet had started slightly at her father's approach but kept her eyes fixed on the blacksmith. In 1921, Wychgate Saint Peters was busy enough to carry not only its own smithy but also a general stores – run by Violet's father, Peter Ball – a railway station on the Midland and Great Northern line, which it shared with Wyckhamby, and two Inns.

'You haven't time to watch, my darling. They'll be waiting for those things up at the Manor.'

Violet was leaning on her father's delivery bicycle, a heavy machine with black enamel frame and cumbersome front basket in which lay a small box of groceries – currants, raisins and sugar in blue soft-paper bags, a small calico sack of flour and a butter pat that was beginning to melt in the May sunshine. She was just fourteen and carried, under the ruffles and folds of her white muslin frock, a newly formed woman's outline with slender waist and developing breasts. She had inherited her father's smooth skin, olive complexion and his dark hair, but had her mother's eyes, so large and deep brown that in certain lights, they looked black. They were intelligent, expressive eyes, quick to reflect her emotions. They could flash with anger, sparkle with humour and then well up with tears all in the space of a few moments. Violet was no more mercurial in her character than most girls of her age but, unlike her contemporaries, she had never felt the need to stifle her emotions. And now, as he worked on the massive hooves of a grey shire horse, she was staring at the blacksmith with a frankness that would have unnerved him, had he not been so intent on fitting the iron shoe.

Horses were so much a part of village scenery in the Twenties, that she hardly noticed them, especially not a lumbering beast like this, bred to pull the plough in October and to cart corn in August. A sleek thoroughbred she might have noted, or an impish pony with streaming mane and tail, pulling a governess cart, perhaps, or carrying a child in a wicker pannier; but not this patient animal, content to have its great strength harnessed and its fiery equine spirit quelled in return for daily oats and hay.

The blacksmith fascinated her, especially his hands. She had seen him take hammer and tongs to pick up an iron bar, heating it until it glowed – a light source deep within the metal – then watched it transform, under the rhythmic blows of his hammer, to a perfect fitting shoe. She had seen him lift the horse's great foot, making gentle noises with his mouth to reassure the animal, carrying, but not expressing a mental power that could master the beast whose physical strength was so superior. She had gasped when the hot metal had hissed on the tissue of the hoof, making a puff of smoke which smelt like singed blankets, only stronger and making the smith glance up.

''Tis only like a finger nail, Missy. They never feels it.' He wore no shirt beneath the high breasted leather apron that protected his body from the sparks and heat of the forge. She watched a small runnel of sweat gather at the neck and run down towards his chest. This disturbed her in a way she could barely define. It was like that with some people's hands. She loved to watch them holding, gripping, palpating – but admiring dexterity was only part of the pleasure. Certain people, especially men, had hands that moved her, so much that sometimes she longed to touch them, to trace the veins on their backs, to test the palms for roughness, or to feel their grip. The smith's hands were scarred with spark burns and the end of his left middle finger was missing. She could see the absence of a nail and the fold of skin over the scar.

'Violet, love, you must get on!' Peter Ball held her upper arm and she turned to him, taking his hand.

'I will, Father, don't fret. I only stopped a moment. Just to have a little think.'

'Daydreaming isn't thinking, Violet. A body *must* think, must keep in the habit of thinking.' In reply, she gave him a little punch on the upper arm. Peter was a progressive, liberal-minded man, driven by hunger for success. He knew he was more intelligent than most of the men who ran things in the world, and he was determined that his three children would be allowed to develop to their full potential. Money no longer interested him, but social recognition was everything.

Violet's brothers, James and Philip, had both won scholarships at Stoneford Grammar School where they excelled in everything they undertook. Violet had no opportunity to join them – Stoneford, in the Twenties, had no secondary school for intelligent girls – but her voracious mind and crystal memory enabled her, with steady coaching from her father and from the rector, to educate herself to a level which exceeded that of both brothers. Peter's fondest dream was that she should go to Oxford. Education he saw as a doorway through which his young would have to pass, if they wanted to transcend into the middle class and beyond.

His own origins were humble. His parents had been farm labourers in Leicestershire and when he reached school-leaving age, before the end of the century, he astonished his family by announcing that he would not be staying on the land at all, but wanted to work in a shop and was going to be an apprentice. They had always known he was odd, because he read so much and asked so many daft questions, but throwing his life away at such a tender age appalled them. They hoped he would soon come to his senses, citing his Uncle Paul as a living example of what terrible things can happen to those who are daft enough to leave the land. 'Fancy having to live in London,' they said, 'all them crowds, and terrible fogs!' But Uncle Paul, who had gone up to Town to see what happened to the potato crop when it had left the farm and been loaded on to railway trucks, had ended up with his own business, selling green groceries, first from a barrow and later from a shop in the East End. Peter wrote to him and was invited to lodge at Whitechapel for as long as he liked, on the understanding that he would have to make his own way.

The prospect of serving, man and boy, in one company was not one Peter could bear. Soon after completing his apprenticeship, he astounded his employers by announcing that he had landed a job with a different firm. He worked in various London shops for eleven years, lodging with his Uncle Paul all that time. He advanced himself with every move and wherever he went, made his employers grateful for taking him on. He gave them new ideas and suggested new products; he devised alternative ways of managing things and showed how easy it was to persuade suppliers to extend their credit. He had been apprenticed in clothing and drapery but soon moved on to groceries and provisions, rising in the small hours to visit London's great wholesale markets at Covent Garden, Billingsgate and the Smithfield meat market. Remarkably, for one so young, he was offered a senior buying position at the famous grocery firm Jacksons of Piccadilly. Delighted with such a big promotion, he returned to Whitechapel early that day, to share the good news with his uncle, but found him lying dead on the kitchen floor. Long working hours, fifty cigarettes a day and a fatty diet had taken their toll, but this was forty years before science was to link such habits with health. The family blamed the London fogs and begged Peter to leave while he was still healthy.

Uncle Paul had been a bachelor with no dependents, so the funeral was a low key affair, with but few mourners. Peter learned, soon afterwards, that he had inherited his uncle's modest estate which included the lease on the shop in Whitechapel and the small, terrace house, which he had owned. There was also a balance of two hundred and fifty seven pounds, nine shillings and sevenpence ha'penny at the bank. Peter had always known that he wanted to have his own business. Now he had the capital.

He chose Lincolnshire, rather than London, because properties seemed cheapest there, and Wychgate, because the village shop had extra land at the back and to one side where he could expand. The business was run down, but soon he was making it pay, marketing everything from leather shoe laces to patent oil-fired ovens.

He met Emily in Stoneford, not long after moving up to Lincolnshire. In such a planned life, she was something of a wild card and shook his conviction that, because Uncle Paul had seemed so happy as a single man, celibacy would suit him too. But within an hour or two of meeting Emily, he knew that he wanted to be with her for ever and since, at twenty-eight, he felt he was of an age, outlined his prospects to her and suggested they marry. She needed her father's permission, being only twenty, but this was happily given and within a few years, the three children had been born.

'I said don't fret, Dad,' Violet laid her hand on his, stroking the backs of his fingers with her clipped nails. 'I'll soon be done.'

'Quick! Give me a quote.' This was a game they played. He would demand a literary quote or a reference apposite to the moment. Education was everything.

'Er . . . "Swifter than the moones sphere" – no, this is better: "I'll put a girdle round about the earth in forty minutes."'

'Then go, my dove!' He steadied her while she put her foot on the pedal and launched forth, groceries rattling as the bicycle tyres bounced along the metalled roadway. The sun was warm on her back – still a welcome feeling this early in the summer – but, wanting to prevent the butter from melting, she steered into the shade cast by the line of horse chestnut trees along the village street. They were in full flower, their blossoms held erect, like white candles and on the road, spent petals whirled up behind her wheels. Swallows were wheeling and dipping along the Dene and the meadows that stretched from the road to the small fragment of ancient woodland, known by the locals as Pyson Wood, were tall with the maturing hay crop. Foxtail, timothy and cocksfoot grasses bloomed here, blowing little clouds of pollen from their plumed flowers. Cowslips, drawn tall by the grasses, were going to seed, but pink ragged robin grew with meadow rue in the damper folds and, on higher, drier ground, the first

white ox-eye daisies and rich blue meadow cranesbills were
coming into bloom. These fields held a rich flora, not only of
familiar wildflowers but also of rarities, and Violet knew them
all. She could lead anyone interested to the moist, peaty zone
at the edge of Pyson Wood to find Yellow Star of Bethlehem,
or to the chalky outcrop where pasque flowers bloomed in
spring, followed in summer by Ploughman's Spikenard. She
knew where Ladies' Tresses appeared in autumn and of one
spot where a colony of Chalk Hill Blue butterflies were on the
wing, every July, their caterpillars feeding on the horseshoe
vetch that grew there.

After a few initial thrusts on the pedals, to gather speed,
she free-wheeled downhill, the wind blowing her hair out
behind, and then turned sharply into the drive of the Manor,
knowing that the deeper gravel there would slow her down
without needing to use the brakes. As the bicycle lost speed
she hopped off, timing the move perfectly so that she was
walking a fraction of a second before the slow speed made
the bike topple. She flushed slightly, proud of herself for
carrying off such a daring manoeuvre, especially wearing a
long muslin dress, and then glanced up to see a face peeping
out of one of the windows. She smiled and waved but the
face disappeared. She began to wheel her bicycle towards the
tradesman's door.

Inside the house, not one but two people had observed
her trick. Upstairs, Michael Pilkington had been sitting on
a window seat in his playroom, gazing out of the window
when she arrived. With Kennedy's *Shorter Latin Primer* on
his bare, suntanned knees and a frown of concentration across
his brow, he was mugging up for the entrance examination to
Barleythorpe. But it was hard for a twelve-year-old – well,
almost thirteen, actually – to concentrate on the irregular verbs
of a two thousand-year-old language, on such a glorious day,
and he had had an awful time trying to keep his mind on
the job. He longed to be back at school and resented the
Scarlet Fever outbreak which had caused all the pupils to
be sent home for a few weeks. It was so unfair, especially
now, when he was captain of cricket *and* likely to become a
prefect after half term. A stray lock of sandy hair had fallen

over his eyes – clear eyes, and almost cornflower blue, with sweeping lashes a shade darker than the hair on his head – and with an impatient flick of his hand he had tossed it back and looked up to see Violet swing into the drive on her bike. Her dexterity impressed him, but he curled his lip and thought, 'What a swank!' When she saw him and waved, he withdrew. Fancy a shop girl being so familiar, he thought, but he would like to have waved back.

Downstairs in his study, Michael's father, Gerard Pilkington, had heard the crunch of gravel and glanced up from his book to see a vision alighting in a flurry of muslin. He froze, one hand poised above his chair arm, his eyes widening in disbelief. 'Could it be?' he whispered, 'Dear God, could it be?' Then the spell broke and it was only the shop girl on a delivery bike. But the ache stayed. Even after nearly thirteen years, it stayed, biting inwards and manifesting itself on his features with premature lines around the mouth and at the corners of the eyes. For the millionth time, that horrid tableau reared up in his mental vision. The midwife weeping with fatigue and frustration, Elizabeth's poor grey face, the huge brown eyes glittering with pain, framed with wisps of sweat-drenched hair. She had been too exhausted to make any more effort but the eyes had yelled a silent outrage at the whole indignity of the thing.

Elizabeth so laughing, so extrovert, so optimistic. 'Come *on*, Gerry m'boy!' she'd say, whenever he slipped into one of his melancholic moods. 'Buck up! Don't be a misery moper!'

She was the very bravest on the hunting field, cutting her own line, outdoing half the men, and she was the most gracious of hostesses. She never forgot a name, or to speak solicitously to everyone, so that even the most retiring souls blossomed under her tutelage, most of them falling in love with her. Elizabeth the unbeatable, brought low by this obscenity of a birth gone wrong. Her labour had lasted for more than thirty hours and all that time Gerard, husband of less than eighteen months, had hovered by the bedroom door, kept out by the midwife and doctor, but unable to go away. As she had weakened, he had prayed that she would not lose the fight. Towards the end, when she cried out – more with frustration than with pain – he had burst into the room and gone to her, dropping to his knees by the bed, trying not to retch at the sight of the blood and the stink in the room. He had stroked her face but she had pulled him closer and whispered in his ear, 'Save our baby. Save our baby. Save our baby.' He had not replied but had held her head in his hands until Doctor Radley had led him out of the room.

'I'm afraid we're at a crisis,' Radley had said. 'It's hard I know, but we may have to make a decision.'

'A decision?'

The doctor had put a hand on the young man's shoulder and squeezed. 'Rather than lose both. If you see what I mean.' Pilkington had paused, struggling to find his voice.

'Did you hear? Just now? What she said to me?' The doctor had squeezed again and had gone back into the room without a word.

The first thing he had noticed about his baby son was the eyes. He had refused to look at him at first, leaving him in the hands of the women – wet nurse, dry nurse, midwife – all woman's stuff and he wanted nothing to do with it. But after a couple of days he had relented.

'They're blue. Hers are brow— were, brown.'

'They always are at first,' the nurse had said. 'They'll probably go brown before long.'

'Really? How interesting!' Being able to talk so calmly, so soon after losing her had made him feel guilty. He did not realise that he was still in delayed shock. The full, purging flow of grief should have erupted later, producing the necessary catharsis, but with Gerard, it did not. All that happened was an internal ache that never went away. He slipped into reclusive habits, shunned the world and took refuge in his library at Wychgate Manor. He never entertained and seldom spoke to anyone other than for essential reasons. By the time Michael was ten and his father was approaching his fortieth birthday, he looked a full decade older.

For the first years of Michael's life, Gerard constantly scanned him for reflections of his mother. None appeared. The eyes did not go brown but kept their intense blueness, almost as if to mock him. His own were grey and, as far as he knew, no one else in either family had blue eyes. When the little boy's hair lost its baby fluffiness, it developed a sandy hue, several shades lighter than that of either parent. In character too, the boy lacked his mother's raucous humour. He had plenty of courage, and spirit, but it was always quieter and frequently more considerate. Elizabeth would spend her time 'bucking people up' but Michael, from a tender age, had more respect for their feelings. This, coupled with his handsome features, and his pluck at sports, made him liked everywhere. But he never took advantage of his popularity.

In Michael's early years, Gerard's housekeeper, Mrs Bull, was the mother substitute and he loved her. His father he met once or twice a day, a towering creature of scratchy tweeds and tobacco smell. He got to know him, in a way, but they never embraced – hardly ever touched – and emotions were never displayed. Even when he was hauled up before his father for some petty crime or other, the ordeal consisted of nothing more frightening than a cold, terse interview which the boy failed to understand but which, somehow, chilled him and made him feel guilty. When he was seven, and beginning his first term at prep school, he thought that all children had that kind of relationship with their parents. Seeing mothers and fathers kiss their sons before leaving them astonished him. Later, when he began to be invited into their homes and saw what happy relationships they all had, he realised what a sad life his father led at home and began to pity him. He valued his friendships far more than most boys his age – he had more to lose – and, at the end of term and during holidays, he pined for school, counting the days until he could go back. Michael's love for his comrades, and his loyalty, was pretty general, but it was not spread thin. He would obviously make a good soldier.

Pilkington saw the shop girl – what was her name? Rose? May? some kind of flower, he was sure – wave to an upper window, obviously to young Michael. He watched her turn, glance at the front door and then begin to wheel her bicycle towards the tradesman's door at the back. How extraordinary, he thought, that he had not noticed her resemblance to

Elizabeth before. He'd seen her in the village frequently enough, but had never really looked. Now that she was growing up, and he had suddenly seen the likeness, it was uncanny and rather disturbing. She even walked like Elizabeth, with the same confident stride and slight roll of the shoulders. Not the walk of a dancer or an actress – more like a country woman, but attractive. Damnably attractive. He remembered that it was Mrs Bull's day off, and that the gardener was probably right down among the greenhouses, so he walked to the front door, pulled it open and called stiffly, an upper-class bray with the accent on the second syllable:

'Hel*leah*.' She had not heard him. 'I say.' Then louder, 'You there!' She stopped and turned. The impact of her large, dark eyes was almost physical. It was as if a young Elizabeth had risen from the undergrowth. He stared. She stared back for a moment and then dropped her gaze. He recovered himself. 'No one below stairs, today, I'm afraid.' He heard himself using tones he would normally reserve for equals.

'That's all right, sir. I usually just leave deliveries on the kitchen table. Would you like me to do that?' He was surprised at her confidence. She was respectful but unembarrassed. He'd have expected a shop girl to giggle, turn red and not know what to do next.

'No need for that, young lady. Here, let me relieve you of your load.' He took hold of the bicycle handlebars, wheeled it to the front door and leant it against one of the portico pillars. 'Now, if you could handle the door, I'll just take this in.' He seemed, to Violet, to be agitated and she couldn't understand why. He began to fumble with the box of groceries, trying to lift it out of the front basket.

'Perhaps you'd better let me, sir. I'm used to it.' He stepped back to give her room. She grasped the sides of the box and swung it easily up. 'Wouldn't do to drop this. There'd be no more cakes and ale!'

'But that's Shakespeare!' A shop girl, quoting literature! 'Do you like Shakespeare?'

'I'm really only beginning to know him. I think I *will* like him but I'm more fond of Tennyson.' Out of habit, Pilkington's reticence was threatening to return. He did not want her to go, but to talk any more would require a considerable effort. There was an awkward, lengthy pause, then:

'Tennyson? Oh, I expect you'll grow out of him.' Another pause, even longer. 'What, um, what else are you interested in?'

'Most things really. Flowers, birds, music, science. Oh, and magic.'

'Magic? Conjuring tricks?'

'Oh no. Real magic.' He smiled. Such an intelligent girl suddenly revealing her childishness. 'I believe in miracles. And ghosts. My aunt's a medium. I expect I've inherited some of her mystical nature.'

'Yes? Yes, well, perhaps you had better be off now.' He had spoken more in the past few minutes than he had all week, but now he wanted to return to his library. And yet . . .

At that point, Michael came down the stairs, two at a time, saw the girl and stopped at the bottom, wondering why his father was talking to her. Pilkington, too ill-at-ease, now, to stay, walked back into his library and closed the door. Being a girl, Violet was quite uninteresting to Michael and he was far too young to attract her and, she thought, he was probably quite stuck up.

'Hullo!' he muttered, looking at the ground, a slight flush of embarrassment on his cheeks and neck. He thought her dress was awful but he liked the colour of her hair – dark brown, but with subtle highlights in russet, like antique mahogany. She seemed so incredibly much older than he, though he knew that the difference between their ages was no more than about eighteen months.

'Thought you were at boarding school.' Her speech, so articulate with Michael's father, turned leaden, confronted by this pretty child. What beautiful eyes and hair he has, she thought, but what a face he's got on!

'Scarlet fever. We got sent home, just in case. I haven't got it.' He shrugged, wondered what to say next and stared at his shoes.

'You look too old for short trousers,' she said. His flush deepened.

'I didn't think *ladies* rode bicycles.'

'Well they do.'

'Not grocer's ones, though.' His cheeks flushed at the audacity of his own remark. She turned her back, strode down the portico steps and, with difficulty caused by the length of her dress, managed to vault on to her bike and speed away, standing on the pedals to make the wheels turn through the thick gravel. Michael felt guilty for having been so unkind.

A moment later, his father re-emerged from the library. 'My boy,' he said, 'I realise that her family is in trade, but that girl seems well educated. I think I could allow you to associate with her.'

'I don't think I'll need to, Father,' Michael said.

'Really?' said Pilkington. He hovered for a moment or two, wanting to say something, but not being able – or willing – to find the words, then, 'Oh well. Probably for the best.'

Michael woke to the sound of bicycle wheels on gravel. The fire had burned low in the grate and the room had grown chilly. His knee ached, but tolerably, and he knew that once he had begun to move his old limbs, the pain would fade. He stood up, pushed a lock of silvery hair off his brow and looked out of the window. A thickish mist had gathered and the trees were dripping steadily now, making a pattering sound on the fallen leaves. At first the garden looked empty, in the gathering twilight, and he assumed that he had dreamt about bicycles. Then he spotted two figures in dun-coloured garb standing on the gravel, supporting chunky mountain bikes, one vivid red and the other an unbelievably lurid green. They had thick tyres with heavy treads, straight handlebars and complicated gearing. One of the riders was studying a map, encased in a polythene bag, presumably to keep it dry. Michael put on the outside light and then walked to the front door. The riders approached and, once they had come within a few feet of him, Michael could discern that they were male and female, in their late twenties or early thirties. It was hard to tell, in the half light, but he noticed that the woman wore eye-liner and lipstick.

'Is this place Wyckhamby?' the young man asked. In spite

of being lost, he seemed to have a rugged self assurance that verged on arrogance.

'No.' Michael felt his hackles rise. During the Eighties, this kind of person had been growing too abundant in the countryside for his liking. Sometimes, they drove their four-wheel drive buggies, like outsize dinky toys, over farmland and frequently, they were found, dressed in extraordinary shooting gear, carrying guns over other people's shoots.

'Are you sure?' the woman asked. They all knew that was a silly question and neither expected nor received an answer.

'*Are* you able to help us?' the man asked, attempting to moderate his tone but still sounding patronising. 'Because we seem to have lost ourselves. We are supposed to be meeting friends in Wyckhamby.'

'This is Wychgate Saint Peters,' Michael said, 'on the Dene. Wyckhamby is on the Venn – a much bigger river – almost three miles west of here, upstream from Kendale. Both villages have certain similarities, except that Wyckhamby is much the prettier of the two.' They seemed wholly out of place. 'Where've you come from?'

'London,' they chorused.

'But not all the way by bike, of course,' the woman said. 'Our friends brought us up in their Range Rover, bikes and all, but we thought we'd like to cycle the last bit of the journey, just from Kendale.'

'That's almost twelve miles from here.' Michael was impressed by their stamina. 'You must have missed the Wyckhamby turning. I'll point you in the right direction.' He walked towards the front gate, giving them time to wheel their bicycles over and then pointed up the street. 'Wyckhamby is over there. You need to go up that narrow lane, there, just past the telephone box, and follow as far as it goes. That will put you back on the Kendale road. Then, after about half a mile, turn left towards Wyckhamby.'

They thanked him somewhat brusquely and pedalled away. Michael was turning back to the house when he noticed a car – very large and expensive – with its side lights on, parked in the narrowest part of the lane, under the trees of Pyson Wood. He wondered what it was doing there. According to that busybody, Ernest Busby, you were supposed to record the registration numbers of strange cars and report them to the Neighbourhood Watch Co-ordinator – who happened to be Busby – so that if there was a crime, the police might be helped. Michael thought the whole thing was rather a waste of time. There had never, as far as he could remember, been a burglary in Wychgate St Peters but nonetheless, he felt like a walk and thought he might stroll down. People often pinched evergreens or even Christmas trees out of woods at this time of year – a seemingly harmless, petty crime – but it struck him as being rather mean for those who could afford such a grand car not to be willing to pay for their festive decorations. In spite of the mist and the gloom, the air was less cold than it had been that morning, so without bothering to put on a coat, he began to walk slowly down towards the lights of the vehicle.

As he got closer, he watched a man push his way out of the wood and then inspect his shoes for mud. He cursed softly and was trying to wipe them on the wet verge-side grass when Michael came up to him. He had intended to walk straight past – just a chap taking an evening stroll – but the man wiping his feet glanced up.

''Ow do!' The shoes, Michael noticed, were narrow and uncomfortable-looking, with built up heels and shiny metal embellishments above the instep, more like small shackles than functional buckles. He couldn't see the point of them. The man wore a dark suit, well fitting, expensive, and a shirt, tie and matching handkerchief tucked into his top pocket.

'Good afternoon,' Michael said. 'A bit damp under foot for that. You seem to be making it worse.'

'Yeah?' The man continued to wipe, losing the gloss on the shoes. His hair seemed unnaturally black and was coiffed carefully forward. In his effort to clean his shoes, he was shaking it slightly out of position. He reached into his inside pocket and brought out a comb, fake tortoiseshell, made by Kent of London. 'Er, what's the name o' this wood?' The accent was Londonish. East End, Michael thought.

'I'm not sure whether it has an official name. It's not very old, but there's a little copse deep inside that has always been there. We used to call that Pyson Wood.'

'Ah!' the man seemed happy to hear the name. 'So this *is* the place.' Michael wasn't sure what he meant.

'The place?'

'It don't matter.' The man seemed preoccupied, gazing into the wood. 'Some o' them trees are falling down. Innit time the place was tidied up? Let a bit o' daylight in?'

'No!' The sharpness of Michael's reply made the man look round. 'No,' Michael said, more gently. 'These were planted in the Twenties, as a timber crop, but the owner sold the land on the understanding that the wood should remain.'

'What for?' Both men surveyed the over-tall, overcrowded fir trees. Michael shrugged. 'Asset of some kind, I suppose.'

'Know anythink about the owner?'

Michael hesitated.

'Look, I'm not sure who—'

'Ains.'

'Sorry?'

'My name. Russell Ains.'

'Ains?'

'Naow! *Ains!*' He spelt it out, 'Haitch – A – N – D – S.'

'Oh *Hands!*' Michael offered his hand, 'Pilkington. Michael.'

''Owdo, er, Mike.' Michael felt his hand gripped, felt many rings and noted a chunky, gold bracelet on the the man's wrist. 'Anyhow, like I said, do yer know anythink about the owner?'

'Not really, Mr Hands. They are rather new here.'

'Yeah?' It was a disinterested sound; clearly he wasn't about to get anything out of this old geezer and needed to end the dialogue right away. He opened his car door. 'Well, can't stop. See yer!' And he jumped into his car, swearing after transferring a small dollop of mud from the ground on to the polished chromium steel door-sill. He opened the glove compartment, snatched out a man-size tissue and wiped the mud off, dropping the tissue on to the ground before closing the door and driving away.

Michael picked it up, crumpled the soft paper round the

nugget of mud and slipped it into his jacket pocket. Feeling the need for fresh air, but finding little in the damp, still twilight, he began to walk on down the street towards the church and river. On his return, he noticed two red pinpoints of light glowing outside Weir House. They were the tail lights of the Jaguar he had seen earlier. Clearly, Hands was paying Imogen Fitzgerald a visit. Michael shuddered. If many more of these disturbing outsiders began to haunt this place, he really would have to consider selling up and spending his last days in his small Pimlico flat.

Chapter Three

━━━━━◆━━━━━

From the sitting-room window of Weir House, Imogen watched the Jaguar slow down and stop outside the front gate. In spite of the gathering dusk and thickening mist, she could see the outline of the driver as he climbed out, smoothed his dark hair, adjusted his tie and checked the pocket flaps on his jacket. Instead of approaching the house, he stood in the lane, looking up at the roof, peering from left to right and then staring right at her window. He couldn't see her, since the room was dark, but his attention unsettled her as much as if he had looked up her skirt. She shuddered and pulled her cardigan – a ruinous item somewhere between beige and grey with stretched and baggy sleeves – more tightly round her. To comfort herself, she reached into one of its distorted pockets for Ted, a small furry toy given as a joke by Marcus on her twenty-first. Ted had once been a pocket-sized teddy bear but was now so worn and dirty as to be unrecognisable.

She had unwrapped the gift in another age, in the company of her closest friends, after the central core of the birthday party had moved from her father's house in Kensington to Zeta's Club. In those days she rode, like a champion surfer, on a great wave of happiness. She was liked! She was loved! Everyone kept kissing her that night, and dancing round her and cheering. When Marcus had handed over the small package, somebody stopped the disco music and a little silence had fallen, as if this might be a solemn moment. With hasty, careless fingers, she had torn off the expensive gift paper – gold and blue stripes, bound with a satin ribbon – wondering what to expect: perfume? Diamonds? An engagement ring? But when she saw the cheap little teddy bear she squealed with delight, waved its tiny orange paw and said, 'Everyone! Everyone, meet, er, Ted. Ted, everyone! It's love, my darlings, love at first sight.' Then she had kissed the toy but she really meant Marcus. Another cheer had gone up and she had kissed Ted again and kissed Marcus, at last, and then the disco began to pump out Heavy Metal and the moment had passed, but not her happiness. That had lasted longer, but not long enough. She hadn't a clue then, that the wave she was riding so fast and so skilfully, could smack so awkwardly on to the breakwater, dissipating itself in a sickening flurry of foam and salt water. It had seemed, then, like a wave of champagne rather than one of tears. She reached into the other pocket for a bundle of sodden tissues to mop moisture from nose and eyes that were sore and sensitive from intermittent weeping and wiping. She was not having a good day.

The sitting-room was dark and dirty, with cardboard boxes and wooden packing cases dumped down at random. Some had scratched the polished wooden floor and only a couple of them had been unpacked. Their contents, a miscellany of household effects, thrown together without method, had been placed at random on pretty well any horizontal surface. A fine eighteenth-century clock – most of its moving parts gone – had been placed inside a huge lidless saucepan, next to an electric knife grinder whose plug was missing. Her only valuable paintings: a Dutch flower group and an English landscape by John Sell Cotman, were wrapped in a vast, hand-embroidered linen table cloth, bought for her by Marcus during their shortened honeymoon in Madeira. The cloth had snagged and frayed where one of the corners had vibrated against the side of the delivery van and inside, gilt had rubbed off the frames, staining the creamy linen. The mess weighed heavily with her. She hated not knowing where to find things but couldn't decide where they should have been in the first place, so she spent much of her time picking up objects, carrying them aimlessly about and putting them down again. She'd get things sorted out one day, she supposed, if only she could shake off this awful, numbing tiredness.

The whole house was in similar disarray, except for Mrs Crowe's private room which sparkled with an almost military cleanliness and even had its own telephone extension. But Mrs Crowe, despite her spreading figure, was an ordered sort of person. She had asked, right at the start, whether she could have a few 'bare sticks of furniture' from Imogen's effects, for her own quarters and had, as with so many requests, assumed that the distracted silence from the young woman in her charge, could be taken as a 'yes'. She had selected the second best bedroom for herself – 'seems a waste not to use it, since we won't ever be having guests, dear' – and had furnished it with a small Sheraton sideboard, on which she placed as much of Imogen's little hoard of silverware as it would decently hold. There was also a pretty walnut Pembroke table, a small chest of drawers in yew wood and an antique commode which served as a bedside table. The bedroom floor, like the rest of Weir House, was of bare, polished oak and, although she'd have preferred a nice fitted carpet, she made do with a vast and intricately patterned silk rug, collected from Tangier in the 1950s by Imogen's father and, when she had grown up, given to her as a birthday present. Imogen had loved it when she was little, partly because of its intriguing pattern whose colours changed from cobalt blue and cinnamon to navy and tan, depending on which end of it you looked at, but also because its texture was so soft and silky. When she was tiny and they were all together, Mummy, Daddy, Jeremy and Philip, taking tea or playing Snap in Mummy's small private sitting-room at Methwold, she would slip off her shoes and socks so that she could stroke the carpet gently with the soles of her feet, loving the electric feel. Mrs Crowe had trouble with the corner of the rug, because it was a bit too near the door of her room, and threatened to catch. She thought of trimming a foot or so off the end, and folding the cut edge under but suspected that that might reduce its value, so she had found a hammer and a couple of nails and anchored it to the floor that way. The bottom of the door chafed the silky pile, but only just.

Mrs Crowe had not been in the family's employ for quite long enough to be classed as an ancient and loyal retainer, but she had certainly won Lord Methwold's heart. Bowled him over, in fact. In spite of his small size and weedy appearance, the peer had a penchant for large, assertive women and, no doubt, it was a mildly sexual frisson that had laid the first cement of his attachment to her. The blouse, relatively tight over the large bosom, buttoned inscrutably at the neck, had suggested a uniform, as if she were a policewoman off duty, and this, coupled with a chin held high and stern mouth below flared nostrils had certainly coloured his judgment. But he also admired what he saw as a mental strength and had never, from the first day of her employment, doubted her integrity or her loyalty to the family. No one who could confront one with such a direct gaze could be anything but honest.

The Crowes had, in the mid-Seventies, arrived as a couple whose references and credentials were too impeccable to be true. They had been hired to manage the Methwold's London house and at that time, Mrs Crowe had not let on that she was not actually married to Mr Crowe, or indeed, that she had only met him five months previously, or that he was, to be precise, the fifth 'Mr Crowe' to have worked with her in double harness. When, less than a year after starting their new job, he had done a runner, and done it, furthermore, with thirty-six of the Methwold's eighteenth-century silver forks in his duffel bag, she had sworn, publicly, to work the rest of her days to recompense the family and, privately, to have the bastard's goolies impaled on two of the aforementioned forks when she caught up with him. Blatant stealing simply wasn't her style – she was for steady milking rather than one-off pillage – and the Methwold family, she knew, could be her lifeblood and her pension. Her resolve to catch up with 'Crowe' had stiffened even further, when she discovered that he had forged her signature, cleared her building society account and that she was virtually penniless.

To survive now, Mrs Crowe knew that she needed to ingratiate herself with the family. As part of the softening up process, she had already expressed an almost unnatural affection for the Methwold children, especially for Imogen who was still, at the time of the fork incident, in the fifth form at Saint Enodoc's, on the south coast. It could be said – and by Immie's closest friends it often was – that Mrs Crowe had something to do with the beginning of her problems. The incidents had begun after the woman's arrival, as far back as her first year in the sixth form, and no one had ever really found out why she had left St Enodoc's a whole year before taking A' levels. Some even hinted that Mrs Crowe actually supplied Imogen with drugs, but Lord Methwold would have none of it and his conviction hardened, over the years, that she was the only person who could really influence his daughter, and for the good.

Much later, when Imogen was well into her twenties and her problem had suddenly intensified into a crisis that threatened the entire family, her mother wrote her off completely, grieving for her as if she were already dead. Her father turned for help, not to any of his equals, inside or outside the family, but to this servant. She, he felt, was the one person who understood, who *really* understood, his daughter. In that respect he was right, she understood her charge all right but, although well intended, his action could hardly have been more damaging to Imogen who, far from being rehabilitated, amounted, now, to little more than a sad human remnant.

It had not taken Mrs Crowe long to know precisely how to turn her employer's confidence to her own advantage and now that they'd moved into Weir House, she'd got Imogen exactly where she wanted her. Her aim was to prolong the period of rehabilitation as much as was possible without actually making the girl insane. Any influence from outside, therefore, needed keeping at bay. She had read, somewhere, about religious cults which managed to entice their recruits by offering salvation but which then held them captive with brainwashing techniques until they handed over all their material possessions, and sometimes those of their families as well. There were several case histories of formerly bright young people becoming mindless husks, living in a trance-like condition. At the basis of such entrapment – of mind, and therefore of body – was the simplest technique of all: starvation. A low protein diet over a long enough period, she read, could turn a genius into a zombie. With Imogen, whose diet was capricious at the best of times, that was the easiest part. Keeping outsiders away would take more doing.

Mostly, she was able to use her aggressive manner to repel boarders but Imogen, who had never shown the faintest spark of aggression and had always been naturally quite friendly, needed to be cowed into reclusiveness. In her present state, though, all it required was an occasional twitch upon the thread to remind the girl that, hate her or not, Mrs Crowe was all she had in the world, and without her she'd assuredly die, or worse. 'We don't want people round here to know *all* the details of our guilty secret, do we dear?' Remarks like that usually did the trick.

Imogen wondered, staring back at the man, through the sitting-room window, what she would do if he came to the door. She didn't dare call Mrs Crowe – she seemed to be in such a mood today – but wouldn't be able to make herself answer the door. The man began to walk up the path and she clutched her toy more tightly, dropped her wad of tissues and put a thumb in her mouth. The bell rang but she kept very very still. It rang again, almost at once, making her start so violently that she nearly dropped Ted. Then she heard Mrs Crowe's heavy tread on the stairs and crept over to the sitting-room door to listen. She heard the bolt being drawn and the door opened.

'Yes?' Mrs Crowe had her battle-axe voice on. She'd been dozing after half a bottle of Bordeaux with her lunch and was obviously cross at being woken up. Imogen could visualise her standing erect, with her feet apart, chest thrust out and arms folded across her bosom. 'What do you want?'

'Ains, is the name,' said Hands, offering a rather soft but sun-bronzed paw on which gold flashed. 'Mrs Smith, is it?' He knew it wasn't, of course.

'No.' Mrs Crowe kept her arms folded and returned his frank stare. He knew that the Smiths had sold both Weir House and Pyson Wood, because he had been under-bidder for the land. In fact, he had been so sure he could get it, and dirt cheap, that he had made an offer but had forgotten to follow it up. With all the other parcels of development land and properties that he was buying and selling in this buoyant market, he had allowed this one to slip through his fingers. At first this had not worried him. After all, he had plenty of other fish to fry, but since he'd been back for a couple more looks at Wychgate, he had begun to realise the importance of his mistake. The place was ripe for development, probably with very little effective local opposition. The villagers might object, but they wouldn't have much of a leg to stand on. The place wasn't pretty; it wasn't even in a conservation area and he doubted whether more than a couple of the houses were listed. However the locals might react, he felt sure he'd have no problems with the planning authorities and above all, there was plenty room for a biggish housing estate.

It hadn't taken much detective work to establish who the new owner of the land was, but what he needed to do now was to find out how he could persuade her to re-sell. Weir House was of no interest – he only went in for what he called 'new build' – but the woodland was begging for development and, once he'd got this Fitzgerald dame sussed out, he'd know how to go about getting his hands on it. Hands usually got what he wanted. Everyone had their price and with land values on the up and up, he was pretty sure she could be persuaded, however snottily this old cow – obviously some sort of minder – was looking at him at this moment. Softly softly, though, he thought.

'He about then?' Nice touch, that 'he'. Made him ingenuous.

'Who?'

'The owner.'

'*She*'s unavailable.' Mrs Crowe kept her arms folded and kept her gaze unwaveringly on him.

'Yeah?' He kept his manner casual, refusing to allow her formidable looks to rattle him. 'It's that wood I was wondering about, really. I was told the sportin' rights 'n' that might be available. On a yearly basis, o' course, only I might be able to take 'em on. It ain't urgent or anything.' In the sitting-room, Imogen was straining to hear more clearly.

There was something in the man's voice that tweaked at her innards. The vowels were drawn out and the consonants hissed, and that repelled; but the timbre was mellow, a pleasant tenor, and that attracted.

'As I said,' Mrs Crowe was about to close the front door, 'she's unavailable.' Imogen felt she must look at the man She needed to match features to that voice, but was terrified of being seen. She wrestled with opposing impulses for a few seconds, almost dancing with indecision, before pulling the sitting-room door fully open. She saw the hall light bouncing off his forehead, slightly glossed with sweat or condensed mist, and took in the neatness of his suit. She observed stubby fingers, be-ringed and cleanly manicured; unnaturally black hair, straight and cut short and brushed slightly forward. She noted his size, not tall, but stocky and strong-looking, quite well-proportioned. He was not bad-looking but he exuded a raw masculine aggressiveness that frightened her; that both attracted and repelled. She began to back into the sitting-room again, then their eyes made contact, and stuck fast. Hunted, grey, hers, looking into small, burning, unwavering black eyes that seemed to lack lids or brows. Within a twinkling – except that these eyes glittered rather than twinkled – she felt what little will-power she could muster draining away. She wanted to get away from that gaze but felt herself drawn to it. She looked away, but her eyes kept twitching back to the glinting stare. The initial encounter took less than five or six seconds but to Imogen, it could have lasted for hours.

''Owdo.' Hands took another step towards the doorway, his breezy voice at odds with the intentness of those appraising eyes. Imogen felt herself move towards him but Mrs Crowe imposed her body between her and the doorway. He stretched out a hand, thrusting it past the large woman who refused to budge until there was almost a tussle, forcing her to take a tiny step backwards to make room. Imogen felt her hand grasped and held. In spite of the cold afternoon, the contact was slick with sweat and that, for some reason, excited her. 'Pleased to meet you.' There was a moment's pause. All three were standing awkwardly close. Imogen could smell his cologne – expensive – mingling with Mrs

Crowe's own special odour of sweat compounded with cheap scent.

'Ahm. Won't you come in?'

'I hardly think so!' Mrs Crowe retorted.

'Cheers,' said Hands, thrusting past the older woman and standing in the hall. At that point he noticed the state of the house. Christ, he thought, this bird really is barkin'. He knew most of her history – everyone who read the gossip columns did – and wondered whether she was still shooting up, or whatever it was junkies got up to. He fixed her with a smile, even white teeth below cold eyes. She loved the teeth; dreaded the eyes. 'Just movin' in?'

'Ahm, actually, yes.' She felt petrified, turned to stone, in an agony of tension. She imagined what a rabbit must feel, when hunted by a stoat. Did they, too, long for the final, sweet bite, the tension draining away with their lifeblood?

'We'ell. Prob'ly not a good time, then.'

'No? For, er, what?'

'Nar. Nuffink, really. I just 'ad a bit of an idea.' He jingled some change in his pocket. 'I'll pop back anovver day. When you're settled.'

'I wouldn't bother, Mr Hands,' Mrs Crowe imposed.

'No. Ahm, do.' Imogen wanted to hear more of that voice but then caught Mrs Crowe's narrowed eyes and amended herself. 'Perhaps, ahm, perhaps better not.'

'D'yer need any help? With all this lot?' He waved at the mess. 'Only, I own a cleaning firm as well, you know. Help get you sorted.'

'We can manage perfectly well, *thank* you.' Mrs Crowe pulled the door open wider and stood by it. Her body language was unequivocal. 'Good afternoon!' she said. Almost before he had managed to clear the lintel, she closed it with a bang and turned to Imogen. 'Just look at you,' she hissed. 'What do you think you're trying to do? You don't seriously think you're in a fit state to deal with someone like that!' She took her by the elbow and steered her back into the chilly sitting-room. 'Oh! Now you've let the fire out, you bloody silly little cow!' With a sigh, she gathered up some pieces of waste paper from around the packing cases and balled them up before putting them into the grate where the dying embers of the old fire ignited them and made them burn away before she had time to delve in the log basket for a few wood fragments with which to build up the fire. She cursed and threw on more paper, ripping off the dust-jacket of a hard-cover novel as she grabbed for fuel. Imogen cowered, clutching her talisman and wiping her nose and eyes. 'Here!' Mrs Crowe demanded, reaching out a hand.

'No!' Imogen cried, gripping Ted even harder.

'Those tissues. They're disgusting.' Imogen surrendered them and reached in her pocket for more but found none. Mrs Crowe threw them on to the fire and heaped on several large logs which were damp and smouldered fitfully, throwing out negligible heat. 'God knows what we're going to do with you, my lady, but you're certainly not well enough to go cavorting with locals yet. It simply won't do – heaven knows what you might tell them.' She raised her voice: 'Sit down!' Imogen obeyed the sharp command. Her thumb crept towards her mouth but she snatched it guiltily away. 'Who the hell *was* that, anyway?'

'I, ahm, I don't know.'

'Are you sure?' Mrs Crowe needed to know everything about all possible contacts. Imogen nodded.

'He seemed to know you.' She narrowed her eyes. 'And you certainly *looked* as though you knew him.'

'No!' Imogen shook her head violently for several seconds. 'No.'

'He's sniffing around after something, that I do know. Probably another news man.' At those words, Imogen's eyes clouded and then filled with fresh tears. 'Oh, for God's sake, girl! You've got to pull yourself out of this.'

'I . . . I know.' But she found it impossible to stop sobbing, a horrible dry, wracking sound. A string of snot appeared from her nostril and when she reached for her tissues she found her pocket empty.

'You disgusting little slut!' Mrs Crowe said, in a cold, quiet voice, and swept out of the room, slamming the door behind her. For a while, she continued the job of unpacking boxes in the dining-room, attempting, without much conviction, to turn a little more of the house from a half-occupied husk into a home. At precisely six-thirty she went into the kitchen, hovered by the telephone and managed to lift the receiver before it had completed its first ring. Imogen did not know, but she had turned off the bell of the drawing-room phone.

'My Lord?' She spoke in low, respectful tones. 'Quite well, sir. Still abstaining . . . She's still not putting on any weight, but we're winning her round . . . I think she's going to be all right, but it will take time . . . Yes, yes . . . Love and kindness always works, in the end. Thank you sir, thank you. Goodbye, my Lord.' She hung up and began to prepare supper.

Imogen continued to sit by the fire, her arms folded tightly across her breast, rocking to and fro, and humming a sad little three-note fall again and again. At the base of her consciousness, she knew, there were weighty matters, matters that one day, would have to come out, to be addressed, get sorted out. But for now, she had barely enough strength to hold on at all. They had managed to wean her off the heroin, and the cocaine, and she had surprised everyone at the clinic by being able to overcome her addictions quickly. It was as if, rather than being addicted, she had been on a crusade of self-destruction. When she had declared, as those well and truly hooked so often do, 'I can give it up any time,' she had, apparently, meant it.

But, after the whole miserable affair had run its course and she had been picked out of the gutter – and out of the hands of the gutter press – by her family, after she had been dried out at the clinic, half rehabilitated and then, virtually thrown out, not just from her home, but from the family, the next move was proving to be something of a poser. 'The family's reputation has suffered enough, thanks to you,' Daddy had said, 'and I'm going to have to see to it that you do no more harm.' He had tried to be stiff and formal, but she could see the tears in his eyes and his shaking hands. Philip and Jeremy had stopped speaking to her altogether – they would never forgive her for Marcus – but that didn't hurt half as much as Daddy's attempt at cold rejection. 'Your capital is gone and so, it seems, is the best of your health.'

The deal was this: all her wealth, most of it granted as part of a marriage settlement, had been squandered and she would receive no more cash. The family, however, would settle her outstanding debts and would purchase a suitable dwelling, preferably as far away from Methwold as possible, where she could live with a paid companion. She would not be given any allowance – the temptation to spend it on drugs might prove irresistible – but her companion would receive a monthly cheque for housekeeping. If she wanted anything more, she would have to earn what she needed. All other ties with the family were to be cut.

Lord Methwold had not intended to be as hard as he seemed. He had realised, at length, that Imogen's only hope of survival was to learn to fend properly for herself. But he wanted to keep an eye – albeit a distant one – on his daughter, without exerting any influence and without her knowing that, even though he was no longer like a father to her, he was still acting as a sort of guardian angel. That was why he had chosen Mrs Crowe. He knew he could trust her, had arranged a large salary increase for her and had promised to telephone secretly, each Sunday. If Imogen ever got to the phone first, he would simply hang up. She would probably assume it to be someone from the press – they were constantly monitoring her movements – and would suspect nothing. No one knew, except Lord Methwold and Imogen's mother, just what a torture this whole thing was.

In her sitting-room, Imogen had failed to hear the telephone. I have no one, she thought. But I deserve no one. Then she began holding herself and rocking again, and humming the little falling scale, 'Hm, hm, hmmm. Hm, hm, hmmm.'

Chapter Four

———

A bright Saint Valentine's morning outside the church of Saint Peter, Wychgate. The line of yews leading from the lane throws a chill shade, but the rest of the churchyard is well lit with short, fine grasses growing between the lichen-covered gravestones. On the north side of the Romanesque tower, a single holly tree, much ravaged by Christmas flower arrangers, has cream variegated foliage but has never been known to bear a single berry. Mid-February is too early and too cold, in these parts, for any primrose plants to venture forth with a flower, but there are drifts of snowdrops, both double and single kinds, and, in the sunlit area by the side door, the turf is peppered with a rash of bright yellow winter aconites.

When Jerome Daniels discovered these and squatted among them to savour their faint honey fragrance, and to enjoy the rich contrast that each golden flower made with its little ruff of green foliage, he felt a surge of joy. The sun was out, days were getting longer; another winter would soon be over, thank God! (An exclamation of delight and relief, rather than an expression of gratitude to a Creator whose existence, in his mind, had grown too indistinct to acknowledge.) He wondered whether to pick a flower or two for his desk. There was a chipped sherry glass at the rectory, saved for the purpose. In June it might hold a specimen rose bloom or, in October, a single chrysanthemum head, but at this time of year, flower and fragrance was at a premium and mostly, it stood empty, water marks staining its sides. If I wasn't so idle in the garden, he thought, I'd have plenty of flowers to pick even now.

His knees began to ache, from squatting too long, so he moved backwards to sit on the kerb of a tomb. The stone felt surprisingly warm, in the sun, even though hoar frost still crusted the grass and gravel under the yews. He relaxed and stretched his legs out, giggling a little at the sight of his loud socks. What a dramatic contrast the purple makes with the yellow aconites, he thought. They hadn't been exactly an original idea, he admitted that. In fact he owed them to Graham Greene's *Monsignor Quixote* which he had read at Christmas. How he had envied the character in the story! A wholly honest priest with such simple faith. Childlike! Jerome wished he too could live such a life – priestly, without all these machinations of the mind. But too many questions flooded in all the time. Whenever anything happened, good or bad, and he was supposed to accept it all as God's Will, he tended to ask why. He constantly demanded answers, even though none had, so far, been forthcoming. What Being, if it purports to be good, and has the power to prevent, could possibly allow such suffering as there was in the world? He wondered about that whenever the news reported yet another child-killing, or more chilling these days, killer children. And how could local farmers, well versed in the selection processes involved in animal breeding, be content to say that famine in East Africa was just part of the evolutionary process? Could they, with their stomachs bulging from a fatty diet, look an Ethiopian child in the eye – a naked child, with limbs like sticks, pot-bellied with parasites and malnutrition – and say, 'Sorry chum, it's survival of the fittest!' And always behind the question: what sort of God could possibly allow all this to go on? was the much bigger one: could such a Being exist at all? With each passing year, as a country rector, religious doctrine and ceremony had seemed less and less relevant. Whenever he read the parts of the Gospel that cover the Passion, his eyes would sting with sorrow for the victim, but he knew he lacked the blind faith that he had been taught was necessary for eternal salvation. Jerome had given up trying to understand eternity, and had begun to doubt its value years ago. More to the point, what was to be done here and now?

Misery was closer to home than anyone round here realised. None of his parishioners knew, as he did, that there were flourishing drug dealers in the quiet country town of Stoneford. He kept his pastoral ear to the ground, and could name them all. The parishioners had no idea, either, that Stoneford had a homelessness problem or, for instance, that fifteen-year-old Jimmy Golby had elected to leave his comfortable middle-class home in the village and sleep rough in the town's lorry park, rather than face what his respectable parents did to him at home. Jerome sighed. The difficulty there was that he was pretty sure he *did* know what had been happening to Jimmy, but hadn't a clue what to do about it. That was something that needed thinking through very carefully before doing anything at all. Well wishers, he knew, could destroy a whole family with as much cruel efficiency as an S.S. detachment might have mustered during the Holocaust. He shivered slightly, despite the sunshine. He may not have had the unquestioning love of God that Greene's saintly priest had, but he did care about his people. His exasperating, back-biting, petty-minded, ignorant parishioners he found hardest to love, but he longed to be closer to the ones that stayed away, that had undeclared troubles or who were unhappy through their own folly but unable to find a solution. Then there were people like poor old Michael Pilkington: outwardly confident, cheerful and well adjusted but, all Jerome's instincts told him, inwardly desolate – a tortured soul. Such people were, in many ways, the most pathetic because nobody really knew what they were going through. He sighed and straightened his vivid socks, smiling at his own folly of gaining comfort from so small a thing, but then feeling a tiny dab of guilt for indulging in what amounted to an aimless vanity.

Jerome heard the click of the new catch on the churchyard gate and his heart sank. The original gate had not been closed since before the war and, when its posts had finally rotted through, back in the 1960s, the verger had taken the wreckage away. Quite why the Residents' Association had thought it necessary to have a new gate now, Jerome couldn't understand. When it was first erected, no one remembered to close it, but the Association had decided, on a democratic vote of fifteen to four, to install a spring. Now, if you arrived on a bike, as Jerome often did, the gate was awkward to handle unless you dismounted, propped up the bike and then opened the wretched catch which was so stiff that it frequently caught one's fingers. He knew, without looking up, that Busby was approaching, and that the encounter was not going to be easy.

It was to do with the gypsies – or 'travellers', as one was supposed to call them these days. The last of them had moved away from Wychgate common, on the village outskirts, the week before, much to the relief of the Residents' Association, but the legacy they had left behind this time had deeper repercussions than the odd missing chicken or uncollected cache of scrap metal. Jerome sighed at the prospect of the conversation that was bound to ensue when Busby caught up with him. He had to admit, the grave was pretty hideous. And he had to admit too, that he had been rather hoodwinked. But when the gypsies had lost one of their matriarchal figures, at a relatively young age, and had chosen Wychgate as her final resting place, he had felt almost honoured. It was obvious that the whole gypsy community had had enormous love and respect for this woman. That they were happy for her to rest here, said much about their opinion of the village.

'Good day to you, rector!' Busby had begun using 'good day' quite recently, considering it a good country-wise greeting. He kept his tweed cap on but unzipped his dung-coloured waxed jacket, letting the ample stomach expand a little, and held out a hand.

'Wotcher,' Jerome said, getting to his feet, then, pointing downwards, 'Oh, do be careful!' as Busby stepped forward on to the winter aconites.

'What? Oh, they're only buttercups, aren't they? I suppose we ought to weed-kill and feed the grass down here next spring.'

'Um, possibly,' Jerome muttered. Over my dead body, he

thought, but it was best to humour the likes of Busby rather than confront them head on. He decided to divert him from his murderous purpose by referring to the reason for their appointment in the graveyard. 'Shall we look at it?'

'Better had. I'm a busy man.' Busby's rounded cheeks already carried a bluish tinge, as if he were unused to being out in the fresh air. Together, they walked to the far end of the graveyard. Among the grey and honey-coloured tombstones, many canted over at odd angles and some so old that the inscriptions could hardly be made out, were one or two newer additions. Moss and lichen had not yet grown on these, but since they were also made of limestone or rough-hewn granite, they blended comfortably with their older neighbours. At the far end, however, a different monument had been set up. This was so large and conspicuous that it had caused a considerable stir among Wychgate's inhabitants and, what was more, it was considered to be all Jerome's fault. He had, after all, sanctioned the thing in the first place and, the Residents' Association felt, it was up to him to do something about it.

'Solidly constructed,' Jerome said, as he and Busby stood at the foot of the grave. And it was. Two huge plates of polished black granite were edged with a kerb, in the same stone, which rested on a white marble base. At each corner, a low post had been carved with a floral motif and gilded. The headstone was a vast granite heart, set at an angle, with a colour photograph of the matriarch permanently bedded in the stone – Jerome wondered how on earth they did that – and a text picked out in gilt carving. 'In Loving Memory of Meg. A dear Wife and Mother' was followed by a few mawkish lines. 'We begged you, Meg, to stay, but the Good Lord wanted you more' and more like that. Lesser members of the family had placed subsidiary monuments on the slabs: planters with plastic laurels and real crocus corms; plaques, in matching granite and gilt, saying 'To our loving Grannie Meg', and 'Loving memories of our darling Aunt' and so on. In a large, town cemetery, this grave would have stood out a bit; here it screamed at its surroundings.

'Well constructed, it may be,' Busby snapped, 'But it just

isn't in keeping. I mean, look at those plastic flowers.' He shuddered. 'You'll have to do something about it.'

'What do you suggest?'

'It'll have to go.'

'Impossible. I gave them permission to install it.'

'Well, you'll just have to un-give it.'

Jerome shook his head. 'Can't be done.'

'Can't it be moved, then?'

'Where to?'

'I don't know.' Busby thought for a minute 'Stoneford?'

'Hardly. They wanted to bury her here.' Jerome shrugged again. Busby was becoming irritated by his manner. The man didn't seem aware of what a mess he'd made, or of how much resentment he'd stirred up.

'But you've got us into this. Can't you do anything to put it right?'

'I have to say, Ernest, that I'm not especially bothered by this grave, not personally, anyway. I don't really mind if it stays. It's a bit garish, I agree, but at least they *care*.'

'And what, precisely, is that supposed to mean?'

'The gypsies – er, travellers. They seem to care rather more about their family, their community, than some of the rest of us do.'

'Community? You call *that* a community?' He jerked a thumb towards the Common. The pitch of his voice crept upwards as his anger grew. 'Did you see the litter they left behind? It took the volunteers a whole day to clean up. Disgusting! I don't know how you can call that, that *rabble* a community. Do they pay taxes? No! Did they ever pay rates? Ha ha! Will they pay this new Poll Tax? The hell they will!'

'Ernest, I know you work very hard for the village, but there are other . . .' he trailed off, catching sight of the scorn on Busby's face. 'Look, there isn't much I can do about this. I sanctioned it, after all, even though I hadn't realised that it would be quite so . . .'

'Common? Naff?'

'Ostentatious. But I will talk to them and see if I can persuade them to take those artificial flowers away, and perhaps a couple of the white plastic planters. That really is all I can do.'

'It won't satisfy the Residents' Association.'

'Ernest, I'm afraid it will have to.' An edge had crept into Jerome's voice, now. 'Whatever the residents may think, decisions about graves in this churchyard remain with the rector and, like it or lump it, that's me.'

As he was speaking, the sun had crept behind the tower, throwing them into shadow. At once, the temperature dropped, reminding them that a hard frost was on its way. Jerome hunched his shoulders and made a shuddering noise. He wanted to take the antagonism out of this encounter, so they could part, at least, on civil terms. 'I'm off to get warm. Want a cup of tea?' He knew the other would refuse.

'Can't spare the time. Some of us have careers, as well as all that community stuff. But I was forgetting, we taxpayers don't really care, do we.' Jerome couldn't think of any reply that wouldn't make the man more angry. He thought of reiterating what everyone was saying all the time. That the village wouldn't be the same without him, but decided that would probably ring a bit hollow. He kept quiet and just smiled, trying so hard to like the man. 'Good day to you!' Busby snapped. He zipped up his waxed jacket before walking briskly out of the churchyard.

Jerome locked the church and then paused by the Pilkington family tomb enclosure near the south door. Among a small group of older graves here, surrounded by cast-iron palings, was a thickset granite headstone. The inscription was simple: 'Elizabeth, beloved wife of Gerard Pilkington, died in childbirth, 14th June 1909'. Jerome wondered why Michael never referred to the grave, never seemed to glance at it on his way in or out of church, and certainly never put flowers on it. No one put flowers on it. Ever. Jerome also wondered, often, what had happened to Gerard Pilkington, and why he was not buried with his wife. He knew that Elizabeth was Michael's mother, and that she had died giving him birth, but he had always shied away, for reasons he couldn't explain, from asking Michael about his father.

*		*		*

The moss roses on Elizabeth's grave had faded, even overnight. It was to be expected in this exceptional weather – 1924 seemed set for a hot June – but as soon as Gerard saw their hanging heads he sighed, turned on his heel and walked straight back to the Manor to pick some more. Less than a quarter of an hour later, he was back, sweating slightly, in a tweed Norfolk jacket – it would have been improper to have ventured out in shirtsleeves – carrying a large bunch, not only of moss roses, but also some of the new-fangled Hybrid Musks hoping that their pale pink blooms might last longer.

As he approached the grave, he noticed a figure, in a white cotton dress and wide-brimmed straw hat, moving among the headstones. He stopped and hesitated. It was important that his grave visits, conducted daily at precisely the same time, were solitary. He was wondering whether to turn back when he recognised, with a quickening of the pulse, the shop girl Violet. As happened whenever he saw her, he was struck afresh, by her resemblance to Elizabeth. As he watched, she walked to the door of the church but, instead of entering, turned towards Elizabeth's grave and stood for a few moments. Gerard held his breath. No one was supposed even to glance at Elizabeth. This was *their* private spot. After a moment, the girl squatted and took a fading rose out of the vase. Gerard gasped. He felt violated. She examined the flower and then dropped it on to the ground. When she grabbed the rest of the blooms, all in a bunch, out of the vase, it was too much for him.

'What, precisely, do you think you are doing?' he demanded, striding up to the grave, his heart pounding and his cheeks burning with indignation. The girl was startled and stood up, dropping the roses. 'Well?'

'I beg your pardon.' When she saw who was addressing her, she was relieved, at first, but now she was shaken by his attitude. 'It was none of my business, sir, but I couldn't help noticing.'

'Noticing what?'

'Your flowers were wilting. I watched you put them here yesterday and—'

'—Yesterday? You were spying on me?'

'No! No sir!' Violet felt her own cheeks burn with embarrassment. 'I've been coming here most days, recently, to study.' She indicated the porch of the church. Three text books and a couple of exercise books rested on the stone bench. 'It's the only cool place in the village at the moment, and I've got such an awful lot of school work to do.'

'I see.' Gerard's breathing was coming a little easier now, but he did not know what to do next. She had ruined his tryst with Elizabeth and yet he felt loath to dismiss her. It seemed remarkable to him that a girl of such humble origins should have such poise. He began to thrust the new roses into the vase that she had emptied.

'I'm afraid they won't last either, sir. Not like that.'

'What do you mean?'

'You need fresh water for a start. Then you should break and crush their lower stems, so they can take up the water. That's what I was going to do with the others, to revive them.' She seemed so capable. Could Elizabeth somehow, be in her spirit? Such thoughts were irrational but nearly fifteen years of brooding had driven much logic from his mind. 'You can do it with this stone, look.' Violet took hold of the stems that he had pushed into the vase and held them against a piece of limestone bedded in the turf surrounding the grave – in this part of Lincolnshire, rock broke through the surface of the land in abundance – and then, spotting a loose fragment within reach, caught hold of it and began to strike the lower parts of the the stems until they were split and crushed. Gerard watched, fascinated by this seemingly destructive act. A greenish, mildly spiced aroma came from the damaged plant tissue and the buff surface of the stone was stained with the juices. 'You need fresh water,' she said, and jumped up with the vase, shooting the foetid dregs onto the grass before going to the pump in the corner of the yard to draw from the well. She jerked the handle up and down a couple of times and cursed under her breath when the hollow clanking sound meant that no water would come.

'It needs priming,' Gerard said, He had followed her to the pump and lifted the full bucket, always left nearby, to tip some water into the top of the mechanism. Violet pumped the handle rapidly at first, slowing down when she felt the sudden resistance, as the vacuum was created and water was drawn up and began to pulse from the spout, rusty red from the pipework at first, then clearing. She rinsed the vase three times and then filled it.

'Better leave a full bucket for the next person,' she said.

'Better had,' he agreed. They walked back to the grave and he stood back while she set up the vase and began to place the flower stems into the water, shaking their buds out and arranging them as evenly as possible. She paused as she lifted one of the Hybrid Musk roses.

'This is lovely.' Her voice had developed a gentler tone, in deference to his wife's burial spot.

'It's new.' He might have explained that it had arrived at Wychgate Manor with several other new rose varieties, in the hands of his new gardener who had previously worked for the Romford clergymen who had bred it. But that would have meant giving an involved exposition and he still found conversing awkward. He was so out of practice.

'Does it have a name?' She slipped the stem into the water, among the moss roses

'Something Greek . . .' he couldn't quite remember, 'Persephone, I think. No. Penelope. That's it, "Penelope". Do you know about roses?'

'Not much. But I love this one. I've never seen quite such a pretty pink.' She fitted the last bloom into the vase, having first, with deft, rapid fingers, removed a blown flower and surplus leaves from the spray.

'You need some ferns to go with these,' she said. 'They'd bring out the beauty of the blooms.' Now he felt unable to answer. He had been planning to spend these moments alone with the grave. He needed, so much, to communicate with the memory of Elizabeth and yet he was grateful to this girl for her considerate ways and her cool confidence. He was beginning to realise that he did not want her to go. He felt more comfortable in her presence than with almost anyone else, including his son, but there was more to it than that. Somehow, she seemed so like Elizabeth, here and now, smiling, talking quietly and helping him with his routine devotions, that the real Elizabeth began to seem less real. In the few times he had met this young girl, and especially now, by this severe headstone, the reality of her presence sharpened his longing for Elizabeth but at the same time confused his memory of her. With this Elizabeth-like girl beside him, alive and breathing, with youthful colour in her cheeks and a light of intelligence in her eyes, it was becoming difficult to build up mental pictures of the true Elizabeth. That made him feel guilty. He had no right; it was unfaithful. He sighed. She noticed, picking up the fallout from the conflict in his mind. 'Would you like me to go?' He was unable to answer. After a few moments, she walked slowly to the porch, to collect her books.

Gerard watched her walking up the path beneath the yews to the lane where she had left her bicycle. At the gate, she turned and waved. His hand twitched in automatic response, but on a stronger impulse, he restrained himself and did not wave back.

He stood and stared at the gate for some minutes after Violet's departure. He could just see, through the yew branches, glimpses of her white dress as she collected the heavy bicycle from behind the end tree and rested one foot on the pedal. He imagined her launching herself into motion with the same grace and ease that Elizabeth would exhibit when she leapt into the saddle of one of her hunters. He wished he had waved back and hoped that not doing so would not have seemed like a snub. He turned back to the grave and began to gather up the faded roses, annoyed by the browning petals that had scattered on to the neat turf, making it look untidy. He tried to pick them up but the task was obviously too great and now a breeze was spreading them for yards around. On the grave itself, the neatly arranged vase – he could never have made the flowers look that good – reminded him of the reason for his visit. He tried to put himself into what he perceived as the 'right frame of mind' but, somehow, it all seemed pointless now. Would she mind if someone else had done the flowers? He hoped not, but could not be sure.

He walked back to the Manor alone, seeing no one on the way. Most of the villagers were hard at work with the hay harvest, gathering up the sweet dried grasses, laced with wild herbs and flowers, into the stackyards, to conserve the summer abundance for winter feeding of their livestock. Later in the afternoon, boys would be swimming in the river, invisible behind the thicket, their sharp, joyful cries sounding over the water meadows; farm workers in shirts minus their Sunday collars, done up at the neck with a stud, would be slaking their thirst with beer outside the Black Pig while their wives tended their front gardens, sowing seeds of lettuce, spring onions and late peas; planting out geraniums that had overwintered on kitchen windowsills and hoeing out emerging weed seedlings.

Gerard, after a brief stroll in his own extensive gardens, went inside and rang for tea in his study. He sat down and took a sheet of letter paper from the ebony holder on his desk and was about to begin his weekly letter to his son when he paused, pen nib suspended above the thick, cream letter paper. Then he began to write, quickly with the pen scratching the paper.

> *Miss Ball,*
> *It occurred to me, after you had left this afternoon, that I had not thanked you for your help. You seemed very taken with the flowers and I wondered whether you might care to visit our rose garden while it is at its best.*
> *Perhaps you would come to take tea on Thursday afternoon at four pm.*

As soon as he had written the last word, he tore the sheet across once, twice and a third time, dropping the fragments into the brass waste-bin by the desk. Then he looked out of the window, and remembered how she had arrived, what? three years before? and had leapt from her bicycle, conjuring up a startling resurrection of Elizabeth. And how, subsequently, he had taken to visiting her father's shop from time to time, to buy objects that he could well have sent a servant to collect. And how, if he had seen her there, or had watched her riding about the village on that monstrous delivery bicycle, or walking in the water meadow – more often than not, with a book in her hand – it was always with a bittersweet surge of emotions. Comfort at seeing her, tinged with guilt about Elizabeth.

He wrote the whole thing out again, folded it once and on the reverse side of the paper wrote: 'Miss Violet Ball, by hand'. At that point, Mrs Bull came in bearing a small tray with silver teapot and cream jug, a single cup and saucer – white bone china with a gold band round the rims – and a matching plate on which sat four small cucumber sandwiches. He cleared an area on his desk for her to set it down and handed her the letter.

'I should be obliged if you would get this delivered, Mrs Bull.'

'Certainly sir,' Mrs Bull glanced at the name on the paper and frowned slightly, puzzled.

'Nothing amiss, I hope, sir.' He glanced sharply up at her, just catching the query in her face before she recomposed it to the usual neutral.

'Nothing at all. Shall you send the new gardener's apprentice?'

'Oh no, sir, he's that absent-minded. There's no telling where he'd be getting to.' Without waiting to be asked, she poured tea into his cup and added precisely the amount of milk he liked. She was well used to serving him and, though there were seldom more than a dozen words expended between them, she was devoted. 'I'll take it up there myself.'

Chapter Five

––––

Whenever Barleythorpe played Tansor, a close-run match was guaranteed. There was much rivalry between the two great public schools, not only in sport but also in academic prowess and in the number of famous old boys each produced. So far, the score on cabinet ministers was exactly equal and both establishments had spawned a generous scattering, across the centuries, of ambassadors, archbishops and law lords, as well as convicted fraudsters and pederasts and, in certain cases, both in the same person.

No one insisted that pupils were good at, or even had to like Rugby Union and cricket, but those who lacked enthusiasm on the playing fields were unlikely to succeed in other aspects of school life. And if you were especially talented – a fleet-footed wing three-quarter, say, or a deadly spin bowler – the chances were much higher that any sins you might commit would be overlooked. Even in the extremes of wrong behaviour, membership of one of the school teams would usually mitigate the penalty.

The captain of Barleythorpe Colts, Michael Pilkington – Pilks to his friends and contemporaries – was about to open the bowling in the second innings of the match against Tansor. In another couple of weeks, he would be fifteen, and therefore cease to qualify for the team. He had already been earmarked for the senior team, and would probably get a couple of games with the bigger lads under his belt before the end of term in, he reminded himself, less than a month's time. But for now, he had the Tansor under-fifteens in his sights and he wanted to concentrate on them alone, and on absolutely nothing else.

'We're all ready when you are, Michael,' Mr Danvers said. Michael supposed that it was quite helpful having his housemaster as one of the umpires, but he felt embarrassed whenever Dreggie – as Danvers was universally known – used his Christian name. It didn't sound quite right, and he knew that only certain boys ever got called anything other than their surnames, with a 'Minor' or 'Major' suffixed, if they had a brother, and a 'Minimus' if there were a third sibling. The case of the Pollack twins had perplexed everyone until Danvers, smirking at his own wit, had come up with the idea of re-christening James 'Castor' and allowing his brother, William, to keep the name Pollack. Before long, the boys in Angmering House and subsequently, through the rest of the school, had amended these to 'Cast-off' and 'Bollock' – the former sobriquet being as painful to the twins as the latter, since the term 'casting off' was school slang for masturbating. But even that was less cringe-making than being called by your first name, just because you were good at cricket, or came top in Latin.

'Thank you, sir.' Michael took one last glance around his field, motioned his slips to move a little deeper and said, 'Ready,' before walking away from the stumps, counting his paces for his first run up.

'Play,' said Dreggie. Michael adjusted his fingers to the seam of the ball. It was a frighteningly tight match and Tansor had the upper hand, but he felt his team could still win, provided they didn't run out of time. The first innings had been pretty disastrous, with an opening partnership of 60 runs before the Tansor star batsman had managed to get himself run out. Thereafter, wickets had fallen fast until, for some reason, Barleythorpe couldn't shift the tail-enders who, with nothing to lose, and little in the way of batting refinements, had knocked Michael's best bowlers all over the field, pushing the final score up to 149. Michael had, at last, managed to catch the last batsman out with his own delivery – a full toss which was knocked sweetly from the middle of the bat straight back up the wicket into his waiting hands.

Barleythorpe had caught up fast and were all out for 128, only 21 runs behind at the beginning of the second innings. But time was not on their side and the opposition would surely dig in after consolidating their lead.

Michael began his run up, his eye fixed on his target, the ball held in his large, confident hands. He gathered speed, swung his arm and delivered. The ball described a gently curving parabola as it sped through the heavy, summer air and bounced exactly where Michael wanted it to, a few inches out of line with the off stump. The Tansor batsman played forward, nicked the ball with the inside edge of his bat and almost played it on to his own stumps. It was an expert delivery.

The ball was tossed back to Michael who bowled an identical looking delivery but pitched, this time, a little further outside the off stump. The batsman, jittery after his last mistake, elected not to play the ball which bounced, turned sharply inwards and knocked his off stump clean out of the ground. Every Barleythorpe boy, watching from the boundary, lolling in the pavilion, lying in the cool grass under the row of lime trees that flanked the west side of the field, leapt to his feet and cheered. Many threw their school caps into the air. Masters, and the wives of those who had them, applauded vigorously from their seats near the pavilion. Visiting masters and pupils from Tansor clapped briefly and halfheartedly.

That evening, there was much celebrating, especially in Angmering House where every boy was re-living, analysing, discuss and rejoicing in the great Pilks hat-trick. In the rest of that over, he had taken two more wickets and the Tansor team, after losing their captain and opening bats before their score had reached double figures, eventually went home dispirited, dreading the inevitable post-mortems, the grilling by coaches and housemasters, beaten by seven wickets. Pilks had gone on to score almost a half century and Barleythorpe had managed to scramble for the runs they needed with less than fifteen minutes in hand.

'Quite the man of the match,' Riversley said. As his special friend, Riversley had been allowed to linger at the baths and changing room while the great captain, having personally seen off the vanquished opposition at the railway station, and then having jogged the mile back, bathed and changed. The rest of the Colts team had already cleaned up and left.

'You didn't do so badly yourself,' Michael replied, climbing out of the bath and taking the towel offered by his friend. Riversley couldn't help noticing how well developed and grown-up Michael seemed nowadays. His own body, he knew, was still gawky and his movements clumsy. He kept dropping and breaking things, besides which, his skin was constantly breaking out in crops of disfiguring spots. Michael's body seemed devoid of blemish; Riversley could not remember ever having seen a single spot or pimple on him.

'Oh pooh! Their bowling went to pieces. They just gave up.'

'No, really, it was touch and go!' He rubbed himself down before pulling a clean white shirt over his head. 'You tonked up the runs quickly. We needed that. We'd have run out of time, if you hadn't been so fast.'

'Gosh, thanks, Pilks!' The boy flushed with pride. His heart leapt so, at such praise from his hero, that he nearly sang out loud. Everyone liked Pilks. Some of the little ticks in their first year at Barleythorpe had lined up, after the match, holding out autograph books to him and had offered chewed fountain pens for him to use. Even the sixth formers displayed an affectionate attitude towards him, something that no other boy of his age enjoyed.

Michael finished dressing and went to his study where his father's weekly letter lay on the desk, unread since its arrival in the first post. Most boys opened their mail hastily, anxious to savour a fragment of home-life. Most boys counted the days left until the end of term; some even drew special calendars with days carefully marked out, striking them off each morning in pencil. But Michael was less interested in home, and term's end loomed on the horizon like a weather front. The holidays were something to be endured rather than to be enjoyed, even though, he told himself, he loved his father and was happy sharing his isolated life in Wychgate Manor.

When he pulled the thick, creamy paper from the envelope, he was surprised to see that, instead of the usual single page, not only were there three sheets, but that both sides of each were covered with his father's immaculate copperplate hand. Assuming that there must be some kind of momentous news, he began to read. But nothing in the opening paragraphs suggested anything amiss. The letter began in his father's familiar noncommittal style:

My Dear Boy
   How quickly the week has passed since my last letter! Everything is as usual here, with nothing exceptional to report. They mowed the water meadow last Friday and have had perfect weather for a good hay crop ever since. Life in Wychgate continues in its uneventful way.
   Last Thursday, the young girl from the shop, Violet Ball, called for tea. She is interested in flowers and, as you may know, Lane re-planted the rose garden last autumn so I decided to invite her to see it.

From here, the tenor of the letter changed and went completely out of character. The tone warmed and the writing, somehow, flowed differently even if the grammar had become slightly suspect:

I do feel, my dear Michael, that we should befriend such people as Miss Ball. During the War, many men from trade, or from even lower stations in life, were given Commissions in the Army; and women, too, from all sorts of strange backgrounds, performed important tasks. Such people, in spite of humble origins, have exhibited a great deal more quality than we realised they possessed.

What on earth was he driving at, Michael wondered. The language was unclear. Did he mean that shop girls were equal with ladies of quality? He read on,

Miss Ball is as intelligent as anyone I have ever met. She

reads Milton and Shakespeare, she possesses enough of the social graces to be able to converse comfortably, even with someone like myself, so many years her senior and, if I may put it this way, in such a different situation.

She exhibits certain eccentricities which, given her youthfulness and naïvety, are excusable. Among other strangely assorted beliefs – including the mistaken conviction that it is proper for women to have been given the vote – she claims to know something of what she calls the World of the Occult. Witches and witchcraft, she informs me, are not by any means evil, or even especially mysterious. She says that the poor creatures who were victimised and tortured in Mediaeval times, were, for the most part, wrongly maligned. They simply used a craft by which they felt they could influence nature. Cures for ills were as much their stock in trade as were spells put on people. She says, also, that she believes it is possible to make contact with what she calls the Other Side – that is, to summon up spirits and communicate with them. All nonsense, of course, but she is, I assure you, most persuasive in her convictions.

The letter ran on in this vein for a while, before reiterating his regard for the girl and, in an oblique way, suggesting that when Michael came home for the holidays, he might care to strike up some kind of friendship with her. The text concluded thus:

Miss Ball is hoping to gain a place at Somerville College, Oxford. Since I know a little about History, I have arranged for her to discuss some of her work each week, over tea. I do hope that, when you are home, you might like to join our little sessions.
Ever your loving father.

Michael read the whole letter through a second time before

folding it with care, and replacing it in the stiff envelope. It was astounding. No one was more withdrawn and reclusive than his father and yet, here he was, writing pages about the local shop girl, a person one hardly noticed. A person who, when they had last communicated, had snubbed him and who, he felt, looked on him and his kind with nothing but contempt. He presumed that she had no interest in cricket or rugby; obviously, she knew nothing about the techniques of trench warfare and anyway, she must be at least a year older than he, and therefore not in the slightest bit interested in any sort of relationship.

Girls, as far as Michael was concerned, were not worthy of serious consideration. Herded with all the other boys at Barleythorpe, life was really too busy to worry about them. The older chaps, he knew, were keen to talk about sex and some of his contemporaries indulged in conversations and activities of so disgusting a nature that they turned his stomach. There were, he knew, certain urges, and in his first year at Barleythorpe, he had been introduced to the practice of 'casting off'. Then, at Confirmation classes, the chaplain had talked to them about the sin of lust, and about forms of behaviour that were unacceptable, not only in the eyes of God but also among grown-up chaps. And what had been innocent mutual fumbling between fellow adolescents, acquired a mantle of guilt and, henceforward, he and most of his classmates adopted a more chaste existence or, at least, gratified themselves only when seriously desperate, and only then, in total secrecy. The ultimate sin was to do it less than twenty-four hours before a house or a school match, because it was said to impair performance at sport.

As for love – that hardly figured in Michael's orbit. He had, he supposed, a dutiful love for his father. Most of his friends, some of whom had lost fathers in the Great War, expressed an ardent love for their mothers. Among codes of behaviour, criticising your own or someone else's mother would have been nearly as unforgivable as 'sneaking' or telling tales to prefects or masters. In a way, he loved his fellows at school. The team feeling, especially now that he was captain of the Colts, was wonderfully warm. He knew, too, that certain boys looked at him with a kind of longing that disturbed him. They offered such little favours as carrying books, running to fetch things or giving sweets with a motive that he knew was there, but which he couldn't quite understand. He also knew that he had a great affection for Riversley, even liking his ugliness. He felt grateful for his ingenuous flattery, he enjoyed similar interests but, as well as all that, he preferred to be in his company rather than not. But that, as his fifteenth birthday approached, was about as close to love as Michael Pilkington had ever been.

Thursday was market day in Stoneford, the day Mrs Crowe made her weekly visit to the town to stock up with provisions. It was the only day she left Imogen alone in Weir House and every week, she expressed the same anxiety about her charge risking contact with the outside world. 'Just make absolutely sure,' she muttered, as she prepared to leave, 'that you answer the door to no one, but no one! Yes?' She buttoned up her gabardine mackintosh, adjusted her head scarf and checked her oilskin shopping bag for purse and shopping list. 'I'll only be gone an hour. Two at the very outside. I know there's nothing you want.'

'Oh, actually, ahm . . .' Imogen wanted to say that she needed some more shampoo but, before she could say another word, Mrs Crowe had slammed the heavy front door of Weir House behind her. A moment later, Imogen looked through the drawing-room window to see the back of her – Imogen's – small Ford Fiesta disappearing up the street. Imogen had a driving licence but had not sat at the steering wheel of a vehicle, since her ban, after the incident. Now, even though the prohibited period was over, she felt incapable of driving.

The little front garden looked neat this morning, with the first of the yellow crocuses opening up to the weak sunshine. She watched a sparrow alight near one of the blooms and could hear it chirruping, in spite of the double glazing. She had never before noticed what beautiful markings sparrows had. The bird's head was a rich tan, with grey cap, a black eye-stripe and pale grey, almost white cheeks. Another sparrow joined it and they chirped at each other for a while before the first bird, presumably a male, since its markings were more accented, hopped to one of the crocus blooms and began to peck at it, snatching off pieces and chucking them aside to grab more until the flower was destroyed and the golden-orange petals lay in fragments on the cold soil. She tapped on the window, to frighten the birds away, but with the double glazing, she couldn't make them take any notice. 'Oh, go away!' she murmured, and went to the front door to shoo them away. Then she remembered that in Saint James's Park the gardeners used to suspend lengths of black thread in a crisscrossing network over young crocuses and primulas. She remembered after a drunken lunch, once, at Overtons, wandering with Marcus into the park and staggering with him along the grass, getting their feet entangled in the threads. It had taken them a while to realise what it was, snagging their ankles and, by the time they had got themselves extricated and had actually fallen on the muddy turf a couple of times, a policeman had begun to stride towards them. They had managed, just, to pull themselves together enough to be able to jog towards the park gates and up Cockpit Steps to St. James's Park Tube station and thus escape. The excitement of the policeman's attention had pumped up their adrenalin and had marked the beginning of a high – sustained by a cocktail of drugs and alcohol – that lasted for days. Or was it weeks? Really, Imogen couldn't remember.

'Thread,' she muttered, and went to find some black cotton. There was a workbasket in the small morning-room on the east side of the house, but it contained nothing more than an old cough lozenge tin full of shirt buttons, a scrap or two of material and a number of small packets of needles and thread supplied for emergencies by some of the more expensive hotels. She rummaged in the kitchen drawers, without success, and then, with some trepidation, crept upstairs to Mrs Crowe's room. Out of timidity, she knocked, even though she knew that her minder would be in Stoneford by now, and peeped round the door.

The smell of Mrs Crowe's scent almost made her lose her nerve, but the sight of this room, so well ordered, and so redolent of the older woman's character, fascinated her. She crept in. She paused by the bed, noting the hospital corners, the neatly fluffed pillow and a bible on the bedside table. Odd, she thought. The Crow had never struck her as being a religious person. She walked to the window and looked out at the garden. Even the point of view, from this room – though it was on the same side as the landing window through which she glanced every day – seemed different, somehow. Better. On the dressing table, beneath the window, was a small porcelain tray in which sat a pair of earrings and a gold ring, set with a large topaz and two small sapphires on either side. Imogen felt sure that Mummy had one exactly like that. Daddy had, she remembered, brought the gem stones back from Ceylon, or Brazil – or somewhere like that – and had got the piece made up by one of the big jewellers in Regent Street. She reached out to pick the ring up but then refrained, not liking, much, to touch something that belonged, so intimately, to the Crow.

With hesitant fingers, she opened the top drawer of the dressing table. Bank statements lay, in an ordered pile, the most recent on the top – her own account, but she knew that. The Crow was supposed to look after things and was even allowed to sign her cheques. She glanced at the bottom figure in the column – £8,735.61 – and was puzzled. She didn't think they had more than a few hundred. That was why there was always so little to eat and why the house was so cold. Even when the Crow roasted a Sunday joint, Imogen was not allowed more than a single, thin slice. A healthy diet, she insisted – though she herself was capable of downing almost a whole bottle of Bordeaux with her slab of rare beef – was part of Imogen's re-hab process. She shut the drawer. Probably misread the figure, she decided. She had never understood money very well. She felt sure she needed glasses anyway.

She found cotton – plenty of it in several shades – in the second drawer down among a well stocked sewing kit. She filched a reel of black button thread, closed the drawer, glanced round the room, hoping it was precisely as she had found it, and crept out, closing the door quietly behind her.

Outside in the cold, bright morning, slightly hampered by her ruinous man's overcoat, she busied herself, breaking twigs from a large viburnum and pushing these into the ground among the drift of emerging crocuses. The cotton she twisted and wove to and fro, making a giant spider web. Every so often she would snap the thin thread and had to stop to tie the end securely to a twig. Just as she bent at an uncomfortable angle, after one of these breaks, tying two short strands together, a car – large, expensive-looking – pulled up close to the gates. The driver emerged. It was Russell Hands.

'Oh shit!' said Imogen under her breath. She bent lower, pretending to be engrossed in her task. The problem was, she had forgotten exactly how to tie a knot – she often had memory lapses – and her hands froze, one thread in each, while she tried to remember.

'Hallo 'allo 'allo!' Hands said, peering over the wall. 'Bit early in the year for gardenin', innit?' She tried not to look up, but felt herself drawn, felt her head move, in spite of herself. He was wearing greenish twill trousers – baggy, with fashionable pleats – and a thick Arran sweater under an expensive-looking navy ski jacket. He looked better in casual clothes than in the suit he had worn last time she'd seen him, and the former pinkness of his face had been replaced by a healthy tan. Clearly, he'd been abroad for a winter holiday. 'Antigua,' he said, reading her mind, 'just got back.'

Imogen said nothing. She was confused. The Crow would get into a terrible rage if she found out about this encounter, but Imogen knew that she would not be able to stop him from talking to her. Unless she got away, quickly, now. She straightened up, and put the cotton reel into her coat pocket. 'Ahm . . .' she said, and ran for the front door. Hands had expected that.

'Oi!' A call so full of sharp command that her body responded instantly. She froze, with her back to him. He said nothing more until she began to move towards the front door again. 'No! Stay!' He might have been instructing a gun dog. She stayed. He softened his tone. 'I only want a chat.' She turned.

'I'm sorry, I . . . ahm . . .' She stood unable to move while he opened the gate and walked towards her. At his approach, she caught a waft of his cologne – a heavy, fruity fragrance, with a hint of musk. Not unpleasant. He stopped in front of her and she was obliged to look into his dark eyes. There was cruelty there, but she also recognised something else: a kind of hunger that struck a chord of sympathy with her own emotions. They were repellent eyes, and yet . . .

'You, um, what?' He smiled. She shrugged and drew her dreadful coat more closely round her shoulders.

'I have to get back inside.' But he held her with his eyes.

'Let's go for a walk.' He indicated the village street. 'You look as though you need some fresh air.'

'Oh, I can't. Mrs Crowe . . .'

'She needn't know.' He took one of her arms. She flinched at first, but then submitted and allowed herself to be escorted to her own front gate. 'I know she ain't there. I saw 'er drive off twenty minutes ago.' It didn't occur to Imogen to wonder why he had been watching the house, waiting to snatch an opportunity to talk to her alone. By now they were walking slowly downhill.

'Where are we going?' There was fear in her voice but she was also excited, partly at the prospect of disobeying the Crowe and partly by the presence of this man. She had not been touched by a male for months. Years even. But she was also afraid of him.

'Why don't we 'ave a butchers at that wood of yours?' He kept hold of her arm, linking it lightly in his own and they walked to the first of the spruces. At the entrance of the track that led into the wood, she tried to hang back but he pushed on and she was obliged to keep up with him. The woodland ride was overgrown with brambles and they kept stumbling, but under the conifers themselves, nothing grew and they soon found it easier to walk. The going, underfoot, was soft now, but resilient because of the thick layer of fallen spruce needles. As he led her deeper into the wood, the light got poorer and she stopped and pulled back, but he would not let go of her arm. 'What you got planned for all this, then?' They were both standing still, now, facing each other.

'I'm, ahm, not sure.'

'Can't leave it like this. All overgrown, can you?'

'Why not?'

'Too valuable to ignore.'

'Valuable?'

'Golden Goose.' He gestured at the woodland. 'Could make yerself a packet.' In spite of her addled brain, and her current depression, caused more by the low protein diet Mrs Crowe was imposing on her than by her previous heroin addiction, the prospect of renewed wealth hove into view through the mists.

'What are you talking about?' Hands caught the interest in her voice, the change in tone. Time to raise the stakes, he thought.

'Obvious, innit?'

'What?' She turned to face him, 'What?' The face was still pallid and, although her eyes had not exactly lit up, they were showing a faint, a very faint hint of eagerness.

'That'd be telling,' Hands said, and smirked. Her reaction surprised him.

'What? What?' she demanded, catching the edges of his ski jacket with both hands and shaking it slightly, 'Tell me, tell me.' Hands continued to smirk. 'Don't be a meany two shoes!'

'Cost you.' He put his hands over hers, still on his jacket. 'A kiss and I'll tell.' She tried to pull away but he would not let go. She was too weak to resist him. She realised, with a mix of revulsion, dread and a little excitement, that she was completely in his power. Whatever he wanted to do with her, he could. The prospect, as all its implications sunk in, almost made her wet herself with fright, but it also set pulses beating, down there, that she had almost forgotten she had. The swirl of emotions made her feel nauseous. He read her hesitation as an assent, but he didn't much care either way and pulled her face to his, clamping his mouth on hers. She clenched her lips together, but when his hot tongue probed them, with rapid stabs, she felt her whole body soften and parted her teeth, anticipating the feel of his tongue thrusting deeper into her mouth. But he pulled back and stared at her face, ready to sneer at her startled eyes. This bitch was cock-hungry. What's more, even though she was barking mad, she knew an opportunity when it got up and smacked her in the face. She wiped her mouth, panting a little and, in those few seconds, managed to re-possess some of what little poise she had.

'I've paid the, ahm, price. Now you have to tell.'

'Timber crop.'

'Oh that.' She deflated. 'I already know about that. We've had it valued. It's over-late for some of the trees, 't'isn't worth that much, really.'

'There's more.' He watched her eyebrows lift again, noticed the glint return to the eyes.

'Yes?' Wary. She wasn't about to be caught out again. But would it be being caught out? Her lips still tingled from his touch but she grimaced at the prospect of another of those invasive, assaulting kisses.

'Build on it.'

'What?'

'Build on it. Good sites are making forty grand a plot round here.'

'But the village.'

'No need to go mad. Just put up three or four 'ouses – nice, executive development.'

'But wouldn't I need, ahm . . . ?'

'Planning consent?'

'Could I get it?' She was warming to this prospect. She hadn't thought things through at all – she did very little thinking anyway – but some instinct told her that to survive, to truly rehabilitate, she would have to find independence, somehow, and this might be a way. 'Could I?'

Hands shook his head. '*You* couldn't. I probably could.'

'How?' But Hands simply shook his head again, and began to walk away. He planned to leave her hungry. It was never his practice to come straight to the point, in any business dealing, and this session, he felt, had gone far enough for the moment. Very nice and satisfactory. What's more, he told himself, this tart could be quite a looker, if only she'd get a bit of meat on her.

'How?' she trotted after him but he increased his pace, thrusting through the branches. One caught on his jacket and, as she followed closely, it whipped back, right into her face, sharpening her temper to a cutting edge. 'Wait!' she shouted, almost in tears from the stinging cheek, but with a suggestion of upper-class command in her tone. 'Dammit, wait, you . . . you . . . *sod*!' He froze in his tracks and turned, seeing the reddening weal the branch had made on her face and noticing that her eyes were watering with the pain. The sight of her, defenceless, angry and smarting, triggered an aggressive impulse.

'Names?' His voice had gone quiet, and a little husky. 'Calling names, is it?' She read menace in his tone and saw venom in the eyes. Now unease turned to fear. He caught her wrist and gripped it so hard she thought it would break His fingers enclosed it fully, the thumbnail actually puncturing her skin.

'I'm sorry.' She was near to tears. 'That branch. It really hurt.'

'Then I'll have to kiss it better, won't I?' He grabbed her head, more roughly than the first time, and clamped his mouth on to hers. While they were thus locked, she felt his free hand begin to knead her buttocks. She was repelled, but could not make herself stop him, even when his hands began to move under her overcoat. Someone as despicable as herself deserved such disgusting advances, she supposed, but this wasn't as simple as a plain case of self-loathing. She wanted him; she hated him. Then, as abruptly as the first time, he pulled himself away and strode out of the wood. This time, he would not be stopped. She trotted behind him, not so much to be with him as to avoid being left alone in the dark wood. It was a horrible place, with an eerie atmosphere and now it would have further associations of unpleasantness.

By the time they got back to the road and he was striding up the hill towards his car outside Weir House, she was quite out of breath. He had the keys out of his pocket several paces before he reached the driver's door. 'That woman of yours go out regular, like?' He spoke without turning towards her.

'Mrs Crowe? Yes. Shopping in Stoneford, every Thursday morning.'

'See yer next week, then.' He got in, slammed the car door and drove off so fast that one rear wheel skidded in the damp at the side of the road, leaving a smeared track and peppering her garden wall with small pellets of grey mud. She stared at the retreating vehicle, putting her hands into her old coat pocket and feeling the cotton reel. Absently, she wound thread round her index finger and then pulled against the reel until it tightened enough to bite into her skin.

Less than an hour after he had left, Mrs Crowe returned to find her in the sitting-room busy with a duster. The furniture had all been moved to one side of the room and, Mrs Crowe noticed, the floor had been swept and the scatter rugs piled neatly in a corner. 'What on earth's going on?'

'Oh, ahm, I thought I'd clean up a bit.' Imogen continued dusting while she spoke. Mrs Crowe looked sharply at her. There was a change in her voice that aroused her suspicions.

'Something's been going on.'

'Hmm, hmm, hmmm' That little three note hum was all she got in reply, but now, it was in a major key. Altogether a brighter sound.

'Something *has* been going on.' The humming and dusting continued. 'Imogen! Look at me.' She stopped dusting and looked. Mrs Crowe spotted the red weal, where the spruce branch had lashed her cheek, just breaking the skin. Eye contact was brief, and Imogen was soon looking at her shoes and fidgeting under Mrs Crowe's scrutiny.

'Nothing.'

'I *can* tell dear,' the older woman's tone softened to a croon, 'I need to know. For your sake.'

'I went for a walk.'

'A walk?' Up to now, the only time Imogen had been permitted, or indeed, had shown any inclination to go out alone, was to church every third Sunday, when Jerome celebrated Eucharist at Saint Peter's. Mrs Crowe, in spite of the bible on her bedside table, never attended religious services. Her motivation for sending Imogen was that it would seem proper – rather than for reasons of faith – and would also give her time to do certain things, alone, about the house. 'What sort of a walk?'

'Just into the wood.'

'Who with?' Imogen had anticipated that question. She wouldn't lie, but she knew she needed to keep quiet about Hands. She simply forced herself to look up at the Crow's inquiring face and shook her head in a vague way that could have meant 'nobody' or, could simply register her puzzlement at everything around her. Crowe appeared to have bought it. 'You've scratched your face.' The girl put a hand to her cheek and coloured, remembering her reaction to the stinging blow and Hands's frightening response.

'Mmm, just a branch.' She turned to resume dusting. 'It's nothing, really.'

'The walk's done you some good. You should go out for fresh air more often.' The dusting, inefficient as it was, seemed a good sign and having Imogen do a bit more about the house might ease her workload. 'On your own, of course.'

'Mmm? Yes, perhaps I should.' The dialogue was as between equals, but both women knew that one, by giving the other permission to make this tiny change in her lifestyle, had tossed her a fragment of freedom.

Mrs Crowe had to unload her shopping from the car. Imogen watched her clumping in and out with cardboard boxes laden with groceries and heard her slam the car boot down. It did not occur to her to offer to help. She thought about her earlier encounter with Hands and knew that she had learned two valuable lessons that day: firstly, she knew that she had, somehow – and God knew why – become attractive to this frightening man, but that there would be danger in the liaison. Secondly, as long as she could shake off some of this debilitating lassitude that dogged most of her actions and could keep her mind awake, she might, to a very limited extent, be able to manipulate the Crow. Both discoveries terrified and excited her. The very thought of Hands chilled her blood. He was like a raptor with a hypnotic effect on his prey, and she was about to become a victim. She knew that. But any captor, she decided, would be preferable to Mrs Crowe.

Chapter Six

———

Hands drove rapidly, using the full strength of his car's acceleration to overtake slower country vehicles and swinging the wheel on the bends as if he were trying to see just how far he could push it before he lost control. The sun was about to set now, on this late winter afternoon and already, an amber light on his dashboard warned that the outside temperature had dipped to within a couple of degrees of freezing point.

After leaving Imogen, earlier that day, he had planned to lunch at a pub down on the Fen, not far from Spalding, before driving on towards the coast to look at one of his property developments. But the feel of her mouth – hard at first, then yielding – had left a tingle on his tongue and he couldn't rid himself of the memory of how slight her body had felt under that ruinous old coat: so bony and brittle, as if a careless move might crush her bones, and yet so warm, so vital and quick in her flinching movements – a feeling that belied the lassitude in her voice and outward manner. She was hungry! And, sod it, so was he!

He had stopped at a junction, indicating a left turn, but had dithered for a moment, and then on an impulse, had turned right, annoying the driver behind him who hooted his car horn. Hands had pressed the electric window button, extended his right arm out of the window and had given an American middle finger salute before closing the window and picking up his car phone. He had pressed one of the preset numbers.

'Shirley? Ains!' Hands had said.

'Russell, love!' The voice was languid, gruff from cigarette smoking, with an east Midland accent. 'Where are you?'

'Never you mind, where's Frank?' Hands had glanced at his watch, flicked his indicator and swung out to overtake a grain lorry, all with one hand, while the other held the car phone to his ear.

'Half way between Plymouth and Bath, I should think. It's his West Country week.'

'Brilliant!' He had swerved back on to his side of the road, managing, just, to get out of the way of an oncoming Jaguar, same year and colour as his own, eliciting a warning flash of headlights from the car and a blast from the grain lorry's air horn. He didn't have a hand free to gesture but had jabbed his brakes, to annoy the lorry driver behind, and then accelerated harder. 'I'm headin' for Boston right now. Be there in fifteen minutes.' He had listened for a moment, then, 'No, girl, lunch is *not* what I need right now. You know what I'm after. Just be ready.' When he switched off his car phone, Boston's narrow church tower, with its unique pinnacled lantern top, was already in view, the only distinctive feature for miles in that flat Fen landscape.

After arriving at the little harbour town, he had driven through to the furthest outskirts and turned up a street lined with a terrace of small houses, all with neat front gardens. The buildings were uniform, pre-war red brick, each having two front windows and a blue slate roof; but many had new front doors in a variety of styles from plain timber, studded with square headed 'Tudor' nails – often with coach lamps on either side – to plainer designs in frosted glass. These had once been council houses but most, now, had been purchased by their tenants who, as a first expression of ownership, had been to the nearest DIY centre to select a new front door.

Hands parked two thirds of the way down the street – for discretion – and then walked back a hundred yards to let himself into the end house with one of a dozen keys bunched on his multiple ring. In the hall, decorated with pink flock wallpaper, was a framed print of a Chinese girl with a blue-green face, and a vase of dried pampas grass flowers dyed blue and pink; he took off his ski jacket, hung it on a hook on the deal hall-stand, glanced at his face in the mirror and called softly. 'Shirley!'

'Up here, love.' The reply was muttered through an open bedroom door, soft and throaty. The house smelt of cigarettes and cheap, musky perfume. He climbed the stairs to find Shirley, sitting in the middle of her four-poster bed surrounded by frilly white nylon 'lace' hangings, bunched and gathered in swags over the structure. She was wearing a vivid pink negligée and, although she had switched on an electric heater, her arms were goose-fleshed and she shivered slightly. She was quite pretty, in a toothy sort of way, blonde hair, out of a bottle, and hazel eyes which were not quite big enough to be voluptuous but which she enhanced, as best she could, with greenish eye shadow and too much mascara.

On the wall opposite the window was a large reproduction of an oil painting showing a vast swan taking off over the ocean in the background while, in the foreground stood a nude male, side view. A tray rested on the bedside table, with two imitation crystal goblets and a bottle of Oloroso Sherry. She reached over and lifted the bottle, but replaced it when he shook his head. He was panting slightly, from running up the stairs, she presumed.

'Not long since you rang,' she said, 'You can't have been far away.'

'I've . . . driven . . .' Hands was having difficulty speaking and tearing off his clothes at the same time – 'like a . . . fucking maniac.' He had yanked off shirt and undershirt, kicked off shoes, dropped trousers and, with more difficulty than usual, lowered and removed his underpants.

'Goodness, we *are* excited,' Shirley had said, manufacturing as much enthusiasm as she could. 'What ever's come over you?'

'Come 'ere, girl,' Hands had muttered, stepping towards the bed and reaching for her.

'Don't you want to have a wash?'

'Leave it out, Shirl!' She had grimaced, but not so as he'd notice, and slid across the bed, to allow him access.

Eleven and a half minutes later, Hands had sat up in bed and said, 'What's for lunch?'

'Oh, Russell, give me a chance,' Shirley had replied. 'You said you didn't want any.'

'Me miss lunch? Never!' He clambered out of bed and, still unwashed, began to pull his clothes back on. Shirley slipped out to the bathroom and then followed him downstairs to her small kitchen where she found him some lettuce and a slice or two of cold ham. She stood by the stainless steel sink unit, smoking a cigarette while she watched him eat. He was framed in the window, the low sun shining right through, so that she could see his outline, but not his features. From his point of view, the light was shining directly on to her, highlighting the sinews that were coarsening on her neck and accenting the pucker lines around her mouth, caused by decades of fag smoking, he supposed. Her eyes had lines too, running from their corners, which deepened when she crinkled them to avoid the smoke. He had watched her take a drag on her cigarette, its tip already marked with her cerise lipstick, saw the smoke hover, dense in her mouth, blotting out teeth and tongue before being drawn into her lungs and then expelled, in a long sigh, towards the ceiling. She always held her cigarette hand up slightly, the fingers half crooked, to avoid nicotine stains on her fingers.

'All right?' Shirley had asked, indicating his meal. He had nodded. Then she had doused her cigarette under the tap, thrown it into the rubbish bin and moved to the table so that she could see his face without the sun dazzling behind. She felt uncomfortable not knowing what sort of expression he was wearing, though you never really knew what he was thinking.

'You got it?' Hands spoke with a full mouth. She could see the ham and lettuce being masticated as he chewed, pink and green mixing, darkening to one dirty hue. 'You got it?'

Shirley sighed. 'Russell, it isn't the full fortnight yet.'

'One day don't make no difference.'

'It does to me, love. I can't just get hold of . . . well, you know.' She was smiling but there were extra stress lines, now, all round her eyes and forehead. He had spotted the fear and, as always when he sensed anyone in a weak position, raised the stakes.

'No. I'll be making it tomorrow. Change of collection day.' Shirley had burst into tears, and had then begun to plead. 'Look,' he had said, 'you're the stupid cow that owes the money. Yer 'usband could afford to pay the lot off. Sudden death. Why don't yer come clean to 'im?' But she cried all the more.

'I couldn't. He'd *kill* me if he knew.'

'Yeah?' Hands got up and tore off a sheet of kitchen roll to wipe his mouth. 'You know,' he went to the hall and returned with his ski jacket which he put on as he spoke, 'we get debtors in my business. Bad debtors, I mean. Debtors what don't manage their affairs well, or, think they can, sort 'a like, get away with not paying – you gettin' my drift?'

'Mmm!' Shirley had nodded vigorously.

'Well, I know a bloke who's, like, dead nifty wiv' a 'ammer. In fact, we call 'im "Sledge". An' 'e don't just break up, you know, *things*.' Here Hands had walked over to Shirley, and had held the back of her head in his hand, just as he had Imogen's that morning. 'No, 'e actually does quite an efficient job on people's legs.' Before Shirley could speak, he had clamped his mouth over hers. She all but gagged on the vinegar taste of salad cream and could feel fragments of food on his tongue. Hands had then released her and strode out, turning his head at the door and pausing. 'In your case, though, five percent a week on four 'undred quid ain't worth a broken leg is it?'

'No, Russell,' she had whispered.

'No. Forty quid tomorrow, then. Oh, and the usual little service. yeah?' And he had driven off, heading south west in the afternoon sunshine, failing to notice the purple daphne bush in her tiny front garden, blooming sweetly.

Now on his way home, he wondered why he bothered. He'd only lent her the four hundred quid as a favour, when she'd got a gambling problem and had snitched cash from her husband's Christmas club money. He didn't need it back, not really, and it was wholly wrong to demand forty quid a fortnight. Poor cow! Every time he went there, he planned to wipe out her debt, but as soon as he'd finished having it off with her, she would put that brave, victimised face on and then he would begin to feel angry. He knew she didn't like having sex with him, not now, and for some reason, that made him want to see her suffer, just a little bit more.

He turned the Jaguar off the main road and chose a back way to Wyckhamby, speeding along the straight but narrow Fenland roads until he reached the low limestone hills that divide Lincolnshire from the Midlands. Here, his progress was slowed by twisting lanes and a series of difficult junctions. By the time he got to the village and crossed the river Venn by the central bridge, it was dusk. He noticed that the drunk old biddy in Bridge House was out in the twilight digging or hoeing or something daft in that huge garden of hers and he wondered, since her hubby was a doctor, why he couldn't do something about her. Then he turned into his own drive.

The Hands residence was the only new house to have been built in Wyckhamby since the 1960s. Separated from the rest of the village by a belt of trees and a two hundred yard lane, it was a large bungalow with white, stucco walls and red roof tiles that would have blended well with the architecture on Madeira, but looked incongruous among the pretty stone houses of this English village. Luckily, it was partially hidden from view in winter and completely invisible in summer, when the trees in the wood were in leaf. To give the interiors an impression of grandeur, Hands had furnished them with outsize items. In the lounge, two vast chairs and a four-seater sofa – Chesterfield style in studded leather – surrounded a chunky coffee table nearly as big as a single bed, made from a two-inch-thick slab of plate glass, supported by six Chinoiserie stone lions.

In the main bedroom, a vast, brass bedstead made the focal point. This was antique-looking, but the period effect was spoilt by a clutter of purpose-built furniture along the walls, housing a small refrigerator for keeping drinks, television and video – both Hands and his wife enjoyed watching pornographic videos in bed – and built-in dressing tables.

Frequent stays at expensive hotels had made them want to imitate the typical five star bedroom.

Hands garaged his car, fitting it between the Porsche and the Mitsubishi – the garage was bigger than most of the houses in Wyckhamby – and went indoors to kiss his wife.

Slender, almost exactly the same height as her husband, with high cheek bones, light chestnut hair and greenish eyes, Doreen Hands was blessed with a natural elegance. But when she opened her mouth, the voice was hard, nasal, and the accent Londonish with pinched vowels and hissing sibilants. Her dress usually said more than she would have liked to declare about her background: always expensive, usually elegant, but she almost always overdid things. A simple silk sheath, in plain cream with navy handbag, shoes and belt might have been fine, but with these she would want to sport as many yards of her gold chains as she could carry round her neck, plus a gold charm bracelet, over-laden with chunky additions, dangling appendages for her ears and at least three rings. Even for housework – which she preferred to do herself than to pay anyone local to come in – she wore an outfit that some residents of Wyckhamby would have considered dressy enough to don for dining out. This evening she wore black trousers and a loose-fitting, long-sleeved silk blouse with a pattern of enormous flowers in vivid colours.

When he went to kiss her she put her arms round him, but then recoiled. 'You're a bit gamy,' she said.

'Sweat o' me brow.' He often wondered if she knew what he got up to during the day. He opened the fridge – a double-doored monster that was plumbed in and could produce ice by the bucketful at a moment's notice – opened himself an extra strong Belgian lager, downed it in two gulps, grabbed another bottle from the fridge, reached above his wife into the cupboard for a glass and carried his drink out of the kitchen into the bedroom. Once there, he peeled off his clothes for the second time that day, wincing a little as his underpants adhered to him, and put everything into the laundry basket. He crossed the expanse of carmine shag pile carpet into their vast *en suite* bathroom and turned on the bath taps. He thought of having a sauna, but there wasn't really time.

The Hands had no children. Doreen couldn't. An abortion, not exactly a National Health one, had gone wrong when she was fourteen, and that had been that. She'd have liked them, but Russell, not. She had a serene air about her, a calm that suggested she might have been a decent mother. He would probably have ended up knocking them about. He ended up knocking most people about, one way or another, but not Doreen. She was different. She was also extremely strong, and, in her quiet way, clever. He came out of the *en suite* bathroom just as she entered the bedroom, carrying a copy of the *Kendale Messenger*.

'Feel better?' He nodded, dabbing the last few moist corners of his body with his towel before opening his drawer for clean pants and socks. 'You won't when you've glanced at this.' She passed him the paper which she had folded to highlight an article on the properties page. He put his towel down, took the paper and spotted the headline: 'Bare Site Busts Record', and skimmed the copy, noting that building land for private housing in one of Kendale's outlying villages had just been sold for £60,000. The local newspaper was hardly a source of news. By the time anything to do with property got published, Hands would have known about it for months, sometimes longer.

'So?' He skimmed the rest of the page. 'Prices are firming up. I told yer.'

'You ain't read it properly.'

'I got the gist,' he read aloud, '"House builders will need to find up to sixty thousand pounds before the first brick is laid."' He read on in silence and then looked up. 'Sixty – per *plot*?'

'You still ain't read it all. It's at Glenton. The Paston Field site.' He stared.

'*My* Paston Field?' She nodded. 'There was only room for two dwellin's there. Three, tops. They won't let anyone build in front o' that soddin' church. That's why I decided to get rid of it.'

'Yeah?' Doreen's mouth was almost, but not quite, set in a sneer. 'But it says there,' she tapped his paper, 'plannin' for six 'omes.'

'Buggeration!'

'At sixty per site, I make that—'

'I fuckin' know what that makes!' He was losing his temper. With any other woman, he'd be twisting her wrist by now and, if she'd got any stroppier, he might be on the point of giving her one in the mouth. But with Doreen there, he simply stood and twisted his towel until the fibres began to snap under the pressure.

'An' you sold it to Beales, what, four months ago?'

'I know!' He fixed her with a glittering eye. She stared right back. 'Don't remind me, don't even *think* of fuckin' remindin' me what Beales paid.' It had been a site that logic told him was a good development bet. He'd bought it from a local farmer for three times agricultural value, feeling sure that, with his influence, he'd manage to get planning consent to build. What he hadn't bargained for was the recent influx of London commuters to Glenton. After decades of inertia, the village had suddenly developed an active Parish Meeting with its own, self-appointed Planning Sub-committee. Since its formation, applications for any kind of development were being blocked as a matter of course and the church, though used by even fewer parishioners than at Wychgate, was suddenly to be cherished and not, definitely not, to have its environs cluttered with nasty modern houses. Rather than erect two small dwellings on the field, tucked neatly away from the church, Hands had decided to cut his losses. He flogged it to an inexperienced developer, name of Beales, who lived in the village. They had settled on just under fifty thousand.

'You made nearly thirty K profit on the deal, what the 'ell.'

'Yeah.' He threw his towel on the bed. It wasn't the missed opportunity that infuriated him so much as finding himself one step behind. And behind such a green competitor. He should have known. He should have soddin' known about this months earlier, not read about it in the bloody paper.

'Beales, though, will have made—'

'—All right! All right!' His face was blotched and fulvous with rage, his hands itched to fetch her one. But she fixed him with a green, glittering stare. 'I know what Beales will have made. Buggeration!' He pulled a sweatshirt out of his drawer and found some slacks. As he put these on, and then fished in his cupboard for slippers, she stayed quite still, watching him. He buttoned his waistband and then closed cupboards and drawers. 'I'll make up for that, though. Don't you worry.' She continued to look at him until their eyes met. Hers cool, appraising. His blurred with anger.

'I know you will.' That was how it worked. She fed him extra strength, motivated his business progress, not by goading him with taunts, or by encouragement, but by feeding his anger. 'I know you will.'

'Matter of fact,' he said, 'I've got somethink up me sleeve right now.' She knew better than to ask what.

Mid Lent Sunday, in Lincolnshire, can be fair or foul. There are years when keening easterly winds drive frost deep into the ground, and others when gales blow-dry the soil surface, ready for urgent spring tilling to begin, only to have it soaked again by the rainstorms that almost always travel behind the wind. From time to time, though, the climate softens to an early spring, with the March wind no more than a gentle westerly breeze and broken cloud allowing lengthy spells of sunshine.

Walking down to Saint Peter's church, on such a Sunday, gave Imogen so much pleasure that she felt guilty. Soon after leaving Weir House, she stooped to pick half a dozen sweet violets – four blue, two white – from the hedge bottom and noticed, in the grass nearby, that primroses were budding among the vivid yellow celandines. She picked one of these, for a closer look at the sheen on its tiny petals – almost like lacquer or enamel – but did not add it to her tiny bunch of violets because she knew the celandine would close almost at once and never open again. Further down the hill, little grew because of the dense shade thrown by the spruces of Pyson Wood, and here she quickened her stride, hunching in her anorak until she had passed the last tree and walked back into the sunlight.

The anorak, discovered at the bottom of a cabin trunk, was

almost new, navy blue with a vivid orange lining. Flattering it wasn't, but anything would have been an improvement on the ruinous Gieves and Hawkes overcoat. After almost a whole winter in Weir House, she had, more or less, finished her unpacking and, though by no means straight yet, she and Mrs Crowe had managed to translate her home from barely habitable to reasonably comfortable. Furniture was in place, books were on the shelves, the kitchen was properly equipped and Imogen had even taken to dabbling a little in the garden. The hall table, now, had a vase of evergreens blended with branches of forsythia picked in tight bud so that the pale yellow blooms would open in the warmth of the house.

Mrs Crowe still endeavoured to keep her charge on a marginal diet and Imogen was, therefore, still abnormally thin, often forgetful and usually listless. But, since her first illicit walk with Hands, she had taken to strolling outside alone more often, and the exercise stimulated her appetite. What the Crow denied her at mealtimes, she partly made up for by nibbling cheese or scrumping biscuits from the cupboard. Whether because of these small changes in her lifestyle, or whether it was simply time that was involved in a healing process, her memory, in spite of frequent lapses, was improving. She was able to take part in conversations without trailing off quite so much, and occasionally, even to give shape and structure to her arguments. But she was still vulnerable and, even though Mrs Crowe's influence was fractionally less strong than before, she still held her captive. Indeed, in some respects, the reviving memory was making Imogen's hold on reason more precarious. Everything she recalled, at this stage, made her feel guilty and miserable and sometimes, when a particular event came into her mind, she would find the pain of recall almost unbearable.

Mid Lent Sunday was also Mothering Sunday, and during Jerome's sermon, thoughts about her family nearly made her break down. Whenever she recalled her father or brothers, it was with sorrow. The coldness of Daddy's final address, belied by the tears welling up in his eyes, always tortured her conscience, but when she recalled Mummy's face, so twisted with scorn and disgust, as if looking at a venomous reptile, the guilt she felt was seasoned with anger. She had spoken to no one in the family since coming to Wychgate and didn't suppose she ever would. A tear fell on to her prayerbook, raising a puckered weal on the thin paper.

Jerome moved briskly through the rest of the Eucharist and, at its conclusion, because he celebrated in plain cassock during Lent, walked straight to the door to greet his congregation. Since that first Sunday, a few weeks before Christmas, Jerome had walked back with Imogen to Weir House every time he had conducted a service in Wychgate. The other parishioners had given up attempting to communicate with her on these Sundays and chatted for a few moments among themselves before dispersing to drive off in search of pubs or country restaurants that served traditional Sunday lunches. Only a minority of Wychgate inhabitants cooked for their own families and an even smaller number lunched with guests. Jerome had seldom been asked anywhere to lunch or supper – well, almost never.

Imogen waited while the rector locked the church. 'I hate having to do this,' he said, dropping the weighty key into his cassock pocket before buttoning his Burberry riding mac and tying the belt in a knot. 'It seems so unkind. People who want to just sort of drop in and sit for a while, can't any more. But with so much thieving and vandalism, there isn't a lot of choice.'

They began to walk. Imogen, as usual, was disinclined to speak. Jerome had no objection to walking in silence. Goodness knew, with most of his flock he would have preferred not to talk, but instinct told him that these short walks were important for Imogen; that she needed a lifeline to haul her out of her sea of troubles. Goodness, how poetic he was getting these days! Actually, to be honest, there was a deal more to it than that. He found her rather fascinating. He had seen, often during his services, the otherwise blank face take on such an expression of sadness that he wanted to stop the liturgy and run down the aisle to comfort her. Other times, there was a desperation in her, the look of someone who cannot carry her burden for much longer. But mostly, her face was a mask, devoid of

expression. And that, he felt sure, was her most dangerous state.

'You look better,' Jerome said. 'Your cheeks have got
colour today.' She said nothing. 'Oh, and I love your
new jacket.'

'Not new.' They walked on. She had a little more confidence in her stride than before, he noticed. That uncoordi-
nated, shuffling step had gone. 'Found it in a trunk'

'Well, it's an improvement on the tweed affair.'

'That is an, ahm, heirloom. My grandfather's.' She spoke
with po-faced reverence, as if describing an eighteenth-
century escritoire or a piece of ancient porcelain. Could
this be the beginnings of humour? Jerome didn't dare risk
a laugh, but he smiled to himself.

'Has something happened?' He asked in as light a voice as
he could muster. Nonetheless, she flinched. 'You seem . . .
happier.' She stopped walking for a moment and, looking at
the ground, said, as if to herself:

'No . . . No. I've no, no ahm *right* to be . . .' She shook
her head vigorously. She had turned paler and began to walk
again, still looking at the ground.

'Guilt,' Jerome said, in soft tones, 'can be a very negative thing.'

'No!'

'It is actually sinful to hate yourself, you know.' Dear
God, Jerry, he told himself, she doesn't want balls like that
dribbled at her! Why don't you shut your mouth. But he saw
her features working and found it almost unbearable to see
these manifestations of the conflict that was going on, under
her skin.

'No! . . . *No!*' She muttered through clenched teeth and
increased her pace.

'And for what it's worth,' Jerome continued, 'I happen to
think that anger, properly channelled, can be a very positive
thing.' The response was one of her abrupt little laughs, with a
hand – pale and thin with blue veining – clapped to her mouth.
They walked on in silence for a few yards, both quickening
their pace as they passed the wood. Even though the breeze
was slight, the spruces sighed with an unnerving sibilance.

'I ought to cut them all down!' Imogen stated, with a tone that edged towards vehemence. 'The whole blasted lot!'

'Oh hear hear!' Jerome said, glad to be on a more earthy subject. 'Let the daylight in.'

'Do you really think I should?' She stopped again and clutched his arm hard, grabbing a piece of Burberry sleeve, cassock and, inadvertently pinching the flesh beneath. 'Do you? Do you?' The strength of her reaction had taken him aback. He responded without thinking of the consequences.

'Why not?' He hated the brooding plantation. 'Make a change. Let the sunshine in. Why ever not?'

'I will!' Her eyes burnt with a feverish zeal. 'I will!'

'Bully for you, my dear!' And laughing, he put an arm over her shoulders and marched her up the hill towards her house. He opened the front gate for her.

'Come in!' she said, her eyes still wide from the excitement of reaching a decision on her trees. 'Come and have sherry.' Mrs Crowe who was waiting behind the front door, swung it open to admit Imogen. 'Oh, Mrs Crowe, Mr Daniels is coming in for, ahm, sherry.' The older woman admitted Imogen and then pushed the door partly to, placing her body firmly into the small space left.

'I think it wiser not, vicar, if you don't mind. You do understand, don't you?' And, as she had on Stir Up Sunday, banged it shut before he had time to remind her that he was a rector, and not a vicar.

He stood for a moment or two on the door step and then turned and walked back into the village street, closing the gate behind him. The prospect of ridding Wychgate of Pyson Wood cheered him, until he began to think of how others might react. The Residents' Association would be sure to try to prevent the clearance. They had their Conservation Group, a cluster of urbanite vigilantes who had been to national conferences to learn how better to impede change in the countryside. Busby would be nagging him about the need to support his action group, but as rector, he would feel obliged to adopt as neutral a tone a possible – however badly he wanted to see the trees removed. Opposition like this he could handle, but it was all a strain on one's patience.

Then he remembered Michael Pilkington. Now there was a problem. The old man for some reason was inordinately fond of the plantation. He never went into it, as far as Jerome knew, but whenever the question arose of tidying up the fallen timber, or felling trees that were too near the road and had become dangerous, Michael would become almost irrational in his efforts to leave the place untouched. Jerome knew that as owner, Imogen had the right do to with the wood as she liked. But he also knew that if the trees were felled, there would probably be trouble, one way or another. He wondered whether he should call on Michael. He might resent his Sunday peace being spoilt but, on balance, Jerome thought it would be better if he did call.

As the rector was pondering these questions, Michael was about to eat a meagre lunch of canned Scotch broth with a piece of French bread. He swore when he heard the front doorbell ring and wondered, for a moment, whether to pretend not to be at home. Thoughts that someone might need him overruled his reticence, however, and he went to open the door. When he saw it was Jerome, his face lit up. 'My dear fellow, I'm *delighted* to see you. Come on in.' Both men were fond of each other but Jerome found the effusiveness of this welcome disarming and entered feeling a little awkward. 'You haven't called for months.'

'I have been tempted, I must admit, but I hate to disturb your Sundays, Michael.'

Pilkington ushered him into the sitting-room. 'Disturb my Sundays?' Michael looked puzzled at first and then burst out laughing. 'What an absurd idea! Have you any idea what I do after church?' Jerome shook his head. 'I walk back. I decide what kind of a tin to open, or whether to try out some new convenience item I may have picked out at that vile hypermarket place. I set out drinks,' he indicated the decanter, water jug and two crystal tumblers standing on the same silver tray that Mrs Bull (now long dead) was wont to use for serving his father. 'Nobody comes, but there's always a hope. And now here you are. A delightful surprise. Delightful!'

'But I've interrupted your lunch, surely.'

'Soup and a crust. Not worth pining over. Scotch!'

'Michael, I could *murder* one.' Without being asked, Jerome sat but then leapt up again, 'I say, I hope this isn't the chair you prefer.'

'Sit wherever!' Michael poured a generous measure of Scotch into the glasses, enjoying the swirl of the warm-coloured amber liquid against the ice cool silvery glass. 'Water?' Jerome shook his head, knowing that Michael's Scotch was always a good straight malt and would taste fine on its own.

The two men chatted amicably, focusing on parish matters at first, but soon ranging to wider topics, each lonely man enjoying the presence of the other. They refilled their glasses twice as the afternoon waned and darkened.

'I'm afraid there's no woman here today,' Michael said, 'so if we want tea, we'll have to make it ourselves.'

'I ought to go home.' Jerome eased himself out of his chair. 'Why not come to the rectory for tea?'

'What? Oh, that's kind of you,' Michael stood up, 'but I don't think I will, if you don't mind. My knee's a bit painful and I'd prefer not to walk any more today.'

He held the door open for Jerome, and they walked along the hall to the front door. Just before leaving, Jerome asked, 'Do you ever walk in that wood?'

'Pyson Wood? Never! You can hardly move in there anyway now, the growth's so thick.' An edge had come into the older man's voice. 'Why do you ask?'

'Oh, no reason really. Except that I've just spoken to Lady Imogen.'

'Oh? How's she doing now? I've never managed to get a word out of her.'

'Rather better.'

'Good job. Those drugs must have fried her brain, poor little thing. That scandal,' he shrugged, 'awful business!'

'Michael, she wants to fell the wood.'

Pilkington froze. His face seemed to collapse. After such an affable afternoon, the whisky-flush drained from his face and he looked, suddenly, old. 'Why?' A dry whisper 'Do you know why?'

'Says she wants to let in the daylight. And she's right, you know. Those horrible firs . . .' He stopped and caught hold of his friend's shoulders as he began to stagger. 'Good Lord, Michael, are you all right? Do you want to sit down?' The old man's face had turned chalky and he was trembling and swaying. Jerome led him back to the sitting-room and helped him to sit down. 'Do you take medication? Do you need a doctor?' He shook his head and made a dismissing gesture, instructing Jerome to leave. 'No chance! I'm staying with you until you feel better. Then I'll go, if you want me to.'

'It cannot be allowed,' Michael was murmuring, 'cannot be allowed. Can *not* be allowed.'

'Michael,' Jerome knelt on the floor, not in supplication, but in order to gain eye contact and to get through to this troubled man. He took hold of one of his hands. 'Michael what is it?'

'Cannot . . . be . . .' He began to mumble incoherently.

'Can't you talk about it?' Michael shook his head, hardly aware, now, of the other's presence. Jerome looked into the blue eyes, willing himself to bring the man out of this unhappiness – or this unhappiness out of the man. Night was falling, and in the gathering darkness of the room, Jerome's pupils had dilated to their fullest extent, making his eyes look dark. Michael seemed to recognise him for a moment but then, not, for he uttered the name:

'Violet?'

'Violet? Aren't you . . . Violet? What happened?'

'You fainted.' Violet cradled the boy's head in her lap while a small circle of onlookers applauded. Someone brought his cadet's cap. Michael Pilkington. Cadet Under Officer and not yet quite sixteen.

'Oh *really*!' The boy, fully recovered now, coloured crimson to the roots of his straw-blond hair and began to scramble to his feet. 'Really, how *too* embarrassing.'

'Steady, Michael.' Violet restrained him. 'You need a little time, yet.' Almost two years older than he, she spoke with what she hoped was an element of authority because she wanted to be able to cradle that head for a few moments longer. The way she felt about him, particularly when he had fainted, was such an odd sensation that she wondered whether she was becoming ill in some way.

She and Michael had grown up in the same village, within shouting distance of each other, and yet their worlds were as alien, one from another, as if they had come from separate continents. On the few occasions that they had exchanged conversations, in the last dozen years, they had been curt and cool. Once he snubbed her for riding a delivery bike. On a later date, she laughed at him for thinking George Eliot was a man and had rejoiced in his sweating, adolescent embarrassment. He had watched her show off while skating on the Long Pond, doing fancy pirouettes and whizzing across the ice backwards when it was all he could do to keep upright. Her most recent snub had been last summer, when Wychgate's main bowler had pulled a leg muscle and he had been asked to stand in. He had bowled the legendary Frank Burgess for eight runs. Frank Burgess! A batsman who habitually scored centuries, making his village team almost invincible. Amid the general applause, she had turned her back on him, angry because of the triumphant smile on his face. He had everything; Frank had only his cricket and nothing else, and to be humiliated by a mere boy must have hurt him terribly.

Then today, this extraordinary thing; this inexplicable event. Walking along the street early this morning, with a bunch of cowslips in her hand, to help decorate the May Celebration table, she had seen the tall figure in khaki uniform marching up the street towards her. The brass fittings on his belt glinted in the sun but she was unable to see who it was because, until they got close, the peak of his cap threw his face into shadow. But as they neared to within a few yards of one another, he threw up his hand in an immaculate, army regulation salute – hup, two, three; down! – and she caught the flash of his blue, cornflower blue, gentian blue, Aegean blue eyes and the straightness of his brow and even the downy surface of his tanned skin around the cheekbones. The encounter had had an almost physical impact. She had faltered and had turned to watch his figure marching away from her, the heels ringing as they struck the metalled surface of the road, the back straight, the small buttocks tight and rounded.

And that image had burned into her being all day. When he had officiated at the flag-raising, hauling up the red cross of Saint George to the sound of a bugle, she had stopped serving ice-creams to little boys to stare. Later, when he had sat in the pavilion marquee, she had watched him remove his cap and seen the pupils of his blue eyes dilate, in the lower light conditions, and had felt faint from a strange kind of excitement, especially when he had looked across, caught her stare, and had smiled, looked down and blushed.

He had cycled the twenty-two and a quarter miles from Barleythorpe, where term had recently begun, that very morning to take part in the celebrations. He had eaten no breakfast and by lunchtime, after such an active spell, his blood sugar had dropped to a dangerous level. Leaping up to hold open the tent flap for a lady, he had dropped, crumpled and unconscious, just outside the lunch tent. Violet had been following the lady. Hardly knowing herself, she had gasped and had leapt to his aid, laying his body out straighter and cradling his head on her lap while she fanned his face with her programme. Someone had gone for water and sal volatile, but he regained consciousness in less than a minute.

As he began to come to, lying in the sunshine, the first object to swim into his fuddled sight was a head, a feminine head, haloed by a wide-brimmed straw hat. The face, blurred at first, gradually sharpened into focus and he found himself looking into a pair of large, dark eyes. Eyes of greater beauty than he had ever, in his life beheld.

'Violet?'

Chapter Seven

———

'Believe me,' Graham Ball said, 'we're well out of it.' He
turned for a moment to give Veronica, his latest companion,
a blast from his large, dark eyes before looking back at the
road. He pushed back a lock of fractionally too long, brown
hair and then rested both hands – large capable hands, but
sensitive, with long fingers – on the wheel of his new
all-terrain vehicle.

Graham was born to command, not sue; but he was a
kind leader with sympathy for everyone who worked with
him. He loved to be challenged. Few projects attracted him
more compellingly than those beset with obstacles. Even now,
instead of taking the direct route, he was driving the back way
from the Great North Road to Wychgate, steering carefully
down the narrow, winding lanes, and was looking forward to
splashing through the unbridged ford about a mile further on,
where the road crossed a small tributary of the Venn. 'Best
thing that could have happened to us. Absolutely the best
thing.' There had been many tears, in the BBC Staff Club,
at his farewell party.

Veronica said nothing but reached over and pressed his
hand. Graham continued: 'We're both exactly the right age
for a change in direction and anyway, who wants to be
involved with that lot now? I mean, would you want your
life run by a bunch of bloody accountants?'

'No, darling.' She squeezed his hand gently.

'And that *cretin* in charge of the network! I mean would

we want that? Would we *really* have wanted that?' His voice edged upwards in pitch while his face began to develop stress lines across the brow.

'Of course not.'

His features had acquired quite a number of new lines in the eleven months that she'd been living with him, Veronica thought.

Since the Broadcast Act had forced the BBC to reorganise itself, it seemed to her that decisions made in senior management circles had been progressively irrational. At first, when the redundancies began, she had thought a little pruning might do the Corporation some good. She had been one of the first to go, but she had gone gladly. Almost a decade, first as a dogsbody secretary and later as a Production Assistant, had acquainted her with most aspects of programme making and, by the time they were ready to replace her with a twenty-year-old graduate in Media Studies, she'd had enough of the political in-fighting and the pettiness. But the out-flow of production people accelerated and she began to realise that the BBC was shedding its talent, replacing creative minds with pedestrian administrators and money men.

With the Act demanding that at least a quarter of all programmes be made by independent production companies, the number of safe positions within the middle and upper ranks of the BBC were bound to erode. Brilliant programme makers who thought they had years of work ahead of them were being summoned to boardrooms and given their marching orders.

Graham's demise had been one of the biggest shocks of all. As maker of one of the most successful and long-running documentary television series ever broadcast, he had felt confident in his future and indeed, was being tipped to take over the running of one of the main networks. But, to everyone's amazement, he became the victim of a 'sweetheart deal'. His series was handed to a rival who, on the basis of receiving the very generous budget allowance for the programme, left the Corporation to start making it for them with his own newly formed production company, Tarquin Television. Graham was then offered the choice of a junior producer's job elsewhere in the Corporation, or redundancy. The motivation was obvious. Those further up the management hierarchy were keen to remove a threat to their own positions. Veronica wondered how much more talent would flow out of the BBC. It had already lost much of its integrity and programme quality, she felt, was declining fast. But what irked her more was the hurt it had done to Graham. He had put such a brave face on things but she knew precisely how insulted he felt.

After the initial shock, Graham had decided on a totally fresh start. 'We can live in the country,' he'd said. 'I can get my book written. You could carry on freelancing anywhere.' Veronica had had to think hard about that. Haverstock Hill, where she shared his Victorian house, may not have been exactly central but it was close enough for easy theatre visits and shopping expeditions to the West End. And, if you wanted fresh air, Hampstead Heath was on the doorstep. The Old Stores at Wychgate Saint Peters was fine for weekends – it was a dear cottage and she loved it – but she had always been grateful to get back to London, to turn her back on the eternal, ubiquitous mud of the countryside and be able to hop into a taxi to Piccadilly, or jump on a tube and lunch with old colleagues at Shepherd's Bush. Now they were going to be in Wychgate for good, it seemed. Residents. Country folk. She sighed and looked up in time to see the nose of the vehicle dip as it ran down the short slope to the unbridged ford. After several wet days, the stream was swollen and they hit the water with a slap, throwing up a thick spray that, for a moment, blotted out everything. Graham turned on the wipers and slowed down to walking speed until vision was fully restored. Looking in the driving mirror, he watched the steam made by water hitting the hot parts of the exhaust system quickly disperse. The Ford had settled back to calmness, seconds after his wheels had whipped it into a frenzied maelstrom. He wondered how quickly his programmes would be forgotten.

'I want to make a splash from time to time,' he said. 'I don't just want to rot away writing books.'

'You won't find much going on round here,' Veronica said, looking over the neatly managed landscape. They were passing from arable fields with developing crops into a small area of pastureland, a rarity in this part of Lincolnshire in the 1980s. There were lambs racing round their mothers in some fields and piebald cattle in others, heads all down, munching in unison at the fresh spring grass, their heads all facing the same way, their tails gently swishing.

'Oh, you'd be surprised.'

'I would. Very.'

Graham slowed right down as they approached the village and steered carefully into the gateway of the small paddock by the Old Store. The shop had long since gone, of course, but the building had made a roomy cottage, L-shaped in construction with a small stone barn whose main door had been widened so that it could serve as a garage. He parked just outside the back door and they both climbed out. Coloured primroses, grape hyacinths and pansies flowered among developing weeds in the narrow border along the wall of the house and there was a large Japanese quince, once trained, but now flopping away from the wall and covered, not with the usual coral blossom, but ivory white with a touch of green and a suggestion of pink in the open blooms. 'Do you know,' he said, indicating the shrub, 'I've never noticed that before.'

'Graham, of course you have!'

'The bush, yes, but not the flowers. Unusual colour.'

'It was flowering the first time you brought me here. More – something, I think. Yes, "Moerloosii", that's it.'

'How the hell did you know that?' He was impressed. She shrugged.

'Mummy had one by the front door at home.'

'Will you garden, do you think?'

'It's a case of having to. I don't think there's a choice.'

'Really?' He thought for a few moments. He hadn't really got to grips with the idea of living in a country house with a proper garden. There had to be less trivial things than that to concentrate on. 'Why?'

'Because it won't look after itself.' Their house at Haverstock Hill had nothing more than a tiny paved backyard. She opened the tail gate of the vehicle and reached in for her dressing case. 'In fact, it takes quite a lot of work. Especially a neglected garden like this one.' He unlocked the front door of the cottage and pushed against the resistance caused by an accumulation of mail on the door mat.

'I'll get the kettle on,' he said, stepping over the litter of envelopes and walking straight through to the back kitchen. 'We can finish unloading later.' The house smelled musty, so he opened the kitchen window, in spite of the chilly afternoon. After a moment Veronica came in, holding his post in her hand.

'Mostly circulars,' she said and put them on the table. He avoided her eyes and turned to stare out of the open window. She caught his expression, reflected in the grass and was surprised at its bleakness.

'What Graham? What is it?' He turned and glanced round the ill-lit room. With the slanting sun throwing orange light into it, the ceiling seemed lower than ever. He could only just stand upright. She walked over to him and took his hands in hers.

'I always forget how small this place is, how . . .' He shook his head. 'When I was little, all this seemed like a paradise. The garden was a universe you could explore for ever. When we did *Fern Hill* in English at school, I always imagined this place. But now, instead of feeling "young and easy under the apple boughs" I feel trapped. It's so mean, so *cramped*.' She put her arms round him, circling his waist – still as narrow in his early forties as it was when he was at Cambridge – and pulled him closer.

'This is silly.' She kissed him. 'We've been coming here practically every other week since we met. You've been coming since you were a baby. It's your main home now, that's the only difference.'

'And we're so isolated. So far from our friends.'

'They can come up from town. Most of them will jump at the chance of a break in the country. Besides, you'll make new ones.'

'And talk about what? Wheat and potatoes?' He grimaced.

'Instead of all that Hampstead bitchery. Effete know-it-alls who only sucked up to you because they wanted to be on your programmes.'

'Christ, Vee, I hope we're going to make it.' He held her so tightly she could hardly breathe.

'Graham! Of course!'

'And you will stay?' Almost imperceptibly, her back stiffened. 'Won't You?'

'Graham!' She took his arms from her waist and stepped back. 'I said I'd come out here with you, yeah?' He nodded. 'And I said I'd see how it went.'

'But now we're here—'

'I'm still not sure I'm the country type.' The desolate expression returned to his face and dispirited her. 'Oh Graham! I said I'd give it a try, OK?' He sighed and nodded. He began to shuffle through the mail, putting circulars and bills on to one pile and personal letters on another. From among these, he picked up a stiffish, pale blue envelope, with the address written in a bold hand in old fashioned ink. 'From my great aunt, I think.' He slit the envelope with a kitchen knife, removed a couple of pages of paper and read. 'Yes, Aunt Violet . . . Good God!' He laughed, and read on. 'Can't be far short of eighty and she's still in harness—' he looked up. 'She says she's working on the ninth edition of her magnum opus——'

'Subject?'

'Mediaeval history. She's Professor Ball – well, professor emeritus now – I thought you knew.' Veronica shook her head. Graham continued reading. 'Oh, and her publishers want her to do a popular book on the same subject. Full of pictures. Coffee table job.' He chuckled a little and then read aloud, '"It seems to me, dear Graham, that you could have the makings of one of your splendid television programmes here: mediaeval occultism may give the impression of being an obscure and dry subject but, believe me, there is much potential."' He put the letter down. 'I hardly think so. Not for the Beeb, anyway. She's not serious, really. Her main reason for writing was to welcome me – us really – to this cottage.' He handed the letter to Veronica.

'Violet? Isn't she the aunt who grew up here?'

'With my uncle and dad. Both clever boys; both got to Cambridge from nowhere. But Aunt Violet managed Oxford without even going to a proper school. My grandfather was something of a legend too.'

'But Violet rose highest.'

Graham nodded. 'With a greater handicap. It was even tougher being a woman in the Twenties than it is now.'

Veronica hugged him again.

'That's one of the things I love you for. You're the most ardent feminist I've ever known – for a man.' She kissed the tip of his aquiline nose.

'Mind you, she had no family; no children to cramp her style.' Veronica read the letter, quickly, and then looked up, handing the pages to Graham who replaced them in the blue envelope.

'Why don't you invite her here?' she said. 'I'd love to meet her.'

'Have done. Loads of times, but for some extraordinary reason, she won't come to Wychgate. She hardly ever ventures outside Oxford at all, nowadays, anyway. She never learnt to drive and now the train service is so lousy, it's almost impossible for her to travel beyond the cities.

'Couldn't you drive her over?' He shook his head.

'I've pressed her repeatedly. Once I even asked her, point blank, what she's got against the place. "Doesn't do," she said, "to stir up bitter memories." Then she simply clammed up. Wouldn't say another word. I get the feeling, though, that it's not just this house. It's something else about the village that puts her off. But, whatever it is, she's got the Ball stubbornness. If Aunt Violet doesn't want to return to her birthplace, nothing is going to drag her here. Especially not wild horses – she'd tame them in a jiffy and send them packing.'

I could stay here for ever, Violet thought, just watching him. Ripples from the stream made patterns of reflected light which danced on his young face. She could see the blue of his irises glinting between the half-closed lashes and, as his hair moved slightly in the breeze, it changed in hue from honey to the colour of oat husks, lighter than his tanned skin. For ever. His eyes opened, met her gaze and he sat up quickly, blushing.

'Hey! That's not fair! It only works if you lie down.'

'Says you!'

'No it does. Lie perfectly still, with your eyes half-shut.'

'Oh all right!' She lay beside him and stared up at the sky through her lashes. Small white clouds were moving slowly across her vision and as she watched them, she got the feeling that her body was gradually losing its weight and she was drifting gently. Michael raised himself on one elbow to look at her profile. Her hair was lustrous in the sunshine and, where weathered, had developed chestnut overtones to the darkness. The cheekbones gave her face a refined structure and her nose, small and fractionally turned up, above full but not over-large lips, was, thought Michael, one of the prettiest he had seen. He had never felt like this about any one before. He didn't know what being in love was and did not, in any way associate these feelings with *that*. But he did want to be near Violet as often as possible and for as long as possible. And even when they didn't speak, he felt a happiness in her company, so intense that he ached with it.

Sensing his stare, she opened her eyes. Large and dark, they reminded Michael of the moist, vulnerable eyes of young calves, but they smouldered with an intelligence and sensitivity that moved him every time he looked at them. Now they flashed with mock anger. She had caught him out. 'See,' she said, 'you're just as bad as me!' They both laughed.

'Right! Once more,' Michael said, 'and no cheating!' They lay, gazing upwards while swifts flew to and fro, high in the blue sky, and insects worked in the grasses around their heads. After a while, Michael said, 'If you lie with your head lower than your body, and do the same thing, it feels like falling off the edge of the world.'

'I wonder if it's your astral body coming out,' Violet said.

'Your what?'

'It's like your soul. Some people believe that when you sleep, your astral body leaves your earthly body. Magicians – witches and that – can do it at will. That's what it means when they fly on broomsticks.'

'Poppycock!'

'Oh but they can.'

'How?'

'Will. They can will themselves out of their bodies. You can get in touch with departed spirits that way too.' Her voice had gone dreamy, a quiet murmur that Michael found exciting. In fact he found the timbre and pitch of her voice much more alluring than the tarradiddle she seemed to be talking. Without looking at her now, he could close his eyes and conjure up an image of her face. He knew it in every detail and found it faultless – had done since their first emotional encounter, when he had fainted that spring. Then, in those few seconds when he had looked up at her, he had noticed how her skin darkened slightly, but looked almost translucent around the eyelids. Girls' faces were so much more delicate than he had realised. The nose and ears so much neater, the mouth more . . . more something. He wasn't sure what. He wanted to kiss her lips – an impulse to do so, from time to time, took him so strongly that it needed an almost physical struggle to prevent himself. But now, the heat of the August afternoon made it difficult not to feel drowsy and he wanted to do little more than just lie there and enjoy the sound of her voice.

'Is that the sort of rubbish you talk to Father about?' Why did he ask that question? And why did asking it bring a tiny shudder of uneasiness, like a chill breeze in the midst of the August heat?

'Sometimes, yes.' He sat up now, and stared at her. She stayed on her back, eyes half closed.

'Really?' Michael could hardly imagine them having a conversation on such a silly subject. 'What does he say?'

'Not a lot. But he listens. Good listener, your father.'

'He's soft on you.' Michael said this as a joke, but he found the whole idea of his father's weekly teas with Violet disturbing for reasons he couldn't quite fathom. His father was a total recluse. He spoke to almost no one in or out of the village. And yet, Violet and he chatted like old friends. In fact his conversations with Violet were a good deal warmer and noisier than the terse, polite exchanges he had with his own son. He could talk to her about the Plantagenets or the Synod of Whitby with a light of enthusiasm in his eyes. Michael had, at the beginning of the school holidays, joined in on these teas, but had felt awkward and had, he felt sure, made his father uncomfortable too. The history didn't exactly interest him and he felt estranged and a little jealous. Gerard had never been so warm with him as he was with Violet. Because she was a girl, he supposed, but he had often wondered what it might have felt like to have been hugged by his father. Some of the fellows' paters brought them to school by car at the beginning of term and then they often hugged them before saying goodbye. It wouldn't have been unmanly, he supposed, if he and Gerard had held each other. But perhaps it was better not.

When he had endured two such teas, longing to have her to himself and fighting his feelings of antagonism, first towards his father and eventually to the whole thing, including himself, he had determined to find some alternative Thursday afternoon activity. There were few people around, of his age and class, but he did manage to find a couple of chaps, both on holiday from their public schools, and therefore at a loose end at this stage of the summer holidays, and had arranged with them to practise in the nets at the Wychgate cricket club.

After the first week, all three boys had found that this routine suited them. They would practise bowling and batting all afternoon, until Violet left the Manor and found them. To his surprise, his companions always made their excuses as soon as she arrived. One had to cycle three miles home and the other had a driver coming to meet him to take him to the outskirts of Stoneford. 'We know you'll want to be alone, old boy,' they would say. And the odd thing was, he *did* want to be alone with Violet, not because he was afraid his friends might think him soppy or girlish but because when she was there, anyone else seemed to get in the way.

Violet felt the same about Michael, of course. But she knew she was in love. Had been since his dead faint and was never happier than when she was with him. During the term, her Thursday afternoons with Gerard were spiced by the knowledge that she was nearer, by proxy, to Michael. The odd thing was that when Michael was home, she found the weekly teas almost unbearable because he seemed so ill-at-ease with his father. On that first Thursday of the holidays, when he had walked her home afterwards, he had seemed to transform from awkward youth to assured young man. At times she could hardly believe he was almost two years younger than she.

But that wasn't all. Gerard's attitude to her was so obviously different than to anyone else, including Michael. He barely spoke to the village people and yet, when Mrs Bull showed her into the study, or escorted her to his favourite spot under the huge lime tree in the manor garden, his face would light up. 'Violet, my dear!' he would say, 'How *delightful* to see you.' And he would leap up to offer her a seat, or would take her arm and walk her into the rose garden. 'Come and look at our latest treasure! A real Persian beauty!' If it was raining, he'd have looked out some obscure essay on the Knights Templar, or the Tudors, and would soon be enthusing about the author's style and approach, even before she had had time to take off her waterproof cycling cape.

There were periods, too, during these visits when his mien would alter. His face would fall, or turn vacant, or he would stare at her while she watched an almost unsupportable sadness take over his spirit. These moods followed a set pattern. The first sign was usually a slip of the tongue or a solecism. He would call her Elizabeth by mistake. Once he stroked her cheek but almost immediately apologised for taking such a liberty, murmuring, 'You remind me so much of . . . ' but not being able to trust his voice. A few moments later that afternoon, when he had sat silently at his desk, waiting for her to leave but not able to summon up the will to dismiss her, she had laid a cool hand on his, as it rested on the tooled leather of the desk top.

'People you've loved often feel close,' she had said. 'Even when they've passed over.'

'Died,' he had said. 'The word is "died".' His tone was flat, bitter. She had shaken her head.

'No. It isn't as simple as that. Or as final. I think you can sense their nearness because they *are* near. Not visible, or tangible, but discernible.

'How?' His voice had a scornful edge.

'I'm not sure. Through other senses, somehow. Senses we don't understand but which the ancient magicians understood.'

'Oh really!' He was dismissive, but she continued in her cool, self-assured tones.

'Don't you think they might want to talk to you? To communicate? To reassure.'

'I do not.'

'I do.' Two words uttered quietly, but with such conviction that he had almost been persuaded. 'I also believe you can summon the spirits. Talk to them. Listen to them. Converse with them.'

'That is nonsense.' He had taken his hand away from under hers. 'It's also irreligious.' She knew she had offended him, but she also knew she had made him wonder. He had sat still, rigid in his seat, thinking. Were those strange feelings he sometimes had *really* a presence? Down by her grave when he was completely alone, he could almost hear Elizabeth's laugh, sometimes could even feel her breath on his neck. If only he could talk to her. Just once, just to make sure he had made the right decision on that hateful night; or if not, to see if she could forgive him. 'Save our baby,' she'd said, over and over. 'Save our baby. Save our baby.' But had she *really* meant it? Had he interpreted her correctly? Had he been right to play God? If only he could know. And if only he could know that she'd be there, to meet him, when his turn came, wherever the after-life might take him. Then, after this brief flight, his thoughts came back to pursue a more logical course. No! This spiritualism stuff was nonsense. Comfort for stupid old widows or doting mothers who had lost their boys in the Great War. It was not for him! But this beautiful, intelligent girl, so like Elizabeth, and yet so much more sensitive, could they be linked somehow?

'I think you'd better leave,' he had muttered.

Violet sat up, in the meadow, and looked at Michael. 'What *do* you mean?'

'What I say. I think Father's soft on you.' In response, she cupped his face in both hands and planted a kiss on his mouth, making his lips even ruddier. It was a chaste peck, swiftly delivered, and before he could respond, or even reply, she had jumped up.

'Now you know who's soft on whom,' she said, and walked briskly away, leaving him sitting in the long grass by the river bank with his senses in pretty serious disarray. After a few moments he stood up and watched Violet's figure diminishing into the heat haze as she walked towards the village. Not wanting to get in her way and not daring to follow up that kiss, he wandered slowly in the opposite direction, along the banks of the stream for a while before turning away, across the flowery meadow into the shade of Pyson Wood.

Few people ventured among these ancient trees. One or two villagers might come, in spring, to gather primroses or bluebells, or to cut themselves a few pea sticks from the hazel bushes, but usually the wood was silent and deserted. He could hear the shouts and cries of little boys from the village playing in the bathing place, but he had the wood to himself. He wandered among the trees, hearing the dry bluebell stems rattling out the last of their seeds as he disturbed them and, occasionally, startling a rabbit from its resting place in the heat of the afternoon. His emotions were in a tangled state as he thought about Violet and the kiss. He realised how much he wanted to kiss her again, and yet, felt there was something shameful about it all, something forbidden. He spotted an oak with a wide limb that curved downwards, and was tempted to climb it. He threw down his flannel jacket, jumped up and caught hold of the branch. It was difficult reaching up with his heels but after two attempts he managed, and began to climb until he was some twenty feet from the ground. He could see the village stretching to the west and, not far away, the naked boys taking turns to swing from the rope and drop into the middle of the stream before paddling feverishly to the bank to try again. This was the only part of the river Dene where serious bathing was possible and even then, five or six brisk strokes brought a swimmer to the opposite bank. The activities of the boys kept the firm gravel bottom weed-free and clean. Michael looked deeper into the little wood and saw something in the distance that reflected the light, but dully. He climbed down and went to investigate, pushing through a dense growth of ferns until he reached an area – hardly a clearing – where the trees were so old and gaunt that they let enough daylight in to allow the ground to develop a grassy covering. To one side of this was an oak so antique and gnarled that it was barely alive. Its great bole had split so that someone could easily stand inside the hollow. A few yards away, near an almost equally ancient ash, lay a large horizontal slab of stone. The irregular shape suggested that it was neither hewn nor carved, but the composition – smooth and worn – and the colour, blue-grey, almost like slate, suggested that it was neither natural nor local. It rose at least a foot from the ground, supported, presumably, by other, invisible stones, and was nearly level. Michael had played in the wood as a child, occasionally, but could not recall having seen it before. Something about the stone – it looked a bit sacrificial – disturbed him and he shivered, in spite of the sunshine, and began to walk back to the edge of the wood. Passing the hedge that concealed the bathing place, he noticed that all had gone quiet. The little boys had dressed and run home to their teas, so he pushed through the small hole in the hedge, looked carefully around to ensure that he was alone, and stripped off before stepping discreetly into the cool, clear water. He could see the small fish, gudgeon probably, darting away from his feet which looked unnaturally white in the water. He swam in the cool, clear river for some minutes before getting out and allowing his body to dry in the sunshine. Then he dressed and walked slowly home.

The emergency session of the Wychgate Residents' Association was not going according to plan. Ernest Busby, in the chair, had been reluctant to hold a full, open meeting in any case, since that always slowed down the decision process, but what he hadn't bargained for was blatant opposition. At first he had been relieved to see how few people had turned up. The Jacques sisters always came to meetings, but seldom spoke; Mrs Maidwall huffed and puffed a bit but invariably supported him and the rector felt obliged to adopt a neutral stance on most issues. Also, it was gratifying to see the old colonel here. Pilkington usually avoided Residents' Association events, considering them to be surplus to requirements. Anything important, he maintained, would be brought up at the parish meeting which was held twice a year. The rest of the gathering was made up with about a score of the usual of nonentities who were anxious to toe the line and comply with the general tide of opinion as long as they weren't asked to do very much. But this Ball geezer, Busby thought, was beginning to be a pain in the neck in all sorts of ways and, being BBC, was probably a liberal as well.

'Well, thank you all for coming,' Busby had begun, 'I think we can get this meeting over pretty quickly. I've called it, as you no doubt know, because of the threat to our environment. For those who don't follow, I'll put you in the picture. In a nutshell, it's this: the new owners of the land at the very heart of our community want to fell ancient woodland, and hence destroy one of our most valuable natural habitats. Now I know we are all opposed—'

'Excuse me,' Graham butted in. 'It's probably rude of me to interrupt' – Busby gave him a look that said, yes, it was, extremely rude – 'but could you be a little more specific and, at the same time, ease up a bit on the emotive vocab?'

'Mister, er, Ball—'

'Graham!'

'Yes, well,' Busby was beginning to look uncomfortable. He usually presided over everyone with ease. 'Yes, if you'd kindly let me say my piece, I'm sure we'll be glad to have you share your comments with us a little later on.' He continued, but modified his tone. 'Lady Fitzgerald is planning to fell the trees of Pyson Wood. Now clearly, we are all opposed to that, but the problem is that I'm not sure whether she needs planning consent to fell or not. If not, we might be able to get her for "change of use" but what I have to tell you is that we may find we have a fight on our hands. Now the purpose of this meeting is to decide how we are going to prevent this appalling act of destruction.'

'Get teepeeos on 'em,' muttered Mrs Maidwall. 'That should settle the owner's hash.'

'Sorry?' Jerome raised a quizzical eyebrow.

'Tree Preservation Orders.'

'Ah.' He thought for a moment or two and then said, 'Who has actually spoken to the, ah, owner?' There was a silence.

'Well obviously, no one. But the colonel—'

'It was I who brought this to the attention of Mr Busby,' Michael said. 'I want to get the thing stopped right away. Nip it in the bud.'

'Mister chairman,' said Graham Ball. Busby preened at the respectful address. 'You seem to assume that no one is in favour of those trees being cleared.'

'Well, obviously,' said Busby.

'Have you sounded out everyone at this meeting?'

'Of course! Well, I have in a manner of speaking.'

'And in the village?'

'Well, not in—'

'Not at all in fact, I think.' Ball fixed him with a challenging eye. 'I know I wasn't approached. Neither were my immediate neighbours.'

'Well, it's pretty obvious you'd be against it.'

'Would I?' Ball said, 'What makes you think that?' He looked round the room at the other faces turned on him. 'In point of fact, I think the trees should be felled. They spoil the lines of the village, they're not old—'

'Some of them are dangerous,' Jerome cut in. 'I'm not at all sure they would be such a loss.'

'Any one else in favour of wrecking our habitat?' Busby asked. The Jacques sisters shook their heads in unison and Mrs Maidwall kept silent but glared at the rector. 'Thank you. Clearly, the meeting is strongly in favour of objecting to this move.'

'Mr Chairman, I think we should have a vote on this one.'

'All right,' Busby glanced at his watch.

Ball continued, 'I would like to propose a motion that this meeting supports plans to remove the coniferous trees of, um, Pyson Wood.'

'Seconder?' Busby put on his briskest manner.

'Jerome's hand twitched.'

'Those in favour?' To his surprise, several hands went up. But the bulk of the room did not vote. 'Against?' A few more hands went up, but the majority was by no means large.

'There is one aspect to this that may have escaped you all.' Busby had kept his trump card until last. 'Development!' If he'd said 'fornication' he would not have elicited a sharper response. There was a common gasp. Followed by general chatter.

'On the site?'

'Houses?'

'Horrible little bungalows, washing lines everywhere!'

'Starter homes. Children! Can you imagine!'

Busby raised a hand. 'Ladies and gentlemen, I'm inviting someone to propose a motion that all planning applications for Pyson Wood, including felling trees or building on the site be fully and energetically opposed.' This time everyone, except Jerome Daniels and Graham Ball, raised their hands.

'Unanimous, I think,' Busby said,

'Not quite,' Graham muttered.

'Would the meeting like me to visit Lady Fitzgerald?' Busby asked.

'Actually,' Jerome said, 'I'd be willing to have a quiet word with Lady Imogen. It might be a little kinder that way.'

Chapter Eight

———

The worst possible thing happened: Hands arrived early.
Mrs Crowe had not yet left and was still in the kitchen
at Weir House, finishing her shopping list. Wringing her
hands, Imogen stared out of the sitting-room window and
watched him stride up to the front door and ring the bell.
She heard Mrs Crowe's heavy footfalls in the hall, heard the
bolt slide back and the door swing open. Imogen crept over to
the sitting-room door and stood still, turning her ear towards
it and even trying to stop breathing in her endeavour to make
out what was being said. If the Crow found out about their
walks together, she'd do something awful. No doubt about
it. But what would Russell do?

'You'll have to be brief,' she heard Mrs Crowe say. 'I've
got to get off.' The two of them walked to the kitchen, and
Imogen heard the door quietly closing.

After almost a quarter of an hour she heard them come out
of the kitchen again and move slowly down the hall to the
front door. Hands left, apparently without asking for her. He
didn't peep into the sitting-room or even glance back as he
walked away, down the front garden path. Imogen watched
his Jaguar speed away and felt a pang of disappointment,
followed, almost at once, by a feeling of relief. The walks
were getting progressively more exciting, especially when
Hands was in a kind or a gallant mood, but they were also
terrifying at times. He could be so vicious. Today would have
been especially horrid because she was going to have to let

him know that she had been persuaded to abandon the whole idea of cutting any trees down or building anything in Pyson Wood. Crowe barged into the sitting-room.

'I'm late now, thanks to your friend.'

'Not my friend.' Imogen shuddered. 'What did he want?'

'My business.' She regarded Imogen for a moment or two. 'Nothing you want in town, I presume.'

'Several things, actually.' Imogen had been ready for this question. 'I've, ahm, made a list.' She walked over to her little knee hole desk and picked up a sheet of paper. Mrs Crowe skimmed the list.

'Tomato plants? Courgettes? You want me to go all the way out to the garden centre?'

'If you wouldn't mind.'

'Well I would mind. I shouldn't have to run around like this for you.'

'I know, but it would be such a, ahm, kindness. I want to try growing things like our own salads and that. Please?' Mrs Crowe regarded her charge. This gardening craze seemed to be doing her a bit of good and it did keep her at home. Now that the Hands creature had visited and told her one or two things, the goal posts were, she felt, slightly on the move. She needed Imogen to be happy and compliant now, if she was to gain anything for herself in all this, and Hands had made it clear that the stakes were high. 'All right,' she said, 'but I'll be a lot later than usual. I might even have a pub lunch and come home this afternoon.'

'Fine,' said Imogen, happy to have a few extra hours of relative freedom.

Mrs Crowe picked up her shopping bags and went out, slamming the back door behind her. After a few moments, Imogen watched her drive away. She stared out of the sitting-room window for some minutes, enjoying the sight of a sulphur yellow Brimstone butterfly working among the vivid purple blooms of the honesty plants that had been seeding themselves in the front garden of Weir House for more years than anyone in Wychgate could remember. She had not yet, this season, spotted her favourite butterfly, the Orange Tip, but expected, any day now, to see one feeding on nectar from the flowers or racing along the hedge that lined the street. She remembered how she had first spotted an Orange Tip lying on her back with Marcus, in long grass on the banks of the Thames. 'That's a pretty butterfly,' she'd said, when one had hovered for a moment over their heads. 'I don't think I've seen an orange and white one like that before.'

'Keep very still,' Marcus had said, and see what happens when he settles. He had held her arms in his strong grip until the Orange Tip had paused over a sprig of cow parsley and, finally, had settled and closed its wings. 'See,' he had whispered, 'look at the underwings.' She had observed for the first time, the beauty of the butterfly's wing design – a green and white tracery that helped to conceal it among the white laciness of the cow parsley.

'It's almost disappeared,' she whispered. 'I do believe the orange is only on the topside but shows right through. I never realised a butterfly's wings were so nearly see-through.

'Not an "it",' Marcus had murmured, 'it's a "he".'

'How on earth do you know?'

'The females don't have the orange wing tips. They're just white and green and black. More sedentary too.'

'Marcus, how clever you are!' Imogen had exclaimed, tracing a finger along the vein that pulsed in his temple. 'All those brains. Do you think it's ruining them, really?'

'What *are* you on about?'

'You know very well.'

'Coke and that? Never! As long as we know how to control it. We're educated. We *know* what we're doing, yah?'

'Oh yah, definitely!' But neither had believed it. Not really.

Memories cut into the raw nerves of Imogen's conscience. She pushed her hands so deeply into her cardigan pockets that the fabric began to tear. 'Oh Marcus,' she whispered aloud. 'What must I do to stop this pain?'

Outside, the sky was cloudy, but for May it was mild, sultry even. When she had had a lengthy cry, she went out to the garden to prepare the ground for some vegetable seeds that she had ordered by post just after Christmas. The physical task of hoeing, raking and measuring out seed drills was soothing and, by the time she had been at it for almost half an hour, she had begun to feel calmer. The warmth of the morning was pleasant.

She was not able to hear the approach of the car but when the front gate clicked and there was a bang on the front door, she heard it quite clearly. She decided to stay where she was, hoping the visitor might go away.

When no one answered the door, Russell Hands assumed that Imogen had gone for her usual walk in the wood by herself. He decided to have a quick look round. He could always pretend he was looking for her if she happened to be in but not answering. He cupped his hands over his eyes and peered through each ground-floor window in turn. The house was certainly better ordered than when he had called for the first time, back in winter. He could see little sign of real wealth, though, and wondered why the little tart had taken so long to decide, finally, to do something about developing the wood. She must need the money and, as far as he could tell from that Crowe woman, she hadn't been influenced by anyone in the village, apart from the vicar. Handy, that little session with Mrs Crowe had been. Very handy. He reckoned she could be counted on as an ally now, and would probably turn out to be useful in other ways, though just how, he didn't yet know.

He walked to the back of the house and was surprised to see how much had been done to pull the garden round. There were weed-free rose beds, neat borders and, although the paved terrace outside the back door was cleanly swept, blue dog violets and lady's mantle had been allowed to grow in the cracks and crevices, softening the harshness of the lines. He was about to peer through the kitchen window when he spotted Imogen in the kitchen garden, partly hidden behind a screen of shrubs. She was marking out a drill before sowing Brussels sprout seeds. He walked over, picking the shortest route and pushing his way between the shrubs.

'Ow do!'

She leapt up, fear showing in her eyes. 'Oh, it's you.'

The acuteness of her fright subsided but left a troubled, wary expression. 'I thought you'd, ahm, gone.'

'Bad penny!' He grinned at her.

She felt a sudden, urgent compulsion to tell him, to get it over. 'I have to tell you, I've changed my mind.' She had to get it out now, quickly, before she completely lost her nerve. 'About the wood, I mean. I'm not doing it now, after all.'

'Yeah?' His voice displayed a studied lack of interest.

'Do you understand?'

He ignored the question and began to wander towards the old Edwardian summerhouse, now used by Imogen as a makeshift tool shed. 'Valuable structure!' He slapped the wooden railing on its small verandah. ''En's teeth, these are nowadays.'

'Oh, yah?'

'Oh yah!' he mimicked, and beckoned to her with his chin. 'Let's have a look inside.' He opened the door and held it for her. As she passed in front of him, he goosed her crudely, making her topple forward and then stepped in behind her, slamming the door. She stared at him, her breath coming in short gasps. He stepped forward, grabbed her chin in one hand and pressed his mouth on hers. As always, she resisted but soon felt unable to forbid access to his stabbing tongue. This time, though, the setting was different and his approach was more brutal, his fingers clutching more cruelly. She pulled her head back to protest.

'Russell, please!'

'You love it, girl! You know you do.' He kept hold of her chin, gripping tightly. 'Now, what's all this about changing your mind?'

'I've just told you.' Her voice sounded odd, her chin clamped in his hand. 'They want me to leave the wood alone.'

'They?' He let go her chin. 'Oh, *they* do, do they?'

She nodded. 'I daren't go against them, Russell. I've got to live here, after all.'

'Daren't? Are you afraid of them?'

'A little, yes. Well, cautious really.'

'You ought to be afraid of me,' he said, fixing her with

his eye. 'Maybe I should make you afraid.' She felt her pulse rate rise. Her mouth went dry and she began to tremble. There was a small kitchen table in the summerhouse, old-fashioned pine with sturdy legs, ancient but still durable. She used if for potting. A small heap of compost was on it, ready for sowing the half-hardy plant seeds when Mrs Crowe brought them home. He grabbed her shoulders and pushed her back until she felt the edge of the table, just under her buttocks. She began to perspire, and to moan in a low voice. He held her neck and kissed her again, assaulting her with his mouth until she was at the point of gagging. His hands began to work over her body, pinching her breasts and then clawing the top of her knickers. She managed to bring a foot up and kicked him, making him stagger a little. In response, he punched her in the stomach, not very hard, just enough to wind her. She vomited down his jacket.

'You mucky little bitch,' he whispered, his teeth a half-inch from her ears. 'You ain't gettin' away wiv that!' He pulled her knickers so hard they ripped, but not before they had cut into her flesh, almost deeply enough to draw blood. 'You don't want me to stop, do you?'

'Please,' she whimpered, 'please, please stop.'

'Because if I stop now, I'll be frustrated. An' if I'm frustrated I could make life *hell* for you.'

She merely whimpered, incoherent now as he continued to fumble, pressing his vomit-spattered jacket against her face so that she inhaled the sharp stench of her own stomach contents. She deserved this. It was mete punishment for Marcus, for everything. She hoped he would kill her and the whole miserable thing could finish. She felt the pile of compost, gritty under her backside and his right hand on her throat, pushing her backwards. He fumbled some more but within a couple of minutes, it was over and he was zipping up his trousers. She was too shocked to weep, or to try to run. She got to her feet and stood, with her clothes filthy and awry, staring at him with blank eyes.

'I'll be kind to yer next week,' he said. '*If* yer tell the villagers you've changed yer mind back again.' She continued to stare, still unable to speak. 'Oh, ah!' he added, 'I'll have an architect with me when I come next time. Make a few drawings. Yer minder knows all about it.'

He left, kicking open the summerhouse door and leaving it swinging. Imogen half sat, half stood, her rump resting on the edge of the potting table, her senses blotted out by a general numbness. For several minutes she stared ahead, seeing little. Then she realised that her bare buttocks were still pressing against the table and she stood up, shuddering with disgust. She adjusted her clothes and dusted herself down. Most of the vomit had landed on Hands but there was a spread of it on the floor and she had spatters down her skirt. She had to get clean. As she walked over the lawn to the house, the sense of revulsion increased until she felt she could contain it no more. But she told herself she had no right to feel self-pity. Someone as low and as filthy as she could hardly be made any lower or filthier, whatever happened. What she had just received was no more than she deserved. No more at all. In fact Hands had seemed to know that they had both been expecting things to reach this level. But what chilled her more, what made her finally break out into a piteous low wail that grew in a steady crescendo, and lifted in pitch to a thin scream, was this: they had not yet, she knew, touched bottom.

With dry eyes and a drier mouth that tasted of stomach acid, she walked to the house, took off all her clothes in the kitchen, crammed them into a bin liner, double tied the neck and then, naked, walked upstairs to the bathroom where she ran hot water into the tub, tested the temperature, running more in until it was almost too hot to bear, and stepped in.

Thirty minutes later, she was still in the bath, the water now down to blood heat, when the door bell rang for the third time that morning. She got out of the tub but then decided not to answer the door. In the bathroom mirror she could see bruises blackening on her thighs and upper arms – actual thumb prints where he had gripped her. She felt an impulse to try to scrub the bruises away as if they were dirt. She put on a towelling dressing gown, stolen from the Shangri-La Hotel in Singapore when she had been on an eastern jaunt with Marcus, tried to wrap a towel round her head in a turban, the way film stars did it on screen, failed, and ended up with a sort of Virgin-Mary-cum-Bedouin head-dress and walked slowly downstairs, planning to have a glass of milk and an apple before getting dressed. She had, at most, another hour of solitude before the Crow got back.

As she got to the bottom stair, the doorbell rang again, making her start so much, her head dress nearly fell off. She uttered a little cry of fear. The bell rang again, and was accompanied by knocking. She opened the door a little and looked up into the kindly grey eyes of Jerome Daniels. His smile turned to an expression of concern when he saw how she was dressed. 'Oh, I'm so sorry. I'll come back another time.'

'No no. Come in!' She opened the door to admit him. She might have wanted to pour out her troubles, to weep, to rail, anything to share the hurt she felt. But that simply wasn't possible.

'I've been meaning to call, ever since I told you about the Residents' Association nonsense on Sunday.' Jerome seemed a little flustered. He couldn't help thinking how much more attractive she was in a dressing gown than in her usual shapeless day clothes. The towel on her head made her look like a someone in a nativity play. 'I'm *so* sorry. I shouldn't have disturbed you, I know. I do hope you will excuse me for being so persistent, but I believe your very efficient chaperone is absent today.' He allowed himself to give her a conspiratorial wink.

'Mrs Crowe? Yah. Thursday is shopping day. Won't you, ahm, sit down,' Imogen opened the sitting-room door for him. 'Would you like some tea? A drink?' Jerome shook his head and then laughed – with a touch of sarcasm in his tone.

'Are you allowed to make such offers, off your own bat?'

'Oh yah!' He noticed the assurance in her voice – she'd been growing emotionally stronger week by week – but today she had a wild, mad look in her eye that he hadn't seen before. It disturbed him. 'I say, are you feeling absolutely all right?'

'Never better.' She sat on the sofa and, not bidden to go anywhere else, he sat beside her and took one of her hands. It was clammy, presumably from the bath, and shaking a little.

'Imogen, I wanted to say to you,' he paused. What he was about to do would be interpreted by many as being disloyal. 'About that stupid, brainless Residents' Association.' He dried again. Unable to find the right words.

'Yah?'

'The fact is, well . . . what I wanted to say was that they don't have the ultimate say, you know.'

'Sorry?'

'I mean, just because the Residents' Association objects to your felling Pyson Wood, doesn't mean they can actually prevent you from doing it.'

'No, but I've got to, ahm, live here.'

'Imogen, there are lots of us who would like to see those hateful conifers chopped down. They're overcrowded and hideous. They throw the whole street into darkness. Do you know, in frosty weather the ice doesn't melt there because the sun never gets on to that bit of the road. I say get rid!' He folded his arms, pushing each hand into the opposite sleeve of his cassock, like a Chinese Mandarin. 'And blooming good riddance.'

Imogen sat, staring ahead, saying nothing. Eventually, almost as if sleep-talking, she said, 'I had already changed my mind again. I will clear the wood. I will sell the timber for pulping.'

'Oh well, fine!' He rubbed her hand for encouragement. 'Bully for you.'

'It will make room for the houses.'

'Houses?' Jerome was startled.

'Houses. But,' she waved a warning finger, 'you're not to tell.'

'I won't,' he promised. 'But I ought to go, you'll want to get dressed.'

She said nothing but continued to stare ahead, so he showed himself out. Gracious, he thought, houses! That really will wake them up. He began to imagine all the righteous indignation that would be exhibited. It would be amusing to watch. But before those thoughts had properly crystallised, he felt guilty for having had them at all. He really should like his parishioners more. He increased his pace, keen to get back to the rectory, to watch the Test Match on television.

Eleven weeks later, on Michaelmas day, Colonel Pilkington called an Extraordinary General Parish Meeting. Practically every inhabitant of Wychgate Saint Peters turned up, so the meeting had to be adjourned, before it began, and was moved from the drawing-room of the manor to the garden bar of the Black Pig. Latecomers were unable to fit into the crowded room and had to stay in the beer garden, clustered round the open French windows like worker bees hanging on their queen.

Imogen Fitzgerald stayed away. Not only was her intention to fell the wood now official, but worse, far worse, she had applied to the West Kesteven District Council for consent to construct three executive-style, two-storey dwellings on the site of the wood.

'Almost opposite the church,' Mrs Maidwall had said to her neighbour, literally spitting with excitement, when the *Stoneford Messenger* had published the application details. 'Modern 'ouses. I *ask* you!' Talk buzzed around the parish. Never had so much concern been shown for the environment; for the beauty of the trees; for maintaining the purity of the village. But the biggest concern of all was that someone, an outsider at that, might be about to make themselves a heap of easy money. There was no way the Wychgate villagers wanted to let that happen.

'And each with a double garridge – bigger than some of us've got 'ouses,' said a regular drinker at the Black Pig, who had decided to stay for the meeting since it had come to his bar. His audience, a couple of young farm workers, nodded dutifully, mindful of the need to charm him into buying them another pint of lager.

The meeting turned out to be even stormier than Jerome had expected. At first there was a general rumble from the crowd, in full and unequivocal objection to the planning. No one could understand how it had got this far without being prevented and during the evening, one individual after another, each claiming to speak for the Village, the Nation,

God, Common Sense or the Conservative Government, stood up to express opposition to the idea of three more dwellings being added to the sixty-one that already existed in the parish.

All the while, Michael Pilkington, looking older and frailer than his seventy-five years, chaired the proceedings, preventing the garrulous speakers from going on too long, and encouraging the shy ones to speak out. Just as he reached the point where he felt everyone had had their say and he could safely sum up, Graham Ball arrived and, politely but firmly, nudged his way through the French windows and into the room, smiling and excuse-me-ing to the front. He caught Jerome's eye and nodded before raising his hand and looking at Michael.

'Please accept my apologies,' he said, 'but I got held up for hours on the A1, outside Colsterworth.' Michael nodded and one or two long-distance motorists murmured their sympathy. 'I've just got back from a trip to Harrogate. On the way up, this morning, I stopped at the West Kesteven Offices to have a good look at these plans for the Pyson Wood site.' He allowed himself to make a dramatic pause and looked slowly over the crowd. 'I presume that's what you are all discussing. Mr Chairman, may I ask what the consensus at this meeting is?' That elicited a ragged laugh. 'Against?' Michael nodded. 'Then please may I speak?'

'The floor is yours, Mr Ball, but I think we've pretty well talked it out.'

'Fine. Er, well, I just wanted to ask first of all. Who, in this room, has actually looked at the plans? In detail?' Not a single hand was raised, not even Busby's. Ball looked directly at him.

'No time, I'm afraid,' Busby said, rather lamely, 'it all came on us so quickly.'

'Well, may I say that I have. And these houses look, to me, to be exactly what this village needs.' There was a ripple of dissent. 'No, my friends please! If I could be allowed to speak,' and Graham Ball, with eloquence and charm, presented a case, not only for building these houses but for allowing further, moderate expansions to the village.

As he spoke, his arguments began to find sympathy with a growing number of the residents, even with those few who had planned to skip the meeting and go to the pub, only to have the meeting find them there. He knew how to be brief but dramatic and was soon summing up. 'I'd like to see this village – and so many other of our wonderful, charming English villages – with its own post office and stores,' he said, 'with a decent bus service and with a healthy population of mixed ages. Plenty of youngsters growing up to take care of the old folk, and to keep that excellent primary school at Wyckhamby open. In short, ladies and gentlemen, not merely a dormitory for commuters, nor a weekend retreat for harassed city dwellers, but a proper, working, living, lovely village.' As he drew his oratory to a close, his audience had grown silent. Even the drinkers at the bar had put down their pints of lager and turned to listen more closely. The applause at the end was loud and enthusiastic, but not universal. Several of the faces glared and a couple of people walked out, making as much show of their exit as they could. Small discussions began within the body of the meeting, many of them acrimonious. Ball went to sit down next to Jerome.

'Well,' said the rector, quietly, 'you've stirred 'em up all right.'

'Had to be done,' Graham said. 'I meant everything I said.'

'Bit fanciful though, isn't it?'

'What's wrong with that? God knows, we could all do with a little more idealism and a little less cold cynicism.'

Jerome loved him for that.

'Hear hear,' he whispered. 'But I'm afraid Michael's going to feel very badly about this. He has a thing about that horrible wood.'

By now the splinter discussions had become noisy. Michael Pilkington began to tap the large porcelain ashtray on his table, louder and louder until, at last, silence fell.

'I think it's necessary,' he said, in a voice grown tremulous, 'that we wind up. But before we do, I think we should make some kind of summary and recommendation, so that I can make an official representation to the District Planning

Department.' Graham Ball had his hand up. 'Yes?' Michael
said, irritably.

'Perhaps a proposal would sum it all up pretty well.'
Michael remembered Ball's proposal at the Residents' Association meeting and hoped this one would elicit the same
response. He nodded curtly. Graham continued: 'I propose
that the application to fell the conifers and develop the wood,
within the guidelines in the application, be given support by
this parish meeting.'

'I see,' Michael was looking decidedly blotchy round the
face. 'Is there a seconder?'

'Yeah!' One of the young farm workers at the bar raised
his hand.

'Mr, um, Althwaite?' Michael asked. The young man went
very red and sniggered into his lager. 'Those in favour?'
Graham raised his hand. There was a brief hiatus, then
seven more were raised, two of them tremulously, one put
up, lowered, and then half-raised. Michael should have looked
relieved, but his colour was, if anything, worse. 'Against?' A
forest of hands shot up. 'Well, ladies and gentlemen. I think
that's it.'

'You haven't voted, Jerome,' Graham Ball whispered.
Jerome shifted uncomfortably.

'Any other business?' Michael's features had now turned
pale. Black bruise-like marks were appearing under his eyes.
'Anyone anything else to say?' There was a silence. 'Rector?'
It was customary, at the end of these parish events, for Jerome
to be called upon to lead a short prayer. Even after routine
meetings, he found this embarrassing but today, he felt he
just couldn't do it.

'Michael, er, Mr Chairman, everyone. I'm not sure I want
to say a prayer tonight. I feel there is too much dissent in the
air. What's more – and it's probably improper for me to say
this – but I'm not sure the right decision has been reached.'
That elicited a murmur of surprise. Jerome continued, raising
his voice a little. 'A village, like any community, is about
people, not buildings. And I thought Mr Ball's remarks about
a living, working society with people of all ages, were some
of the most relevant of the evening. I suppose, as your rector,

I should keep neutral, but on this one, I feel I can't. Progress and growth are not things to be shunned. I'm sorry Michael, I know you have strong feelings about it but I'm afraid I'm on the side of the developers.' He looked at the old man's face, clear grey eyes looking into clouded blue. He had seldom seen such bleakness of expression.

There was little reaction in the room – just a few mutters and then silence. When he had spoken, Jerome had felt he'd been making a major decision which would have significant consequences but, he thought, looking at faces other than Michael's, I might just as well have kept my mouth shut. A feeling of helplessness began to invade his spirit. He'd had a pretty dire week all in all, and wondered really why he bothered. Just three in church on Sunday morning and only seven in Wyckhamby for Evensong. He – or his function as rector – just didn't count for anything these days. People seemed to look to their newspapers or television for guidance now, or to their doctors. Spiritual leadership was a thing of the past. He wondered, yet again, what he was doing wasting his time here. The people around him were waiting for the chairman to wind up the meeting formally, but Michael had snatched up his papers and was already on his feet, striding towards the door. He passed Jerome on the way out.

'Michael?' Jerome said, but he didn't stop to listen. Jerome walked out after him and followed him down the street. 'Michael!' The old man turned, looked at him for a moment and then turned back, walking slowly, his shoulders hunched, his gait irregular. In spite of the soft, September air, Jerome felt chilled. Michael was wrong on this one, he knew that well enough, but Jerome had hurt the only person in this village who, he felt, had totally honest principles. What was more distressing was that he had hurt the only person he really liked.

September was mushroom month and 1924 was a bountiful year. Most of the pasture-land around Wychgate Saint Peter carried horses at one time or another and therefore, most grew good mushrooms. No one knew quite why horse dung was so beneficial to the fungi but uneducated people thought they were actually spawned by horses and that without them, mushrooms could not appear. In the meadows surrounding the small copse known as Pyson Wood, white discs, some as much as ten inches across, had appeared in their hundreds every morning, and early-stirring villagers were able to gather them to fry with their eggs and bacon for breakfast. Peter Ball, with his usual enterprising spirit, had been selling freshly gathered wild mushrooms at the village stores for nearly two weeks. Those who were too grand or too idle to gather their own, could have them delivered with their groceries at the cost of a penny farthing per quarter or fourpence the pound.

Thus, each morning at six-thirty, Violet Ball would walk into any of the fields that ran along the river Dene with a large osier basket on each arm to gather ware for the shop. This morning, as she trod a zigzagging course across the land, pausing to stoop and to pluck up a mushroom cap that was at exactly the right stage of development, she kept glancing back towards the village. Pretty soon, she knew, she'd see a figure working through the dewy grass towards her. As the clock on Saint Peter's church struck seven, she saw him, vaulting over the top gate and trotting at a steady pace towards her. He ducked under the wire fence that enclosed the field she was in, almost without slowing down his speed, but slipped in the dew and nearly fell before recovering his balance and his speed. Within a few seconds he was up to her, only slightly out of breath, with a flush on his cheeks that made the blue of his eyes look more intense than usual. She put her basket down and reached out both arms. He took her hands and held them.

'I knew you'd come,' she said. He stood still while he recovered from his run. His breathing soon returned to normal but his heart beat more strongly as he looked at her face. Her hair was slightly untidy, with so much bending for the mushrooms, and some tresses were falling across her brow. He reached up and, with a reverent tenderness, stroked them away, feeling the smoothness of her cheek and the warmth of her body on his hands, in the chill of the morning.

'I'm dying to get back to Barleythorpe,' he said, 'but I can hardly bear the thought of not seeing you until December.'

'It'll soon pass,' she said. 'You'll be busy. So will I.' They began to walk, looking at the ground.

'I can only stay about half an hour. My train goes at eight-forty-one.'

'I know.' She bent to a mushroom the size of a dinner plate and reached a hand under the cap to grasp the stem and tug gently, until it came out of the ground. Underneath, the gills were pinkish, evenly spaced and close together, but with tiny spaces between, like the leaves of an old, often-read book. She stroked the smooth cap, enjoying its unique texture – velvet but smooth, like living skin – and ran her finger lightly across the pink gills. 'This is where the spores come from,' she said, 'millions upon millions.' Michael looked with scant interest. He was watching her face as she spoke. 'They could blow – the spores, from this mushroom – all the way round the world. Several times.'

'How?'

'They're so small and light. Microscopic. They get up into the atmosphere and blow and blow. Wherever the wind takes them.'

'What a lot you know!' They only had minutes together and the the thought of a three-month separation caused a horrible dragging sensation in his chest. The church clock struck eight. 'Violet, I want to . . .' But he couldn't go on. She put her baskets down again. 'Here, let me carry them for you,' he said.

'Don't be silly. They're not even half full yet.' She reached for his shoulders; he pulled her closer. They brought their lips together and kissed. A heavy sigh came out of him and he hugged her so hard she felt her bones creaking.

'I've never felt like this,' he murmured, in her ear, breathing in the scent of her skin. 'Never!' She pushed him from her. Almost roughly.

'Go!' she said, sharply. 'Go. Now!' She managed a bright smile. He hesitated. 'Go *on*!' She turned away, to prevent him from seeing her eyes fill with tears. He ran, without stopping, all the way to the manor where Gerard was waiting in the hall, with his overnight case. His cabin trunk had been sent to school in advance, wheeled to Wychgate station on a handcart.

'Good walk?'

'Yes thank you, Father.' Michael stood, a little stiffly. 'I must change my shoes before I go up to the station.' He went into the kitchen where, ready polished, his black uniform shoes were waiting. Mrs Bull picked them up and handed them to him.

'You've gone and got damp on your trouser cuffs, Master Michael.'

'Oh, that won't matter, Mrs Bull. It's a warm day – or will be when the sun gets up more – they'll dry.'

Mrs Bull thought she detected a sadness in the voice. 'Bit upset at having to go, are we, dear?'

'No, not at all.' He glanced at her and she was surprised to see the moistness of his eyes. Before, he had always seemed to keen so get away from this lonely household.

'Soon be Christmas.'

'Several pretty important rugby matches before then, Mrs Bull,' Michael said, standing up after tying his shoes. She saw through the effort of cheerfulness but was glad that he seemed to regret leaving. She assumed it meant that he and his father were getting on better with each other. Not that they were enemies at all, but their relationship had always seemed so cold. It must be that Violet girl softening the old man up a bit, she thought. What a lovely influence she was turning out to be.

'Well, goodbye, Master Michael.' She'd have liked to kiss him but that wouldn't have been proper, so she put out her hand. He shook it formally, with just the right degree of grip.

'Goodbye, Mrs Bull, and thank you for looking after me so well.' He strode through the house, his nailed heels ringing on the flagstone floor of the hall and joined his father, waiting by the front door.

'I won't walk up with you, if you don't mind.'

'Of course not, Father. I can manage.' He grasped his small case and put out a hand. 'Goodbye, Father.'

'Goodbye, son. The best of luck with your sport. I know you'll try hard.'

'Of course, Father.'

Gerard was at his study desk before Michael had closed the front door behind him. Ahead lay a ten-minute walk to the railway station, the short, two-stop journey to Barleythorpe and thirteen weeks of Latin, Maths, French and, above all, rugby, glorious rugby! The whole prospect thrilled him, but then he thought of Violet, and a feeling of sadness blotted out the joy of his anticipation of the new term.

Sixty years later, on a sunny October morning, Michael Pilkington was walking exactly the same route, slowly and with the aid of a stick. The site of the old station was now a warehouse for agricultural machinery and, in spite of being a mild, moist autumn, there were no mushrooms. The best mushroom field had been planted with conifers in 1926 to become the expanded limb of Pyson Wood. The rest of the land around the village was largely arable now, with winter wheat crops and sugar beet grown where, half a century before, cattle, sheep and horses had grazed, kept in their fields by huge hedges which provided shelter when the harsh east winds blew. In spring those hedges would blossom with hawthorn, wild rose and purging buckthorn; in early autumn they would stage multicoloured displays of wild fruits: orange scarlet rose hips, blood crimson haws, blue-black dogwood berries and luscious ripe blackberries, plump and juicy – perfect companions to the tart apples garnered from the cottagers' moss-coated trees. Now there were few hedges and those that remained were flailed to within three feet of the ground by whirling machines that littered the roads with chips and fragments of white wood.

Passing Weir House, Michael noticed how Imogen's work in the garden was beginning to show results. The sun lit up tall, white Japanese anemones and threw the shadows of their outlines across the cropped lawn. How pretty they looked, he thought, with those deep blue asters in between. But Michael could not feel happy with the sight, reminded by it, that this misguided girl had brought on all the misery of recent weeks. Never had he seen the village so up-in-arms, so torn and divided between those few who wanted change and the great majority who abhorred the thought of it.

As he passed, he noticed Imogen, head down in the border, pulling weeds from between the perennials. He crossed to the opposite side of the street and looked ahead, determined not to speak to her. From her crouched position, she could see him and knew that he would not greet her. She stayed low until he was out of sight, but she felt guilty for causing him so much anguish. Really, she'd have liked to drop the whole thing but dared not, now that Hands had his plans all drawn up.

For weeks after the assault in the summer house, she had teetered on the edge of breakdown. The tattered overcoat had come out again, and she would sit hunched in the back garden, in spite of summer heat, with the rough tweed wrapped closely about her. At other times, she had prolonged weeping spells, slipping into the shrubbery and emerging an hour or more later with bloodshot eyes, ready to blame her appearance on hay fever. Frequently, during the first part of summer, she had refused food, and grew so thin that even Mrs Crowe was alarmed. She had felt quite unable to confide in anyone. She had never dared confront Hands with the incident and he made no references to it. On her return, that day, Mrs Crowe had gone to put the tomato and courgette plants into the summer house and had discovered the vomit. After swabbing the floor with bucket and mop, she had remonstrated, 'Really, I do think you might clean up your own mess. What made you so sick?' Imogen had looked alarmed but had said nothing.

Hands kept returning, the visits now approved by her minder, and Imogen was obliged to keep seeing him. Each time he came, she found her revulsion a little easier to cope with, and to conceal. And, as the months passed, even the reality of that hateful experience grew blurred. Could she have imagined it? Could she have magnified a minor assault into a rape? It was so hard, sometimes, to give shape to her thoughts and it was less painful simply to push them away.

In some respects, she hoped that planning consent would be refused. Then she could forget about Hands altogether. And yet, money from the development could be just the lifeline she needed. Now that she was beginning to recover from her past, edging towards leading a normal life, she realised that she was a captive – not only of her family, by proxy of the odious Mrs Crowe, but also of Hands. She still needed the Crow to look after her, especially during her depressions. Hands, she needed too, for without him, there was no chance of getting planning consent. Her instinct for survival was getting stronger by the week and it told her that the only way she would ever get herself fully rehabilitated, would be to buy independence. That meant freedom from absolutely everyone and for that, she needed money. Quite a lot of it.

Had she bothered to open her post that morning, she would have known that the seeds Hands had sown on her behalf were already germinating and looked set to provide a rich but bitter harvest. Up to this moment, the village had been squabbling about a theoretical situation. Most of the wiser folk knew that planning consent was unlikely for a variety of reasons. The village street would not take the added wear and tear. The junction with the main road was already dangerous and would be more so with extra traffic. Proximity to the river would create sewage and drainage problems and anyway, the West Kesteven usually said 'no' on principal to almost everything that was not part of its overall county plan. But the villagers did not know that Hands was interested in exploiting this opportunity to the full, or that he had clout with almost everyone in the planning offices of most local authorities in the county and its neighbours.

Michael was walking up to leave a note in Busby's letter box, to inform him that he would be resigning as Parish Chairman, after more than twenty years. It was a short, formal note, but the old man felt a log-jam of bitterness clogging his breast. His family had resided at Wychgate Manor for generations but he no longer felt at home there. He felt estranged, victimised, unsafe in his own village. The removal of the conifer wood was unthinkable. It had been planted to cover, to expunge, and if the cover went, there was too much to lay bare. He could not be here when that happened. He simply could not.

When, later that day, Imogen did open her post, she

discovered that permission to erect the houses was granted. Tree felling could begin as soon as she liked. A copy of the document had been sent to the Parish Chairman, which was why he had resigned. But no one, not even Imogen, had the slightest suspicion that Russell Hands' ultimate designs on the village of Wychgate Saint Peters were more far-reaching and more pernicious than any of them would have thought possible.

PART TWO

———————

SAINT LUKE'S SUMMER

Chapter Nine

The most abiding feature of the countryside, thought Graham Ball, is neither birdsong nor the scent of newly mown hay, nor the gambolling of little lambs, nor the beauty of the ripening corn. It's mud – tacky, filthy, shit-coloured, inglorious mud! He looked down at his brogues, noticing with disgust that in spite of walking down the tarmac surface of Wychgate's main street, the soles were soiled at their edges with a slimy suspension of yellow-brown pug. In the arable fields surrounding the village, sugar beet and potato harvests were in full swing and the lugged wheels of tractors, bearing loads of lifted roots from field to farmyard, threw clarty deposits all along the main roads. Wet weather and passing cars spread these, leaving a film of muck across every inch of the highway. Along footpaths, treacherous nuggets of mud lay in wait for shoes which came into contact and then walked it into houses, daubing carpets with marks that were replicated with every footfall. Later, when the weather dried, mud turned to a fine dust which coated roadside vegetation and penetrated cottage windows.

After a warm, golden September with misty mornings and duck-egg skies, October had begun in a sour mood. Persistent light rain was borne on a cutting easterly wind, making everyone seek out winter jackets and switch on their central heating systems a week or two early. As he walked down the sticky street, Graham hunched his shoulders, kept dry by his oiled Barbour jacket, and wished he'd worn his new tweed cap after all. 'Close bosomed friend of the retiring sun' my arse! he thought.

To say his book was going badly would have been something of an understatement. It wasn't going at all. He had not written a word since coming to Wychgate and wasn't even giving thought to the synopsis. All the bright ideas and beginnings of story lines that had intruded into his concentration when he was making documentaries at the BBC, seemed to have evaporated, or to have collapsed during their development phases. Characters, so strong and vivid in his former imagination, shrank when he tried to develop them, or became implausible when he attempted to fit them into a context that matched his literary aims. Anne-Marie, his powerful and acerbic literary agent, though making positive noises about his plans for a novel, was keener for him to develop non-fiction projects. 'Write something a publisher can put a budget to,' she had said. 'Something scandalous. Or, better still, do a TV series with a book to go with it. That could pay the bills and give you time to indulge in fiction.' She was right, of course. But Graham had had enough of television and loathed the prospect of doing yet another hard-hitting series. He wanted to exit the real world for a time, and to indulge his fantasies. That was why he'd come to the countryside, why he had set up the shop's old store room as a study and why – as soon as he and Veronica had finished unpacking – he had, with a tingle of anticipation in his fingertips, turned on his Macintosh computer, created a file entitled FIC/PROJECT, and typed: 'SYNOPSIS' at the top of the first page and *Dramatis Personae* at the top of the second. But after almost seven months, all he had written was a short series of articles about farm subsidies for The *Guardian*, and a number of letters to the broadsheets on the demise of British Broadcasting. His FIC/PROJECT file was still virtually empty and story ideas in his head no less scrambled or jejune than they had been last spring.

He knew, too, that Veronica was unhappy. Twice in the past fortnight, he had woken to the sound of her blowing her nose and, when reaching out in the dark, had encountered cheeks wet with tears. On both occasions, he had held her in his arms and tried to provide the comfort she needed, but she had been unable to express what, exactly, was depressing her. He was pretty sure he knew. She was bored and was pining for London. He felt sympathy with that, but was not ready, just yet, to chuck in the sponge and return to the capital.

So deep was he in brooding introspection – you could hardly call it constructive thought – that he walked right past Weir House without noticing. He cursed under his breath, turned and retraced his last few steps to Imogen's front door. Her eyes widened with surprise when she saw him, as if she had been expecting someone else. He noticed the alarm in her expression and apologised. 'Sorry for coming without phoning first, but I just wanted a quick word. Should I come back another time?'

'Oh no!' I'm, ahm, more free on Thursdays than on any . . .' A car approached. She started at the noise and craned her neck to look over his shoulder, and peer up the street. Slender, pretty neck, Graham thought. If he'd been writing his novel, he'd have called it 'graceful' or even, 'gazelle-like'. She was a little *distrait.*

'Were you expecting someone?'

'Well, no. Actually, ahm . . .' She was expecting Hands, but he liked her to retain complete secrecy about their meetings. Also, she was uneasy about being seen in his presence. Their backgrounds were profoundly different; they had nothing in common but, deeper than that, she felt contaminated by her association with him. 'Perhaps.' She made no attempt to invite Graham inside. He tried to meet her eye but she either looked down or over his shoulder and her mouth kept twitching in a way that suggested more than mere nervousness. Her clothes were horrible but the gentle curve of her chin and the refinement of her features attracted him. She seemed, so much, to need protection, to need sorting out. He knew something of her past – who didn't? – and that she was ignored and probably despised by pretty well everyone in Wychgate. The idea of an effete, over-privileged person coming unstuck through her own folly should have made him scornful, but all he could feel was compassion for this girl. He also sensed that his very presence was causing her anxiety and so decided to say his piece and withdraw.

'Some pretty unkind things have been said about you – *à propos* of this planning thing. I'm sure you've heard.' She glanced directly at him and for the briefest moment saw kindliness in his eyes. 'I just wanted to say that I support your ideas, and that I think it disgraceful that anyone should conduct, or condone a personal vendetta against you.'

'That's kind. That's, very ahm . . .' He noticed her eyes moisten.

'If there is anything,' he took her hand, 'I mean *anything* I can do for you, do, please, let me know.' He hadn't meant to take her hand, but had simply responded to the protective urge. As he was making his little gesture, Russell Hands's Jaguar drew up in near silence. Imogen uttered such a gasp of fright that it made Graham start and turn round. She had snatched her hand out of his.

'Go!' she said. 'You must! Now!' And, though the wildness in her eyes disturbed him, he knew he must obey. Hands was emerging from his Jaguar as Graham walked out, holding the gate open for him.

'Ow do!' Hands said.

'Hullo!' Graham replied. Keen observation and an ability to make rapid judgments of character – essential qualities for a journalist – enabled him to guess what Hands was about. It was just a hunch, but he had to confirm his assessment. 'I say, are you to do with all that?' He gestured towards Pyson Wood.

'Eh?'

'Development. The wood?'

'Nar!' Hands shrugged and then cocked his head towards Imogen at the front door of her house. 'Friend o' the family. That's all.' He gave Graham a conspiratorial wink and walked up to Imogen. 'Ullo girl!' he said, and gave her a chaste peck on the cheek before glancing back at Graham to check that he was moving safely out of the way. Then he turned back to Imogen and pushed her inside. 'You been talkin'?' His voice had at once grown colder. She shook her head vigorously. 'Good,' he said, closing the front door behind them, ''n' that cow gone shoppin' as usual?'

'Ahm, yes.' Imogen decided not to add that Mrs Crowe would also be away for lunch. She began to tremble – the hall was chilly but she was also afraid. Whatever happened though, she mustn't show it.

'Let's go up then.'

'What, ahm, now?'

'Whasser matter?' He grabbed her wrist. 'Ain't you in the mood?' She shuddered with revulsion, but he interpreted the shake as sexual excitement. 'See! Yer always in the mood!' He turned her towards her own staircase and gave her a little push. 'Go on!' His voice had grown soft and menacing. She mounted the stairs slowly, Hands following very close so that she could feel his breath on the back of her neck.

When she had first seen him, she had harboured a kind of fascination. He had both repelled and attracted her. Now he merely disgusted her, but she felt bound to comply with his desires. Partly, she felt it necessary to punish herself, and in that respect, he was like a form of executioner. He was also her route to freedom. Without him, she could not develop Pyson Wood and thus generate the capital she needed to buy herself a new life. But if she were strictly honest with herself, she derived a certain satisfaction from his abusive treatment, as if each degrading session were notching up a score, neutralising a debt that could only be paid off with instalments of suffering and shame. And beneath those feelings ran another realisation more chilling than any ill-treatment Hands could dream up: though her every cell should have loathed and feared the abuse, some inner strand of her being was beginning to accustom itself to his cold brutality, and almost to enjoy the pain and humiliation he administered. That was the cruellest aspect of her punishment.

He pushed her into her bedroom and gave her a sharp command: 'Undress!' She complied, and soon stood naked in front of him, arms folded across her slight breasts. He made no attempt to remove any of his own clothes. 'Turn round!' She obeyed. 'Get dahn. On yer hands and knees!'

His voice had become hoarse. 'Get yer face right dahn, on the floor.' He stood directly behind her, still fully clothed. 'Don't you dare move a single muscle. If you do, I'll fucking kill yer.' Then, in a low monotone, he began to recite a litany of insulting language. For several minutes, the words were meaningless – just filth – but gradually the venom in his voice, the hatred began to focus on its target. He knew just enough about her past to lash her with key words that unlocked the monstrous guilt. Tears began to flow and, as he detected this, he altered his tone a little, developing an even crueller edge. She sobbed, once. He was ready and slapped her so hard that she cried out with pain and surprise. 'I told yer to keep fucking still!' He dropped to a kneeling position behind her. 'Now you're dead.'

The actual sex act, though painful, was soon over. Afterwards, he strode out of the room. He hadn't even taken his jacket off. She spent a while in the bathroom and then came downstairs to join him in her sitting-room. She had dressed in a pair of men's jeans and a thick, cotton blouse, navy blue, with a black belt that looked wrong. She went to the drinks table and poured him a generous measure of Scotch. He addressed her as if none of the previous scenes had happened, one business associate talking to another.

'I bin thinkin' about our little project.' He took the glass and gulped down a generous mouthful.

'Oh?' She sat, carefully, on the edge of the sofa, facing him.

'Yeah. Bin 'aving second thoughts.' He eyed her, enjoying the look of alarm. 'Don't think I'm going ter buy the wood after all.'

'But we've got the planning permission. It's, ahm, all agreed!'

'Is it? I don't remember signing nuffin.'

'But you've got the contract. It's all ready for you to sign.' Panic was entering her voice. 'You've *agreed*!'

'Yeah?'

'If you don't – you know – sign, I'll have lost everything.'

'Nar!' He swallowed another mouthful of Scotch. 'What's

three 'ouses these days. Yer stand to clear sixty gees, after costs, and then yer'll have ter pay around forty percent in tax. What's the bleedin' point?'

'Well, the, ahm point is. I'm depending on—'

'Listen. You could make a bleedin' fortune on this.'

'I don't want to make a fortune, I just want enough to, to . . .' to do what? Buy respect? Acquire freedom from the past? She knew that was impossible and sighed.

'Here's how it goes.' Hands leaned forward and fixed her with his eye. She listened, childlike. 'That site, if it were all cleared, would give us room for, what – thirty, maybe forty 'ouses? If we both developed, going into partnership I mean, we could raise the loan capital jointly, and then build. The 'ousing market's going bonkers at the moment. At worst, we could clear fifty grand profit per 'ouse. That'd make a cool two million.'

Even to someone with as moneyed a background as Imogen, two million pounds was an impossible concept to grasp. Unreal. But the sixty thousand in hard cash that Hands had already agreed to pay for the wood, was an amount she could visualise, could invest, could convert into a modest income. Just enough to buy herself a ticket to independence.

'You *promised* to buy it,' she said, near to tears, 'you promised to sign the contract.' He stood up, walked over to the sofa and grabbed her wrist.

'Don't be a completely stupid bloody cow,' he said, through a clenched jaw. 'Don't you see? I'm givin' you another chance – a big bloody chance. I could have bought that land off of yer for peanuts and then pocketed the jackpot meself.'

'But you *promised*.' She seemed unable to see beyond the possibility of losing the sale.

'Yeah? Well now I've changed me mind. What are *you* goin' to do about that?' He threw her wrist down with a contemptuous snort. She began to tremble again. He put his hand under her chin and cupped it, quite gently. 'All right, all right. No need to take on. We've already got plannin' for three. Kind of a fallback situation, yer might say. But before

I exchange, I'm puttin' in fer more. If we get it, you'll be laughin', girl. Believe me, I'm doing you a favour.'

'But I don't understand. Why can't you just, ahm, sort of buy the wood from me and then develop it yourself?'

'Security – share the risk. I've got that many bleedin' irons in the fire I need a partner on this one.' He knew, with all his other commitments, that raising so much finance, on his own, would be difficult, but that he could probably work something out with her on board. She might improve their chances of getting expanded planning, too, if he could use her in some way. He wasn't sure how he'd manage it, but felt he had a better chance with her as partner than without. He tightened his hand on her chin, pinching and distorting her features, making her eyes water with the pain. 'Even a half-baked bitch like you. You're upper class, see. Titled.' He laughed at the thought of this addle-brained junkie being more respectable than himself and gripped even harder.

'Pluse R'ssell,' the words sounded odd through her pinched mouth.

'Worlds apart, girl, you and me.' He laughed, still holding on to her chin, 'Worlds apart.' Then he lowered his face so that her eyes were less than a couple of inches from his. 'But all these plans are just between the two of us, OK?' He began to shake her head to and fro. 'Just the two of us.' He pushed her head back against the wall, banging it enough to hurt but not to injure, and left, slamming the front door. She had a headache all afternoon.

Truly, we are worlds apart, Violet thought, looking frankly at Gerard's face as he dozed in the opposite seat of their first class railway carriage. In sleep, his features relaxed a little, but even his physiognomy was patrician. The eyebrows were naturally arched; the nose, more aquiline than his son's, had slightly pinched nostrils and the hands, white, smooth, with veins noticeable but not prominent, had been neither moulded nor distorted by any kind of manual exertion. Michael's hands, in contrast, were muscular, sun-tanned, even in winter, with firm, smooth skin and palms roughened from sport, but with slightly tapered fingers, suggesting sensitivity. Violet thought about Michael often, but her longing for him always sharpened when she was in the presence of his father. So much about him reminded her of Michael, and yet he was so different. With Michael any feelings of belonging to a different class had vanished since the May Festival, when he had fainted and she had cradled his head in her lap. His accent was different from hers and his manner inclined to haughtiness, but she no longer noticed. She felt more relaxed, more comfortable with him than with anyone else.

Yet, Gerard had displayed nothing but kindness to his young protégée. He seldom spoke to anyone in the village, except for the briefest moments, but for more than a year, had received Violet at least once a week to assist her with studies to meet the entrance requirements for Oxford. Recently, she had taken the necessary examinations, had been interviewed, and was waiting to hear whether she had been successful. There was no longer a need for the two to meet, but the study sessions seemed to both to be too valuable to discontinue. Twice, in the past two years, they had travelled together on day-long trips, once to Lincoln, to visit the Minster, and to attend the public gallery at Lincoln Crown Court and today, they had been to London to see a matinée performance of *Hamlet* at the Old Vic.

For both, the experience had been memorable. Violet, whose experience of theatre was limited to a couple of amateur productions at Stoneford and the annual village pantomime at Wyckhamby, was entranced. She knew the play well enough – having read all Shakespeare's works, and studied the major ones in some detail – but she had been quite unprepared for the emotional impact of the drama. From the moment of Hamlet's encounter with his father's ghost on the battlements, to his demise at the end of the play, she had been enthralled. It would probably be ages before she could see another play, but she knew that whenever the chance came, from now on, she would grasp it. Oxford, Gerard had told her, had some quite excellent theatres, and would also provide her with opportunities for acting herself, if she happened to be that way inclined, without in any respect compromising her reputation.

The day was to have a deep effect on Gerard. He had arranged for them to meet at Wychgate station for the local train. They would change at Essendine and take an LNER express to King's Cross whence a taxicab would take them south of the river to the theatre. After the play, Gerard would dine with Violet at an inexpensive restaurant, and they would catch the 8.12 p.m. express back to Lincolnshire.

When he arrived at the station, she was already waiting by the ticket office. Against the October wind, she wore a full-skirt, an old but neatly pressed British Warm – re-tailored for the female figure – and a red tam o' shanter. Her outfit was so utterly unmodish, so against the modern trend of cloche hats, dropped waistlines and straight skirts, that he almost laughed. She was no more than a schoolgirl – one who had had to do most of her own schooling. But when she turned her face, fresh and unmarked – not even so much as a dab of rouge on her cheek – and when he took in the beauty of her dark eyes, widened, slightly, with anticipation of the excursion; and when he noted the slight downiness of her upper lip, like the cleft of a ripe apricot, he felt as though he was seeing her for the first time in his life. The emotional impact almost took his breath away. Until today, he had enjoyed her company because she reminded him so much of Elizabeth. Her voice had a similar timbre to Elizabeth's – their laughs were remarkably the same – and many of her mannerisms were like hers. But now he realised, for the first time – though this had been creeping up on him for months – that his ache was not only for his dead wife, but also for this beautiful, intelligent, lively young girl.

Unable to police his expression, he nodded curtly, and went straight to the window, to buy their tickets. On the platform, he answered her polite enquiries about his health and her hopes for the day in vague, distracted monosyllables. On the short journey to Essendine, he buried his head in his copy of *The Times* so she fished out a small volume of Milton. On the main-line train, he finished reading his paper and watched her studying her poetry; watched her lips move and her eyes dart back to a couplet that particularly affected her. A casual observer would mark her down as a slow reader, but Gerard knew that she was committing sizable chunks of *Paradise Lost* to memory.

As he studied her, he attempted to compose his feelings. This new turn of events was dangerous, unhealthy. Should he cease to see her altogether? He should! It would be entirely unfair to do otherwise. Could he bear not to see her? Well, could he? And wouldn't she be terribly hurt at a sudden brush off? She might think she had done something wrong, and he couldn't have borne that. He'd have to be honest, to explain exactly what was happening to him, and to tell her that to go on associating, therefore, was simply not possible. Not to do so would be disloyal to Elizabeth – treacherous, in fact. She looked up, saw his intense gaze, blushed a little, smiled and maintained her cheerful expression, even though he could not smile back, managing only a little lop-sided grimace.

As Gerard agonised over this latest predicament, Violet stole surreptitious glances at him, while conning her Milton. She was fond of him, when there was room in her head to think of anyone other than Michael, but she wished he could be happier. Ever since their first meeting, she sensed that he had been attracted to her. That he liked her was obvious and, as their relationship had warmed, she presumed that, like men in romantic novels, he might have developed a soft spot. But he was so utterly devoted to the memory of his poor wife that it was unhealthy. There were moments, like now, when an expression of such unendurable sadness crossed his face that she felt an urgent need to smooth his misery away. But she had no idea how that could be done without seeming to pry or to be insubordinate. He was old enough to be her father, and then there was his station in life, compared with hers. As it was, he was making a great concession by associating with her at all. She knew that whatever happened, she must never overstep her mark, never become familiar.

At King's Cross they had walked together to the taxi rank and soon, he was able to indulge in his own quiet thoughts, in the darkness of the theatre. By the time *Hamlet* had concluded, he had quite recovered himself. With what passed, for Gerard, as normal composure, he had conducted her over Waterloo Bridge and along the Strand to a fish restaurant. They ate oysters, which she had never tasted before, and was not at all sure she liked, followed by Dover sole, grilled, on a bed of spinach. He drank most of a bottle of Chablis – she sipped half a glass – and, after they had eaten apple Charlotte for dessert, and he had rounded off his meal with a piece of Cheshire cheese and a dry biscuit, they took a taxi back to King's Cross to catch the evening train.

Peter Ball had walked up to Wychgate station and was waiting to meet his daughter. 'Father!' she cried, as he held his arms out to her, 'You came to meet us! What a sweet thing to do!' They hugged each other for what, to Gerard, seemed a wholly unnecessary length of time. 'We've had the most *wonderful* day. Oh, and father, why didn't you tell me what Shakespeare was like, on the stage? I *loved* it.'

'Steady, my dove, steady,' Ball had difficulty maintaining his balance with her enthusiastic embraces. 'Steady!' But she hugged him again, and then suddenly remembered that she was in the presence of Gerard, and quickly composed herself. Ball handed her an envelope. 'I opened it, as you said I could if it arrived in your absence.' He turned to face Gerard, 'I walked up sir, because I wanted you to be the first to know, outside the family, like. After all, you have been responsible, in so many ways.'

'Ball? What *can* you be saying?'

Violet held out the letter. 'I've been offered a place. At Somerville. And I've won a scholarship.' Gerard looked befuddled at first. Then it sank in.

'Oxford! Oh my dear girl! My dear, dear girl!' He said, and then quickly led the way into the darkness, away from the station lights so that neither of them could see the tears that overflowed from his eyes.

Chapter Ten

'But it seems so cold, so businesslike,' Graham Ball said. He was standing at the dormer window of the main bedroom, looking down at the garden of the Old Stores, and at the village stretching downhill to the Dene. Veronica had worked hard, all summer, renovating the two borders that flanked the lawn, weeding the rock garden and restoring fertility to the strip of land outside the garden wall so that it could be converted to a productive kitchen garden. He had helped, gradually learning gardening skills and lending what would have passed in Hampstead as brute strength to her artistry. He had hacked and hewn overgrown shrubs and trees, lifted and re-laid flag stones that had gone cockly over the years, double dug bindweed-infested patches and had even attempted, without much success, to re-build the small rock garden that Violet's Mother had laid out to celebrate the end of the Great War. He turned and looked at her. 'I mean, after everything we've achieved together here.'

She said nothing and continued to fold garments before placing them in a green canvas-clad suitcase. Downstairs two other bags, gravid with her small share of their movable possessions, stood by the front door.

'Achieved?' Veronica closed the lid of the case, now over full, pushing down on the top to force lock and sneck into contact. 'What *have* we achieved, Graham?' In response, he gestured, indicating the house, the garden.

'All this.'

'House Beautiful? Homes and Gardens? Crap like that? Is that what we're about now?'

'A new way of life,' Graham said. 'It suits me.' He made no attempt to help her to close the case. After further struggle, she abandoned the task and straightened up.

'No it doesn't.' He shrugged and turned back to the window. 'It doesn't suit you at all. You're only happy when working to a killing deadline, or teasing out the most challenging story, or trapping the most artful politician. In fact, you're hopeless, except in a crisis.' She attacked her suitcase again, with renewed anger, kneeling on the lid and bouncing until the gap narrowed and the locking parts were aligned. The catch snapped shut.

'I want to write. I can do that here. It's peaceful.'

'Why do people think they need peace to write? I'd have thought conflict had to be at the heart of anything worth reading.' He shrugged again. She was right, of course. 'Anyway, you haven't written a thing in months. I've looked into your computer. It must have been the most unproductive summer you've ever had.'

He walked over from the window, stooping, because of the low ceiling of the cottage bedroom. 'I know, but I want . . .' He took both her hands in his. 'I want to try for a bit longer. I *can't* move out now, it would be too much like giving up. Plus, my roots are here.'

'Doesn't mean a thing.'

'Perhaps not, but I haven't been here long enough to find out.'

'Haven't you?' She reached up to stroke the back of his head. Her anger had evaporated, but not her resolve. 'I don't know what it is you do want. I don't think you know yourself, do you?'

'I want *you*, Vee.' His voice was muffled because his lips were buried in her hair.

'No, Graham. I don't think you do. Not really. And I don't think I can do any more for you. I certainly can't give you what you seem to need.'

'And you've just got to get back.'

'I agreed to try it out down here. And I have tried, we both have.'

'I *would* make sacrifices for you.'

'Graham, even if you came with me to London, I'm not sure I would want us to stay together. Not now.'

There was really nothing more to be said. Graham lifted the case and carried it down to the kitchen. She followed him.

'I'll drive you to Stoneford.'

'Don't,' she said. 'I've phoned for a taxi. I want to go straight to Kendale, to pick up the London train there.'

'You can't get away quickly enough, can you?'

'Don't be bitter Graham, it's out of character. I'm going in as soon as I can because they want me to start work tomorrow.' After what seemed like half an hour, but was exactly seven minutes, the taxi arrived. Graham carried the two heaviest cases out; Veronica followed with the rest of her baggage.

'How on earth will you manage?'

'I'll get a porter at King's Cross.'

'In this day and age? Ha bloody ha!'

'They have trolleys. I'll be fine.' Out of earshot of the driver she said, 'I'm afraid it's finished, my darling, and I'm so sorry.'

'Christ, I'll miss you!

'Of course, but not for long. You'll be OK. Especially when you get a project of some kind going.'

'A project!' His scoffing response was almost drowned by a roar of diesel engines as a large yellow digging machine trundled past, followed by an old green van, heading for Pyson Wood.

'Oh, you will.' She kissed him one last time and got into the taxi. He watched it pull away and gave a final wave to her shadowy outline, visible through the retreating back window.

He couldn't face going back into the empty house, not just yet, and pulled the door shut before locking it and walking slowly down the hill. After almost continuous rain, during the first half of October, the weather had improved. Even some of the mud on the main street was beginning to dry. He walked, under a pale blue sky, in milky sunshine which lit up the gold and russet foliage on the limes and horse chestnuts along the village street.

From Weir House, Imogen watched him pass and hoped he might call. She knew the Crowe would try to keep him out, and would almost certainly succeed, but if he came to the door, it would provide a diversion from what was becoming an uncomfortable conversation. She was beginning to like Graham, not just because he seemed the only one – apart from the rector – who was reasonable about her plans, but because he was comfortable to be with. But he walked past without even hesitating by the gate and, in an instant, her mind jerked back to the unpleasant reality of Russell Hands.

'I do know he comes here,' Mrs Crowe said. She was sitting with her back to the window, looking intently at Imogen. 'I've seen his car by the wood, twice. What's more, every Thursday, when I come home, you're different.'

'I, ahm, I don't know what you're talking about.'

'Oh, I think you do.' Mrs Crowe pulled her brown woollen jumper down over a bulging midriff. She had gained several pounds over the last few weeks, and her clothes were beginning to feel tight and uncomfortable, particularly at the waist. The condition made her a little breathless at times, and even more irritable than she had been before. 'And you're going to tell me about it. Everything.'

'What?' Imogen looked startled. To have to reveal her secrets to the Crow would be too humiliating to bear.

'This development. You're hatching something.'

'But you know all about that. You've been with me to, ahm, to deal with the solicitors.' Indeed, Mrs Crowe had done most of the communication necessary to arrange the sale of Pyson Wood, with planning for three superior dwellings. But now that Imogen was ready to exchange contracts with Hands, something had happened to hold things up. Hands, too, had been less than forthcoming. After promising to keep her in cahoots, even to the point of including a commission for her own services, she had heard nothing from him.

'There's more. You're rigging up something else.' Remembering her headache, from being banged against the wall a week ago, and Hands's threats through gritted teeth if she blabbed, Imogen shook her head. 'Oh yes there is,' Crowe persisted, 'you must be doing something with that, that *creature*.' Imogen stared at the floor. 'You're going to have to tell me. One way or another.' But Imogen began to shake her head slowly, looking vacant and humming her little cadence.

'Hm, hm, hmm!'

'Oh, don't try that "fried brain" act with me,' Crowe snapped. 'I know you well enough by now to tell that there's a good deal more going on, between those pretty ears, than you like to let on.' The humming continued. 'You fancy 'im, don't you?' A wild shot, but it found its mark. The humming stopped and Imogen looked sharply at her minder.

'No!'

'You do!'

'No!'

'We'll see.' Mrs Crowe stood up and, again, tugged her jumper into position. 'I shall stay home tomorrow and we'll confront the man together. I can go to Stoneford this afternoon, instead.' Imogen knew that Hands would punish her if Crowe was there when he came. She had to warn him off somehow, just absolutely had to. But she couldn't think how. Fear was driving out her reason.

'You can't. You just, ahm, can't do that.'

'Can't what?'

'You don't know what he might do.' Imogen had folded her arms round herself and was shaking. She began to rock to and fro, and tried to hum but the sounds came out as little shuddering moans. Mrs Crowe was surprised at the depth of her reaction. It was months, now, since the girl had got anything like as bad as this. The behaviour may have been partly genuine, but she was sure much of it was play-acting. With a sudden movement, she swung her extended arm and slapped Imogen hard across the face, twice, forehand and backhand. The girl screamed and put up her hands to protect herself.

'Pull yourself together!' A burst of sobbing followed, making Mrs Crowe lift her hand again, but then, dropping it. She still needed to get to the bottom of the mystery and would sandwich brutality with kindness. 'I'm sorry, dear, but I *had* to do that.' She sat beside her and put an arm around her shoulders. 'You were getting hysterical, you see.' The sobbing subsided but Imogen moved away out of reach. She blew her nose and made an effort to control herself. Mrs Crowe edged closer.

'Leave me alone.' Imogen got up and walked to the other chair. 'Just leave me alone.' Such an abject creature elicited a dab of pity, even from Mrs Crowe. She wondered what Hands could possibly have been doing to have made her so frightened.

'I'm not afraid of him, even if you are,' she said. '*I* have no reason to fear the man at all. And I don't see why you should either – or at least, why you should fear him when you've got me to protect you.'

'Ahm, protect?' This came as a brand new concept to Imogen. After the Crowe's last encounter with Hands, she had assumed that, if anything, the two of them would combine against her. But, if she had someone as strong as Crowe on *her* side, she could cope with Hands on a more equal basis. But should she confide in this odious woman? What alternative had she? Could she mention the physical aspect of her relationship with Hands? Her stomach and mind revolted in unison. She couldn't, absolutely could not share that awful shame. But if Hands arrived, and Crowe was there, what then? Imogen sat in silence for some minutes, then:

'OK, yah! I'll explain.' Crowe was startled at the change in tone, and in mien. 'Everything.' Except the disgusting things, she thought.

'Well?' Crowe sat down again and listened while Imogen explained about Hands's plan for re-applying for planning consent, not for three or four houses, but for forty.

'Then why the hell hasn't he signed the contract?' Crowe seemed mystified.

'I think he, ahm, wants me along as some kind of partner. Also, he thinks it will be easier to get permission, if I'm a, ahm, joint applicant.'

'Mm I can see that. And he may want to use your family

name, to raise capital. Probably sees Lord Methwold bailing
you out if it all comes unstuck. But we both know that
the Methwolds mustn't be involved at all, don't we dear?'
Thinking hard, she began to pace for a bit, then stopped and
turned to Imogen. 'But don't you see? He's laid himself open.
We can take big advantage of this.' She thought some more,
and paced some more. 'Ye-es. We can all do very well out
of this. As long as *you* don't do anything completely bloody
stupid.'

'Oh, I ahm, I won't, ahm . . .'

'No, you're bloody right you won't. I shall act for you.'

'Oh, but I—'

'I'll see to it that you get the best deal, dear. But I'll want
a commission.'

'But I——'

'Ten percent. OK?' Mrs Crowe's frame stood between
Imogen and the window, blotting out the light. It was an
awesome silhouette. Imogen knew that she'd make a better
ally than enemy.

'Oh, yah. OK.'

'Good. That's settled then. Oh, and another thing.' She
cupped the girl's chin in her hand, much as Hands had done
the week before. 'This is completely secret. Not a word to
anyone – not the vicar, that BBC bloke or anyone. Clear?'
And she too gave Imogen's head a shove backwards.

Further down the hill, on a small triangle of grass at the
western end of Pyson Wood, the JCB and green van had
parked. A Land Rover soon joined them, driven by a man
in a tweed sports jacket and cavalry twill trousers. As soon
as he emerged, the other drivers also got out of their vehicles
and formed a respectfully attentive duo. Graham Ball, coming
slowly back up the hill, after his lonely walk, saw that a
conflab was about to ensue, and slowed his pace so that he
could hear.

'The idea,' the man in cavalry twills was saying, 'is to
create a small infrastructure within the stand so that we can
get our vehicles right inside and load the timber easily. But
first, we have to remove all the dangerous trees, and I suggest

we begin along the roadside. We may have to close the road off for a while, from time to time, for safety.' At that point, Ernest Busby's Ford Sierra Ghia Estate approached rapidly and stopped, level with Graham, just past the point where the foresters stood. He jumped out, neat in shiny grey suit trousers and unbuttoned shirtsleeves, folded back to reveal pink wrists and fat forearms. His suit jacket hung on a special hook just behind the driver's seat.

'You see!' He strode past Graham as he spoke. 'See what happens when people won't support the community? Now the damage begins.' He marched off towards the assembled men. Graham heard him address them. 'Good day, gentlemen!' Then he observed the man in tweed and cavalry twill turn towards him, introduce himself and offer a hand which Busby ignored. Time to bugger off sharpish, Graham thought, not wanting to get involved in a verbal village punch-up, particularly not with Busby. But as he walked slowly past the group, he heard the Parish Meeting chairman, Residents' Association spokesman, Neighbourhood Watch coordinator and God knew what else besides say: 'We'll be resisting your every move. Every single move. The entire community is united against what is going on here. And we intend to put a stop to the ruination of our countryside, in the face of unbridled greed and selfishness.'

Graham felt a surge of ill-temper rising within him. Those few presumptuous remarks from the man he had begun to despise within seconds of their first encounter, back in April, opened a chink in the dyke that had held back months of growing anger. His demise at the BBC had laid a bedrock of resentment and the pain of Vee's departure, still fresh and sharp, was the catalyst, but Busby was the main agent of this catharsis. Frustration at his own inability to get to grips with anything here, where the soporific countryside lulled you into a relaxed attitude, or enticed you into a retreat from anything too unpalatable, had grown in parallel with his developing love for the place of his closest ancestors. This flawed paradise, where mud softened the edges, and eroded resolve; where the image of rustic romanticism was at such variance with the hard-nosed business of modern farming; where commuting residents thought country values were important, but where they preferred to watch telly than help with hay harvest or walk over a rough shoot. This place was his home now, and he was realising that if he wanted to come to terms with living here – and he desperately wanted to be happy and fulfilled here – he would have to start taking action. Chipping in with a little common sense at meetings, as he had done in the past, was simply not enough. When men like Busby – irritating, stupid, small-minded men with no vision, no ability and all the wrong values seemed able to tyrannise the rest of the apathetic community, he knew that he had a mission to open people's minds. Not that this had the stature of a major television exposé – this wasn't unearthing a drug baron, or getting to the bottom of a political scam – but it was a bloody good start. He loved this place. His roots were here. He loved the countryside too, especially this border zone that divided East Anglian Fen from the gentle hills of the Midlands, but he hated what was happening to it. He turned, and strode over to the group.

'Just one moment, Mr Busby,' he said, thrusting his way in. 'Just one bloody moment!'

Thursday came, and Imogen's anxiety sharpened. She was afraid of what Hands would do when he found out that Crowe had muscled in on their arrangement. She was more terrified that he might tell Crowe something of their sexual liaison and bring about a process of humiliation that even she could not tolerate.

The actual logistics of what was to happen – as masterminded by Mrs Crowe – were quite simple, really. The Crow was to park her car out of sight and leave the garage doors open, as usual, so Hands would have no inkling that she was around. Then, after he had arrived and was safely installed in the house, Mrs Crowe was to make an entrance. That way, Hands couldn't, as Mrs Crowe put it, 'scarper' to try to preserve the secrecy of his liaison. As soon as she had got him cornered, Imogen was to keep quiet and let the Crow take the initiative. She was not, her minder said, to make any attempt to leave the room, but was to stay put, just in case any strong-arm tactics were needed. If anything ugly happened, Crowe was to keep the man at bay – God knew how – while Imogen dialled 999. It was ludicrously cloak-and-dagger, but Imogen knew, better than Mrs Crowe, that Hands was not at all inhibited by the thought of using violence. The horrific part was, though, that Imogen was afraid Hands might try to initiate something that might reveal their loathsome secret before he realised that they were not alone in the house. She was fairly sure he would, in fact, and didn't know how she could prevent it, since she was completely in his power.

It must, she supposed, be part of her punishment that she should be the victim of these two people. She accepted her position, but her thought patterns were changing nowadays. During the previous winter and long, warm summer, she had been irrational more often than not. Depression had wiped out her powers of judgment and had taken away great chunks of memory. Whenever she looked back over events since Marcus – and here, even as she reflected, a dragging bolus of guilt weighed down on her being and made her inhale a sharp, sobbing breath – she had only the vaguest notion of their order and sequence. Most memories of previous events were indistinct, except for those that were more deeply seared into her tortured conscience. But reflection over these past few months had become easier, more fluent, and recall more ready to spring up in her mind. There were pleasant occasions to be re-lived: walking back from church with Jerome; harvesting her first tomatoes and slicing them to make a Greek salad with garlic, olive oil and real Feta cheese, brought, grudgingly from the Stoneford delicatessen, by Mrs Crowe; meeting Graham Ball, the only other person in the village to treat her as a fellow human, rather than a mental retard. There were horrible moments too, such as the look of betrayal in the old colonel's eyes; the whispered taunts she half thought she heard uttered by some of the villagers and, above all, the hateful attentions of Russell Hands. But most of these she felt she could contain – or at least, could contain for most of the time.

This new situation unnerved her, but it also gave her hope. A year ago, it might have been meekly received as more of the same divine retribution being meted out to purge her wicked soul. Now she saw it all, to some extent, as a means to an end and, since there was so much to lose, but also much to gain, her emotions were different. She glanced out of the window, gulped another draft of air – a hybrid breath and sob – and then groaned *sotto voce*, for Russell Hands was quietly opening the front gate.

She opened the front door to him, met his eye and looked instantly away. Amid the feverish activity of her brain, she was astounded to see herself observing that he had had his hair cut – it was cropped and gelled, sticking up in the current trend for a startled look – and he wore a loose-fitting, dull green, double-breasted suit, with a generous cut at the shoulders, narrowing at the waist, with wide trousers. He actually looked more attractive than she had ever seen him. She had avoided the eye-contact after the first encounter, and now, making a great effort to look him in the face again, managed only to raise her eyes to his mouth. It was on the small side, for a man, but with lips that did not lack appeal, held slightly open, so she could glimpse the even teeth. She found it hard to believe that such filth could have issued from that mouth last week. It was innocent, a boy's mouth. But the voice chilled, when it came, and the East London pinched vowels, made the lips distort so that she was repelled as suddenly has she had been drawn.

'Well, girl.' He closed the front door behind him but before he could get his hands on her, she giggled slightly, and slipped into the drawing-room, leaving the door open for him to follow.

'Want a, ahm, drink?' She walked towards a table in the corner on which stood bottles and glasses.

'All right. He came up close behind her. 'Scotch.' She picked up a decanter – heavy, Edinburgh crystal – removed the stopper and poured about a pub double into a thick, wide-bottomed tumbler. He sniggered. 'What the 'ell d'you call that?' He stood close behind her, breathing into her ear. 'You just pour. I'll say when.' She poured, the level continued to rise, he put both hands under arms and groped for her breasts.

'Don't. You'll make me spill it.'

'Spill it then, you moronic little twat.' He bit her ear, hard enough to make a mark. She ducked, banging decanter and glass – now very full – down on the table, chipping one of the other glasses. He intercepted her feint and held her against the table, holding her between his knees and with his hands gripping the table on either side of her. Mrs Crowe had come quietly into the room. 'Did I tell you to stop?'

'Mr Hands?'

'What the fuck . . . ?' Hands leapt back. Imogen stayed, hunched at the table. Both the women were too calm for this to have been a chance encounter. Hands looked, first at Mrs Crowe, framed in the open doorway and then at Imogen, straightened up now, but still with her back to him, and breathing rapidly. 'You pair of . . .' Quickly, he controlled himself. Got to think. Got to keep on the ball. He changed his tack. 'Yer girl got 'erself into a bit of a state, like. I thought she was going to faint.' He gestured to Imogen. 'All right, now, love?' It wasn't going to work. Mrs Crowe had guessed that the man had had some kind of hold on Imogen, and that it was probably sexual. She came straight to the point.

'Sit down, Mr Hands.' By her tone, it was clear that Mrs Crowe would brook no argument. Physically, Hands reckoned, she could probably give him a pound or two, and she didn't look the type who would dither before laying about with a poker or some such. He sat. Imogen continued to stand by the drinks table, gazing out of the small window that looked onto the back garden. The petals are blowing off the last Japanese anemones, she thought, trying not to shake.

'Forty houses,' said Mrs Crowe. Hands looked startled but said nothing. 'Take the value of each building site at, say, twenty grand.' She paused to allow herself a little dramatic strength. 'Makes a total of exactly eight hundred thou.'

'Yeah?' Hands was stuck for a better return of serve.

'Yeah?' Crowe mimicked the cockney interrogative. 'Build 'em for, what, fifty-five . . . sixty thousand each?'

Hands shrugged. 'Dunno what you're rabbitin' on about, Missis.'

'Yeah?' Crowe had caught the disinterested tone perfectly. 'Put on today's market at . . . ooh . . . hundred and ten, hundred and twenty, maybe. Could make you another thirty gees per site.'

'Wha— ?'

'Mmm. If the price holds. You could toddle off with a cool million net profit. More, if the market carries on doing what it's doing.'

Hands refused to have his bluff called. 'Would you mind telling me what the fu—'

'Mr *Hands*. There is absolutely no call for that kind of language.'

'Then would you mind telling me what you are talking about?'

'I think you know.'

'Yeah?' The word was beginning to annoy both of them.

'Yeah! Pyson Wood development. We want the contract back. We haven't signed it ourselves yet and—'

'We?' Hands looked over at Imogen who now had the edges of the drinks table in both hands, knuckles whitening. Mrs Crowe ignored the interruption.

'We want to sell you the property. We don't know chapter and verse, but we've a pretty good idea of what you can make on it, and of what price you'd be prepared to run to. We know there are other developers who would wet themselves to get this site. But we're not greedy. All we want is half the value of each building plot.'

'What? That'd be nearly twenty times the price we've already agreed.'

'We'll give you a choice, then.' She hadn't moved from the doorway. But now she came into the room and stood in front of him as he sat, upright, at the edge of the sofa. 'You can buy subject to planning consent. No consent, no sale.'

Hands thought for a whole minute. 'OK. But yer figures are way out.'

'Probably, but that needn't concern you. You'll make a huge profit anyway.'

'OK. If I get consent. Fer forty 'ouses. I'll pay yer ten grand per plot. Can't say fairer than that, eh, Lady, er, Imogen?'

Imogen turned, startled.

'Oh, ahm no. Quite.'

'I told you not to say a word,' Mrs Crowe snapped. She turned back to Hands. 'No, you don't get it quite that easily. The deal is this. Either you pay, let's say,' she paused to pop in a bit more drama, 'two hundred and twenty thousand now. Today. And take the risk on extended planning. Or, you pay a minimum of four hundred thousand pounds for the whole piece – or, ten thousand per plot, whichever total is the greater *after* getting consent. One way, we take the risk, the other way you do. It's as simple as that. As you know, you're getting them at half-price or less.'

Imogen felt she had to sit down. The air was electric – almost as if anything she touched would spark or give her a shock. She could feel a pulse drumming in her throat and she knew her hands were shaking so much that she would have found it difficult to hold on to the glass she had filled for Hands. Nevertheless, she made a concentrated effort to pick it up and carry it to the man who had tormented her, more or less, with her consent, every week for months; she stood before him and offered it.

'I think you might need this,' she said. She looked at his face. It was not an ugly face and his new hairdo suited him well, made him look fitter. But his expression was loathsome. She could see that he hated the fact that Mrs Crowe and therefore she, by proxy, had the upper hand. He could have walked away from the humiliation, but greed was likely to overrule his desire to save face. He ignored the offered drink, letting Imogen hold it out, and then feel silly. She was about to apologise and take it away again but remembered that now she need not fear this man. 'I think it might be polite if you, ahm, said something.' He snatched the glass, slopping a little scotch over his wrist.

'Cheers!' He raised the glass to both women, standing in front of him, and fixed Imogen with a look of the coldest fury he could muster. She stared back. When he glanced away, she almost felt sorry for him.

'Make your decision quickly,' Mrs Crowe said. 'There are plenty of other developers who would die for such an opportunity.'

'I'll phone next week.' Hands said.

'Too late I'm afraid,' replied Mrs Crowe.

'Jesus Christ, woman, there's financing and all that to see to.'

'Your problem.' Mrs Crowe walked to the drawing-room door and held it open. Hands stood up. His new jacket had creased at the back, where he had sat on the material.

'I'll give you a bell tomorrow, then.' Before going out, he turned to Imogen. 'I'll see *you* later,' he said, through clenched teeth.

'I don't think so.' Imogen felt calmer now. 'Probably not on my own, anyway.' In response, he leered at her, winked and walked out.

Mrs Crowe heard him slam the front door, almost hard enough to crack the glass in the fanlight above it. 'Temper temper,' she murmured, and walked back to the drawing-room. She had been impressed by Imogen's behaviour throughout the discussion. She had obviously picked up most of what was said. She had also, clearly, been up to more than merely talking, with the man. That look she gave him, when he ignored her drink offer, was almost pitying. It was clear to Mrs Crowe that the previous close control of her charge was likely to slip from her. The girl was on the mend. It was also clear that Hands was more dangerous than she had realised, and that Imogen would need protection from him.

'I think you're well enough, now, to come shopping with me, each week, dear,' she said, when she re-entered the drawing-room to find Imogen, not vacantly staring out of the window, as she had expected, but sitting at the small escritoire, writing something down on a piece of paper.

'Sorry?' Imogen, continued to work. Mrs Crowe didn't repeat herself. 'I was just trying to work out what sort of, ahm, tax bill there might be. But I'm so hopeless at sums, I can't seem to get it right. Can you do percentages?'

Chapter Eleven

—■—

Busby, crimson-faced and almost tearful with rage, had driven away in his Ford Sierra Ghia Estate. Graham Ball, also breathing heavily, but quickly calming, stayed behind. He wanted to apologise to the forester for having pushed him into such an embarrassing situation. He also wanted to find out a bit about what was actually involved in felling the wood.

'I'm really sorry about that,' he told the man whose name was Gilmore, and who was the head forester on the Cranston estate. 'I don't usually behave like that. I do hope you'll forgive me.'

With its own sawmill, not far from Stoneford, and more than four thousand acres of woodland of all kinds, from ancient ash and small-leaved lime coppice to newly planted Sitka spruce, the Cranston estate was the best equipped local firm to process the timber of Pyson Wood. Imogen's solicitors had recommended the estate's forestry company to Mrs Crowe who had relayed the suggestion to Imogen. Her only reservation had been that some members of the Cranston family, particularly the Marquess of Stoneford, were friends of her father's and she was afraid they might realise who she was and contact him. She did not want her family to be involved in any of her machinations and felt it best if they remained ignorant. With her large commission at stake, Mrs Crowe was wholly with her on that one, and had set her mind at rest, pointing out that this was a small job, for an outfit so huge, and that her family name need not appear in the books anywhere.

Gilmore, an intelligent and kindly man who, after finding that a degree in English Literature, even from Cambridge, was pretty useless at launching him into the kind of career he wanted, had gone on to study forestry and now, in his mid-thirties, was happy in work that kept him outdoors for most of his working day. His job earned him enough income to live in modest comfort, and yet was undemanding enough to allow time for his passion, which was to write. He had already published three novels, under a pseudonym, all given ecstatic reviews by broadsheet critics, but none selling more than a few hundred copies per edition. He didn't mind, really, since the reviews gave him as much comfort as might handsome royalty statements.

'It hasn't been one of my best days,' Graham said, 'one way and another.'

'Trees are rather emotive,' Gilmore answered. 'We often get reactions like Mr Busby's, even when we're clearing up dead ones.'

'Perhaps if you showed me a little of what is about to happen with this wood, I might be able to rustle up a fragment or two of goodwill in the village. Or, at least, calm the resentment.'

Gilmore explained the procedure as they moved along the woodland margin. Graham had never been tempted to walk the eastern edge before, finding the brooding spruces dark and forbidding. He was told that the value of the woodland had fallen because it had grown over-mature. Gilmore described how the trees along the village street would be the most tricky to fell, because of the risk to the public. Once the foresters had begun to clear the interior, they would bring in machinery that would strip boughs from the trees so that the trunks could be transported clean. Side branches would be pulverised for compost. The site could, after the trees' removal, be cleared of its stumps, or simply re-planted with young whips for another stand of timber which would be ready, if conifers were planted, in about thirty-five years. Hardwood forest would take at least twice as long.

When they had moved to the end of the stand and turned, now following its southern edge, Graham was surprised at the change in habitat. Here, instead of blocking out the sun, the trees reflected it, offering a smiling face and a warmer environment. And here, wildflowers grew in the long grasses at the base of the outermost trunks. Though most species were dying back for autumn, Graham spotted a few remaining blue scabious, purple knapweeds and a yellow Saint John's Wort. Over the decades, as the firs had developed, the headland of the field adjacent to the wood had been allowed to widen so that now, even though the land was frequently ploughed – and, that afternoon, was gold and brown with wheat stubble – a strip of ground, some twenty feet wide ran alongside the conifers. Here, smaller trees and shrubs had taken root. Some were common weeds elders, blackthorn, dog roses – but there was also a holly, whose berries were beginning to suffuse with blood, spindle berry and some field maples. At this point in their stroll, Gilmore uttered a crow of delight. 'I *thought* there might be one or two of these around.' He had stopped before a small, rounded tree loaded with a crop of crimson fruits and leaves that were turning from dark green to gold, russet and red. 'A wild service tree,' he explained. 'This is special. There has to be some ancient woodland hereabouts for this to have popped up.'

'What makes you say that?' Graham took hold of a branch to study the colours. Each leaf, slightly lobed, was shiny on top but covered in greyish down below. He had not realised, before, how beautiful wayside plants could be. Should he take up painting?

'Seed. The seed that grew this was probably dropped by a bird, and I suspect that the parent tree is not a million miles from here. The old ordnance survey plan has a fragment of ancient woodland, marked in the middle of the conifer stand, but I presumed that had been done away with to plant this lot. Now I'm not so sure.' The two men walked back towards the road. 'You know,' Gilmore went on, 'this little strip of wasteland here has taken nearly half a century to develop its habitat. It'd be a pity to spoil it. Especially with that wild service tree. You can be sure there'd be some interesting plants here at other seasons, too. There are lots of cowslip seed capsules and look, here's quite a rarity,' he stooped to pluck a leaf, browning with age, but much divided and curled, almost like parsley.

'Some kind of fern?' Graham ventured.

'A member of the rose family. Dropwort. Close relative of meadowsweet but far less common.'

'Would you be able to fell the timber without spoiling this bit?'

'Oh yes. But once those trees are removed, the farmer who owns this,' Gilmore waved a hand indicating the stubbles, 'will probably clear the strip and plough right up to the boundary.'

'Could it be preserved?'

'Difficult. The farmer has a right to do his job as efficiently as possible, but there *is* a way. If enough special plants are found here, it could be declared a triple ess eye.'

'A what?'

'Site of Special Scientific Interest. No one is allowed to touch those.' Graham was quick to spot an opportunity to neutralise the village activists and, at the same time, snatch some advantage out of this whole site-clearing episode. It would make sense for everyone and would reduce the pressure on Imogen, who could proceed with the felling, knowing that she had at least preserved one vulnerable part of the environment. Gilmore gave him the name and telephone number of a contact at English Nature.

If Graham had had any doubts about the rights and wrongs of getting rid of this brooding fir forest, they vanished like mist in an August sun as he walked back from the warm southerly strip to the sullen, shaded margins on the opposite side. Here, where even at midday, the street was still coated with a film of mud-laden moisture, warning signs had been erected but the foresters had disappeared into the gloom. Graham hastened his stride, pausing only for the briefest instant when he heard the first rending buzz of a chainsaw echoing among the trees. If they'd had those things when Chekhov wrote *The Cherry Orchard*, he thought, how much

more effective the noises off-stage would have been, rather
than blows of an axe.

The Emergency Conservation Action Group of Wychgate
Saint Peter's was settling down, in Ernest Busby's living
room, for its fourth meeting in a month. Between them,
the three men – Busby, Bert Tighe, the foreman who ran a
four-hundred-acre satellite farm belonging to the prosperous
Wyckhamby Estate and Richard Barton, a London weekly
commuter who had recently moved into two of the labourer's
cottages on Church Farm, now knocked into one – now had
everything in the village pretty well buttoned up. It had
made a lot of sense to Busby, to have formed this little
inner cabal, because of the need to cut out waffle and get
to the heart of things. This was an emergency, like a war,
really, and the village simply could not afford the luxury of
a democratic process. Of course, not having the rector or that
pinko BBC type helped enormously, but Busby knew that he
could depend on the other two for unequivocal support in
pretty well anything he suggested. Tighe was a man with a
grudge, a would-be anarchist who liked nothing better than
to embarrass those he saw as 'moneyed'. This Lady Whatsit
at Weir House was obviously moneyed and it stood to reason
that she should be thwarted. Richard, who was too new to
understand much about the country, and too meek to gainsay
Busby, assumed that since his aims were to retain the kind of
lifestyle one read about in such magazines as *Country Living*
or *Country Life,* he deserved full support. Richard could not
yet know that such lifestyles simply did not translate from
glossy magazine pages to real life.
  'It's a bit early to tell,' Busby said, 'but I think I've
managed to pull something off.' He paused to invite con-
gratulation, and continued. 'All to do with wildlife.' He let
them wait for another moment. 'I've been in communication
with the Department of Terrestrial Ecology.' He omitted to
say that it was they who had contacted him, as Parish
Chairman, informing him that a certain Ordnance Survey
reference was under review and might be subject to restriction
of certain agricultural practices. 'And it seems that we have,

in our own parish, a site of special scientific interest. '*And*,' he rubbed his hands, 'it is in Pyson Wood, or rather, at the edge of it.'

'What might that mean?' Jeremy asked.

'Rare plants, usually,' Tighe, said. 'Bloody nuisance. Buggers up yer farmin'.'

'It means, gentlemen,' Ernest Busby stretched and placed his hands behind his head, 'that we've got 'em! Work at Pyson Wood will have to stop. Henceforward.'

'Bit late isn't it?' Tighe's mouth was creased at the corners from being permanently turned down. ''Alf the soddin' wood's bin cut.'

'But apparently,' Busby said, 'the southern end is the bit that really matters. And that is still untouched.

On the following Sunday, Jerome Daniels was walking up the hill with Imogen. He had been in the habit of escorting her home after Eucharist for almost a full year now, and though each encounter was fairly brief, he had grown fond of her. At the beginning of every service, when he progressed from vestry to altar, he would scan the draughty church until he spotted her, always sitting in shadow, always apart from the handful of regular worshippers.

Since all the brouhaha over the felled woodland, Jerome seldom saw the other person with whom he had come closest to a deep friendship, Michael Pilkington. He had stopped worshipping at Saint Peter's altogether, preferring, now, to drive to Stoneford, to visit the Grammar School's sixteenth-century chapel. Last time they had approached each other in the street, the old colonel had looked him directly in the face – angry, faded blue eyes, almost fearful, looking into compassionate but troubled grey ones. A muttered greeting, as open a smile as Jerome could muster, a curt half-nod from Michael and then they had passed, Jerome upbraiding himself for having missed a perfect opportunity for attempting a reconciliation.

'If I'd known what a terrible, ahm, mess, they'd make,' Imogen said, as the two of them walked slowly up the hill, 'I'd never have got the trees felled in the first place.'

'Yes, it is a bit mucky.' Jerome looked at the road, filthy with smeared mud, and at the space alongside, where the trees had stood. Trunks and branches had gone, leaving an expanse running almost a hundred yards back from the road, pocked and ruptured with track marks, and with scars made by trees having been dragged across the ground. Some of the stumps had been pulled out by machine, and were heaped to one side. It was said that these were to be burnt. 'It is a mess, but do you realise that we are walking up this street in sunlight? No one's been able to do that for nearly half a century.' There was just enough watery, November sunshine to make two slanting shadows of their bodies, across the murky surface of the road.

'Well, I'm stopping it for a while now, anyway.'

'You are?' He didn't know why, but felt disappointed. 'Why?'

'Oh, ahm, various reasons.' A pale hand that Jerome found so in need of holding, moved to her mouth, as if she was about to suck her thumb, and then was snatched away again. Jerome knew the movement well. He kept silent, but took hold of the hand. It was warm, in spite of its whiteness, and surprisingly rough from gardening. She allowed him to hold it. 'Well, there's this wildflower thing.' A long pause. Jerome still kept silent. 'And Graham says—'

'Graham?' Jerome felt a different emotion now. Not jealousy, of course – there was no cause – but disquiet. She could be so easily damaged again.

'Mm. He thinks there might be some, ahm, ancient site there, or something. Wants me to stop until he's found out more.'

'And will you?'

'Have already. The forester, Mr, ahm, Gilmore, says it's getting too boggy to work easily now and anyway, they've got things to do on the estate. He wants to pack up until spring.'

'What about your house building?'

'Oh ahm . . .' She paused and her hand twitched in his, making him release it. Her eyes slid away too, when he glanced at her. 'I don't want to start building anything.

Not until next year anyway.' She was obviously leaving much unsaid.

'But your project is going ahead?' Jerome had supported her development plans because he saw them as a means for her to complete her own rehabilitation. He knew – or thought he knew – that she wanted to create an independent existence for herself. Clearly, she had no drug problem now, was rational and appeared to have her depression under control, but as far as he could tell, she had yet to come to terms with her guilt. He wasn't sure whether, or when she could do that. He was also keen to have more people living in the village. He had welcomed the idea of two – or was it three? – new houses, even though they'd almost certainly turn out to be smart executive residences and become homes to green wellies and 'all-terrain' vehicles. Even members of the Kensington Coup, would improve on the stagnant pool of indifference that made up the current population. There might be new families, with fashionably, but unhealthily skinny young children. Tristrams, Angelicas and Jocastas, he supposed, spending most of their childhoods at prep schools, and their holidays being fed on low fat yoghurt, twigs and berries. They'd be driven off, by achievement-mad Mums to attend sports events at Stoneford Leisure Centre, and would probably all sneak out, before being collected, to supplement their Belsen diets at the chippy. He smiled at the image of the kids trying to disguise the chip fat on their breaths by chewing sugar-free gum and then sighed at the manufactured guilt dished out by the parents. People would always need sorting out, as long as there was guilt.

'Oh yah!' Imogen's voice disturbed his thoughts. 'We've cleared enough space to, ahm, build a couple already.'

Jerome was surprised, at the end of this exchange, how lucid and articulate she was becoming. There had been steady progress, over the whole year, but something had happened recently. Something had clicked, had loosened her tongue and had rid her of the despairing look that haunted her features, sometimes flickering across her face, like a small cloud over the sun, other times infiltrating her body language, so that her posture became hunched, with folded arms and bowed head.

The next event surprised him even more. She held the front door of Weir House open for him to enter. As expected, Mrs Crowe emerged from the kitchen which, through the open door, he could see was slightly fogged with steam from roasting beef and boiling vegetables, and advanced on them both.

'Oh Mrs Crowe,' Imogen said, as she closed the front door behind an astonished Jerome. 'Mr Daniels has popped in for a, ahm, drink.' She turned back to Jerome, 'and you can stay for lunch, can't you?' Jerome was too thunderstruck to answer, but nodded. 'Good, then we'll be two in the dining-room.'

'As you like, *dear*. I'll go and prepare some extra vegetables,' said Mrs Crowe, as equably as she could, but her lips compressed as soon she had finished speaking and she turned and slammed the kitchen door behind her. Jerome looked at Imogen, trying to detect a an expression of triumph. There was none – or at any rate, nothing more than the flicker of an eyelid – so when she held the drawing-room door open for him, he walked past her, eyed the drinks table, noting with satisfaction that it carried an enticing selection and waited for an invitation to sit down.

'Oh, do, ahm, help yourself,' Imogen said.

'What about you?'

'I, ahm, don't.' Jerome assumed that a drug free existence, for her, included alcohol. She read his thoughts.

'Oh, I, ahm, I could. But I prefer not to.' And for the first time, that day, the hunted look returned. To rescue her from whatever thoughts might have obtruded into her mind, he said:

'Tell me about this archaeology thing.'

On the sixteenth of December 1924, Michael said goodbye to his fellow sixth-formers and boarded the train, at Barleythorpe station, for the short journey home to Wychgate. His luggage had gone on ahead, and had been wheeled, the day before, to Wychgate Manor on the station handcart, pushed, or rather, held back from running down the hill, by the aging, red-faced and puffing porter who was also Wychgate station's ticket inspector, platform attendant and station master. His Midland

and Great Northern Railway uniform strained at the bulging midriff, but his gold watch chain was looped with precision across the waistcoat.

The boys' customary joviality hid Michael's sadness at having to be parted from his class and team mates, peerless friends like Jumbo Gray, Dasher Gordon – whose prowess as a wing three-quarter was legendary at Barleythorpe – and his particular friend, Riversley. He would miss Riversley's ugly face, with its snub nose, pockmarked cheeks and wide, honest eyes. When you got the ball cleanly out of the scrum to Riversley, you knew it was in a safe pair of hands, knew Riversley could be depended upon to remember all the surprise tactics the team had rehearsed in pre-match practices, and to come up, from time to time, with his own special feints and false passes so that the Barleythorpe first fifteen was, according to Mr Danvers, a team that succeeded because it played with its head, as well as with all its might and main. The school had enjoyed an unbroken run of victories that term.

As the train – three rather ancient carriages pulled by a small tank engine – puffed its way out of Barleythorpe West station, Michael's heartache, at parting with his friends, was tempered with a happier anticipation. In previous years, the prospect of four and a half empty winter weeks would have filled him with gloom. Mrs Bull usually tried to make Christmas at the Manor as cheerful as possible, but there was so little to do in the endless evenings and so little company in the village. But today, even though his eyes had moistened and his feelings for the gaggle of boys who had just seen him off before starting their own, London-bound train journeys, had been of an almost unendurable tenderness, he thrilled with every mile the train chugged towards Wychgate. *She* would be there, waiting at the platform. She couldn't know what train he'd be on – he had only decided which one to catch that morning – but he knew she'd be there.

There was hardly time, on the short journey, to open a newspaper or settle to anything useful, so he stood, in the corridor, his small pigskin overnight case at his side, and watched the countryside slip past. Smoke from the engine, billowing over the grassland, appeared grey against the hoar frost, but showed white against the freshly ploughed land. He passed farmyards, their strawstacks gone, or half-gone, as the sheaves of wheat and barley were fed into thrashing machines, driven by steam traction engines with huge, whirring flywheels. There were no cattle to be seen, since beef and dairy herds had long been enclosed in yards, to be fed with stored hay and imported oilseed cake, but sheep grazed in rows, on fields of turnips, kept in line by hurdles, erected across the crops. No one came to punch his ticket, but he was far too honest even to have thought of keeping it to use again.

He opened his carriage window, as the train chugged into Wychgate station, peered out to see if she was waiting and then alighted the moment the train had stopped. The platform was deserted apart from two crates containing live laying hens, set down from an earlier train and awaiting collection. They seemed content, in their cramped habitat, but Michael hoped someone would soon come to deliver them to the freedom of a yard or field where they could scratch in the chilly ground to find grain and insects. Beady yellow, avian eyes regarded him through the wooden slats of the airy crates as he walked past and the hens clucked to each other confidentially. Feeling disappointed, Michael walked out of the station building, ready to trudge home alone.

She came pedalling into the yard as fast as she could, the tyres of the heavy delivery boy's bike cutting a track in the gritty surface and losing speed as the gradient increased. She hopped off, keeping perfect balance – not so much as a wobble – and laughed at his astonished face. 'I promised myself I'd meet you, but Mother would have me drop off some orders first. And she's that tired, with her Christmas cooking and all, that I just had to give her a hand with pressing the tongue and then making almond paste. But I knew you'd be on this train.'

'Violet!' After weeks of anticipation, the moment was anticlimactic. She wheeled her bicycle towards him. He experienced such a mixture of feelings brewing up inside that he thought he might burst. Her winter coat was shabby and unfashionable, an old wartime thing, but she looked wonderful in it. Her hair was bunched up under a narrow-brimmed hat, with dark billows ready to tumble out from underneath; her eyes, large and dark, were not soft and yielding, as he had anticipated time and again in his daydreams, but glittered with intelligence. He wanted to touch her, to embrace, but that would have been wholly unacceptable. No one was in sight, on this drear December morning, but the station yard might have been as public at Piccadilly Circus – more so, in fact, because whoever might have seen them in physical contact mattered.

'Congratulations about Oxford.' He'd written, of course, as soon as he heard, but this was the first time they had been face to face since she had won her place. 'I should think you'll do jolly well.' His voice came out rather wobbly and made him feel even more awkward.

'Michael, Michael.' She took his case and put it into the metal carrying frame over the front wheel. Her face was flushed, partly with exertion from pedalling up the hill so fast, but mostly with the desire to hold him. 'Michael, I so want to—'

'Don't, Violet.' He placed his hand over hers, on the handlebars. Both were gloved, his in brown leather, hers in woollen mitts.

'Michael.' Repeating his name made her feel warm inside.

'I know.' They stood for almost a whole minute, simply gazing at each other, their only physical contact buffered by cloth and hide. Then the spell broke. He took the heavy bicycle from her and wheeled it as they walked at a snail's pace over the frozen ground.

'Your father's not home at the moment. He's gone to Stoneford.'

'Really?' Michael did not expect to be received on arrival, even by his father. Their greeting would be effusively polite, but cold. Both males would then move independently through their days, meeting at lunch and dinner but otherwise doing very little together. It seemed odd, though, to be receiving the information from Violet. 'How do you know?'

'He told me on Thursday.'

'You still come to the manor, each Thursday?' Michael couldn't understand why, since she now had her place at university. Violet nodded.

'I'm allowed to use your father's library. We're working together, too. A special project on ancient history.'

'I see.' Oh, lucky, lucky Father, seeing her so much!

'I don't have to carry on.' Violet turned again to catch another glimpse of his profile. She loved the look of his eyes from the side, their blue so dark, the dilated pupils making him look so sensitive. 'But I do, partly because I love the work, and also because your father is such a lonely man.'

'Really?' Michael knew that well enough, but he could not help feeling envious. Violet caught the edge in his voice. She was sensitive with everyone, but with Michael, her antennae were super-receptive.

'Oh, now you mustn't mind, my love.' Those last two words smothered any resentment. He could hardly speak.

'Violet!' It came out in a gulp. This time it was she who put her gloved had on his, as he wheeled the bicycle along the drive of the manor to the back door. In the kitchen, Mrs Bull hesitated, wondering whether he wasn't a bit grown up to hug, but then gave way to her impulse and caught him in her burly arms, giving his embarrassed cheek a peck before stepping back to say:

'Master Michael, you look as though you want a bit of feeding up!'

'Oh, I'm, um, fine, Mrs Bull, thank you.' Both young people removed coats and gloves, sat at the kitchen table, drank a cup of tea and ate fruit cake, before going through to the study where Mrs Bull had lit a fire and set a small vase with Christmas roses and holly on the desk. Michael had been quiet and preoccupied throughout. Now, in the study, he sighed.

'You don't seem very pleased to be home.' Violet said, standing very close to him.

'Oh Violet!' He trembled slightly, as he took one of her hands. She immediately circled his waist with her arms, and then took his face in her hands, exactly as she had the last time they had met, in the September mushroom meadows, by the river. As their lips met, he felt a tingling thrill, running down his spine. Her cool fingers on his cheeks, her soft lips, her huge eyes, out of focus now, they were so close. He felt the smoothness of her skin, at the back of her neck, the dark hair was caressing his hand and, as he moved his arms down her back, he felt the bumps of her spine and the thinness of her waist. The electric sensations in his body tuned themselves to an ascending pitch. He felt his throat go dry, his heart-rate increase and, to his shame and confusion, an involuntary stirring in his groin. He hated his body for doing this, but knew that it was beyond control. He pushed her from him a little and turned his body away. She wondered at this abrupt change. He longed to hold her again, but was anxious to divert himself, to take the heat out of the moment. She hoped she did not disgust him. Did he, after all, mind terribly that she was a shop girl?

There was a piano in the room, an old Broadwood upright, rather out of tune but with a tone that was soft at the edges, and belonged to an age half a century before, when families and guests regularly sang for each other after dinner. Gerard never played and Michael's skill was limited to a few set pieces learnt for music lessons at school. His sight reading was rudimentary. Nevertheless, to create a diversion, he pulled out the piano stool, lifted the lid and ran clumsy, hesitant fingers over the yellowing keys. Violet had a natural ear and, like her two brothers, was a competent musician.

'I've never heard that piano played before,' she said, and sat beside him. He took his hands off the keyboard. She played a series of chords and arpeggios, wincing at the pitch of some of the notes. 'Wants tuning,' she said, 'but what a lovely tone it has.' She began to play *In dulci jubilo*, first the simple tune, and then a series of improvised variations. Michael sat spellbound, overawed by her skill and loving her with such an aching tenderness that he felt he could hardly bear it. But he dare not touch her for fear of the embarrassing arousal which he felt sure she would notice, and which would offend her. Nothing, absolutely nothing must be done that could risk losing her. He contented himself by watching her hands play, now *cantabile*, with caressing gentleness, now with a deft *staccato,* sinews raised along the backs of her half-cupped hands. Occasionally she faltered, or played a wrong chord whereupon she would stop, re-work the harmony and nod to herself at the improved arrangement. She hummed, softly, under her breath as she played. Michael sat beside her, his eyes trying to follow her hands, basking in the sunshine of her presence.

That was how they were when Gerard came into room. The music had drowned his quiet entry into the house. Hearing the sound, he had walked straight into the study before removing his top coat. Michael froze for a moment while Violet brought her improvisation to a hasty conclusion. Gerard noted something he had never before seen in his son's features: a flicker of guilt, as if he had been caught in the commission of some misdemeanour. But the look vanished as the boy leapt to his feet and offered a hand.

'Hullo, Father!'

'Michael, Violet – how pleasant to see you both!' Gerard caught Violet's look now, turned briefly on himself and then back at Michael. He noted the expression change from polite greeting smile to a softer, more affectionate glance. His son was, he supposed, becoming quite attractive to women. He resisted the resentment stirring the sediment at the base of his mind – such feelings were wholly unworthy – and addressed the girl.

'Shall you take luncheon with us?'

Much later, after a leisurely meal of cold mutton, pickles, steamed cabbage and boiled potatoes, Michael and Violet were sitting alone in the kitchen, while Gerard went through the motions of work in his study. During the previous summer holidays, Michael had found a heap of photograph albums in one of the attic rooms, and wanted to show her. 'My mother, it seems, was a great photographer. She took all these in the few years before I was born.'

'I'd love to see photos of your mother.' Violet began to leaf through the first of the albums. Each black sugar paper page was separated with a leaf of tracing paper on which dates or captions had been pencilled.

'You won't find any in there,' Michael said. 'She was always behind the camera.'

'But I'd so love to know more about her. Your father says that portrait in the drawing-room is not a good likeness at all.'

'Maybe not,' Michael sat beside her as they leafed through the album. 'But that is all I have to go on.'

'Don't you wonder what she was like?' Violet was surprised at the lack of emotion Michael displayed whenever the subject of his mother cropped up. He shrugged.

'Father won't talk about it. I really don't know.' She could hardly know that 'mother talk' had never been allowed, in this house, and that Michael's warmth and affection had always been strongest for his fellows at school. Such feelings had never been overshadowed by love, received or given at home and only now had been exceeded by his feelings for her.

'But don't you wonder what sort of a person she was? What interested her? What sort of things did she say?' Michael shrugged again. 'Michael?'

'Mmm?'

'Do you ever try to imagine what your mother's voice might have sounded like?' Michael pondered for a second.

'No,' he said. 'I think that's rather a morbid line of thought, don't you?'

'Perhaps.' She resumed turning the pages. There were pictures, mainly of Gerard. Gerard on a horse; Gerard in the uniform of a Guards officer; Gerard on an elephant, with dozens of native Indians in attendance; Gerard with his foot on a dead tiger; Gerard in white tie and tails, outside the Royal Opera House; Gerard and friends at the Chelsea Flower Show. There were pages and pages of pictures, all of Gerard and his associates doing things that were adventurous, that involved travel, that were expensive. 'Your father seemed to do an awful lot more then than he does now.'

'He was younger.'

'He's not that old now. People his age do loads of things.' Michael shrugged again. He didn't really mind what she chatted about, as long as he was here with her. He soon lost interest in the photographs. He had looked through them several times, giving some of the albums no more than a cursory glance, after scrutinising the early pages. He found them, frankly, rather boastful.

'Why don't we go for a walk?'

'Better not, perhaps. It's getting a bit dark.'

Violet slowly turned page after page, studying each picture. 'Now here's a different . . . Oh, my goodness!' She was staring at the page. 'Oh Michael, look!' He moved the oil lamp a little closer, so that its warm light could sharpen the features on the photographs. On the page were a couple of landscape pictures, side by side, of a rocky stream, presumably taken in Scotland. At the bottom of the page was a photograph with its horizon crooked, and its subject slightly off-centre – obviously shot by an inexperienced photographer. The subject was a young woman, facing the camera flat on, holding a large salmon with her fingers hooked through its gills. In her other hand, was a long fishing rod, its handle resting on the ground. The young woman's face bore a triumphant smile. Michael looked more closely. He had not noticed this photograph before.

'That portrait in the drawing-room is nothing like,' he said, after a lengthy silence. 'Absolutely *nothing* like,' he murmured. He had to think for a moment. Things were moving; he felt his stability threatened. The portrait on the drawing-room wall meant little. It was his mother, just as the face on a tuppeny stamp was the king's. But this amateur snap, for all its fuzziness, its brownish grey tones, and its small size, was of a person who suddenly was there, sharp in his mind, replacing the misty image of she who had given birth to him but not stayed to bring him up. This faded photo was of a person who could live, breathe, laugh, get angry, love. It was an image of a person he could have known, could have loved. It was the image of the person he *did* love. He could barely trust his voice but felt he must speak. 'She's *so* like you!'

Violet had turned very quiet. She was thinking of all the little signals Gerard had made, of all the remarks, the long glances, the moments of silence. The woman in the picture, she knew, was more than a mere resemblance, more even than a *doppelgänger*. The eyes held precisely the expression of triumph that Violet felt, when she had achieved anything difficult. The clothes, ridiculous fishing gear, said nothing, but the way she wore them was the way Violet could have seen herself wearing them. The hat brim, she would have folded in exactly the same way. She would even had held the fishing rod in the same way and posed, just like that, for the photograph. In one glance, Violet understood why Gerard found, in spite of his lack of appetite for other human company, her presence so valuable. Is he only seeing her in me, she wondered, or is it actually me he desires? Oh, let it be her, not me! To comfort herself a little, she reached for Michael's hand and gave it a squeeze.

'You're quite right,' she said, managing to create a convincingly breezy tone, 'your mother did look a little like me.' And she closed the album with a bang. Violet had never been one to linger in front of a mirror.

Chapter Twelve

———

Seeing the photograph reminded Violet why, in spite of his aloofness with everyone else – even with his own son – Gerard had always been so warm with her. It was obvious, since she resembled his wife so closely, that he felt comforted in her presence. Had she lived, Elizabeth would be approaching forty by now but in Gerard's mind, she would always be a very young woman. Those facts Violet was quick to absorb, and she found them discomfiting though not unbearable. But when she began to reflect on how his manner had evolved in recent months, she suspected that his hunger was no longer merely for a surrogate Elizabeth – even if it had been all that time ago when he had found her touching the flowers on Elizabeth's grave – but for herself. Thus, in spite of her intelligence and her liberal upbringing, she found herself in a predicament that needed more experience and sophistication than she possessed. What could she do? She had not the slightest stirring of sexual attraction for Gerard. He was nearly three times her age, and any suggestion of carnality, or of physical contact of any kind beyond a formal handshake would never have occurred to her. But Gerard must not be hurt. That was crucial to her deliberations. He was a dear man, a loving uncle, wholly unworldly, but wise and kind. If she rejected him now, if she stopped seeing him, it would be an act of gross ingratitude. But how could she prevent him from suffering? How could she divert his attention, to someone, or something else? And if to no one living, could she help him to re-focus on Elizabeth?

Above all else, even Gerard, Michael must not be hurt. She loved him, probably naïvely, probably irrationally, but with the whole of her heart, and with a physical intensity that made her feel faint with excitement whenever she thought of him. Whatever happened, now, with Gerard, she knew that Michael would be affected. Jealousy could poison the purity of their relationship – Michael was already uneasy about her visits to his father – and if mishandled, she could lose him. She would rather die than have that happen. She did not want to live without Michael, ever, and would do whatever was necessary to stay with him, and have him stay with her. Their age difference was nothing, even though it was unconventional for girls to consort with boys more than a year their junior. Their class difference would have presented deeper difficulties, but now that she had a place at Oxford, she held a key that could admit her to Michael's class. Gerard's obvious desire created too complex a puzzle for her to unravel. She had no idea what to do about it at this stage, but it seemed likely that Elizabeth held the other key that she sought.

No one took much notice of the great four-wheel-drive tractor trundling down the hill towards Pyson Wood, even though it was not quite four in the morning. Few of Wychgate's inhabitants understood the warp and weft of modern agriculture, but everyone knew that there were busy seasons when implements would be moving about the village or at work in the fields, regardless of the time. Even between midnight and dawn, it was common to observe heavy tractors on the land, lit up like slow-moving ships at sea, ploughing or cultivating in the farmer's constant bid to keep one step ahead of the weather. This frosty March morning might have tempted many an anxious 'arable' man to snatch a few hours while the ground was still frozen, and therefore possible to be worked without damaging the soil by compaction, to prepare friable seed beds for his late-drilled spring crops.

In the Old Stores, Graham was woken briefly by the

machine's roar but turned over, in his lonely bed, and drifted back to sleep. For almost a year, after his move to the village, his sleep pattern had been unpredictable. Bouts of frustration, caused by his inability to get to grips with his writing or long spells of despondency about his treatment by the BBC would come, like unwelcome companions to his bed and lie heavily on him until he felt unable to keep still under their pressure. He would rise, frequently, make himself tea in the small, cramped kitchen or sit in the old store room, attempting to read but, in reality, staring at the print while trying to make some sort of sense of what was happening to him.

Veronica's departure had been the most recent blow – one more failure to pile on the heap – but after his run-in with Busby and his immersion into village politics, he realised that when she had finally decided to go, she had taken his malaise with her. Village affairs, in themselves, were paltry – microcosmic struggles with stunted intellects – but they had helped to wipe away his self-pity, clear his brain, and to make him apply himself with determination and direction, to what he saw as the next phase in his career. There were three projects in his sights now: a documentary series for Channel 4 called *The Countryside in Crisis*; a brand-new and utterly convincing idea for his novel – he had already mapped out a synopsis, dashed off a trio of chapters and sent these to his agent, and Imogen. He thought fondly of each in turn, sighed with content and was asleep again before the noise of the tractor engine had faded away.

In Weir House, the subject of Graham's third project woke with a start and knew, even though it was still dark, that she would not sleep again before day. She alone in the village discerned threat in the tractor's engine. She had been the target of too many aggressive incidents in recent weeks, to allow her to rest easy about anything, and she felt more friendless, now, than when she and Mrs Crowe had first come to Wychgate Saint Peters. When she had decided to clear the wood, the previous summer, opinions had been divided. Those like Busby and Mrs Maidwall, who had made the loudest protests, were actually in the minority. Most villagers had, with quiet satisfaction, watched the gloomy trees recede and few had been bothered about the proposition to build three new houses. Some were actually looking forward to seeing them go up since, it was said, a thriving community helped to boost the values of other houses in the village, and no one saw that as a bad thing.

Then news of the expanded plans had broken and opposition grew stronger and noisier. To counter this, villagers were told of a special public meeting in the parish hall, arranged by the would-be developers, a firm that called itself Saint Peter Properties. Until its appearance, Imogen had been held solely responsible for all the trouble that the new development was bound to cause, but now, instead of the blame being diluted, a fresh load of ill-will was dumped on her for bringing profiteering outside developers to this rural spot. Everyone assumed that Saint Peter Properties was a large, established firm but in fact, it was merely a front, set up by Russell Hands, and was not even, yet, incorporated as a limited company. Imogen had felt quite unable to go the meeting and Hands had had no intention of being anywhere near the place. Indeed, he was not yet ready to admit to having anything whatever to do with Saint Peter Properties.

Those few parishioners who had attended were treated to canapés and wine – more would have gone, if they had realised that the comestibles were to be free of charge – and a presentation on what was proudly called the Saint Peters Field Development Project. A public relations man, backed up by his anorexic assistant, spoke of the 'enhanced rural experience', of 'environmental conservation', of 'habitat-friendly dwellings', and of something called 'starter homes for first-time buyers'. As he spoke, slides were projected on to the cobwebby whitewash walls of the village hall. The handful of attenders, sitting meekly like a church congregation, saw artists' impressions of a sprawling estate built in a mishmash of architectural styles that had borrowed the worst features from previous centuries, or from Spain and Mexico. There were louvred shutters, fulvous pantiles and dormer windows designed to exclude, rather than admit light. These pictures were interspersed with wildlife photographs of exquisite beauty. Between images of a song thrush, poised by her clutch of sky-blue, ink-blotched eggs, and a Maytime woodland scene of bluebells in slanting sunshine, viewed through a bridal veil of hawthorn blossom, there was a half-timbered and yellow brick residence, with an unconvincing oak door, fronted by a concrete and brick patio on which languished containers of exotic plants that looked as though they were feeling the cold, and flanked by an intrusive double garage that appeared to dwarf the dwelling. 'The Burleigh,' said the speaker, in reverential tones, 'faithful to our Tudor ancestry and top of the range for this particular development.' More pastoral scenes had followed, and then a succession of genuine village streets – someone felt sure they recognised Hemingford Grey – followed by more clusters of strange new dwellings, each built from different materials and in mismatched architectural styles. The effect was of a random collection of toy houses made with plastic kits. 'Fascinating in its architectural complexity and charming with its different styles, er, ladies and gentlemen, the Traditional English Village, updated for Quality of Life for the Eighties,' continued the PR man, 'and I'm sure you'll all agree, the perfect place to bring up children.' No one in the room, other than the speaker's assistant, had been of child-bearing age.

The special presentation, programmed to coincide with the official application to build forty houses on the Pyson Wood site, had failed and now a huge majority in the community was against the development. Jerome had spoken to Imogen at length, several times, in the hope of persuading her to revert to her original plan, or at least, to cut back. 'I know we are now on the overall county plan for expansion,' he had said, 'but, Imogen, an influx of that size can't be healthy. We'd just be swamped.' She had listened, but had not reversed her decision.

Graham, too, had paid her a visit, to try to persuade her to change her mind. He felt guilty because he suspected that his original words, at that early parish meeting, might have encouraged her to have embarked on such an ambitious project. At this suggestion she had merely given him a smile that would have made the Mona Lisa look ingenuous. But she had warmed to him, and had begged him to stay. They had had tea and she had shown him her garden, talking at length about mulching, propagating and planting ideas until, noticing that he was shivering in spite of his thick anorak, she had apologised far more profusely than was necessary and shepherded him back indoors. He could hardly believe that this lively, almost feverish girl was the same person as the wan creature who, formerly, would dart into gateways to hide, if approached in the village street, and would slip into the church, each Sunday, long after everyone else had arrived and would skulk in the shadows. He had responded to the light in her eyes by giving her a small kiss, not on her cheek, but directly on to her parted lips. But then he had said, 'I'm so sorry, Imogen, but I think I will have to oppose your scheme. It's just too big.' And he had left.

Hunched in the foetal position, in bed, Imogen tightened her arms around herself and thought of Graham, and of that initial kiss, and sighed. How she needed a gentle man!

Shortly after Graham's visit, the ugliness had begun. At first, they were small acts of aggression: mud smeared over the planning announcement that had been nailed to a telegraph pole; litter thrown over her garden wall; phone-calls, either with silent callers or with staged heavy breathing. It got worse. Objects fouler than waste paper began to arrive in the front garden. Something too fleshly pink, and too like human tissue made her scream when she spotted it on the lawn from an upstairs window. It turned out to be a dead piglet and, once she had identified it, and had been moved to pity by the little hairless body, the closed eye and tiny snout, half snarling in death, she buried it at the back of a mixed border under a winter-flowering cherry. Someone threw sump oil onto her lawn and a firework was posted through her letter box. These acts had frightened her but, rather than persuade her to abandon her plans, they strengthened her determination to proceed. She was used to ill-will – receiving it had been part of her life for a fair while – and as long as she had Mrs Crowe in the house, she felt relatively safe from physical harm. The woman was untrustworthy, but Imogen knew that it was in the Crow's interest for the plans to go ahead and that she could therefore rely on her for support and protection.

The sound of the tractor that had woken her in those small hours was a reminder that within a few weeks, Gilmore would be back with his foresters after their winter cessation, to finish clearing the last of the trees. In a few weeks, too, she would know the outcome of the planning application.

Michael Pilkington also heard the tractor go by, in spite of the thick walls of his manor house. He seldom slept for more than an hour or two at a stretch nowadays and, since the beginning of felling operations, had become as reclusive as his father had been. His housekeeper was commissioned to buy what little food he needed and he answered the door to nobody. Most of his wakeful hours were spent in a torture of aimless, cyclical thought. It was impossible for him to focus on actual events but with every tree that fell, his anxiety increased. The wounds had never healed, but over more than half a century he had developed an insulating shell – layer upon layer of horny keratin to protect the raw, exposed nerve endings beneath. The shell had been strengthened with a lifetime of dedication to his fellows: loyalty to colleagues in the army, kindness to acquaintances within his milieu and selfless service to his community. But the surface of this shell, made bright with a gloss of *bonhomie* and good manners, had loosened and been sloughed off with the felling of the first trees. Michael's last visitor had been Jerome but he had been asked, curtly, never to call again.

Jerome did not hear the tractor. His modern rectory was too far from the street for him to be able to hear anything, but he seldom slept easy. This whole planning affair, and the behaviour of the villagers, made him wonder whether he should not only move out of Wychgate, but also whether he should leave the Church and find something more usefully pastoral to do. His small congregation had shrunk to a dismal remnant who refused to sing at services and who shuffled away afterwards before he had time to emerge from the vestry to greet them. He had always been irritated by the most faithful among his flock, despising their self-righteous attitudes, and wondering how they could be so complacent about their own salvation, but he had always been able to find some sort of love for them. Now he wondered whether such spoilt, selfish prigs deserved much love. And for once, he didn't feel guilty for thinking of his parishioners that way.

He did feel guilty and miserable about Michael, a harmless and charming old man whose life seemed to have been ruined by this development thing – and God knew why that was.

He was also guilty and miserable about Imogen. Guilty because he felt he may have led her into all these difficulties by encouraging her to fell the wood and to develop – though not on the scale she now seemed to envisage. And miserable about her because he loved her – not pastorally, you understand, but was *in* love with her. He wanted to be with her, wanted her. Ridiculous, of course, absolutely ridiculous! With such an age difference, and with his *useless* prospects – he really thought he would leave the Church, at some stage – a marriage, even a liaison, was simply not possible. Besides which there was the small matter of her attitude to him. She, obviously, quite rightly, had no desire for him at all, even though she was coolly friendly. He groaned and for comfort, slipped a hand beneath the waistband of his blue and yellow poplin pyjamas.

The tractor, a huge John Deere 4240 towing a trailed sprayer, belonged to a farmer from the other side of Kendale. It turned down the west side of Pyson Wood, running along the felled section, past the remaining standing timber and turned again, on to the strip of rough grasses and shrubs that constituted the newly designated Site of Special Scientific Interest. The driver, a muscle-bound creature whose neck was wider than his head, stopped the tractor, unhitched the sprayer and then took a massive chain out of the cab. This he fixed to the hydraulic linking arms on the back of the mighty vehicle before scrambling up the steps back into the cab. He backed his tractor to the largest of the trees, the wild service that Gilmore had found with Graham, and got off again to wind the chain round its trunk and then fix the hook on the link arm. Then he climbed back up cab steps, reached inside the door and pressed the hydraulic lever to lift the arms. The huge 120 horsepower engine barely changed its note as the chain tightened and entire tree was lifted gently from the ground and fell. Before unhitching it, the driver towed it to the edge of the grassy strip. He repeated the procedure several times and before long, a couple of fifteen-foot hollies, several hawthorns and the field maples were lying along the side of the strip, their roots exposed, their bruised crowns lying along the ground. He then drove back to the sprayer hitched to the tractor and extended the booms so that they reached almost thirty feet across. It took less than two passes to spray the entire area with a cocktail of potent herbicides. By dawn, the grass would already be showing signs of scorch. Within a couple of weeks, the whole plant population would be dead. The job took less than an hour. Once over, the great green and yellow tractor sped across the blighted field, along the wood and turned sharp right, up the hill and away. No one had seen it in the darkness, even though Imogen, wakeful, watched its headlights reflected on her ceiling as it passed.

Imogen gave up even trying to sleep two hours later and rose to a sharp, clear morning. Her eyes felt gritty with fatigue and her head ached, but she was accustomed to meeting each day feeling under par. Even on the odd occasion when she had slept peacefully through the night, her body still took some time to nurse itself into activity. This was also the time of day when she often felt the need for some kind of crutch to help her face the challenge of existence, the time when an alcoholic would reach into the back of the wardrobe for a pre-breakfast nip, or would clean his teeth and gargle with scotch – purely medicinal, of course. She had never weakened, and felt confident that she never would, but these early post-dawn moments, even now that she was making excellent progress back into the real world, were often the most difficult to get through.

She sat at her dressing table and began to brush her hair. Hands was coming, she remembered. She groaned aloud and paused in her brushing. It was to be the first time they would meet alone together since Mrs Crowe had come into the scene as an ally. The sexual thing was wholly behind her, but she was afraid he might try something. Physically, she was stronger now than she had ever been, even before her period of addiction. Days spent in the garden, long walks and, since Christmas, when she had given herself a bicycle, even longer excursions, had made her lean body more muscular and resilient than anyone would have thought possible. Her skin, though naturally pale, had a healthier glow now, and her mind was more consistently alert than it had ever been. Addiction, on her young body, had caused little more damage to her liver and kidneys than a regular whisky drinker might have sustained, and her subsequent healthy lifestyle had more than made her whole. It was as if she had shrugged off the effeteness and indulgence of her aristocratic background along with the addiction. Her mind, though, had yet to complete its purgation. Daily, she was tortured. Frequently, tears of remorse or leaden feelings of shame made her falter at whatever she was doing. In her mind, series of events had sprung up so often that now they had become encoded in small, trigger images. These, in turn, would be flashed into her conscience by some trivial event – a chance remark, an object, certain smells – and she would have to stop whatever she was doing until the whole sequence had run its course.

Yesterday she had heard on the local news about a child who had fallen into the Dene downstream from Stoneford, where the water was deeper and swifter, and had been rescued and revived by a local first-aid expert who had applied the kiss of life. The term 'kiss of life' sounded heroic but more grisly images flashed across Imogen's mind. A body on the grass, one leg twisted unnaturally under itself, the head almost roughly jerked back by the paramedic in his haste to revive. Mouth forced open with finger and thumb and a sour plug of vomit and mucus hooked out with two fingers. Then the paramedic's mouth mashed on to Marcus's and the farting noise as he tried to breathe life into the broken body. Later, when he knew he'd failed and stood up, Imogen could see the yellowish stain of Marcus's vomit round his lips and on his moustache. She had begun to giggle. She couldn't stop, even when she felt the hot stream of piss running down her leg, even when the paramedic looked at her with cold, black eyes and when the police-woman took her to the waiting car.

Her mind switched back to the present. How *was* she going to handle this odious guttersnipe? Mentally, she felt she could nearly match him now, but if things became physical, what then? He arrived a little late and, to her annoyance, let himself into the house. More than simply a display of bad manners, it felt like a violation, or rather, a reminder of the series of violations that she had, sort of, consented to. He was in the same blue-green suit she had seen him wearing for the first meeting with Crowe. Well-cut, expensive, attractive. She was sure he was losing weight and that made him look better still. She nearly found herself wanting him to touch her.

'Where's yer old bag, then?' Hands had noticed that the car was missing. 'Shoppin', is it?'

'Shall we get down to it?' Imogen was anxious to get the meeting over as soon as possible.

'Down to what?' Hands moved closer and reached for her bottom. She ducked, stepped back and stood facing him with her arms folded. It was the first physical contact they had had since last August and she had no intention of any resumption of that depraved union, even though something inside her, even now, responded to that brutal touch. A pulse quickened, a small warm ember kindled.

'I don't think there's any need for that,' she said. 'We both know that that's over.'

'Yeah?' Hands stepped forward again. Imogen held her ground.

'You've too much at stake to spoil it for the sake of a bit of vileness.'

'Yeah?' His face set into a sneer, but he knew that the person he was dealing with now was a different kettle of bloody fish than the pathetic bird he'd mishandled before. He composed his features, met her eye and then looked at the ground for a moment before adjusting his cuffs and brushing an imaginary speck of fluff from his jacket. 'Yeah, well, we'll have to see about that, won't we?' Since she still owned the land on which he wanted to build, and could probably now find another developer if she wanted, he'd better watch out. What's more, he had more to ask of her this morning.

'You said you wanted to discuss something special.'

'Yeah.' He sat down. She remained standing. 'I've got some good news.'

'Really?'

'Well, good and bad.'

'Let's have the, ahm, bad first.'

'The application ain't going in until the June Meeting.'

'But that's almost three months away.'

'Yeah. And that's the good news. I 'appen to know who'll be chairin' that one, and who, on the committee, is likely to be away on their 'olidays. Strengthens our chances, see!'

'I see.'

'In fact, it makes the whole thing virtually a dead cert.'

'Does it?'

'Oh yeah.' He remained sitting. She walked to the window and then back to stand in front of him. 'And there's more good news. Concerns you.'

'Ah!'

'Yeah! 'ouse prices are still shootin' up.

'But I'll hold my original price. I'm as good as my, ahm, word.'

'Oh, I know yer will. I wouldn't've mentioned the prices, else.' Hands leaned forward, sitting on the edge of the sofa. 'Thing is this: you could make a killin' if you came in a bit more with me. As a partner, like.'

'How do you mean?'

'Well, you stand to make four 'undred thou already. Why not develop the site with me – re-invest yer sale proceeds into new build? You could make a cool million. Possibly more.'

'Ahm . . .' Imogen pondered briefly. 'I'm quite happy, actually, with what we've already agreed.'

'No, no, hang about!' Hands began to shake his head. Imogen detected, beneath the affected casualness, a note of urgency. 'Think it over a minute.'

'I don't need to.'

'*You* may not need to, but . . .' He realised he was beginning to make himself look weak and dried up.

'But?' She recognised the plea, even though it was well disguised. There was no problem with the site, once permission had been granted, Hands knew that, but he had too many projects up in the air at once. With two other substantial developments down on the Fen and now this Pyson Wood thing, the stakes, already huge, were getting out of line, and so were the risks. All in all, he might have to finance the building of twenty or more houses at a time before actually selling a single one of them. That could mean that the banks would be into him for a couple of million short-term financing – and that was costly as hell – before revenue from sales started trickling back.

Looking at the bright side, though, he was making up to fifty thousand a house pure profit on some of the estates. And, as long as prices kept rising, it made plenty of sense to go out for as much development as he, or his bankers, could possibly afford. But how much more *could* he afford? And what if prices began to level out or even, to fall? That was why he felt, increasingly, the need for someone with whom to spread the risks. He knew that Imogen was in a position of strength anyway – if he'd been in her shoes, he'd have raised the price – but he also knew that she was a woman of principle, in spite of everything that he knew about her recent past. If he could persuade her to come into partnership with him on this project, she would be less dangerous and he would be able to go on expanding.

'It's a brilliant opportunity for you.' Hands appeared to have regained his composure. 'Serious money!'

'I'll think about it,' Imogen said. Hands opened his mouth to remonstrate. He needed her to reach a decision pretty damned fast but knew, by looking at her, that he would be risking a flat refusal if he put any pressure on her now.

'Yeah? OK then, love.' He adopted as breezy a tone as he could muster and went to give her a kiss. She had anticipated his approach and side-stepped him by jumping to the door, opening it and then running to the front door and opening that. Outside, in the narrow front garden, her first primroses were joining the crocuses – already cottoned against sparrow attack – in a chorus of cheerful yellow. Hands dared not try to kiss her again, especially since someone was coming and, to her relief, he jumped into his car and sped away.

Imogen recognised Graham Ball and waved. He waved back and hastened his steps, arriving slightly out of breath. 'I'm so glad I caught you. Fact is, I've some rather interesting news.'

'Oh?'

'Mmm. You could be the proud possessor of an extremely important archaeological site.' He jerked a chin at the remains of Pyson Wood. 'It's amazing what comes to light, once you start delving. 'Specially in a place that's been left undisturbed for nigh on sixty years.'

'What? What *are* you on about?'

'Ancient artifacts. Ancient woodland.' On an impulse, he leapt over the small wicket gate, resting one hand on the post, as a pivot, and alighted by her side. She uttered a little shriek of surprise mixed with delight.

'You'll do yourself a, ahm, nasty—' Her hand leapt to her mouth, to suppress a giggle. It was quite natural, and rather sweet, she felt, that he should want to do something like that. Sort of gallant. She held her hand out to be taken and enjoyed the warmth of his grip. 'Show me,' she said.

Chapter Thirteen

———

'There's so much more I want to tell you.' Graham kept hold of Imogen's hand all the way down the hill. 'At last, it's beginning to work out pretty well for me.' He gave her hand a squeeze, 'you'll be happy with what I've got to say too, I think.' He led her to the fence, erected along the roadside where most of Pyson Wood had stood until the previous autumn, to keep out trespassers. It was nothing more than three strands of barbed wire, stretched between chestnut wood posts about twelve feet apart, hardly enough to discourage pedestrians but it prevented the passage of cars or all-terrain vehicles which, until its erection, had been arriving in increasing numbers to raid the wood for pieces of branch and the ends of trunks, too narrow or distorted to use as timber, but valuable for logging. Some of the drivers had been extremely offensive when stopped by Gilmore, and told to surrender their booty. It was generally thought, by members of the Kensington Coup, that fallen timber was without value and anyone's to have.

He widened the gap between wires for her, pulling upwards on one strand and holding the other down with his feet. She bobbed under and he followed, moving through before she had time to widen the gap for him. His jacket snagged on a barb, but she managed to unhitch it before he tore the material. 'Oh, I say, do look!' She had noticed that the ground, wherever it had been tortured, had greened over with seedlings. Nature was claiming back territory after a half-century of sunlessness.

'Ah, but wait until you come inside the wicked wild wood!'

'Oh Graham. I'm, ahm, not sure I want to go in there.'

He was surprised at her reluctance. 'It's perfectly OK,' then, archly, 'I won't try a thing on, I promise.'

'It isn't that, it's just . . .' Memories of Hands were still too recent to be comfortable. It had, after all, started in the spiky, sighing darkness of the wood. She hesitated a little longer and then shrugged. 'What am I making a fuss for? Most of the trees are gone anyway,' and they continued, hand in hand through the last of the standing conifers. Soon, it was difficult to move through the thickness of the growth.

'It's hard to find and almost impossible to get into,' Graham said, pushing his way, backwards, into the matted branches. 'You'll have to come right close to me.' He caught her slight body in his large arms and, protecting the top of her head as best he could, by cradling it on his breast, he continued to thrust himself backwards through the last of the thicket. They burst through, Graham staggering, almost falling and almost pulling Imogen on top of him. They both giggled, and then dusted one another down. Their hair was full of tiny spruce twiglets, dead so long they had lost all their needles. Then they turned and, side by side, hand in hand, they moved into the clearing.

'Ancient woodland,' Graham said. 'Only a fragment, but it could go back to pre-history. To Merlin, Arthur, Gawain and the Green Knight – all that jazz.'

'I don't like it.' Imogen folded her arms. 'What's that great stone? It looks man-made.'

'I think it probably is. And it's not local. There's no stone like that anywhere near here. It has to have been brought here.' They wandered about in the clearing for a few minutes and noted the dozen or so old broad-leaf trees and the pair of yews. In contrast to the spruces' regimented shapes, these had great, spreading limbs and were gnarled and twisted with age. Imogen seemed keen to get away. 'I keep trying to find the place where I first went through,' Graham said, 'but its almost as if the trees snap shut behind you.'

'We shouldn't be here,' Imogen said, her teeth chattering in the cold hostility of the place. 'Can't you feel it?'

Graham put a hand out, as if testing for rain. 'No, I don't think so. I get the impression it's rather a religious place. But then, I have the advantage, because I've read up on it.' He sat on the great tablet and patted the stone at his side for Imogen to sit. She shook her head but stood close to him.

'I can't keep it from you any longer,' he said. 'I've got the series. I'm doing *The Countryside in Crisis*. It'll be filmed over the next six months and screened in the autumn. Channel Four.' His eyes gleamed with the prospect 'Oh, and you *will* let me shoot this thing here, won't you? I want to do a whole programme on planning policy and this is an absolute honey of a location. Good story, *great* human interest, with that Busby creep getting hot about all the wrong things, this wonderful find here in the wood. And, on top of all that, there's the archaeology thing.'

'What archaeology thing?'

'What I've been banging on about all this time. They'll want to do a dig. This could be an important site.'

'Dig?'

'You will co-operate, won't you, Immie?' He turned her gently to him, and looked down into her eyes. 'And you won't chop down this ancient fragment will you? It hardly affects your building plans and it would be vandalous to do away with it.'

'Yes, I, ahm, suppose it would.' No one had found out who was responsible for spraying herbicide and pulling the wild trees out of the special strip along the south side of the wood, but most people in the village had assumed that it was she who had arranged for it to be done, to clear the way for more development.

'It could make a little oasis, among all those ghastly houses you want to put up.'

'Oh Graham, I'm not sure whether I want to build them anyway. Not all of them.'

'But if you do, you *will* spare this little bit, won't you? It can't be more than half an acre.'

Imogen nodded. 'And I think we should keep pretty quiet about it, at this stage,' she said. 'Who knows beside you?'

'Gilmore. He's the guy who alerted me to the archaeological potential. The only other people would be those old enough to remember before the forest grew up.'

'Old man Pilkington.' Imogen sighed. 'I feel *awful* about him. Awful.'

'Oh, there's more to tell you.' Graham wanted to prevent her from dwelling on the old man's enmity. He hated to see her hurting. 'I'm offering you a job.'

'A job?' Imogen laughed. (Me? A job? What a concept!) 'What job?'

'I wondered if you'd like to help me make these programmes, as a researcher. I couldn't pay you very much, but I need someone who knows a lot about the great land-owning families. You seemed the obvious choice.' Graham wanted an excuse to keep her near him.

They heard the first cuckoo calling from the great oak by the altar rock. The little river Dene, which widened at the boys' bathing place, was swift and clear with swathes of green-water crowfoot waving in the current. The meadow was dotted with yellow cowslips and, here and there, purple spikes of wild orchid, both green-winged and, nearer the fragment of ancient wood, early purple. Violet had picked a small posy of cowslips to which Michael had contributed half a dozen blooms of the orchids. The purple spikes made a pretty contrast with the fragrant yellow umbels. 'That's early,' Michael said, when the cuckoo's two-note song rang from the trees, 'we're not half-way through April yet.'

'Let's see if we can find it,' Violet said. They walked to the small piece of woodland, stooping under elder and wayfaring tree to get into the centre, where the altar rock showed through the sun-dappled trunks. She stood before the rock for a moment, silent, as if in respect for the place.

'Don't you find it spooky in here?' Michael asked. She paused for some time.

'No,' she murmured, at length, 'there's something very special about this spot.' Her hand moved in his, a slight twitch, as she watched shadows of the ancient tree make a dark tracery on the surface of the stone slab. The air where they stood was as still as a sealed chamber, but the slight breeze at the treetops made the shadows move across the stone, forming a slowly changing pattern. 'I feel sure this is something of a holy place.'

'How do you know?'

'I *feel* it.' He caught the intentness on her face and was moved with a kind of hero worship. Her pupils, dilated in the half-light, made her eyes look large and gentle. He felt the warm tide of her presence wash over him.

'Violet.' She turned, saw the love in his eyes, even saw tears beginning in them, not enough to overflow, but softening the edges and clotting the lashes.

'Michael!' They stood close, held each other and were silent for quite sometime. Then Violet said, 'Michael, don't *you* feel this place? Doesn't it affect you?'

'In that it does you.' His voice was was unsteady.

'I feel . . . I don't know . . . a presence. Things have happened here – sacred events, perhaps, centuries ago. Perhaps even before Christians got here.'

'Violet, I . . .' He wanted to say 'I love you' but the words simply wouldn't form on his lips. What he felt was far too big for such a hackneyed little phrase. He imagined a cinema sequence, the piano music going all soft and squashy while hero and heroine mouth the words at each other.

'I know, Michael. And I love you.' The words said simply, matter of factly.

'I want to be with you for ever. To marry you.' It sounded a comic suggestion. He blushed with embarrassment.

'We're too young.'

'I know. But we can wait until I've finished Sandhurst. I want to make a vow to you. This is the perfect place. It's almost like a church.'

'A vow? But before whom?'

'You. Me. With whoever you think is watching.' His suggestion was supposed to be facetious – he hadn't supposed that witnesses would be necessary – but her face was perfectly serious.

'Yes.' She paused, and then looked slowly round the clearing. 'Yes. Before whatever ancestors are here, whatever spirits. The Wood God, the Power, the . . .'

'The one God. The Lord of Lords.' He had caught her seriousness now. His neck hairs bristled with the solemnity, the enormity of what was about to happen. They faced each other. It was obviously his cue, but he faltered for a moment, wondering how to put his intentions into words. After a moment, with both her hands in his, he dropped to his knees, gently bringing her down so that they faced each other, kneeling before the altar. 'I, Michael William Thornton Pilkington hereby, er, pledge to you, Violet . . . um, I don't know your middle name.' She did not reply. Her eyes were tight closed but she squeezed his hands, willing him to go on. 'Violet Ball, that I will, for the whole of my life, be true and faithful to you alone. And that I will become your husband as soon as I am, um, of age.' That seemed about all he could say. Now it was her turn.

'I, Violet,' she kept her eyes tight shut, 'before this congregation of spirits here present . . .' the words chilled Michael. He could not believe in the spirits himself, but that someone as intelligent as Violet should do so was significant. '. . . will be the true and constant lover of you Michael, to the exclusion of all others, for the rest of my life here and . . .' here she faltered slightly, '. . . and during my life hereafter.' They both opened their eyes again, each looking deeply into the other's. It was a natural move to seal these solemn words with a kiss, mouth to mouth, tongue to tongue. After a few moments, they stood up. Without thinking, when they had held hands, Violet had put the bunch of cowslips and orchids on to the altar stone. Now, as they began to walk away, the flowers still lay, a small token of their betrothal. The chill stone would keep them fresh for several days.

'We have to tell our parents,' Michael said. It was quite out of character to be able to conduct a deceit of any kind. 'Not about the wood. Just about how we feel.' Later, at the gate of Wychgate Manor, he said, 'Come in, now. Let's talk to Father.'

'Perhaps better not,' Violet said. 'Better if we each talk to our own.' They parted. Michael watched her lilting stride as she walked towards the village stores. His spirits fell at her parting. He resented every moment that she was not with him. He walked in through the front door of his father's house and knocked at the study door.

'Enter!' Gerard's voice was muffled through the thick timber. Michael went in. His father was at his desk, writing his journal, the faultless copperplate handwriting flowing swiftly and easily from his pen. 'Son!' he said, colouring a little and closing the book after hastily blotting the ink.'I thought it was Mrs Bull. Do sit down.' Michael sat, feeling nervous. 'I hope you are finding plenty to do during the holidays.'

'Oh yes, Father, thank you.'

'Excellent.' Gerard seemed anxious to return to his journal. Michael knew he should come quickly to the point but felt his courage ebbing. 'Is there something?'

'There is, but I don't know how to say it.' Michael blushed and felt even more tongue-tied than usual with his father. Gerard, though wholly introverted, was not unsympathetic. When he saw his son's embarrassment he divined that, since the boy was sixteen – soon to be seventeen – it was probably to do with sex. They had never discussed anything so personal before – Gerard assumed that that kind of thing would have been dealt with at school – but for a couple of years, he had half expected the whole sordid business to come up.

'What is it about? I might be able to help.'

'Father, what happens when you fall in love?'

'Ah!' So it was to be an embarrassing interview. It would do the boy a disservice if he were not as frank as propriety would allow, but he wished the conversation that was about to ensue would soon be over. 'Well, I'm not sure how much you know about the so-called facts of life, but you are bound to understand that your anatomy is different from that of a girl and—'

'Oh Father, I know about that!' Michael wanted to stop his father from making himself feel ashamed. Even so, he felt slightly shocked that his father could touch on the same subject as countless whispered dormitory discussions, and of a certain slim volume, *What Every Married Woman Should Know*, that was passed furtively from hand to hand to be read under bedclothes by flashlight.

'Oh, I see.' The relief was evident in Gerard's eyes. But not for long.

'You see, Father,' Michael swallowed. 'I think it's happened to me.'

'What *can* you mean?'

'I think I'm in . . . that is . . . I care very much for someone.'

'Nonsense, boy! In love, at your age? An absurd concept!' Gerard picked up his pen and began to write.

'N-nonetheless, sir, I think I am,' Michael took a deep breath, 'with Violet Ball.' The pen jerked, flicking the steel nib which made a large blot, surrounded by a scattering of smaller ones. The hand that reached for the blotter trembled and, instead of applying a corner, so that the ink soaked in slowly, Gerard dabbed and spread the blot further. He put down his pen and pulled out a cotton handkerchief to wipe his inky fingers.

'That is a *wicked* thing to say.'

'Father, I cannot help my feelings.'

'It is quite the most ridiculous idea I have ever heard. She is older than you. At least two years older.'

'Seventeen months, Father.'

'She is from a completely different background. A *shop* girl.' Veins in his temple were pulsing; his hands, resting on the tooled leather surface were shaking so much that they rocked the desk. 'And you are still a *schoolboy*.'

'She loves me, Father.' Michael could not know why these words hurt his father so much.

'No!' Through his entire childhood, Michael had never heard his father raise his voice. 'Damn it. No!' He stood up, placed his journal in the centre drawer of his desk and locked it with a key from his waistcoat pocket. 'This ludicrous notion has got to stop at once. It is clearly a stupid puppy infatuation. I forbid you to speak to the girl, or to see her again. I *forbid it*, do you hear?' But Michael had fled, running to his lonely bedroom at the top of the house. He closed his door, turned the key in its lock and then he sat on his window-seat gazing out at the green, green meadow running to wood and stream. Gradually the scene blurred and, although to weep would have been unmanly, the two bitter tears that overflowed on to his sixteen-year-old cheeks, were so hot they seemed to scald.

At the same time Violet slipped into the shop, lifted the trap door in the counter to let herself behind and, seeing that her mother was serving a customer, walked through into the kitchen. At the pine table, Peter Ball was totting up the day's takings. He looked up and saw her radiant face, the eyes full of sexuality, the lips slightly parted, the breathing shallow and fairly rapid. His heart sank. He knew that she was fond of the Pilkington boy and, for all his liberal attitude, he knew no good could come of it. Even such just-minded people as the Pilkingtons would, he felt sure, close ranks at the threat of an interloper from the lower orders. And, more important than that, he wanted nothing, absolutely nothing to distract Violet from Oxford.

'Oh Dad, I've got something I'm bursting to tell you.' In matters of importance, she always confided in her father first, knowing that he would, in turn, discuss what she had said with her mother later. It just seemed easier for them all to work that way.

'I think I've an idea, Missy, what it might be.'

'Oh, you couldn't have.' She spooned tea into the pot, moved the hot kettle from the side of the range to the centre, to bring it to the boil and then poured water into the teapot before setting it onto the baize cloth. She took two cups and saucers from the dresser and at last, sat at the table opposite him. 'You see, I'm in love.'

'Aha! Young Pilkington.'

'Dad, you're so clever. You know *everything*!' She jumped up and walked round the table, putting her hands on his shoulders and squeezing. 'And he loves me, of course.'

'Of course.' So full of excitement, she failed to notice the bleakness of his voice 'Oh, I forgot the milk!' She went to the cool larder and returned in a moment with a large stoneware jug. In a moment the sides were damp with condensation. 'Tea?' She passed him a full cup.

'Thank you, Missy.'

'I know he's got to go back to school, and to Sandhurst and all that, and I'll miss him so much that—' and here to her surprise she found she was suddenly in tears. Joy? Desolation at the thought of all the absences before they were finally together? Which, she couldn't say; probably both. Peter made no attempt to comfort her. She recovered herself. 'We want to be together, Father, for always.' To her annoyance, she began to cry again. Peter put his arms round her waist.

'Now just hold off for a moment, my dove. Just stop and think a bit.' He pulled out a clean handkerchief for her to wipe her eyes and blow her nose. 'I know you love the boy. I'm not surprised, he's a pretty fellow, but you have to be realistic. They are gentry. We are not. You are clever. Very clever. He is, well, just ordinary in the brains department. *They* don't need to be as clever as we. They tend to get it all handed to them. You have that rare combination – brains and beauty. You could be a top . . .' he tried to think of a profession in which a woman might excel. It was always difficult. 'A top writer or something. He will be an army officer. Would you be happy in some dreary barracks in India or Africa?'

'Father, I'd be happy anywhere, as long as he was there.'

'Well I think you should clear your mind, Missy. You've everything to lose. I can't stop you seeing the boy – you make your own decision about that – but for goodness sake, try and get it into perspective. Get him out of your sight for a while. See if you can concentrate on something else.'

'I cannot, father, I can only think of Michael.'

'You'll feel that way about a hundred young men before you make your final choice.'

'Father, I won't.'

'Oh you may not think so, now, but you will.'

'Did you, Father? Fall in love with other women before Mother?'

Peter shifted on his hard kitchen chair and sipped his tea. 'It was different for me. I was so busy trying to get on in the world. I knew no one before your mother came along.'

'But, with her, you *knew*. Didn't you?' Peter, looking bleaker than ever, nodded. 'Exactly, Father. And I've made my final choice.'

Chapter Fourteen

———

. . . for only by making such a sacrifice, wrote Jerome Daniels, *can we understand the truth about ourselves and our relationship with God. The sacrifice has a physical, practical side – it feeds, it clothes the poor, it preserves, somehow, the habitat that we occupy – and it has a spiritual core. By giving of ourselves, we are sharing a greater common good. By foregoing that which we hold most dear, we gain the love, the power, the energy that will sustain us.* 'Oh, what a load of bollocks!' he shouted, and threw down his pen, upsetting the small glass that held a handful of fading bluebells. Stale flower water ran across his sermon notes, making the ink run.

The basic problem was that he couldn't make himself believe now, at all. Faith had, for the last couple of decades, and by degrees, slipped away. First to go had been the concepts of virgin birth, resurrection and the miracles. All those Bible accounts, wonderful though they were as stories, were too improbable for anyone with half a brain to believe, except by a total cancellation of logic. In religion, such suspension of rational thought would be a virtue called Faith; in any other sphere, the same mental blanking would be derided as ignorance or prejudice.

The idea of redemption had sustained his faith for much longer. The Pure One, saving mankind by making the ultimate sacrifice, that had kept him going in his ministry for years. But that story, too, was little more than myth, he realised.

The Romans had been in the habit of nailing to a cross almost anyone who happened to dissent from their colonial law, and a man with such revolutionary ideas as Jesus would have got right up everyone's nose. But regardless of what mystical elements the Christian religion might contain, Jerome had come to believe that the practical implications provided a perfect working basis for modern society. In fact, he was sure *that* was what Jesus was really driving at. Where man sacrificed self for man, society would surely thrive. Whatever happened after life – and as far as Jerome could reason, nothing happened after life – selflessness on Earth was an excellent code to live by. That was what, lately, had kept him reciting the Creeds and the Collects; had him miming the nonsense of turning bread to flesh and doling out salvation to sinners in the form a wafer that stuck dryly, like guilt, to the roof of the mouth and could then be washed off with a moistening draft of sweet wine. It was humanism in a formal overcoat. You could always scrub out the past and begin again. That was how it worked.

In recent months however, he had grown to despise the whole machination. He no longer saw the liturgy as a means of enabling people to focus their altruism, but as a shelter from their real obligations. Far easier for them, especially those in the conveniently re-packaged Anglican form of Christianity, to babble their shortcomings and then seek the comfort of a conventional forgiveness in the Chalice, than actually to *do* something about the mess they were all helping to make. He had, he decided, had it up to here with Christianity in general, and the C of E, in particular. Involuntarily, with these thoughts, his hand marked a level of intolerance somewhere between his left brow and his receding hairline. He longed to do pastoral work at the sharp end, where the misery was *really* at. 'I've got to talk to the bishop,' he told himself.

Recent events had sharpened his dislike for the locals. In Stoneford, a couple of weeks before, there had been a murder outside the town's one nightclub. A young man – a simpleton, as it happened, so it didn't matter quite so much to some people – had fallen foul of a gang of youths, and been stabbed several times. He had been left, bleeding in the street for almost an hour, before the services had been called. The casualty unit at Stoneford was closed – it only operated on week days from nine to five – so he had to be transported twenty miles to Kendale. He was dead on arrival. There was no relative to hold his hand while he died in the ambulance and no one to await his arrival at the hospital. The sad event affected Jerome deeply because he had known the young man – one of his ex-youth club supporters – and because any unnecessary death filled him with rage. In Wychgate, even though it had been the first Stoneford murder for decades, there was little reaction. The street where it happened was considered rough and sleazy – no one in their right mind would go there.

Jerome's sense of anger had sharpened when, the following week, the lead story in the *Stoneford Messenger* had been about a small group of men, two of whom were more or less eminent members of the local community, who had been arrested for acts of indecency in a public lavatory at an out-of-town beauty spot. That, many of his parishioners seemed to imply, was a greater moral outrage than the murder of a mentally retarded man. How these people hated anything to do with sex, and yet, how obsessed with it they were, lapping up the dirt every Sunday, when hands that had so piously taken the sacrament would grip the *News of the World*. 'I *must* talk to the bishop.'

No one in this village was about to make any sacrifices. That was for sure. The campaign of hatred against Imogen, which had gathered momentum for the whole of spring, had now risen to an intensity that frightened him. From a roughly divided position, attrition from the pro-developers had continued until Imogen was alone, without a single supporter. Forty houses was simply too much. The wood felling had created an appalling mess and then the vandalising of the Special Site, followed soon by the arrival of the archaeologists, had convinced the last few stalwart progressives that there was more to lose here than they had previously supposed. Imogen had promised to preserve the fragment of ancient woodland, and the plans had been changed to incorporate this into a small green area near the edge of the proposed housing estate.

Then, when details of the proposed sewage plant had come to light, feelings had become even more hotly roused. The actual site would be tucked away, on the bend in the river just upstream from where, in the 1920s, the little boys' bathing place had been. It was to be a small, highly efficient unit that would process sewage from houses on the estate – and other village dwellings, if desired – pouring only purified water into the river. It would be odourless, and considerably kinder to the environment than the dozens of septic tanks that would otherwise have leaked unpurified foul liquid into the ground, possibly to find its way into groundwater reserves from which the county extracted much of its drinking water. But it was a sewage works and that was unacceptable. Even Jerome had had qualms about that.

Imogen, though, seemed to be weathering the storm. The more he watched her in her adversity, the more he admired her steadfastness and the more he loved her. She had received hate mail, telephone threats, dog excrement pushed through her letter box and litter was constantly thrown over her lawn. She managed all that with equanimity. The ostracism that might have destroyed others did her little damage. She was already a complete outcast and had been ever since she had arrived, firstly because she had been unable to communicate very much with anyone, and later, because once people had got out of the habit of trying to talk to her, they didn't bother again. They didn't know what they were missing, Jerome thought. The slight, but attractive young woman who lived in their midst now was quite different from the haunted, gibbering creature that had arrived eighteen months before. Only Jerome had persevered with her. Only Jerome had, at first, gently wooed her into conversations. He had been attracted, but had never pursued her for selfish ends and had had no notion of falling for her. But now, having grown so used to her vague moments, her sudden changes of subject and her apparent oddness about men, he had come to love her voice and to need her companionship.

His bachelor existence was, from time to time, spiked with

sexual hunger, but loneliness was a greater problem and she had banished that. Even knowing she was but a short walk away comforted his nights. He knew that there was too great an age difference for them to have a proper relationship, and that he would have been a wholly unworthy partner, and one with dismal financial prospects. But he loved her nonetheless, with a full passion, both sexual and spiritual, and he hoped she would never go out of his life, even though she merely skimmed his stratosphere like a loosely bound satellite.

He was beginning to hatch a scheme in which Imogen could play a pretty central rôle. A scheme where, side by side, they could, possibly, develop a loving and working relationship. But he had to speak to the bishop.

Jerome picked up a note that had been pushed through the rectory door and re-read it.

Dear Jerome,

I'm not sure whether you know, but we will be making a television series on the village over the next few weeks and hope that you will be able to spare us a little of your valuable time to contribute. I'm not sure, yet, whether this will be as an interviewee or something behind the camera. Imogen is one of my researchers, and will probably talk to you about this before long.

See you about the village,

Regards,

Graham.

Jerome didn't know, precisely, what Graham's relationship was with Imogen, but he was pretty sure he was keen on her. He felt no jealousy about this, he told himself, just regret that he was not Graham's age, and therefore not eligible. But he hoped Graham was capable of looking after her and that his intentions were honourable. He liked the man, but you could never tell where sex was concerned, or rather, where sex ended and love began. Or should that have been the other way around? It was so complicated. Jerome groaned. However logical he tried to be about it all, he knew he couldn't really bear Graham to have Imogen. Then he felt guilty for thinking that way, and for thinking of Imogen as someone who could be possessed. 'God! What am I doing?' he asked aloud. 'And if I don't believe in Him, why am I invoking Him?' And that thought, uttered aloud, seemed so brazenly atheist – rather than agnostic – that it actually made his neck hairs stand up, and made him glance guiltily up at the ceiling, as if ready to receive the thunderbolt that would settle the question and damn him in a single stroke.

He turned to his text, crossed out the last sentence and wrote, *By giving up those things which we hold most dear, we gain. We gain the love of God. We gain the Divine Energy that will feed and sustain our spirits through times of temptation and bring us to salvation.* But the paper was still wet with the flower water and smudged so that it became almost illegible. 'Just as well,' Jerome said, picked up the phone and dialled. 'Daniels here, Wychgate Saint Peters. I need to speak to his Lordship, if he's available.' The female voice inquired what it might be about. Jerome answered promptly. 'Crisis of faith . . . not a parishioner's . . . mine.'

The Whitsun heatwave of 1926 was not sensational enough to be widely documented and followed too closely on the heels of the General Strike to be much remembered. Few in Wychgate had been affected by the strike, but most thought it a political outrage. Violet had been asked to go to Stoneford to help as a post office volunteer, but had refused. Even if eligible, she would not have been a member of the Trades Union Congress, and was certainly not a Socialist, but she felt that the miners' cause was just and that the general strike had, on the whole, been justified. When the TUC had caved in, she had felt sorrier for the miners' families than had anyone else in the village.

In spite of the excitement of recent political events, however, Violet's mind was almost wholly preoccupied with Michael. She had not seen him at all for the remainder of the Easter holidays. Peter had given her a large task in the stores that kept her indoors for hours at a stretch and even if she had been able to get out, she would not have looked for him. The morning after she and Michael had made their vows in the wood, Gerard had come to the shop, nodded to Violet and had said, 'I'd like to speak to your father. Alone.' She had gone, without a word, to the kitchen to send Peter out to the shop, and had stood by the half-open door, trying to catch what the two men were saying while her mother washed up breakfast dishes in the scullery.

'Mr Pilkington. Anything wrong?' Peter had put on his grocer's smile.

'Ah, Ball. I'll be brief.' He had leant forward slightly and lowered his voice, but she was able to hear him say, 'My son, it seems, has got himself rather hot under the collar about your daughter. I think it best if they don't see each other. I'm sure it's just a puppy thing, and he'll be safely back at Barleythorpe in a couple of weeks. But I think you'll understand.'

'Yes, sir, of course.'

'As you know, I'm very fond of Violet. I'd hate to see her studies come unstuck because of this. Perhaps she should take a couple of weeks off now, and come back to the manor on, what? Fifth of May? I'd like her to continue with our History Project. If you are willing, of course.'

'Of course, sir. We're very grateful for all your help. I'll tell her.'

'Much the better thing. You know what youngsters are like.' And he had walked out of the shop. She had cried, not openly but internally, until safely away from the shop and able to take refuge in her fragment of Pyson Wood. She had hoped he would come there, so that they could have a chance meeting.

To her surprise, the flowers of their tryst were still fresh on the cool altar stone. She picked up a couple of cowslips and then noticed near them, a whole violet plant, lifted from the woodland floor, its roots placed on a small pad of moss. She could not recall their having pulled the plant up and held it, devoid of flowers, to her nose to smell the violet fragrance of the leaves. There was a small twist of expensive, cream paper tucked among them. She unfolded it and read the note, written in pencil.

I knew you'd come back to our place. I knew, if you found the violet plant, you'd pick it up to smell the leaves. Father has forbidden me to see you and I cannot disobey.

These words were written in his bold, legible hand. The following sentences were rougher. The writing less regular, some of the letters gone over a second time

I will always love you. Wait for me.

It was not signed. How she had cried! She had folded the note and saved a cowslip and handful of violet leaves. These she had taken home and pressed into her prayerbook.

Weeks without Michael dragged, and Violet saw a long, lonely summer in prospect before going up to university in October. If she had wanted to stop seeing Gerard, she would have. She already had her place at Oxford, and all current learning and reading was really as much for enjoyment as for education. But she had the ghost of her *alter ego* to lay, or rather, to raise, since she had come to the conclusion that the only way she could divert his attention from herself was to re-kindle his feelings for the memory of his true wife. He had never really let out his grief. That was at the root of the problem and, poor naïve girl, she thought she could bring about the catharsis he needed, to purge his in-turned mind of nearly eighteen years of pain.

With Michael at school, and with the resumption of Violet's weekly study visits, Gerard had managed, almost, to push the problem of his son's claims of loving his protégée behind him. But now the long exeat was approaching, and he did not want his son to be tempted or, more likely, to be embarrassed by what would probably turn out to be an unwanted reunion. The two young people were unlikely to come across one another since Violet visited the manor on a Thursday and Michael would not cycle home for the exeat until Friday afternoon, and would leave again on Sunday evening, but during those few days, they would be in the same village. He knew that he could trust his son not to look for her, but he had no such confidence in Violet. Much as he loved her, he knew that her upbringing was different, and that the standards and morals of her class were less rigid. The possibility of a secret meeting between the two of them bubbled up in the calm of his mind like thunder clouds on a hot June afternoon. The thought of Violet in his son's arms, of Violet and Michael kissing, made him feel physically sick. It felt almost incestuous. He could not bear it to happen and knew he must ensure that they be kept apart.

He paid another visit to the village shop. This time Ball sympathised with the problem but was less cooperative. It was the weekend of his annual stock-taking, when all the family were expected to help and no, he could not let Violet off, and could not suggest where she might go for the weekend. He would, however, ensure that she was so busy in the shop, she would not have time to go looking for anyone, let alone young master Michael. Gerard was satisfied, but he would have been happier if the girl had gone away for a few days, or if Michael had gone to a friend for the exeat.

The eighteen-mile cycle ride was long in the dusty afternoon. Hay was almost a yard high in the meadows, the hedges creamy white with fading hawthorn blossom and the air sickly with its fragrance. Michael had taken the journey at a steady twelve miles per hour, never stopping, never slowing, even for hills, but never exerting himself on the level. He knew he could shave almost fifteen minutes off his journey time, if pushed, but the afternoon was too drowsy, and the air too warm to make much effort. He left at three. By four-thirty he was freewheeling into the village. He was not tired, but his body felt stiff and sweaty. He decided, before turning into the drive, to go on to the bottom of the village, to leave his bike by the hedge and, provided the bathing place was deserted, go for a dip.

When he got to the meadow, he realised that it would be difficult to reach the river because the hay was not yet mown. But he had so set his mind on swimming, that he decided to try to push his way through. The alternative was to take the central footpath right across the meadow to the small wood, and then to cut through to the river from there. It would be shorter, but would tread down some of the farmer's hay, and that would not be right. He scratched himself a couple of times, on the blackthorn hedge, and tore his shirt on a dog rose, but after much pushing and shoving, found the way along the hedge and through the blackthorn tunnel to the discreet bathing spot.

It was clear that no one had used the entrance for some time. The village boys would not begin swimming for a few weeks yet. Bathing by convention and date, rather than by weather, it would not have occurred to them to enter the water this early in the year, despite the heat-wave. The grassy river bank was warm and dry, in full afternoon sunshine and he lay for a few moments, enjoying the solitude. Then he sat up and began to take off his shirt. Shoes came next – pulled off without undoing the laces – and socks, revealing white, well-formed feet with clipped toenails. He undid his fly buttons and lowered grey flannel trousers folding them after removing them and, after a last furtive glance to left and right, and over shoulder, unbuttoned and slipped off his knitted cotton underpants and walked, naked, into the water. The cold caught him by surprise. He gasped, and then, with an exertion of will, lowered himself into the icy stream. The clear, cold water exhilarated him. It was lovely, splashing, jumping up and down, swimming the few strokes to either side of the small pool.

He swam and splashed about until he could bear the cold no more, and crawled out, remembering, then, that he had no means of drying himself. He decided to sit, in the sunshine, on the short grasses of the bank. In spite of the pleasant warmth of the afternoon, his exhilaration soon evaporated. The pain of being separated from Violet had barely receded all half-term, but he had been able to lose himself in work and sport. Cricket had got off to a difficult start – the school was short of good medium-pace bowlers – and that had helped to take his mind of their enforced parting. But now, after the relief of the cold water and the relaxing of muscles stiffened by the bike ride, he was beginning to realise that being here, so near her and yet forbidden to speak to her, would be unendurable. He uttered a low groan and spoke her name. ' Oh, Violet!'

In spite of both parents' precautions, it was pretty likely that they would have come together, and sooner rather than later. She had not planned to catch him. She did not try to make him disobey his father and she certainly had not intended to shame him or humiliate him. But she simply could not keep away. Catching sight of him as he coasted past the window, she had made an excuse and walked out of the shop, down the hill. She had watched him jump off his bicycle, right at the bottom of the village, and guessed he had decided to walk by the river before going home. Surprised that he chose the route along the hedge, she had planned almost to stalk him, just to see him, from the distance.

Keeping low, bent nearly double, in fact, she had moved along the footpath until she reached the safety of the great oak at the edge of the fragment of woodland. She saw his white shirt moving along the hedge, and then watched him duck and go through the twiggy tunnel. She crept nearer. It took some time, and soon she heard a splash, followed by his gasp. A series of splashes, little cries of delight, in his wonderful voice. Then the splashing stopped. She crept to the entrance and could just see the outline of his bare back as he sat facing the sun. A little closer and she could see the hair on his head, haloed in the sunlight. The tenderness she felt, the longing to stroke that golden head, was almost too much. Then she heard his groan of despair and her name, lovely on his lips.

'Oh, Violet!'

'I'm here, my love, I'm here.' She saw him start. Saw his back stiffen. She went through the gap, stooping below the canopied blackthorn, and before he could cover himself, before he could utter a cry of surprise, she stopped his mouth with hers. There were tears, of course, in both their eyes, but he forgot, for a moment, that he was naked.

'Don't move,' she admonished. I want to be the same as you.' She unbuttoned her boots, took off her belt, unbuttoned her blouse.

He began to be shocked. 'Violet, I—'

'Shh.' She removed her clothes deftly, folding them and placing them on top of his. He looked at her body. Its sanctity appalled him. This was forbidden. He saw where her breasts ended in russet nipples, her narrowed waist, rounded hips and buttocks and, after years of the boys' changing-room at Barleythorpe, the extraordinary absence at her crotch. Just a dark triangle; nothing else visible. She sat beside him. Her touch filled him with fright, making his skin grow goose flesh, but it also kindled a longing that he could only appease with his mouth. They kissed, his tongue creeping into her mouth, he kissed her neck, her breasts, her stomach. He could not prevent his fingers from exploring her groin, and when she flinched, he cursed himself for being so clumsy. Though focusing entirely on her, he could sense that his penis was strongly engorged, but he knew there was no need to feel shame. She stroked the inside of his thigh, and then held it, gently tugging him towards her.

'Come into me, Michael,' she whispered into his ear. 'But do it gently.'

Afterwards, they lay in each other's arms until evening advanced and they began to feel cold. He noticed her wince slightly, as she got up to dress. 'Did I hurt you?'

'Only a little, my love. I suppose it does, first time.' The first time! He realised, with sinking spirits, that he would be back at school the day after tomorrow, that he had Sandhurst and she had Oxford. He felt as though they were victims of a conspiracy to keep them apart. He helped her with her clothes and quickly dressed himself. They walked, neither consulting the other but both knowing, to the small wood, and up to the altar stone. Here they knelt, just as they had when they vowed loyalty, and embraced.

'You have defied your father for me,' she said.

'I never want to be away from you,' Michael said. 'Let's run away together.'

She held him tighter and cried. 'Michael, we cannot, we cannot.'

He kissed her again, and stroked her dark hair. 'I know.'

'But we can meet tomorrow. I'm not working in the afternoon.' They held each other for a while longer, and then walked slowly back to the footpath. Violet hung back, giving him time to collect his bicycle before she walked up to the stores.

On Saturday, there were more people at large in the village so they needed to be more careful. He walked to the wood straight after lunch but she was already there. They found a concealed spot at the back of the clearing where cowparsley, taking advantage of the sunlight, had established a small, aromatic stand of dense ferny foliage and lacy blooms. Here, each luxuriated in the other's body. Neither had seen anyone of the opposite sex without clothes before. He marvelled at her contours and wanted to kiss every part of her, noticing, as he did, both the scent she wore, and her natural fragrance.

She loved him as an entire being – his laugh, his features, his gentle kindness. But his body, if she had imagined it at all, was more glorious to her than she could have hoped. The smallness, and neatness of his buttocks she found exciting and, though she might have been repelled by an excess of hirsuteness, she loved the straw-coloured hairs on his chest which, now and then, she caught between her lips and tugged. His thighs were hard, from active sports, and she loved that, but she was not yet used to the sight of male genitals. They seemed so unnecessarily complicated, ruining the sleek lines of his body. She felt his penis grow, as she held it. That was very exciting. As if she had some sort of control over it.

'How come they're always so much smaller on statues?' Violet asked. Michael didn't know. They lay together for some time and then, as evening came, the temperature fell and hunger motivated them, they began to dress. It was time for their short honeymoon to end.

'We have to wait until July,' Violet said, tearful. 'I can hardly bear it.'

'Nor I,' Michael's voice choked. 'But we have to be strong.'

They came out of their cowparsley patch, the plants now somewhat crushed, and knelt for a last time, by the altar, facing each other and holding hands.

'Is what we have done wrong?' Michael asked.

'Do you feel that it is?' He shook his head.

'I love you.' The words tripped off his tongue, but not with the glibness of the loyal husband. There was still an enormity to them that dwarfed him. Then he changed key. 'Society would condemn us, and the Church. We are not married.'

'But we are, in our way, by our vows made here.' She looked carefully around the tiny woodland clearing. The tree tops, dark now, against a violet evening sky, nodded. 'These spirits are our witnesses and our wedding guests. They are our congregation.'

Never had Wychgate seen such drama. As the small team of archaeologists moved out of the fragment of ancient woodland, the tree-felling team moved in. So did the demonstrators. Busby had worked feverishly to get support to try to prevent further removal of the conifers of Pyson Wood, but his achievement had been dwarfed by a tiny item on local television news. In the process of making his series, *The Countryside in Crisis*, Graham Ball had alerted BBC news departments to the opposed plans for Wychgate. As it stood, the story was pretty bland but the news department was soon able to twist it, giving the impression that developers had thrown the archaeologists out, rather than wait for them to finish their investigations. The story was even fed to national television news and got a short mention on the main evening bulletins. Soon reporters and hoards of demonstrators began to arrive at the village. All the conservation pressure groups were there, and not a few spectators.

Graham was delighted. The results of his careful placing of information had worked perfectly, and now he had the opportunity to shoot plenty of dramatic footage. It was the kind of thing that would bring his documentary series to life. Nothing better, to demonstrate a crisis, than to have screaming people, insulting one another, and hurling themselves, body and soul, against the establishment. The weather was a little awkward. Sunshine and showers. That made things very difficult when they came to edit because, if some scenes were shot in sunshine, and others in rain or dull weather, they would not be able to mix and match different bits of different takes to make it more exciting, to tone up the violence or slant the shooting the way he wanted. He warned the single camera crew, and his production assistant, and Imogen, standing by as researcher, to be extra careful about continuity.

'Oh, I, ahm, I think I ought to be right out of this one.' Imogen had said. 'It's far too close to home.' And she had fled.

Gilmore said goodbye to the archaeologists and then, with a hand signal, instructed the two JCBs to start their engines. The last of the trees that made the thicket to the north of the ancient fragment were too densely planted to be of commercial use and were simply to be bulldozed out of the way. The ancient fragment was to be left intact, but bereft of any surrounding timber. When the plumes of smoke issued from the exhaust pipes of the diggers, and the roar of their engines was heard across the muddy expanse that had been the bulk of the wood, the demonstrators began to move. Some were aimless, wondering where to put themselves. Others, mostly members of Earthlove, Natural Alliance and other ecological organisations, moved with precision, forming a line in front of the machines and then sitting, with arms locked together.

Ernest Busby, who had hitherto run from group leader to group leader, alternately giving orders and then counter-manding them now began to shout to his small handful of local protesters – actually only five in all – to join the what he called the main picket line. Graham Ball, who was nearby with his camera crew overheard this and said to Busby, 'I'm surprised you want to be included in something called a "picket line", a hard-bitten anti-union man like yourself.' Busby ignored the taunt and ran off to a group of spectators to try to get them to join the demo. They shook their heads and laughed at his suggestion. A minibus with fourteen policemen was parked on the lane. These now emerged and began to march in formation to the line of demonstrators. Other police vehicles were drawing up in the village, obstructing the road. 'Where's your law and order now, Busby?' Graham asked.

It was over pretty quickly. As the JCBs advanced, the police helped the sitting demonstrators to their feet and out of the way. Tree-dozing began. Within a few minutes, a growing heap of small, starved conifers was forming at the west end of the wood. One more sweep and the ancient woodland would be exposed.

The accident might have been avoided, if the driver of the inner JCB had been a little more alert. As it was, the last thing he expected was to see someone jump out of the thickest part of the undergrowth right into his path. The old man had been dressed in army camouflage and had obviously intended not to be seen until the last minute. He had also not given any regard to his own safety. Indeed, he seemed to want to kill himself. With as much effort as he could muster, he had simply launched himself out of the thicket and on to the bucket of the advancing digger. His leg was trapped underneath the metal and broken; his head hit the upper rim of the bucket, hard enough to injure him quite seriously, but no one could tell, at that stage, whether or not the blow had been fatal.

Instantly, the engines stopped, the demonstrators re-grouped and stood quietly. After what seemed an age, the Stoneford ambulance arrived and trundled over the dried ruts of the cleared woodland. The inert body, surprisingly light, was lifted gently onto a stretcher. A paramedic inside took the wrist in his hand and shook his head. Then the vehicle began its slow journey towards the town.

Imogen, Graham, Jerome and the camera crew stood by the television production company's van. People were beginning to go home. Later, the diggers would finish their job but this was not quite the right time. Gilmore was too sensitive to allow that.

Hands, who had kept away the whole time now arrived on the scene. He walked up to Imogen.

'All a waste of time, as it 'appens,' he said. 'Plannin' Consent's been refused. We've 'ad it.'

PART THREE

NUNC DIMITTIS

Chapter Fifteen

———◆———

Guy Fawkes Night. For once there was harmony in Wychgate Saint Peters, as the whole village – with one or two exceptions – turned out to enjoy the drama of bonfire, rockets and Roman candles. Wychgate had no tradition of celebrating the Gunpowder Plot of 1605 and most of the villagers would have felt that letting off fireworks, even if they had been cheap, would be a complete waste of money, and at current prices, it was dafter than burning banknotes. Someone else had offered to pay for these, however, and as there was no admission fee, everyone came along to enjoy the display.

And what a display! The original idea had been Jerome's. He had suggested to Imogen that perhaps a way to get back into the village's good books – if she wanted to – might be to make some kind of gesture of goodwill. She had thought about that for months, but could come up with no idea of what kind of gesture until walking up the hill with Jerome, after church on the last Sunday in September, she had received inspiration from him. He had pointed to the piles of brushwood and waste timber on the site of the wood and asked what she planned to do about them.

'Oh, ahm, they'll be piled up and burnt,' she had replied. 'All the usable wood has been taken away.'

'Then why not save it for bonfire night?'

Graham Ball had suggested raising funds for fireworks – he wanted to shoot footage of a country fireworks display for his television series – but no one on the Parochial Church Council or any of the village committees felt able to sanction such frivolous expenditure. Graham had then managed to work a small allowance out of his television programme budget and, wanting to neutralise a little of her unpopularity, Imogen had matched the fund with a similar amount from her own bank account. The result, on this mild, dark night with the gentlest of westerly breezes taking all the smoke and gunpowder smell away as it was generated, was a display that delighted everyone.

Michael Pilkington was not at the wood. After almost eleven weeks in Kendale hospital, the bones of his leg and contusions on his skull had slowly knitted and mended, but the wounds to his psyche continued to fester. For the remains of summer, after he had been brought home to his manor, he hobbled about with crutches, or was wheeled in a borrowed invalid chair by a full-time nurse. She helped him to feed himself and assisted him with such necessary functions as bathing and dressing but, when his physical recovery was more or less complete and her period of appointment came to an end, he was left to his own devices. He would speak to no one in the village and, after a few rebuttals, no one dared make any further attempts to visit him. He began to neglect himself, seldom taking any form of exercise and failing to give himself an adequate diet. Sometimes, especially on wet days, he was unable to find the motivation to get out of bed, and even when he did rise, he would spend hours in his study, staring at the dead ashes in the fireplace or gazing at *The Times*, open but unread, on his knees. Now that winter was setting in, his house grew cold in its bones, but he seldom lit a fire and had forgotten to order oil for his central heating system.

Ernest Busby had intended to boycott the fireworks but had changed his mind at the last minute. He had felt that Graham had been too high-handed, taking over the organisation of the event without consulting the proper people, and he would not speak to Imogen at all anyway, after all the damage she had done. Her original plan, for no more than three houses, was still to go ahead and he had sworn undying opposition to that, but he was in the minority. The relief of not having to watch the village spoilt by forty new homes springing up in its midst had been so intense to the anti-lobby, that they had, almost to a man, sanctioned the reduced proposal. But not Busby. He and his two-man *junta* were still intending to fight any development plans every inch of the way. The next step in their campaign was to question the builder on the matter of the drains. Busby thought they could prove that septic tanks would be unsafe this near the river. With the fight still on, he had felt it politic to try to persuade people to boycott the bonfire night celebrations. But when he realised that most – if not all – were looking forward to the event, he decided to go himself, after all, and began to turn the facts so that he could acquire as much credit as possible for the whole affair. One or two villagers, who recognised his face in the light of the bonfire flames, acknowledged him and offered congratulations.

'Yes,' he replied, several times, 'we thought the parish deserved a bit of a treat. That's why the committee gave permission for this.'

Imogen stayed in the shadows, wanting to speak to no one. After looking forward, with some pleasure, to the night, now it had come, she was troubled. The morning's meeting with Hands seemed to have cast a shadow of gloom that, for her, doused the hilarity of whooping boys, throwing sticks on to the fire, of laughing adults, crowing with delight at shell bursts of green, red, silver and blue stars; at rockets that hissed skywards and exploded in scintillating showers and at catapulted sparks that look insignificant, but that exploded like cannons, with a blue-white flash that showed before the sound reached their ears. Until the news broke – that the whole wretched business was starting all over again – Imogen had not fully appreciated the enormous relief she had felt when planning consent for the forty houses had been turned down. Now it was all back in the melting pot, she wasn't sure whether she could go through with it. Seeing people beginning to come her way, she moved back a little to stand closer to the ancient trees of Pyson Wood. Their shadows made a denser blackness in the night and, though the wood fragment rather gave her the creeps, she was glad she had preserved it. The feeling that emanated from the centre of that group of trees was strange. It should have been frightening but rather, it made her feel uneasy, uncomfortable, as if someone were looking at her, almost as if someone were trying to capture her attention. When she felt the hand take hold of her elbow she uttered a little breathless scream. With all the noise by the fire, nobody heard. She turned, to face her attacker but as she did he spoke and she recognised Russell Hands.

'You ain't told 'em yet, then?' She was too startled to speak for a while but stood, trying to see him in the darkness. Not being able to see his hands, or the expression on his face was unnerving. 'Prob'ly just as well. All hell's gonna break loose wiv 'em when they find out.'

'Russell, I . . .' She wanted to say that she didn't want to go through with it all. Not again. But, really, she had made up her mind that she needed the capital. If she was to get rid of the Crowe and to set herself up with a reasonable standard of living, she would have to go through with it. At one stage, she had thought of moving, probably back to London, but since then, she had been developing the garden at Wychgate, and she liked the anonymity there, where villagers actually made a point of leaving her to her own devices. Occasionally, the press would try to contact her and from time to time she had seen young men she was sure were reporters, lurking about the village but by and large, she seemed to be forgotten by everyone and that suited her. In London, she could not be sure that the nightmare of her other life might not surface and give her problems.

'You what?' Hands squeezed her elbow but she pushed his hand off.

'I want to get it over quickly. I want to sell the whole thing to you now. Lock, stock and barrel.'

'Negative.' He took her arm again, more gently this time. 'I've got the partnership's financing all fixed up, girl.'

'I don't care. I'll . . . I'll halve the price.' That made him stiffen. At less than half a million, he could finance the rest of the project more easily, *and* keep all the profit. She'd really served her purpose, adding respectability, with her title, to the appeal. He'd got what he wanted.

'You serious?'

She realised she was probably giving away a fortune, half a million or more. She dithered. 'I, ahm, I'm not . . . sure.'

Impatiently, he pushed her elbow away with an exasperated snort. 'Look, girl. If you ain't got the bottle, *I* 'ave. All you've gotta do is tell this lot tomorrow, or wait 'til it 'its the local paper.'

The last salvo of rockets went up with a whoosh, like the tearing of a hundred yards of calico. Imogen heard her name called and then three slightly embarrassed cheers called across the field, each one a little louder and more assured than the one before. She would have to tell them. But not tonight.

Next morning, Jerome called early at Busby's house, but found out that he had already left for his office. He would be back late in the evening. Jerome was disappointed. His whole day was coloured by the unnerving prospect of having to tell Busby, chapter and verse, of what Imogen had told him: that when planning had been refused by the local authority, Saint Peter Properties Limited had appealed to the Department of the Environment who had, after some four months' consideration, reversed the local authority decision. Forty homes would now be built, with all the necessary infrastructure of roadways and, as before, a sewage processing unit, down by the river, just upstream from where the boys' bathing place had once been. Jerome, uncomfortable with Busby at the best of times, was dreading this meeting.

Michael lay awake, covered only by a sheet. Agincourt, the only dormitory on the ground floor of the House, was well lit, with large windows, all of which could be opened, but the night was still and sticky. In all his years at boarding school, Michael had never, until now, been unable to sleep. The sounds and smells of the dormitory, the animal companionship, had always been more comforting to him than his lonely bedroom at home in Wychgate. It had never even occurred to him that a dormitory might be a noisy place. But now, with the air so still and so stale, he felt hardly able to tolerate so noisy nor so noisome a place. Around him, boys were breathing regularly, some snoring, others occasionally muttering in their sleep, or turning over, or farting. Earlier, he had detected the swift, accelerating hand strokes of someone quietly casting off under the bedclothes. He felt sympathy with the boy's frustration for, whenever he thought of Violet, his own member would swell to an aching hardness. And yet, he knew it would be wrong to, as Dreggie would put it, pollute himself: wrong to himself, perhaps, but definitely wrong to Violet. But when he did sleep, his dreams were so full of Violet, and of the scene, re-lived, by the river, that frequently, he awoke after a shuddering climax, with sticky belly and feelings, not of shame and guilt, but of a crushing sadness that she was not in his arms and would not be for weeks.

By day, after such restless nights, his performance was beginning to suffer. He had not played cricket at all well this season and there was even talk of swapping places with his Vice Captain for a match or two. School work was going reasonably, but he had to struggle to keep alert, especially in Dreggie's classes which were always in the afternoon, and always numbingly boring. He felt jumpy and restless in class but lethargic and slow-witted on the sports field. The company of other boys dispirited him as never before, and he felt odd, out of sorts with them, even with his closer companions. Riversley had been quick to notice this and invited his confidence.

'It's a girl, isn't it?' he had said, when he and Michael were changing after a game of fives. Riversley, whom Michael usually beat, but never by a very wide margin, had thrashed his great friend. Even when he had let up a bit, and allowed Michael to score an extra point or two, the pair were not evenly matched and that was unusual. Michael had not answered but had shrugged and dressed quickly, to get away.

As the term progressed, Michael became more able to cope with his separation from Violet. He forced himself to concentrate in class, and went into training for sports with a self-mortification that seemed almost masochistic. He got into the habit of rising an hour before breakfast, and taking himself off for long cross-country runs. Riversley, anxious about his greatest friend, offered to get up and come with him for company. At first, Michael refused, hurting Riversley with his brusqueness. Then their eyes met and Michael, seeing the anxiousness in the other boy's face, agreed, and they had begun a daily routine of running two miles before school, and then of swimming at least eight lengths of the school swimming bath before evening prep. Both were in the peak of fitness, but whereas Riversley had a wolf-like appetite, and slept soundly at night, Michael's pining continued and he began to lose weight.

My mid-June, he was able to slip two fingers between collar and neck on what had been his tightest and least comfortable shirt. Then, one morning, just as the two boys were setting out across the playing fields to the edge of town, on their daily run, Michael's steps faltered and he fell. In a second, Riversley was down with him, first putting Michael's head between his knees, then gently slapping his cheeks. Before he came fully to, Michael cried out and wept, briefly. Riversley felt his heart would burst for his friend. Within a moment, though, Michael had come fully round.

'What's going on?' he enquired.

'You tell me,' Riversley said, his own pockmarked face pale, his eyes wide with concern.

'What? Oh nothing. Must be lack of breakfast.'

'Pilks, you've *got* to tell me.' The pleading tone of Riversley's voice made Michael look at him more closely.

'Rivers? Have you been blubbing? I do believe your have!'

'Michael, don't be unfair. It simply isn't you.' Riversley's use of his Christian name had the necessary effect. Coming from his housemaster, it sounded unctuous, but from his classmate, it sounded solemn, heralding an important moment where confidences were expected to be exchanged.

'Do you swear to keep this utterly to yourself?'

'Michael, how *could* you think anything other?'

'All right, um, Edward, all right.' And Michael, in the space of about five minutes, while they both sat on the dewy grass at the edge of the outfield, told his friend all about Violet. Everything he told was true, but he censored his story. This was no recounting of a sexual conquest, and what actually happened between him and his love was no one else's business. But Riversley now knew the depth of Michael's involvement. He felt a mixture of envy and jealousy – he had had no luck in attracting girls yet – and these feelings made an acrid contrast to the admiration and, one supposes, love that he had for his great friend. 'But you will keep counsel, Edward?'

'Michael, I swear it.' After that, Michael's pining was no less acute, but it comforted him to know that he need not face the whole thing alone, that he had a sympathetic ear. And now, at one in the morning, with a waxing moon shining through the curtainless windows on to his face, Michael took comfort in Riversley's closeness. He would trust him with his life. Raising himself on one elbow, he glanced at the sleeping form, one arm stretched out above the sheet and extended half-way across the space that divided the beds. On an impulse, Michael took hold of the hand. Riversley stirred in his sleep and Michael felt his fingers gently squeezed before he extricated his hand, turned over and, at last, slipped into a dreamful sleep.

'A bird in the hand, dear,' said Mrs Crowe. 'Your decision, of course, but just remember that what goes up can come down.' She was standing at the edge of the lawn while Imogen, on her hands and knees, cut back perennials. Mrs Crowe never gardened. A week had passed since the firework display. Everyone knew about the revived plans and, as before, Imogen was *persona non grata* in Wychgate. The difference, now, was that people seemed to know they were beaten.

Busby had had all the fight knocked out of him and had run out of ideas on how to combat the appalling situation. He even thought of getting out of Wychgate while the going was good. Graham's last episode of *The Countryside in Crisis,* to be shot over the next couple of weeks, was to take the form of a kind of epitaph for his own village. He, too, had thought of putting the Old Stores on the Market and, though she did not yet know it, he was developing a plan for the future that involved living somewhere else, possibly in north Norfolk, since that was still largely unspoilt, with Imogen as his partner or perhaps even his bride.

Imogen, however, was getting used to the idea of living in a busy village with some two hundred more inhabitants. She had no intention at all of moving anywhere, since her house and garden were becoming her main loves. Her period of abject submission to Mrs Crowe was over and had been replaced by an uneasy association which both knew, would not last beyond the completion of their mutual business aims. Imogen would be happy alone. This she knew. Sometimes she missed her father; constantly she felt guilty about what she had done, but Family was behind her – as if she had died and gone on to another life, which, of course, she had. Meanwhile, she had to admit that, unintelligent and lumpen though the Crow might be, she had plenty of low cunning, and that was what was needed, particularly when dealing with an animal like Russell Hands.

'If I sell now, I stand to make about four hundred thou.'

'More, dear. The price has gone up, remember.'

'Oh I'd stick to the original, ahm, price.'

'But what about inflation?'

'There hasn't been much.'

'There has in houses. This one is worth more than twice what you gave. In two years!'

'Well, I wouldn't go more than about twelve thousand a site.'

'Even at that pitiful rate, you'd gross nearly half a million. Cash.'

'But if I wait, and share the building with him, I could make several million.'

'Once you've sold all the houses.'

'Oh yah, of course.'

'Like I said, dear, a bird in the hand.'

'But houses are selling like hot-cakes. Someone paid, ahm sixty thousand for little more than a cupboard in Knightsbridge.'

'Wychgate is not exactly a stone's throw from Harrods.

Are you sure you could sell forty little boxes at a hundred thousand or more each? There's no bus here, remember, no post office and no pub.'

By Thursday, when Hands was due, Imogen had made up her mind. 'I'm reverting to my original plan,' she told him, confident with Mrs Crowe by her side in the drawing-room of Weir House.

'Yeah?' Hands failed to register any surprise. He had been expecting this. He'd have to phase the building and finance over a longer spell. No problem. 'You must be stupid, throwing away a couple of million like that.'

'So all we have to do now is fix, for the final time, the selling price,' said Mrs Crowe.

'What? But it is fixed.'

'Almost,' said Imogen, 'I want twelve, ahm, thousand, per plot.'

'Jesus, woman, that's another eighty grand to find. Do you *know* what's happening to interest rates at the moment? They could kill the market.'

'Which,' said Mrs Crowe, 'is precisely why we're sure you'll want to exchange at once and close the deal.'

'Oh, I'm in no hurry.'

'But we are. And there are other companies interested.'

'Never!'

'Does the name Beales mean anything – Beales Homes?'

'Buggeration!' Hands had not meant to react, but mention of his strongest rival rattled him. Once before, Beales had shown a little more vision than he, and had taken a trick. Ever since, he had followed every move his competitor made with obsessive attention. Hands knew that the housing market was getting too volatile, that things could overheat, that a lot of people with big commitments could get their fingers burnt. But he also knew that this was a good development. As long as he hurried, he could get this one up and running and start to bring revenue in before the crash, if there were to be a crash. And he'd keep one step ahead of that bastard Beales. He assented.

Once the verbal agreements were completed, the legal work followed with alacrity. To her utter amazement, Imogen found that she had succeeded in selling off the twenty-five acre site, with ancient wood – encumbered with a lengthy tree preservation order – and cleared land bordering the river Dene.

Within another six weeks, just after Christmas, the enormous cheque was cleared and Mrs Crowe had been paid off and gone, taking all the silver out of her bedroom and her large commission. There were no fond farewells. Imogen knew that with her funds, she could now protect herself. The older woman believed she had milked Imogen and her family enough to have generated sufficient capital to begin her own enterprise. There was much demand, she had discovered, for old people's homes which, it was said, were highly profitable to run. Furthermore, she suspected that there would be further rich pickings, if one admitted only the weakest and wealthiest as inmates.

Imogen was wealthy again. Not knowing what to do with such a huge sum she put it on a high-interest, short-term money market and was amazed to see that in three months, her four hundred thousand would make her a profit of almost eleven thousand. In a year, she would have recovered the Crowe's commission.

On the fourteenth of January, when it was too cold to go into the garden, she sat brooding by the fire in the sitting-room. She had not realised quite how much work Crowe had done about the house and, though it was wonderful to be rid of her bullying ways, she felt rather lonely. She was wondering whether to get up to make herself a pot of tea when the phone rang.

'Imogen? Immie?' The tone was plummy, Sloaney 'This is Rupert Lilliwhite.'

'Rupert! He*leah!*' She heard her own voice click into an upper class bray in response to his patrician tones. She had spoken to no one outside the village, besides Hands, for over a year. Crow had always manned the phone, indeed, Imogen had only just discovered that the bell on her drawing-room extension had been turned off ever since she had arrived at Wychgate.

'Imogen, your father has asked me to ring.' Lilliwhite

faltered for a moment. 'Immie, I know you've rather been been through it lately. And I . . . um . . . I'm really sorry to have to tell you this, but I'm afraid your mother has just died.'

'Who?' said Imogen.

Chapter Sixteen

———

Mr Danvers always insisted on 'lights out' at ten-fifteen, even in Agincourt, where the average age of occupant was sixteen years and four months. Normally, this was an irritation, although the boys were so active during the day that the majority of them were sound asleep within fifteen minutes of darkness descending. Tonight, Michael counted it a blessing. He had plans. Only Riversley knew about them, and only he because of the risk involved.

Michael waited until the dormitory was quiet, then he felt for Riversley's hand, in the dying light of the evening, and squeezed it for a moment before slipping out of bed and closing the dormitory door quietly behind him. In one of the cubicles of the boys' lavatory, he hastily shed pyjamas and pulled on the cycling pantaloons and shirt that he had stuffed down his front. The next move was the most dangerous. Dreggie usually wandered from dorm to dorm a couple of times before retiring and an encounter in the corridor would have been disastrous. He waited, listened and, when satisfied that the house was completely silent, slipped out of the side entrance to the bicycle shed. He had leant his bike just inside the door that afternoon, and hoped it would have been left untouched and accessible. It was. He wheeled it to the gate and, as the last of the daylight was replaced by a rising moon, slipped down Barleythorpe High Street and on to the main road, gathering speed as he went, pushing his feet harder and harder on the pedals, determined to cover the ground in as fast a time as possible.

What he was doing was folly. He risked expulsion, disgrace at home and, cycling this fast, at night without lights, he was in physical danger as well. But he had to do something to wipe away the pain of being kept from her. He pedalled frantically until, after half an hour, a cramp in his thigh told him to pace himself more judiciously. Luckily the wind was on his back and, in the moonlight, he had the sensation of flying.

The journey seemed to be taking for ever but, whenever he looked at his watch, only minutes had ticked by. When he finally pedalled, at top speed, down the main street of Wychgate Saint Peters, his watch registered one minute to midnight. He had completed eighteen miles in one hour and seventeen minutes. An average speed, he worked out, of nearly fifteen miles per hour. By now, the moon had risen enough to illuminate the pathway across the meadow. The hay had been cut, turned and had dried rapidly in the heatwave. Now it was piled into a series of haycocks, waiting to be carted and stacked in the farmer's yard. He lifted his bike over the stile and re-mounted, to pedal towards the wood.

He could not explain why, but he had known she'd be there all the time. He had told himself, at first, cycling along the streets and suburbs of Barleythorpe, and later, on the long hill up through the limestone villages and then down along the rim of the huge Cranston estate, that she was receiving his thought messages; that she would know; that she was sure to be there. And with each mile, the possibility that she might not be there diminished until, as he dismounted near the little wood, he was ready to greet her. He laid his bike on the grass, near the path so that it would be easy to find again, even if the moon went behind a cloud, and walked quietly into the wood. The altar stone lay ahead, catching the moon's rays, shining dully, like pewter in candlelight. The wood was deserted.

All the frenzied activity of the preceding hour seemed, now, to have been a complete waste of time. As rational thoughts began to intrude into his romantic fantasy, he realised that the likelihood of a young girl slipping out of her house in the middle of the night to wander in the wood, was a pretty remote one. He cursed his folly. He wished he could be rid of his obsessiveness about her but he so badly wanted to see her.

There was a certain fragrance, weak but constant on the air that made him catch his breath. It was not from a flower, but its redolence caught his breath and made his pulse quicken. He could not tell where it came from, but it seemed to increase as he approached the altar stone itself. He approached the stone and then walked behind, absently pulling at the foliage of the tall weeds that grew there. Cowparsley! With the strength of fragrance from the crushed stems, memories of their afternoon together among the herb came flooding into his mind with such strength that he felt he had to sit, to lie among the plants, to re-live those few beautiful moments, those tiny hours that had sped like seconds. Those dashing fragments of time had stopped for them, had held them both suspended: he, breathing in her presence, listening to her voice grown husky with love for him; she, warm in his arms, musky with love for him. Michael felt the ferny foliage caress his cheeks and thought, she is here! Her spirit, her *essence* is here, with me now. He knew, at that moment, she was awake and thinking about him. He *knew*.

He began to stand up, ready to leave the little wood when he realised, with an icy grasp of fright, that he was not alone. Someone was standing, not twenty, barely ten yards away, at the edge of the clearing. The shadows were too dark to be able to discern any features, in fact the outline was so indistinct that he wondered whether he was imagining this vision. Violet's talk of ghostly witnesses and congregations in this supposedly hallowed place had stimulated all sorts of fanciful ideas but no, the figure had moved; it was there! He sank down again, afraid that it might be someone from the village who would recognise him and even more afraid that what he saw might not be a person at all. The figure moved into the clearing, came up to the altar and, with a surge of relief, he saw that it was, unmistakably, Violet. He recognised her gait, her profile in the moonlight, and her voice as she murmured, 'not alone'. He was ready to leap out of his hiding place and into her arms but was loath to frighten her. Also, he wanted, for a few moments, to savour his joy at seeing her. He *knew* she would come and, clearly, she had expected him, for now she raised her head and seemed to be trying to scan the dark herbage. 'Not alone,' she repeated, dreamily, to the shadows, 'You'll see.' She held out her arms and spoke again, softly, confidentially, 'We must join hands.'

He wanted to jump up, to shout for joy and throw his arms around her, but the reverence in her tone touched an instinct that made him keep still for a second or two longer. The moment had a sacred feeling, in this special place, and he felt awed. What force could have brought them together in such a spot and at such an unlikely time? What could have influenced his level-headed nature to such an extent that, for the last few hours he had been driven by a string of irrational impulses, riding through the dark at reckless speed and risking expulsion for breaking out of school at night? In those seconds, he realised he was witnessing, no, he was taking part in a miracle.

Then he felt the physical shock of surprise in his body before his brain understood. He froze half-standing, half-kneeling, but not heeding the pain in his calf and thigh muscles. She was not talking to him. She was not talking to her spirits, or to the trees, or to herself. Someone else was there. The second figure to emerge from the shadows was not only larger – obviously a man – but more furtive, apparently worried about being detected. He approached the altar stone hesitantly. They both knelt, facing each other, just as she and Michael had done weeks before. A chill gripped his spine, running from groin to scalp and making the hairs on his neck bristle; he stopped breathing and bit his lip so hard that his teeth punctured the ruddy skin and were stained by the drop of dark blood that swelled on them. He could not tell whether the metallic taste in his mouth came from shock or from the blood.

The man held out his hands. He began to whisper, gripping Violet's hands. Michael strained to hear and recognised that the snuffling sounded almost like weeping and, as his ears adjusted, he could make out occasional whispered words.

Then the voice was raised, and he knew how sour and corrupt was the core of his miracle.

'Elizabeth? Oh, Violet! Violet . . .' Michael heard his father say, but then his head began to swim and he sank back on to his knees. The blackness that swelled before his eyes blotted out the greyer darkness of the night and there was such a pounding of his pulse that he felt the blood vessels in his neck might burst. Any sound, now was smudged out by a hissing roar in his ears. A little time passed – seconds, minutes, Michael had no idea – but he found himself on all fours with his head held low and tried to make himself breathe normally. The hurt was profound, he knew, and yet a numbness crept over him now, giving a temporary blankness to his feeling. Only a part of his brain seemed to work, as if giving the rest of him instructions from the outside.

He had to get away, to run. But he had to be so silent. He *must* not be detected. Creeping, still on all fours, hardly daring to breathe, he managed to get back to his bicycle unnoticed and was soon pedalling, flat out, across the field. He barely stopped at the stile, hurling his machine over and vaulting after it. He was almost blind, his tear-blurred eyes hurting in the head wind. He barely knew the effort he was making, as if his body was simply a machine, pedalling on its own while his mind howled. It was a long, long journey back to Barleythorpe.

While he waited for his tea, Rupert Lilliwhite took stock of the room. He had been told to expect a mess, but here was order. He had been told that Imogen would probably be irrational, but here was reason. He had been warned that she would probably be raving with withdrawal symptoms, or would be on a high of some kind, but here was a girl in full possession of all her faculties. And, oddest of all, he had been told she'd be protected from the worst of her excesses by a formidable minder, yet here she was living alone and coping very well. The garden outside was bleak, in midwinter duns and browns, but was well-maintained, with clipped hedges, neat shrubs and the climbing plants on walls of the house all carefully trained and tied in. In the drawing-room, the oak floorboards between the Persian rugs were well polished, the cushions and upholstery plumped and fresh flowers – snowdrops and winter aconites, obviously plucked that day from the garden – stood in a tiny silver vase on the table beneath the window. Rupert could detect their faint honey scent. There were books in the bookshelves, quite a lot on gardening, he noticed and, open on the low table by the sofa, a hardcover copy of *The Remains of the Day*, propped open with a copy of the *Royal Horticultural Society Journal*. Imogen's entry startled him. Spotting the large tea tray she was carrying, he leapt to his feet to help.

'I'm not quite used to all this, ahm, domestic thing,' she said. 'I've lost my helper.' Rupert watched her pour tea, hold out cup and saucer – thin, almost translucent porcelain. Sèvres? Worcester? 'Just as well, really, I'm pretty sure she was pinching things.' She pointed to a covered silver muffin dish. 'Ahm, not muffins, I'm afraid. Crumpets, though they seem to call them pikelets round here for some reason. Help yourself. Oh!' She emitted a little laugh and clapped hand to mouth. 'I've forgotten to butter them.' She leapt up and left the room again. Rupert watched her leave. He had not spent time on his own with her before but had known her since his early teens.

He had never, until now, understood why Marcus had been so besotted. At Eton, he hadn't seemed very interested in girls at all; in fact his obsession with nature had always been regarded with suspicion by the other boys, as if, in itself, it had been some kind of perversion. Why would anyone have wanted to lie about in long grass studying beetles if not for some strange sexual dalliance? But later, just after Cambridge, when he and Marcus had both managed to get fixed up with jobs at the City, Marcus had changed so much. He had always been obsessive about things, cycling for miles, Sunday after Sunday to the same spot, quartering a hundred acres or more of farmland, searching for some elusive wild orchid that was reported to have grown there, but never obsessive about people. Then, during the endless round of parties of their early twenties, Marcus had been introduced to Imogen. He had been warned, by several close friends, that she had a 'problem' but this had made him keener. Gradually, he became less fun, attaching himself to her and excluding others, even Rupert. He chucked his job but really, Rupert had heard only days before, he would have been sacked. He was hardly ever at the bank anyway, and the days, even of the richest merchant banks carrying salaried passengers, however nobly born and whatever status they might bring to the establishment, were fast going. Rupert had lost track, then, of both Marcus and Imogen. After their over-publicised wedding, they had dropped out of the social circle completely, but occasionally, a note or two appeared in the gossip pages of the tabloids. The last time Rupert had seen Marcus was near Saint Bride's church, where he'd attended a memorial service for another Etonian who had become a foreign correspondent and had been killed in a road accident in Durban.

After the service, Rupert had fallen in with a small group who planned to lunch at a new wine bar quite close, behind the Old Bailey. It had been a rather subdued little party, with moderate sipping of a chilled Sauvignon de Touraine and a shared plate of mixed sandwiches. After a while, he and his companions had become aware of a gatecrasher, with a matted beard and ruinous clothes who loitered near them and began to address some of their number. Whether he knew who they were, or had picked up their names by eavesdropping, no one knew. The man was clearly very drunk. Then Rupert heard his own name called, loudly, in the braying tones of his class and looked more closely at the interloper, hoping to shut him up or get rid of him. As the two men's eyes met, Rupert recognised Marcus Fitzgerald. He was filthy and looked unwell, with bloodshot eyes and yellowish skin.

'Jesus Christ, Marcus, just look at you!' Rupert had said, advancing on his old friend and taking his arm. 'You don't belong here!' And he had propelled him firmly towards the door. At first, Marcus began a blustering protest, but seeing the hard eyes of his former contemporaries all turned on him, he dropped his shoulders and allowed himself to be ejected.

At the door, he raised a finger and pointed waveringly in Rupert's face

'Problem is, Rupert, old *mate*,' he said, 'where do I belong?'

Within a couple of months – just short of his twenty-seventh birthday – Marcus was dead. Rupert wondered what really had happened with Marcus in the end. He supposed he would never know. He wondered, even, if Imogen really knew. After all, she was pretty well gone on the hard stuff when it happened. It was a wonder she was still alive to tell the tale, actually. Not that she seemed about to be telling any tales.

Imogen returned with the muffin dish. 'I did a fresh lot,' she said, handing him a plate and putting the hot dish by him, on a small table with leather inlay. 'Oh, that's OK. It won't, ahm, hurt, it's only repro.' She busied herself pouring tea and then sat. She felt only slightly awkward – because it was so long since she had seen him, or anyone else from her former life – but she enjoyed his being there, with her and longed to know what he'd been up to. 'How's the City?'

He finished his crumpet and wiped his mouth before speaking. 'Odd,' he said. 'Very odd.' She waited for him to expand. He wasn't sure how much she understood – probably very little, he assumed. 'Things are happening. The October crash. Lots of people are losing jobs.'

'Oh? Why?'

'There's a nasty change on the way. Everything's down – or looking as if its down. The trade deficit worries City folk, but they're more concerned that Maggie's losing her grip. Advertising is in a terrible slump and some people are saying that means a recession's on the way.'

'I, ahm, I see.'

'And there's property prices, of course. This mad spiral. It can't continue – not with interest rates where they are, and with everyone borrowing so much.'

'No.' Imogen imagined a helter-skelter, with hundreds of Russell Hands, all in Armani suits, skidding down to land in a heap of cockney squabbles at the bottom. She giggled and put a hand to her mouth.

'Oh you can laugh, Immie, but a lot of property speculators are about to lose their shirts. And the amazing thing is, they don't seem to see it coming.'

'Rupert, I, ahm, I'm not laughing. Really I'm not!' The helter skelter image wouldn't go away. She felt her shoulders tremble with suppressed giggling. Rupert watched her for a few moments.

'You seem pretty well all right now, anyway.'

'Oh fine. I've done quite well, in fact.' Imogen explained about her property dealing to him. 'It seems that I was, ahm, right to sell and pull out,' she concluded.

'I'll say.' Rupert watched her drink her third cup of tea and then put cup and saucer on her side table. The grace of her movement, and fine bone structure touched him. She was delicate, almost frail, he decided, but not weak. He realised, now, that he had rather missed her company in recent years. In spite of what had happened to Marcus, he was pleased to be with her, even though her hands were soil-stained, the nails worn down with gardening and even though the tendency to giggle was disconcerting. 'What about personal things?' he said, wishing at once that he hadn't sounded so arch. 'Who's looking after you I mean?'

'Oh, ahm, no one. I don't have any real need, now that I'm no longer, you know, *dependent* on, ahm . . .'

'No, no, no – I don't mean like that.' He did not want to embarrass her. 'I mean, you know, relationships . . . friends.'

'None really.' She shook her head. 'Apart from our rector.' Rupert noticed her eyes grow fond.'

'Is he nice?'

'More than nice. He's been *such* a friend.' Her daydream intruded for some seconds. Rupert paused, but then had to say, not without an element of envy: 'I believe you're soft on him.'

Imogen looked at him, and then stared out of the window. 'Actually, Rupert, I adore him.' A longer pause. 'He's not remotely interested in me, of course – well, not in *that* way.'

'Oh?'

'Besides, he's a lot older – at least fifty – and, well, he's a rector and all that.'

'Is there a Mrs Rector?'

Imogen shook her head. 'He's just doing his job. Keeping a fatherly eye on me.'

'Like a shepherd and his wayward lamb?' These words, humorous though Rupert had intended them to sound, made her blush. He moved to her sofa.

'I shouldn't have said that. Look, I'm jolly glad to be here, but can't we see the garden before it gets too dark?' It was natural for her to slip her hand into his as they abandoned tea things and gently burning logs to wander outside in the gathering afternoon mist. She showed him her new borders, shrubs that had been planted that autumn, a newly paved terrace, to the west of the house, designed to catch late afternoon sun, and her kitchen garden, where winter cabbage and Brussels sprout plants made plump outlines against the darkling sky. On her way out, Imogen had picked up a small wooden trug basket and now began to pick sprouts into it.

'Let me help.' Rupert began to handle the plants, surprised at the amount of water that came off them, and at the numbing cold of the sprouts. He watched how she deftly twisted each sprout, snapping the stem and dropping them into the basket when she had three or four in her hand. He struggled to twist a single sprout, using both hands on the plant and considerable effort to break the stalk. In a moment, his trouser leg was wet through.

'I should just chat while I pick,' Imogen said. 'Won't take more than a few moments.' Rupert was glad to be relieved of the task and watched her with somewhat revised respect.

'Have you spoken to your father?' Imogen's hands stopped, mid-pick. She paused for several seconds before dropping the handful into the basket. 'I do know that he'd like to talk to you.' She shook her head, picked some more sprouts, now beginning to struggle slightly to break them from the stem. Her fingers were numb from the cold and ached.

'How was the, ahm, the funeral?' The tone was assured,

but there was a slight tremble in her voice, possibly because the damp coldness of the air was beginning to penetrate her clothing.

'Haven't you got enough sprouts, now, if it's just the two of us?'

'Three,' she said. 'I thought I'd ask Graham Ball.'

'Who the hell is Graham Ball?' Rupert found it impossible to suppress his disappointment that they were not to spend the evening on their own together.

'Just someone from the, ahm, village.' She handed him the basket of vegetables and bent to pick some sprigs of thyme and rosemary from the low hedges that bordered the kitchen garden. 'You'll like him.'

After a brief but troubled morning stroll in the garden, Gerard went to the dining room. Noticing that his appetite, capricious at the best of times, had all but dried up in recent days, Mrs Bull had made him a special breakfast of his favourite lamb's kidneys, bacon and scrambled egg which she served with a small flourish, failing to notice his queasy grimace. He picked up his knife and fork, and set about slicing one of the kidneys, trying not notice the fresh blood, or the urinous odour that emanated from it, but put his knife and fork down as soon as Mrs Bull had left the room to collect the morning post. This she set beside him before topping up his coffee cup and then leaving, quietly closing the door behind her. He noticed an envelope bearing the Barleythorpe School crest. The letter it contained absorbed him so much that his breakfast began to congeal, unnoticed.

Dear Mr Pilkington,
I felt I must write to you about your son, as I'm extremely concerned about him. Until recently, his school career has been an example to everyone here. His gallant contribution to House and School Rugby will long be remembered, and his prowess at cricket has been such a major contribution to our performance against other schools that I can hardly bear to think how we will do without him, after his remove to Sandhurst next year.

*Academically, too, he has excelled himself, and shows
every junior boy the right way forward.*

*I have to report to you, however, that there has
been an extraordinary change in your son over the
past few weeks. Not only has his game lost its edge,
but his attitude seems to have become one almost of
nonchalance. Things he was so passionate about before,
no longer affect him. When, in the match against Oundle
last week, he was bowled for naught in both innings, he
showed no concern at all, and then left the field before
the end of the match, showing a lack of good manners
to his fellow team members and to the visiting team.
This is so unlike him.*

*In class, he has started to hand in work of a standard
that is only barely acceptable and appears inattentive
and disinterested. Furthermore, he has been unable to
complete his meals, and is growing noticeably thinner
and seems to take little trouble with his appearance.*

*I wonder, therefore, whether anything might have
happened to him at home to cause this extraordinary
change in behaviour. Sometimes the bereavement of
a close relative or some other change can be more
damaging than we realise, particularly to a young man
in his teens. Has he experienced anything like that?*

*I'm so sorry to burden you with this, but do hope
you can throw some light on to the matter because I
am extremely anxious about this boy. He is too good a
pupil, and too valuable an asset to the school to see go
to waste in this way.*

Gerard re-read the letter several times before leaving his
breakfast untouched, walking to his study and closing the door
behind him. Outside the open window, a white climbing rose
issued sweet fragrance into the room and a song thrush, whose
mate had nested in the rose plant, sang from the branches of
the holly tree by the gate, but Gerard noticed nothing. Almost
every part of his mind was filled with Violet, and the small
part that wasn't nagged him about his son. He knew that this
problem with Michael also had something to do with Violet,

in fact Violet's influence seemed almost universal. Obviously, the boy had been besotted with her, and presumably, he had been brushed off, but this did nothing to ease the pain he felt about her himself. In fact it sharpened it.

Whenever he thought of that appalling incident in the wood, he groaned with a blend of anguish and shame. He knew it had been folly even to consider meeting for a séance in such a place, and at such a time. Supposing they had been seen? What a mad risk he had taken, and what a stupid negation of his self control! But she had been so lovely in the moonlight, her eyes so wistful, such a look of expectancy on her features, her lips slightly parted. If she'd been a doe, her ears would have been pricked, straining to hear the slightest stirring from what? The spirit world! Oh, what a humbug it all was. And the awful part was, that with the adventure of creeping out to the trysting place, the pulsing excitement of hearing her, of sensing her there among the trees, and the uncanny feel that they were not alone, that they were observed – in all that quickening flurry of fear, of excitement, and finally of sexual arousal – he had not thought of Elizabeth at all.

As Gerard folded Mr Danvers' letter and slipped it into his jacket pocket, Michael lay in the school sanatorium, pale, nauseous, exhausted but sleepless. What had started as a summer cold, had worsened to a fever and Michael had, after stumbling like a drunk into the prep room, been escorted to the sick bay where his temperature was recorded at 103 degrees. He lay, recalling again and again, every moment of that horrible night.

His last sighting had been of his father holding Violet in a clumsy embrace. He had managed, only by the greatest presence of mind, to get away undetected and had then begun his night-long cycle ride. Almost blind to his surroundings, guided by a kind of automatic pilot, he had pedalled furiously, not towards Barleythorpe, but in the direction of Kendale. He did no know where he was going. He only wanted to pedal away from the pain. He knew he could never go home. He knew he could not return to school. The very idea of school seemed ludicrous, miniaturised, to him now. Mile after mile, he rode, through Kendale, over the river Venn, on and on, thinking to head south, perhaps to run away for good, he didn't know what.

And gradually, as he rode, the emotional flood began to subside. It dawned on him that here was much more to lose. His love was gone, but he still had to live. He had promised Riversley he'd be back, and now poor Riversley would have to carry the can for him. That would make a single betrayal into a double one. He stopped his bike and looked at his watch in the moonlight. Almost two in the morning. Already, there was a noticeable violet pallor in the east.

He turned and began to cycle back to Barleythorpe, using the main road from Kendale to Stoneford and then riding cross country along a pattern of byways. He had to be back before anyone got up. As he rode, his limbs began to cramp. His muscles, even in one so physically fit, were fatigued, but not half so much as his mind. He stopped frequently now, taking rest and massaging his calves. The problem of his father kept coming to him. How could he stay in the same house? How could he ever look at him again? But as he neared Barleythorpe, and as the landscape became familiar again, he knew that somehow, he would have to. He knew that he depended on his father to get to Sandhurst; knew that people at school depended on him. Especially Riversley.

At almost six in the morning, stinking of sweat from his exertions, so tired he could barely stand, Michael crawled into bed just as Riversley's honest eyes opened. 'Lordy, Pilks! Have you only just made it?' Too tired to reply, he slipped the bedclothes over his head and screwed his eyes tight shut. Even in that tiny haven of bed, with his great friend by his side and half the cricket team in the same room, he felt more exposed and isolated than he had ever felt in his life.

He had not felt properly well since that frantic night, even though much of the summer term had lapsed. He groaned and turned over in the hard sanatorium bed. Presently, the school matron walked in. She was a kindly woman, widowed in the Great War and nearly killed herself when, as a VAD, she had been working in a hospital near Ypres that was shelled. She was strict, but gentle with boys whom she knew to be genuinely troubled.

'Pilkington, as you know, the term is almost over,' she said. 'I've asked Mr Danvers write to your father so that you can go home as soon as you are well enough to travel.' She came and sat on his bed, reaching out a hand to brush the straw-coloured forelock from his brow. 'You grind your teeth at night, did you know?'

Rupert carried the last of the washing-up out of the dining-room into the kitchen where Imogen was drying cutlery with a linen tea towel decorated with the London Underground route map. 'That's the lot,' he said, as he placed dessert plates and a glass dish, sticky with the remnants of a crème brulée, on the shelf by the sink and then ran the cold tap to rinse his hands. 'You were quite right, I did like him.'

'See, I told you.'

'And he likes you.'

'Oh, I, ahm, I don't know.'

'Oh come on, Immie. He was gazing at you all evening.'

'Well, you see, he's my, sort of, boss.' She had explained about *The Countryside in Crisis* and, over dinner, they had talked about little else. Rupert had felt quite locked out. 'And he's been, kind of, ahm, supportive, too.'

'Well, God, Immie! I *know* that!' She turned, surprised, from the dresser and saw the affront in his eyes. The expression he wore was the same that Marcus had affected sometimes. Obviously a kind of Eton look. She froze, remembering. He saw the shadow of anguish cross her features. 'Oh God, I'm sorry!' He walked over.

'Sorry for, ahm what?'

'For you, for everything. And I think the way you've managed to – you know, get over it all. Well, it's brilliant!' He stepped over to her, took her not too gently, by the shoulders and kissed her. She recoiled to any man's advances, since Hands, and he sensed the revulsion and stepped back. She wanted to melt, to give in, but could not. Graham's attentiveness, too, was fresh in her memory. Less than two hours before, he had leapt up to help her carry hot food out of the kitchen, and had squeezed her elbow gently, indicating the guest in the dining-room and muttering into her ear, 'Old family friend? Or old flame?'. She had not replied, but the question had made her wonder just what Graham's intentions might be.

'Rupert, no.'

'Immie, please.'

'I'm sorry Rupert. But, no.' Gently, she took his hands off her shoulders and then busied herself finishing the washing up.

Chapter Seventeen

———

This, thought Jerome Daniels, is the Great Crossroads of my Life. He walked briskly down the steep hill, with the Minster rising up behind him, the secular part of the city spread for a couple of miles below and the slow, lazy river beyond. He wished he had his car. He had a prolonged journey ahead of him involving a rail-bus link at Peterborough and an expensive taxi ride from Stoneford. He had been determined to try the thing with public transport and had regretted his decision from the start of the day when the only bus of the morning from Wychgate to Stoneford was twenty minutes late and turned out to be crammed with noisy adolescents on their way to the Endowed Schools at Stoneford. The train was late enough to make him miss his Peterborough connection by a few minutes and then the last leg of the journey had been spent in a smoking carriage with a gang of youths who had rigged small loudspeakers to their personal stereo which issued a muffled but infuriatingly monotonous beat. Even songs that had slow, interesting introductions degenerated, within a bar or two, into the same mindless thumping. He had been almost half an hour late at the bishop's house and had then been kept waiting for almost an hour because some politician had come, without appointment, to discuss the Church's attitude to policing the inner city.

The interview with His Lordship had been the lodestar he needed – not into deeper faith, but out of the Church. He realised that now, after he had had time to cool off and gather his tattered thoughts. But, at the time, he thought he would hit the man. The bishop's main preoccupation had been with money. He was obsessed with the stuff, so that whatever topics they had covered, it had come back to the question of how much income he thought the churches in the smaller parishes could be expected to raise towards their upkeep.

'Our church building is wholly redundant,' Jerome had said. 'The scout hut would be too big for our congregation – even my garden shed would be.'

'What's your point?'

'Sell off the church, let someone else keep it up. Continue parish activities elsewhere. Anywhere, even in my sitting-room.' The bishop had not taken kindly to that, suggesting that Jerome had an attitude problem.

'I'm afraid you'll have to go for bums in seats,' he had said. 'Try to spend a little less time with the homeless in Stoneford. *Are* there any homeless in Stoneford? And concentrate more on fund-raising in our parishes. Couldn't you do more in the way of events? Jazz evenings, barbecues, that kind of thing?' And the more Jerome had insisted that his parish didn't need help, and that there were people in the cities who did, the less interested the bishop had become.

'I don't see you as a crusading urban guerrilla of a priest,' the bishop had said. 'You need to be more like Mother Theresa for that.'

'A fundamentalist bigot, you mean?' Jerome had got pretty near to shouting by this stage.

'A living saint, many would say.'

'Without enough brains to distinguish Catholic dogma from the real will of God? She said she'd have sided with the Church against Galileo, for Christ's sake!'

'She's a shining example of how to succour the poor, the needy.' The bishop had kept infuriatingly calm.

'The poor and needy around here need a different kind of help. They are hungry, but not starving. They are lost, confused, miserable. They've lost sight of the boundaries, of where it's at. There are youngsters whose parents have bashed them up and thrown them out of their houses, or worse. There are alcoholics who have no one to sort them out. They don't want to be told to stop drinking, or even how to stop drinking, they just need to be made to *want* to stop drinking. And there are heroin users' – Imogen's face had flashed through his mind as he said this, and he had faltered, thinking of the sadness at the core of her being – 'addicts who don't know whether there's anything about life that's worth having. Their habit is dearer to them than anything.'

'Then offer them salvation in Christ.'

'They don't want "salvation in Christ". They just want a few clues on how to get by.'

'Christ is our business.'

'Is that how you see the Church of England? A business? Roll up, Roll up. Salvation for sale – a weekly quid will buy you a warm church and so much more! A nice warm feel about praying for the starving masses; freedom from guilt; peace of mind – ah that! How cheaply we sell peace of mind to our faithful flock. Mind you, we don't want women clerics dealing it out – not unless they're only deacons, of course. Oh and gays need not apply – for peace of mind, that is – even though half the clergy are bent.' The bishop had shifted uneasily at this remark. He had voted, at Synod, to outlaw what was disgustingly called 'genital sex' between members of the same sex, even though he knew that by doing so, he was possibly betraying some of his most faithful followers. And there had been that dreadful time when he had been confused about his own orientation and had . . . but really, that was so long ago.

'Oh, I think you're being a little hard on the clergy.'

'It's about time we were a little harder on ourselves.' And he had gone on to explain to the bishop that he felt he no longer had the faith necessary to propagate the gospel. That the Church of England seemed too steeped in genteel respectability to be able to function as a militant body, fighting for righteousness, and concluded by saying that he was 'coming out of the priesthood'.

'But for what purpose?'

'To take up *really* pastoral duties. I want to do some good. I've *got* to do some good.'

And here he was, walking down to his train, as good as

defrocked. At first, the feeling had been one of exhilaration. I'm free of the cant, of the claptrap, he had thought. But then the awful sense of responsibility had begun to settle itself firmly on his shoulders. What he wanted to do would take courage. It would also take away his income and his home. He pulled his Crombie overcoat more tightly round his shoulders and firmed the expensive Bates wide-brim trilby onto his head. What *have* I done, he asked himself, with a mixture of dread and exhilaration, what *have* I done? A man in a similar trilby walked towards him and raised it as he passed.

'A'dernoon, vicar!'

'Rector actually,' Jerome said, 'but not for long now!'

'Eh?' the man half turned, but Jerome hurried on, anxious to get home so that he had time to plan the next step.

Mr Danvers knocked and walked into the sanatorium room without waiting for a reply. Michael was sitting up in bed writing a letter. Hastily, he covered what he had written so far with a piece of dark green blotting paper. 'Sir!'

'Michael, how are you?' He came and sat on the bed. Michael only just had time to move his legs out of the way. 'All the fever gone now?'

'Sir.' There was a silence lasting a minute or more.

'That's a handsome writing box.' Michael closed it, not out of a craving for secrecy but to demonstrate how it worked. The brass-bound walnut box opened into a kind of sloping portable desk with compartments beneath the green tooled leather lid.

'It belonged to my grandfather, sir. A present for my seventeenth birthday.' It contained, as well as writing paper – stiffish, cream-coloured, tied up in a blue ribbon – ink, envelopes and pencils and a small bundle of letters, six in all, from Violet. Only one of these had been opened. It was dated the twenty third of June – two days after Michael's illicit bike ride to the wood. It contained trivial news of the village, and several declarations along the lines of how Violet missed him, how she thought of him every day, and how she longed for the holidays, when they could be together again. No reference was made anywhere in that letter to the events of midsummer night. Sometimes, a day or two after it had arrived in the post, he had scanned the neat writing again and again, half-hoping to find some explanation. He had fantasised that there was a missing page, that the explanation would be there, or at least some reference to his father. Anything. The second and subsequent letters had come approximately every other day. Michael had not opened them, but could not bear to discard them. They still lay, tied with another piece of ribbon, beneath the false bottom of his writing box. After receiving the sixth letter, he had been able to bear the contact no longer, and had written her a terse note.

> *Violet,*
> *I think we should conclude our relationship forthwith.*
> *I will never stop loving you. I only wish you had been*
> *able to return the feelings but I know, now, that you*
> *cannot. Please do not attempt to make contact again.*
> *I could not bear it.*
> *Yours,*

After that, the letters stopped coming.

Writing those words had taken so much effort that he had felt quite exhausted afterwards. There was no way to make things less cruel, even though this felt like carving the condemnation of their relationship into the delicate flesh of her face.

'Penny for them?'

'Sir?'

'I wondered what you were thinking about.'

'Oh, nothing sir. I just get a bit worried about Sandhurst sometimes.'

'Have you been having second thoughts about the army?'

'Oh no sir.'

'Well, I'm sure you'll do very well, once you've got your present little hiccough sorted out.'

'Yes, sir.'

'I'll say goodbye properly, of course, but I believe your father is coming the day after tomorrow, to accompany you home.'

'Yes, sir.'

'I'm so sorry you will have to miss the End of Year celebrations.' Mr Danvers tried, almost with success, to keep reproach out of his voice.

'Yes, sir. I'm sorry, sir, really I am.' Michael's Adam's apple bobbed a couple of times and his voice wobbled. He could hardly believe his entire school career was about to end in such an anticlimax.

'Yes, well, here comes Matron.' Mr Danvers stood up and adjusted his gown on his rounded shoulders, held out a damp hand to be shaken and scuttled out of the room, nodding briskly to Matron who had entered carrying a white pot mug of tea and her copy of *The Times*. It was her routine to pass her paper on to any boy who might be in the san when she had finished it. She even did the crossword – when she had time – on a piece of grease-proof paper held over the real thing, so the boys could also do the puzzle. The problem was, the pencil marks usually pressed through so that it was easy to see the words. Michael took the paper absently. He seemed more distrait than before.

'Oh, thank you, Matron,' he said, remembering his manners just in time. He was thinking about going home in less than forty-eight hours. How, he wondered, am I going to be able to face Father?

'The fact is, Imogen, I've been and gone and done it!' Jerome was almost light-headed. 'When I think of the wasted years, the frustrations, and how I feel now, I can hardly understand why I didn't make the decision yonks ago.'

'What decision? What *are* you talking about?'

'Yesterday I went to see my bishop,' Jerome said. 'I have decided to get out of the Church. On Sunday, I will announce it to the Congregation of Wychgate Saint Peters, such as it is. You're the first to know.'

'Oh I see.' Imogen was disappointed. When he had phoned last night, and invited her for coffee and a serious talk, she had assumed it would be about them, rather than about him. Then she realised this news might mean his going altogether, out of the village. 'Where will you

live?' The prospect of his absence filled her with a sense
of doom.

'What?' She seemed to be reading his thoughts. 'I haven't
thought properly yet.'

'But you can't go on living here.'

'In Wychgate? Why not?'

'I mean in this rectory.'

'I should hope not. It's a vile house and I've always hated
it.' He glanced around the little sitting-room, wondering
whether he would miss the place. Outside, now the hateful
firs were all gone, you could see right across the site of the
felled plantation to the remnants of Pyson Wood. He spotted
rooks, flocking over the tree tops and tried to imagine what
the watermeadows might have been like, when they were full
of wildflowers, with footpaths worn to the river. He turned to
Imogen, looking a fright in her gardening clothes – where on
earth had she found that horrendous tweed skirt, and why did
she wear such a vast, man's pullover with it? He was moved
by the proud rake of her shoulders and long neck, with a few
strands of back hair broken loose from the sort of entangled
knot that the rest of it was in – like a collapsing haystack on
the top of her head – and he added: 'but I should hate to
leave this village.'

'But where will you live?' And there she had a question.
Where *would* he live? What would he do? 'What will you,
ahm, do?' She was at it again. Mind-reading.

'I don't know. No, that's not right at all. I do know what
sort of thing I want to do, but I haven't really thought how
to get started.' Imogen watched while he struggled to express
himself. 'You see, I've thought about working with people
who really need help, but I haven't exactly worked out how
to go about it. I'll probably start, doing something with one
of the charities for the homeless.'

'Not too much of their work needed in Wychgate.'

'No. But there is in Stoneford, and more, of course, in
larger places.'

'But you want to stay here all the same.'

'I do have reasons for wanting to be in the village.' He
tried to look composed and relaxed as he said this but found,

nonetheless, that he was sitting on his hands and had crossed and uncrossed his legs. 'And I do have reasons for wanting to talk to you in particular.'

'Oh?'

'You see, I happen to think you are rather special.' He fidgeted some more. He always found it much easier talking to people as they walked, rather than face to face. She looked so lovely, even in those appalling gardening clothes, that what he really wanted to do was kiss her, love her, hold on to her. She looked back, cool and composed.

'I think you're pretty, ahm, special too.' He was so anxious not to alarm her, or to put her on guard, that he had failed to notice the body language, the softness of her eyes. She waited for him to continue.

'Special in that you have, well, you've had *experiences* which—' He stopped, seeing her face cloud over. 'Oh shit, Imogen. I'm sorry, I really am so oafish, I didn't want to—'

'No, no. It's OK. Tell me what you, ahm, wanted to say.' She was touched, as always, by his concern for her own feelings.

'I don't want to dredge up anything painful. But I'll be dealing with a lot with people on, um, you know, drugs and I feel that your experience and your wonderful strength in getting out of the habit might—'

'Getting out of the, ahm, habit is not the hardest part, you know.'

'You see!' Jerome smiled at her. 'You see! That's exactly what I mean. You know so much more than I about these things. People in this village see society as a . . .' he paused, trying to think up a metaphor, 'a beautiful ocean liner. She gleams, white in the sun, her paintwork perfect. But if you use your eyes, when you go below decks, you see the rust blisters under the paintwork, you hear the pumps, constantly pumping out the filling bilges, you notice how, beneath that surface aroma of furniture polish, clean varnish and fresh sea air, there's a constant under-pong of sewage. Now *you've* managed to get back on board the creaky old rust bucket that people round here might call "normal society", and I want to help the poor sods who have gone overboard and are still floundering in the sea of . . . of . . .' He had run out of inspiration.

'Trouble?'

'Unacceptability.' Dear God, it sounded so limp. 'I mean, I want to try to do something about the mass of people who've fallen through the safety net. This growing underclass who, these days, are accused of being destructively poor, as if it were some crime. And they're the ones I think you might be able to, well, to help me to help.'

Imogen stayed silent for some time. She wanted to say, 'Wherever you are, I'd like to be.' She wanted to explain to him that although she looked contented these days, that was surface, and underneath, there was still an awful lot to get sorted out. She wanted to tell him how much she needed his gentle counsel, his support, just his reassuring presence. She wanted to say that he made her feel safe, comfortable, that she rather badly wanted him to hold her, and just to hang on to her for, ooh, a few hours – or perhaps a hundred years or more. She wanted to tell him that only he could take away the feeling of shame and revulsion she had felt – since her beastly affair with Hands – whenever any male began to make sexual advances. And as she watched him sitting on his hands, like an awkward little boy, she wanted to tell him that she wouldn't mind, at this actual moment, getting into bed with him, being made love to by him, gently, and for so long that time would become a kind of irrelevance. She avoided his eye, lest he read her thoughts and was shocked.

'OK!' she said.

Mrs Bull took extra care over the cucumber sandwiches. She had spread butter thinly on the white bread, had honed her kitchen knife to razor sharpness, before cutting fresh cucumber into slices – with peel still on, as he liked it – so thinly you could see through them. These she had laid on the buttered bread, and had taken a different knife to remove the crusts. She garnished the sandwiches with a sprig of fresh parsley, picked from the little bed outside the kitchen door, and then put four of her home-made vanilla shortcake biscuits on a second plate. Finally, she poured boiling water into the 1789 silver tea pot, to warm it, emptied it, added two measures of Earl Grey tea and refilled the pot and hot water jug. The gentle fragrance of tea, mingled with bergamot, wafted from the tray which, after a final check – milk, sugar, tea cup and saucer, plate, knife, spoon – she carried to Gerard's study.

She was worried about her employer. She was quite used to the brooding periods he went through from time to time, but this was different. His depression seemed to be preventing him from eating, from rising until very late in the day, and from doing anything useful at all. Whenever she brought tea or coffee into the study, or came to inform him that a meal was ready, or that the post had arrived, he would be sitting in almost exactly the same position, staring out of the window, across the sloping meadows towards river and wood. It was as if he were waiting for someone to come up to the window.

He seldom ate more than a mouthful or two of his meals, even though she had worked harder than usual to produce delicacies that would tempt him. His voice, throaty from lack of use, sounded toneless; every movement appeared to tire him and yet, he'd go for walks that lasted for hours. When he returned, instead of having coloured cheeks and brighter eyes, Mrs Bull would note a pallor, sometimes dewed slightly with sweat on the forehead, and would see no improvement in his demeanour at all. She knocked, a quiet respectful tap, on the study door, and entered.

'Good afternoon, sir.'

'Oh, Mrs Bull, I'll not take tea. I think I want to go for a walk,' Gerard said, as he rose and slowly walked past her.

'I did make cucumber sandwiches specially, sir.'

'No matter.' And without another word, he walked quietly out of the front door, without picking up cap or stick. Mrs Bull was hurt, not because her lovingly prepared tea was spurned, but because she did not know how to allay his unhappiness. Tomorrow, Master Michael would be coming home. She hoped he would be able take his father out of himself a bit, but she rather feared that he wouldn't.

Some time later, he sat alone on the altar rock. Its cold stone was soothing to his hands in the summer heat, but no balm could ease the discomfort in his mind. He had not spoken to a single soul in seven weeks, apart from Mrs Bull. He went regularly to the altar rock because he felt closer to her there than anywhere else, but the pain of remembering tended to wipe out the comfort of imagining her presence. He had not seen Violet since Midsummer night, when they had parted so suddenly that he still felt the wound – as if they had been wrenched asunder. If only he had exercised more self-control. He had known all the time, really, that agreeing to meet her in the wood was a terrible mistake, but he could not, at the time, bring himself to his senses and put a stop to the whole stupid plan. After that night, he had hoped his life could go on as normally – or what passed for normally – as before. But she did not arrive for her usual tutorial and, next morning, he had walked to the shop. Peter Ball had been behind the counter.

'I'm really, very sorry, sir,' he had said, as deferentially as possible, 'but I'm afraid Violet has asked me to let you know that she would prefer not to come to the manor any more.'

'I see.' Gerard was terse. The man was clearly embarrassed.

'I . . . we are really grateful, sir, for all you've done. But, well, you know how young girls can be, I'm sure, sir.' Then Gerard had noticed, through the door of the little kitchen room, the movement of a white muslin dress.

'Violet!' he had called.

'That's my wife out there. I'm afraid Violet isn't able to see you, sir.' Peter Ball's hands were trembling on the counter. 'I don't mean any disrespect, sir, really I do not.'

'Quite!' Gerard had snapped, and had turned and left. He had walked slowly back down the hill, and had then set out across the water meadows to the little wood, had stopped in its centre and had sat brooding for an hour, on the cool altar stone. He had gone to brood again, when he had received Mr Danvers' rather odd letter about Michael.

Chapter Eighteen

———

The trill of his car phone startled Russell Hands into the
present. His hands twitched on the wheel of his Jaguar and
made him swear. Luckily, the motorway was fairly free of
traffic. He picked up the hand set.

'Yeah!'

'Um, hullo. Could I speak to Mr Russell Hands please?'

'This is 'Ains.'

'Ah, my name is Lilliwhite. I'm with Keil, Overbland –
the merchant bank, you may—'

'Yeah. I know it.'

'I'm acting for Lady Imogen Fitzgerald. I wonder if I might
take a moment or two of your time?'

'Yeah?'

'Fact is, I happen to be in your area and would rather like
to visit you this afternoon. I have some information which I
think could be of some interest to you.'

'Yeah?'

'Yes.' Rupert paused. 'If today is inconvenient, some other
time perhaps?'

'No, er, no. This afternoon's fine. You'll 'ave ter come
to me 'ouse. About five?' Hands gave directions and then
dialled his own phone number. He heard his own recorded
voice, on the answering machine and waited for the bleep
before delivering his message. 'Jesus, Doreen, where the fuck
are you? We got comp'ny at five ternight. Posh git name o'
Lillicrap or somesuch. Merchant wanker. 'E'll need lookin'

after. Be there, girl!' He rang off.

He slipped off the motorway and headed east, for a brief diversion to Boston before driving home. He found he needed a lot diversions, these days, to help him to stop worrying, mainly about money. He had too many unsold houses on his hands, in spite of having dropped his prices, twice, and he knew that his plight was shared by most other developers. Housing that had already been developed *had* to be sold – he couldn't unbuild the homes – but the two large bare sites he possessed were an even bigger headache. He had planning consent but why build when there was no market? And who in their right minds would buy building sites in a slump like this? If he were a multimillionaire, there'd be no probs. He'd simply have waited until things came right again and then develop. But it wasn't that simple. Every day, every hour, every minute, he was clocking up a huge interest charge on his borrowings, and he was beginning to run out of earnings to service these loans. A few sales, just to bring a couple of hundred thou in – that'd help to put things right – but at the moment, absolutely bugger-all was happening. The market wasn't just slow, it was dead. Nobody was buying or selling. Nada, nought, sod all was going on. He chewed the nail on his forefinger until it bled, and then tried to nibble off the hangnail, ripping the skin down to the quick. He just had to find some dosh. And find it fast.

He drove through the outskirts of Boston to Shirley's street, parked at the end, and then walked down to her house. With his key, he opened the door and called. There was no reply.

'I know you're up there, Shirl.' He took off coat, jacket and shoes, and crept silently upstairs. Her bedroom door was ajar and, peeping in, he saw the sleeping form under the bedclothes. Being careful to make no sound, he removed the rest of his clothes, folding his shirt and laying his trousers carefully over the chairback. Then, as he pulled the bedclothes back his heart froze. The hand, that was revealed, was hairy, attached to a hairy wrist. The body, hitherto concealed under the duvet, was large and powerful and belonged to Shirl's husband. In a flash, the body sprang to life, first with the opening of an eye, brown and dark with loathing, the eye-white yellow and veined, then with an arm that shot out with lightning speed and with faultless accuracy. Before he could move, Hands felt his privates in a steely grip that tightened, driving all the air out of his body. He dare not pull back, he dare not move. He could barely speak. 'Frank!' he managed to gasp, even getting a touch of nonchalance into the greeting. Frank sat up, without releasing his grip. Even sitting, he overshadowed Hands. To have put up any sort of a fight would have been a waste of time. Hands had known Frank was big, but not that big. Shirley had also told him, that very morning, that he was in Cardiff. Treacherous cow, he thought.

'Shirley's up at her mother's. I know all about you,' Frank said.

'Yeah?'

'Everythin'.'

'Yeah?'

'Yeah!' Frank released his victim. 'I should get them clothes back on, if I were you. He looked at his hand in disgust. 'I've gotta wash me 'ands. Then I'll be back. He left the bedroom and Hands heard water running in the bathroom. He dressed himself, in frenzied haste, and made a dash for the stairs. Before he could descend, the bathroom door opened and Frank aimed a kick, which missed its mark, but which made Hands lunge forward, miss his footing and tumble down the stairs, landing in an undignified heap. His back was bruised and forehead grazed, but he suspected, as he picked himself up, grabbed his jacket and coat, and ran for the door, that nothing was broken. He pulled the key from his pocket and threw it, hard, at the window. It actually chipped a small piece of glass from the pane, and fell on the ledge, to be retrieved later by Frank, who would test the chip with a calloused thumb.

Over the road, behind swags of net curtain, Shirley's mother watched Hands leave. 'He's gone,' she said. 'I don't suppose you'll be bothered by 'im no more.' She turned to look at her daughter, sitting hunched, with a purple-black eye and bruised cheek on a chair by the gas fire. 'Honestly,

Shirley, you should have told *me*. I could've squared it with the bastard. Frank need never've known.

'It's better this way, Mum.'

Hands drove quietly home. He was not really frightened of Frank and knew, anyway, that he was brighter and cleverer. He'd been getting pretty fed up with Shirley and he had a feeling she wasn't that keen on him any more. Plus, he wanted to stop the money thing. It was a touch too criminal, that, and as far as he was concerned, he was well out of it.

At home, in Wyckhamby, after a hasty bath and with a sticking plaster over his left eye, Hands composed himself, in readiness for Rupert Lilliwhite's visit. Doreen had arrived home to the message, and had laid on tea or sweet sherry, if he preferred. In the event, Lilliwhite only stayed about fifteen minutes, and took neither.

After the briefest exchange of pleasantries, Rupert got to the point. 'I expect, like many other developers, you are confronted by the problems of a falling market.'

'Yeah?' Hands had said, giving Doreen the signal to scarper. Doreen stayed put.

'I work in the City, as you know, and I can assure you that you are not alone. There are already a lot of bankruptcies and there will be hundreds, possibly thousands more.'

'Yeah?'

'Naturally, I have no idea of your financial standing. One can merely guess. But I dare say, a sale or two would come in quite handy at present.'

'Yeah?'

'I'm acting on behalf of Lady Imogen Fitzgerald and, as I said to you earlier today, I have a proposition.' Rupert tried to keep things formal. He was very keen for the man not to say 'yeah' like that any more.

'Yeah?' Rupert swallowed before continuing.

'Lady Imogen would be prepared to buy back the land at Wychgate Saint Peters. All of it.'

'You're *jokin*'!'

'Indeed not.'

Hands thought for a few moments. 'Why?'

'She feels, for various reasons, that it was a mistake to have sold. She has been the butt of a good deal of ill-will at the village, and has had increasing doubts about the benefits of quite such a large development in so small a village.' Rupert watched while Hands absorbed this.

'Same price?'

'Hardly. Property values have slumped.'

'Oh *now* I get it. The cow wants to make a fast buck.'

'Mr Hands, I don't think you can afford to make insulting references, do you?' Hands shrugged. 'You might feel you were being handed a lifeline.'

'Yeah?'

'She would offer a realistic market price.'

'Such as?'

'A quarter of a million.'

Hands worked hard not to react. The *bitch*, he thought. The fucking little cow. She'd virtually halved the price. 'But she'd make two hundred gees, more, on that deal.'

'That's not a matter for this discussion,' Rupert muttered. 'She would be in a position to provide hard cash – she could complete the purchase almost at once. And I suspect a liquid injection of that size would do your business no harm in the current climate, Mr Hands.' Hands clenched his fists. He needed the cash, but what a loss! He glanced at Doreen, who sat demurely on the edge of her sofa, and read her minuscule nod. So did Rupert.

'It's a fucking liberty!' Hands shouted.

'Yeah?' said Rupert, fishing in his briefcase for the contract.

Michael spent nine days in the school sanatorium, before being sent home two days before the official end of term. During that time, with a maturity remarkable for his seventeen years, he managed to sort out the components of misfortune that had compounded to create his life's crisis, and to come to terms with his situation.

Violet – and whenever he thought of his lost love, he almost wept – was now of his past. He knew that there was a risk that he might see her once the holidays had begun, but that he would have the courage to keep clear of her. As long as he thought of her betrayal, he was able to harden his heart. But, he could not believe, really, that it was she who had betrayed him. He knew his father had grown so attached to her that he had become obsessive. After seeing the faded photograph of his mother – so much more real than the stylised portrait in the drawing room – he had realised how like Violet she must have been, and he understood how his father would have latched on to that. He felt sympathy, anyway, for his having fallen so much for her, in fact, it was a source to wonder to the boy that Violet did not have a string of suitors all the way to Stoneford and beyond, so lovely was she. He had lost her, but he would never forget her. And he would always be true to her. Always.

Gerard was a separate problem. His own father, a betrayer – that was almost impossible to swallow. And soon he would be expected to go home, to treat his own parent with respect, to live with him in the same house, to dine at the same table. He was not sure whether he had the strength to do that. Often, he thought of the snuffling, sobbing man, unmanned by the presence of his, *his*, love; the embrace in the wood; her frank declaration of the presence of the spirits in which she believed: 'We are not alone'. Whenever his mind was crowded with such visions – his father's stooping, furtive approach, his sideways glances, his fumbling advances – he felt his gorge rise, his pulse race and sweat break out on his brow, as if he had consumed some poison.

His spell in the sanatorium, under the gentle ministrations of Matron, was not a healing period – the wounds to his young spirit would never heal – but it was a respite in which he could gather his strength. He knew, now, that he would survive. His upbringing, his entire education had been one of learning about worth, about service to his fellows, and to his country. Well, henceforward he would devote his life to service. He would go to Sandhurst, he would be as good a soldier as he knew how and he would perfect his spin bowling. Whatever he did, he would do with all his might. And in those nine days of convalescence, he began to realise that the example his father set, of a brooding, introverted existence, was a poor one. What a wasted life! Whatever happened, he would never forget Violet. Would never stop loving her. But he would never allow morbid thoughts of her to get in his way. He would not, ever, become like his father. As he approached the last hours of his school career, and in effect, the last hours of his boyhood, Michael realised that he despised his father. Going home would be an ordeal. But one he could bear.

Imogen had never been in an editing suite before. The experience was, at first, fascinating, but after a couple of hours, she found it terribly to difficult to pay attention. The same pieces of video were played again and again, with cuts, blends, mixes and so on, turning what Graham called 'rushes' into the edited programme. The first episode of the series had already been transmitted, to considerable critical acclaim, and Graham was at work on the last item of the last episode. Imogen had been fascinated to see how the bonfire party had been tweaked and massaged from a small, village affair, into a noisy, colourful spectacular, with enormous fireworks, a bonfire that would have made Hercules' funeral pyre look humble, and crowds everywhere. 'A lot of it is done with camera angle,' Graham explained. We need to make the whole thing look dramatic, that's why we've got lots of restless, hand-held stuff. All those sudden glimpses of anxious white faces, the little boy running – there, look . . . and there – away from the bigger boys. It looks as though they're chasing him. To make it more convincing, we've put in more shots of running kids – there, look – and now comes a shot of the little boy, out of breath, cornered. See?' Imogen watched the white face, the panting breath of the little boy, his tongue slightly protruding, his eye wide with fright.

'That's horrible.'

'No, just effective. He is actually just resting. The others have given up chasing him and are off in search of another quarry. Look at the original of the same footage.' He pressed some knobs on the console, and on a different screen, Imogen saw the same image, of the scared little boy, but this time the face stayed in vision for a few seconds longer. The breathing subsided a little and then the boy's face broke into a wide grin, before he took another deep breath and yelled,

'Oi! Keith! Over 'ere mate!' in loud, rounded Lincolnshire vowels.

'It's such a deception,' Imogen said. 'So dishonest.'

'It can be, in the wrong hands.' Graham agreed. 'Look at what Goebbels was able to do.'

'But why do you do it like that?'

'It's good television. You agree with the theme of the series – the countryside is in crisis – yah?' Imogen nodded. 'These pictures just make it entertaining. If we cut it to look the way it does every day, it would be boring. That's why amateur videos are so deadly.' He sensed that his crew wanted to finish the edit. 'I think we're in the way,' he said. 'Seen enough?' Imogen nodded. 'Then let's go over the road to the pub.'

Once there, with a pint of ale in front of him, and a mineral water for Imogen, he said, 'Apart from seeing how the series has come together, and to thank you for such fine research work, I invited you over for another reason.'

'Oh?' Imogen sipped her water.

'I wondered whether you would like a more permanent job.'

'I'm, ahm, I'm not at all sure.'

'You're good, you know. And you know plenty of the right people. Or you know where to contact them.'

'The fact is, Graham, I'm not, ahm, sure exactly what I want to do next.' Imogen drained her water. 'You see, I'm changing my plans somewhat, at Wychgate. I've bought back the land. Pyson Wood, did you know?'

Graham was surprised. 'Were you able to afford it?'

'Oh, yah. In fact, I've done rather well out of that. Bought it for rather less than I sold it for in the first place.' She picked up her glass, and put it down again. 'Might I have another? Those bottles are always so tiny.' She was used to drinking great drafts of water from the tap that was fed by a natural spring in the garden at Weir House. He went to the bar, bought another water and topped up his beer with another half-pint. When he had put the drinks down he reached across the table and rested his hand on hers.

'Imogen, there's something of a subtext to the job offer.

I'm sure you realise that I'm really very fond of you, very fond indeed.' She smiled and turned her hand round on the table so that she could grasp his fingers in hers.

'Graham, I know you are. And I'm really very fond of you. You've been, ahm, such a help.' She squeezed his hand a little harder and went on to say, 'I think I know what you may be about to say and I want to save you any embarrassment.' She sipped her water, more carefully this time. 'You see, I know I'm not that good at sorting things out for myself. It isn't long since I got rid of that horrible Crowe woman and, if you take childhood, boarding school, and . . . ahm . . . and . . .'

'Marriage,' Graham prompted, as gently as he could.

'Well, what I'm saying is that I've, ahm, never really known what it's like to be . . . independent.'

'I wouldn't dream of compromising your independence.'

'And then there are, well, *things*.'

'I'm sorry, I'm not with you.'

'It's hard to explain. But there are still things that I have to, sort of, work out.'

'I see.'

'Oh Graham, I don't think you do. Not really. But I do hope you'll be understanding.' Graham was silent at first, and then a smile, just a touch cynical, played round his mouth.

'So we can take it that's a "no", can we?'

'Graham. I *so* enjoyed researching your series. I would like to do more, but cannot because I will be tied up with building and things at Wychgate. I'm going to develop that site myself.'

'Are you, by gosh? Is it a good time to do that?' She dismissed his query with a slight shake of the head, and kept to the subject.

'And the other thing is, I like you very much, and I think you're terribly, ahm, attractive. But I'm afraid my feelings for you, affectionate though they are, are not – well, gosh, I don't know – sort of absolute.' He sat quietly for some minutes, staring at the dregs in his ale glass. 'I'm sorry, Graham.' She squeezed his hand. He had known, really, that the conversation would turn out like this. Better to have cleared the air, probably, but now he needed to save face.

He took back his hand and played, for a little while, with his empty glass.

'Come to supper on Saturday,' he said. 'At Wychgate.'

'I don't think I can.'

'Please? We can talk about Pyson Wood.'

'Oh! Pyson Wood! Sometimes I'm so sick of hearing about the damn place, I wish it would disappear.'

'But you bought it back and I know you'll look after that ancient fragment. That has to be good news for the village.' He reached out again to squeeze her wrist, but restrained himself, as if to do so now might be too much of a liberty. 'Do come, your friend will be there.'

'I haven't got any friends.'

'Jerome.' He noticed the change in her expression, from bland to wistful, and continued in as breezy a tone as he could muster. 'We're going to eat an amazing Thai meal that I, personally, will be preparing from scratch. It's a sort of try-out for a new series I want to make called *Novice in the Kitchen*. You must come!' After a little more hesitation, she accepted. After all, Jerome would be there.

Chapter Nineteen

———

The first encounter shocked both father and son. To Michael, Gerard had always seemed pale – the result of spending too little time outdoors – but now the slight paunch and jowls, developed over years of inactivity, had all but disappeared. His neck skin hung loose, like that of an old man; his hands and wrists showed clearly where the bones enlarged at the joints, but it was the eyes that disturbed Michael so much. He could never remember much in the way of sparkle in his father's eyes but now, they showed no animation at all. It was almost as if he were looking into a pair of dark, empty shadows, cast by the jut of the brow. As he rose, it was clear that his stoop was more noticeable and Michael noted the effort he seemed to be making, simply to get himself up out of his chair.

Gerard was shocked by the sight of his son. At the beginning of term, he had said goodbye to a young boy, but now he was rising to greet a man. Michael, too, was thin – too thin for his age with a pinched-in waist and a jacket that hung loosely on the shoulders. The bone structure of his face was nearer, now, to the surface of his skin, with prominent cheek bones showing and a greater strength in the jaw. Michael's eyes, vivid blue, alive and flashing, were filled with animosity. Gerard registered this as little more than a developing fiery spirit but he knew, from his son's upright stance and direct gaze that from now on, he would defy him if necessary. He offered a hand. Michael couldn't know how much his father had rehearsed this first meeting in his mind, or what an effort it was for him to speak at all.

'Welcome home, Michael, for your last summer holidays before Sandhurst. I hope you have an enjoyable time.' No amount of rehearsing could have prepared him for his son's response.

'Thank you, Father. I won't be much in your way. I have managed to get myself a holiday job.'

'I *beg* your pardon!'

'I'll be working at Stoneford. At the White Hart Hotel, as a receptionist. They want me to live in for most of the time.'

'Good God!'

'Father, the pay is really little more than pocket money, but I've no intention of being dependent upon you for a moment longer than I need.' Gerard was ready to remonstrate about besmirching the family name, by working in trade but, catching the sharpness of the look, from the clear blue eyes, he held his peace.

Michael kept out of his father's way, and out of Wychgate, for most of the summer. He played cricket, not for the village – for fear of seeing anything of Violet – but for a Stoneford club. He also discovered tennis, a game that required far more strength and skill than he could possibly have imagined but at which, with his natural sportsman's eye, he quickly became adept. The Stoneford Tennis club was a jolly place too, with a smattering of young adults from the town. One or two had odd accents, but he had no difficulty in mixing with them and found their company undemanding and refreshing. Several of the girls at the club lost their hearts to him, but at no time were their feelings reciprocated. Michael loved Violet, and always would, regardless of what feelings she might, or might not have had for him.

It should have been an idyllic summer, a prelude to the strenuous training period that would soon ensue at Sandhurst. But in spite of his free and easy social life, his tiny but growing bank balance, and the quiet satisfaction of earning his keep, there was a constant nag in his mind, and that eroded his happiness. Violet was not it. She would always be in his thoughts, a sad, regretful reminder of what might have been, but that episode was closed.

The nag was, rather, an unanswered question about Gerard. What had happened to his relationship with Violet? How would he able to live with his betrayal – of his own son? Judging by his appearance when they had met, Gerard wasn't coping with his conscience very well. But was he still seeing Violet? Michael was almost sure not. Whatever the *status quo*, he felt he had to clear things up with his father. It would take such courage as he hoped he could muster, and it would probably mean that he could no longer call Wychgate Manor his home. He would have to find an alternative life: a prospect that frightened Michael less, than it might a young man with loving family ties to break. He felt, too, that in spite of everything, he owed much to his father. He had been well educated, properly cared for and as a child had lacked nothing other than warmth and affection – a commodity that Gerard would surely not have denied him, if he had had it to give. Michael knew that if he were to face his future with courage and honour, he would have to air all these things with his father.

The summer sped by, and his short term of employment came to an end. He took the train to Wychgate two days before he was due to leave for Hampshire, having spent the previous day in London, collecting some of his uniform and purchasing items that he thought he might need for the Military Academy. Once he had got home, he felt he could not delay the inevitable confrontation a moment longer. He went directly to the study, knocked and entered without waiting for a response.

'Father, we must talk.'

Gerard was standing by the window, looking across the watermeadows. He half turned. 'Michael! We've seen so little of each other.' His voice lacked expression.

'Father, are you still seeing Violet Ball?'

'Seeing?'

'Does she still come here?' Gerard stared at him for several seconds, with eyes that seemed to be viewing a different world. 'Well, does she?'

'Miss Ball has not been here since Midsummer.' Gerard

turned back to the window. After another long pause and a deep, wracking sigh, he said, 'Why do you ask?'

'Father, I have to ask you this.' Michael felt his courage beginning to ebb. This was such a destructive question. Whatever the answer, it would change their relationship for ever. 'Was there ever anything between Violet and . . .' his voice tailed to a whisper, 'and yourself?' Gerard continued to stare out of the window. Slowly he shook his head. 'Father, I m-must know.' Gerard turned, but kept his eyes downcast.

'I cannot imagine what you could possibly mean. Miss Ball was merely my pupil. Her studies simply . . . came to an end.' Michael kept his arms straight down by his sides, fists clenched, thumbs held straight along the seams of his cavalry twill trousers, as if standing on a parade ground. He held up his head and subjected Gerard to the full power of his blue eyes. His voice was unreliable but he managed, just, to keep it steady.

'I am very sorry Father, for what I have to say. But, that night, I *saw* you.'

Gerard swung away, his mouth sagging.

'What are you trying to say?'

'I was there, on Midsummer night. I broke out of school, I cycled over to Wychgate and hid in the wood. I saw the two of you – you and . . .' he could hardly get the words out '. . . Violet. By the altar stone.' There was a long pause, during which Gerard stared out of the window. His next words were carefully chosen, delivered in measured tones:

'I do not know what your implication might be, but it sounds like fanciful poppycock.'

'Do you deny it?'

Gerard turned again and looked, at last, into Michael's eyes. The boy had wanted to press him, to obtain some kind of confession, but now he read such despair in his father's face, that he felt he could not bear to continue. He just wished the moment would pass.

'There is nothing to deny.' Gerard said.

In mid-October that year, a Saint Luke's Summer lit up the countryside with vivid sunshine. Ploughboys whistled as their patient teams of Shire horses pulled single-furrow ploughs slowly across the weedy stubbles, turning the soft earth easily and cleanly. Behind them, flocks of black-headed gulls whirled and swooped, picking up worms, grubs and beetles exposed by the turning of the soil. The landscape was a patchwork of brown ploughland, green striped fields of emerging winter wheat and golden woodland. At the Royal Military Academy, Sandhurst, Michael was so immersed in his training that Wychgate and its horrible associations, though still gnawing at his peace of mind, had faded enough, just, to let him get on with the start of his career. He was considered to be one of the more promising cadets of that year's intake and seemed, already, to have made plenty of friends.

Violet, too, was making her mark. Barely half-way through the short, intense Oxford term, she had astounded everyone, not only with her academic prowess, but also with her retentive memory and gentle assurance. Students, into whose milieu she had moved with grace and ease – in spite of her alien background – were astounded at how widely read she already seemed to be. Her tutor, realising very quickly that she was destined for high achievement, demanded more and more of her, and was not disappointed.

She managed to gain acceptance, not for her social standing, but for her intellectual status, and that transcended most of the class barriers – not that many female undergraduates came from the top echelons of society. Higher education for women, in the 1920s, was still considered by the nobility to be somewhat infra dig. Males, of whatever walk in life, no longer interested her except on a purely social level. She was constantly attracted to them and had, at first, allowed several of them to wine and dine her. There was even a pretty young man, son of a west-country baronet, who almost tempted her into his bed. He was under the impression that having a considerably more humble background than his own, she would be quite willing; she was drawn to him because his colouring and frame were reminiscent of Michael's. But within a very few days, she realised that the resemblance was but superficial – not even skin deep, for he had clear skin, and Michael had a peppering of small freckles on cheek bone and wrist – and their relationship petered out.

That episode had lasted less than a week, but represented a milestone in her newly constructed life, helping to reinforce her determination to remain true to Michael, in spite of his action. She would not be the one in the wrong and one day, she hoped, she would find out what had happened to make him cut himself off from her. She had burnt his terse letter of dismissal but its text, especially the paradox of the first two sentences were always fresh in her mind: 'I think we should conclude our relationship forthwith. I will never stop loving you.' Well, she would never stop loving him, and her quickly aborted dalliance with the handsome son of the baronet had laid the foundation stone of her determination.

Meanwhile, she wanted to stay in this wonderful city for as long as she could – perhaps for her entire career. To achieve that she would need a First, and would have to impress everyone enough to make them feel that the college could not do without her. Nothing could replace the part that Michael was to have played in her life, but carving an academic career for herself, in the subject she held so dear, would provide some of the consolation she so badly needed.

Gerard received no mail from Michael through the whole of October and into November. When his son did finally write, the letter was so brief and formal that he didn't even bother to re-read it. It informed him that he had been invited to spend Christmas with a fellow cadet in Yorkshire, somewhere near Harrogate, and that he would not, therefore, be coming home.

He felt no resentment at his son's obvious desire to stay away. He wrote an equally formal reply, and as he did so, it came to him that for years, his relationship with his son had been wholly unnatural. His letters, even to the little boy at prep school had been curt and free of any expression of emotion and school holidays had been periods when they had instinctively kept themselves apart from one another. The poor boy had had no mother, of course, and Gerard supposed that might have had something to do with the coldness of their past life together, but there had never, until now, been any kind of animosity. The harrowing events of recent months weighed so heavily with Gerard that they quite overshadowed the years of unhappiness since Elizabeth's death. And for the first time, he realised that those years were also, to the day, the length of Michael's life. In those moments, he knew, more clearly than he had ever realised before, just how much he had failed his own son.

His thoughts turned to Violet. He had failed her too, had betrayed her innocent trust, had allowed silly emotions to affect his judgment and had distressed the girl to such an extent that she would never, now, contact him again. And he had so looked forward to following her Oxford career and beyond.

Over recent weeks, as the days had shortened and the November scenery had taken on its usual mushy drabness, with rotting leaves everywhere underfoot and a grey, milky sky that blended with the constant, chilling mist, he had tried to put the events of the whole summer into perspective. Michael's inexplicable decline at school had mystified him. Adolescents, he supposed, tended to go through odd phases but such a setback, after a young lifetime of stability and solid achievement, seemed out of proportion. Memories of Midsummer night were almost too painful to bear, but what nagged at his conscience most was the fact that Michael's decline, and subsequent change in demeanour had begun soon afterwards. Those damning words, 'I saw you, Father.' How could he have seen? How could he have been there? Did Violet inform him about the shameful events that night? And if she did, what motivated her? With a sinking feeling, Gerard concluded that she would have felt obliged to tell Michael so that she could bring about the severance she so obviously desired. How repellent she must have found me, he thought. Before Midsummer, Gerard's life had been unhappy and unfulfilled, but it had its compensations, mainly in Michael's success but more, he had to admit – compounding his feeling of guilt – in Violet's. After Midsummer, he felt himself so different, and so distant, that occasionally he wondered if he had not died, right there in the wood, at Violet's feet, and that his existence now was some kind of limbo.

Guilt about what he did in the wood had forced Gerard to make a series of practical decisions. Down in his watermeadows, in the fading November afternoon, thousands of trees were in the process of being planted. A group of foresters, with bundles of tiny seedling trees, each no more than a foot long, were following allotted lines. In one hand each forester held a short-handled mattock. With this, every two yards, he would stoop to chop out a divot. With his free hand he would pull a baby tree from the bundle on his back, push its roots into the exposed earth and then tread the divot back. Eventually, almost twenty-two acres were planted with the new woodland crop.

In subsequent years, as the trees grew, the same foresters would return to scythe between them, to reduce grass and weed competition while the plantation developed. After almost a decade, the trees would be large enough to fend for themselves. The rabbit fence, consisting of wire mesh, bedded into the ground and held erect by posts every ten feet, erected all round the perimeter of the plantation, would gradually rot away. By the time Hitler had been defeated, and the atom bombs dropped on Japan, the trees would be tall enough to mask the view of the original fragment of ancient woodland known as Pyson Wood.

The old name slipped naturally on to tongues for the new plantation and the villagers became accustomed to the lengthening shadows thrown by the densely planted trees. Soon it was difficult for the little boys to get through to the river to bathe in summer but anyway, Stoneford opened its first public swimming pool just after the war, and many of them would take the bus there, of a Saturday morning, their woollen swimming trunks rolled in their towels. By the time Michael had returned to the manor, after a creditable career in the army, the wood was wholly overgrown, sealing in all the secrets of the past.

But on that grey November afternoon, in 1926, Gerard stood for more than an hour, motionless at the study window, while he watched the men planting the last of the young fir trees. He saw them gather their tools, throw the last few saplings down by the new gate in the rabbit fence and then walk up the street, tired after their day but happy in companionship, nudging each other in the ribs and guffawing at some mutual joke. Not one glanced up at the manor as the group passed.

Gerard did not envy their comradeship, indeed, he hardly noticed them at all. His thoughts were focused on none but his own failures. He had been disloyal to Elizabeth, abandoning her memory and pining like some lovelorn youth for a young girl. He had destroyed his relationship with Violet, the one person whom he could call, truly, his friend. He had betrayed his own son, first by default, returning a lifetime of loyalty with indifference, and then, as he had come to realise in recent months, by poisoning the innocence of Michael's first love with jealousy. He knew too, that deep inside himself he had always resented the sacrifice of Elizabeth's life for Michael's. And he had, at last, made himself admit that the lovelessness of his son's home life had been caused by an inner grit of resentment that had chafed at his being for nearly two decades. Instead of seeing, in Michael, a part of Elizabeth that had survived, that he could have loved, nurtured, watched develop and mature, he had turned his back, preferring to live alone, crab-like within his own hard carapace. That, perhaps, was his worst betrayal.

When he knew the last worker had left the site, and would not return, Gerard unlocked the bottom drawer of his desk and took out a chafed leather case. He did not bother with a coat, in spite of the cold, but carried the case outside, walking down to the gate in the rabbit fence that surrounded the new wood, across the old course of the meadow footpath to the ancient woodland fragment and sat, cold and alone on the altar stone.

Muffled by the trees, and too distant to be clearly audible from the village, no one heard the pistol shot. Gerard's body was not discovered until several days later, during a search initiated by an anguished Mrs Bull. He had been thrown back by the impact of the bullet so that his body lay on its back across the altar stone like some kind of sacrifice. The head, out of sight at first, behind the stone tablet, was almost blown away, the two arms outstretched hanging just off the stone, made a cruciform shape.

Michael was collected from Sandhurst, by the family solicitor. In spite of everything that had happened he grieved for his father and would wish, to the end of his days, that they had parted on better terms. Now, he was quite alone.

The solicitor, it turned out, was to hold the estate in trust until Michael's twenty-first birthday. There were rumblings, in the village, about burying a suicide in the hallowed ground of the churchyard. No one had been close to Gerard, but those who ventured any opinion at all suggested he should share his wife's grave in the family tomb. As the only surviving close relative, Michael was, naturally, consulted and his wishes heeded most.

'I believe my father would rather have been laid to rest where he was found, than to lie with my mother in the churchyard,' he said. 'That ground, I believe, has an ancient history. Certainly, it will be hallowed enough for him to rest in.' Michael was glad the new wood had been planted and understood, now, that his father had wanted to enwrap the fragment and to close it off, for ever, from the rest of the world. Certainly, he told himself on his way back to resume his military training, I will see to it that this new curtain of trees remains drawn over the whole business.

Loose ends, thought Jerome, I must sort out the loose ends before I go. There were many. He had had no say in the selection of his successor, but he had agreed to stay on at Wychgate, if the village wanted him, until the new priest arrived. It was possible that he would be released by the autumn – Christmas at the very latest. He hoped it would be sooner, but could not begin to think about his departure until he had everything sorted out. Outside his study window, blossom from the Bramley apple that leant over the crumbly red-brick wall of the old rectory, shading the area that had become the new rectory garden, was shedding pink and white petals which slowly browned after they had settled on his rather unkempt lawn and weedy gravel pathways.

Thoughts of leaving Wychgate made him sad, not because he was especially attached to the village – in some ways, Jerome felt, it was a hateful place – but because he was especially fond of two of its inhabitants. He had not spoken to Michael Pilkington for almost a year now, but his fondest hope was that they would be reconciled. It grieved him to think that such a kindly old man should have felt so injured as to have cut himself off, completely, from all his associates. Jerome would have to do something about that. He felt he must, somehow, relieve the pain the man obviously felt but first, he had to find out its cause.

And Imogen of course. How he hated the thought of not living near her! But he hated more bitterly the prospect of leaving her behind un-whole, since it was obvious to him – if to no one else – that for all her new-found assurance, she was still suffering from a debilitating guilt about her past. That was another loose end which had to be tied up.

Then there were various practical conundrums. What was going to happen about that bloody building site? No one seemed to have a clue. And, thinking of housing, where the hell was he to live, once the rectory had been handed over to its new incumbent? He had very little capital – well, none really – and no likely salary, so no prospect of buying anything even on a hundred percent mortgage. Jesus had said, 'sufficient unto the day' but he'd managed by spending his ministry on the scrounge. Nothing dishonourable in that, of course, but *someone* had to provide and this was the Enterprise Age, where services had to be paid for.

He had resolved to begin working, in earnest, on all this unfinished business, as soon as the Easter weekend had passed. The final task of ending his duties as a clergyman could be accomplished later but now, since the last Easter hymn of the year had been sung, it was time to take the first step. He decided to pay Imogen a visit.

She was ready, with tea things set out on her new terrace. 'I thought we might brave the, ahm, outdoors,' she said. 'It's so sunny.' Jerome found it difficult to concentrate. She was wearing a tropical-looking, loose-fitting rough cotton blouse – off-white with ferny vegetation on it in vivid green, and a pair of men's trousers far too big around the waist for her, but done up tightly with an old leather belt. Her hair had been cut short enough to stand up slightly at the back and revealed her ears which stuck out very slightly but which were small and neat. He could hardly bear to be so near her and yet unable to touch her. He decided to try to get the business side of their meeting over as quickly as possible.

'Imogen, people are a bit concerned about the wood site. I know your partner has gone bankrupt—'

'Ex. In fact, Russell Hands was never really my partner.' She effected a dismissive little flip, as if shooing away a wasp. 'He's, ahm, history.' Jerome noted her slight eye-movement and looked away, waiting for her to continue. 'I've bought all the land back from him. And I've no intention of building that huge, ahm, estate. None whatever.'

'Oh, Imogen, that's the greatest news.'

'Really?' She looked sharply at him. 'I thought you wanted more people here.'

'Not *that* many more.'

'No. Well what I thought was this.' Imogen outlined what, to Jerome, seemed the best of all possible worlds. She was to develop the part nearest the road, with three, or at the most, four houses. Two would be modest – affordable for first-time buyers – and one or perhaps two would suit people on larger incomes. But the most exciting part was that she planned to donate a large area of the ex-woodland to the village. The ancient fragment would be kept intact and the couple of acres around it would be given back to the archeologists to excavate in for as long as they needed.

'Are you sure they will be interested? Wasn't the place ruined when all those heavy vehicles came in?'

'I've been in, ahm, contact. They are thrilled with it. It will actually be part of the university until it is no longer of archaeological interest, then it will be preserved for the parish, with full public access.' While she spoke, Jerome watched her face, lit up with the excitement of these projects.

'Have you discussed all this with anybody?'

She shook her head. 'Only with Mr Busby. He didn't seem terribly impressed. Said there had to be an, ahm, catch. Said he couldn't see what it was, but I could rest assured, he'd find it.'

'Fat head!'

'He told me the parish would, naturally, oppose any development.'

'So you reminded him that you already had full permission for forty houses and were, in fact, only building four?' Imogen nodded and smiled, enjoying the conspiracy with Jerome. They had both scoffed about Busby before, not overtly, but their shared feelings about the man had been implicit. Jerome felt, as ever, a tiny spike of guilt for thinking ill of the man at all.

'You'll have made peace with the village and, oh, Imogen, you'll have done us all so much good.' He squeezed her hand. He wanted desperately to kiss her, to hug her, to ravish her, here, among the spring flowers. To distract himself, and to break the spell, he leapt up. 'It's getting a bit chilly, can't we wander?'

'Come through to the orchard,' Imogen said, also standing up. 'I planted a thousand daffodils bulbs in the grass there last autumn. Rupert said they're, ahm, rather vulgar, but I think they look wonderful in this bright sunshine.' Hand in hand, they walked from the terrace into the garden.

Chapter Twenty

———

The most difficult loose end, Jerome decided, would be sorting things out with Michael. But it had to be done. He simply could not leave the village and his ministry, such as it was, without achieving a reconciliation. Several times during the previous year, he had tried to speak to the old man, but always had been treated to a terse rebuttal. He had tried telephoning, but Michael had seldom answered and when he had, he would hang up as soon as he heard Jerome's voice. Eventually, the rector had more or less given up, not wanting to make the old man even more unhappy. But now that Imogen's plans were in place, and went such a long way to repair the damage done in the village, he felt he might – he just might – be able to begin the process of patching up the poor old boy's wounds.

Thus, two days after visiting Imogen, he purchased a bottle of Glenlivet Single Malt. It was, according to the label, twenty years old, a straw-coloured liquid that had cost Jerome an absolute bomb at the snootier of the Stoneford wine merchants. 'Cheap at the price, if it works,' Jerome had muttered aloud. Now, as he left the rectory, he slipped the bottle into the poacher's pocket of his Barbour oiled jacket. This was not a garment he would, under normal circumstances, have been seen dead in, but some visiting member of the Kensington Coup had left it on a pew a year before and, since it was still unclaimed, Jerome had taken to wearing it. With his wide-brim trilby, it made him look more

like a country auctioneer than a clergyman. He wished it had
been a brighter colour, instead of this awful cowcrap khaki.
It was known, privately, by him as the bullshit jacket.

The garden at the manor house looked weedy and neglected.
Paint was peeling, too, from the window frames, and one of
the downstairs windowsills had rotted to such an extent that
it was falling apart at its centre. He pressed the bell button,
and heard it ringing deep in the house. There was no response,
so he rang again, and then banged the door knocker as loudly
as he could. After several minutes, as he was about to walk
away, he heard slow, shuffling footsteps. A bolt was drawn,
on the front door, and he heard a heavy iron securing bar
being lifted from it. He giggled. This was getting to be like
one of those clichéd horror films. Slowly, the door creaked
open, no more than a crack. 'Michael?' The door opened a
little wider. The voice that answered was reedy, chesty.

'We've nothing to say to one another.' The door began to
close. Desperate, giggling, half with embarrassment, half with
mirth, for the situation was utterly ludicrous, Jerome jammed
his foot in the door, like a brush salesman.

'Michael, I *need* you. I'm desperate.' It was an impulse
to put it that way, but it worked. The door opened more
widely. Jerome was shocked at the old man's appearance.
He was unshaven, possibly had been for days, his clothes
were filthy and an unwholesome smell issued from the door.
Jerome wasn't sure whether it was from Michael, or just from
the house. 'May I come in?' He produced the bottle of malt
whisky from his inside pocket.

'You think you can buy me with that?' The question was
intended to be offensive; Jerome took it as a joke.

'I should hope so, it cost me an absolute fortune.'

Michael, in spite of everything, almost smiled. After a
moment, he stepped back to let Jerome in. 'I'm in a bit of
a pickle, I'm afraid. My woman hardly ever comes in now.'
He shuffled to the study, followed closely by Jerome. In spite
of the mild spring weather outside, the house felt cold and
damp. The old man sat down while Jerome busied himself
with glasses.

'These need a rinse, I suspect,' he said. The kitchen was

relatively tidy, but filthy with ingrained muck round the sink and cooker and the floor tacky with something spilt and inadequately wiped up. Soon, both men were sitting in comfortable chairs in the study, tumblers in hands, as they had been in the habit of doing when the firs still stood in Pyson Wood.

'Michael, I can't tell you how good it is to see you again.' Michael did not respond, but he sipped his malt. Its peaty, aromatic flavour, and the smoothness of the spirit conjured up happier times, and Jerome watched his friend's blue eyes fill with tears. Both men sat in silence for what seemed like a decade. Michael finished his drink and had his glass promptly refilled. The silence continued, but was becoming companionable rather than tense.

'It may not look like it,' Michael said at last, 'but I'm actually not one for self-pity. Never was.'

'You could have fooled me.' This was pushing his luck, but Jerome knew he would need a sizable dollop of good luck to carry this off. Michael looked up sharply.

'None of you can know what happened. Why the trees were planted.'

'Not very easy for anyone to know, Michael,' Jerome was glad the light was fading, since it would be easier to talk in the shadows, 'unless you tell.' The old man shook his head. They had several more drinks, as the twilight deepened, and a song thrush sang with loudmouth gusto in the holly outside the open window. After so long alone and miserable, Michael felt, gradually, that the presence of the other man had brought comfort. Jerome was careful not to force the pace but slowly, hesitantly, a conversation began. At first they talked randomly about the village, about Michael's youth, about Jerome's years in an urban parish, before coming to Wychgate. Jerome told Michael about his decision to leave the church, and his reasons. Finally, he managed to steer the conversation gently round to the wood, the trees, and Elizabeth's lonely grave in the churchyard.

Much, much later, rather drunk, but happier than he had been for months – years, even – Jerome strode back to his rectory in the moonlight.

*   *   *

Graham had decided to hold a book launch anyway. The publishers of his first novel, *Burnt Acres,* had said that launches weren't really all that helpful these days, and that word-of-mouth was likely to be the best way to sell. That seemed, of course, a contradiction, but then publishers, it seemed to Graham, were fuelled by caprice, rather than logical management practices. They had also said that even though he had a giant reputation among television producers, this would do little to sell books. Now if he had been a presenter, however brainless, but often seen on screen, his sales expectations would be much higher and a book launch would have been a great idea.

So, at personal expense, he had defied the marketing director, a wispy creature, fresh out of her teens, with an inability to speak other than by stringing clichés together and a wholly unbroken record in unreturned telephone calls, and had held his own bash. He spotted about five percent of the London literati he had invited – and a couple he had not – making rapid work of the champagne which the Buster Keaton Club provided at an obscene price per bottle. Several had copies of *Burnt Acres* under their arms, as if they planned to drink swiftly, but copiously, and then dash off. The first guests had arrived at a minute past six and the last were on their way out by two minutes to seven, seeking more salubrious dining places elsewhere in Soho. Few of those that mattered had commented. One, who wrote scatological works of inordinate length, without structure or story, but who was adored by broadsheet critics said, 'Crap, dear, pure crap!'

'You liked it, then,' Graham answered, wondering how he had had time to read the whole book since his arrival about twenty minutes before.

'Oh, lah sir!' cried the author and occasional guest reviewer. 'Do hear me out. It's crap, but I dare say you'll sell like hot cakes.' And then they were gone, and he was left in the somewhat shabby upper rooms of the Buster Keaton, alone with Imogen, who had agreed to help hand out review copies and cheese straws to the guests.

'Well, that's it,' said Graham. 'That's got Project Two

launched. A successful telly series as an independent producer, and now that bloody book is on the shelves at last.'

'What is, ahm, Project Three?'

'Oh, Immie,' Graham looked wistful. He took a half empty
glass out of her hand, 'I've a feeling you suspected that at one
stage it was you.'

'I'm pretty sure it was.' He began to lift the glass to his
lips. She put a restraining hand on his arm. 'You should be
more careful, you've no idea who drank from that one.' She
handed him a clean glass which she filled from a half empty
bottle. 'You should be more careful about how you select
your partners, too.' He sipped and shrugged.

'Will you be OK with that city bloke – all plums in the
mouth – what's his name?'

'Rupert? Oh ha ha!' She giggled for quite some time.
'Rupert!'

'I'm sure he fancies you.'

'I'm sure he does. But our relationship, ahm, has been
purely, as they say, business. He has advised me on investments, and he handled the buy-back at the village. That's
all.'

'But Imogen, will you be all right?'

'Of course, why shouldn't I be? Actually, Rupert has been
rather cleverer than even I could have hoped. He's made me
quite a rich woman – rich enough for my simple lifestyle,
anyway.'

'I didn't really mean about money,' Graham said. By the
twitch on her arm – he still had hold of her hand – he doubted
whether she was quite all right. He doubted it very much.
But he had no idea what might have been wrong, and felt
quite unable, now, to do anything about her. Two successful
projects out of three was not, he supposed, too bad a batting
average. Still . . . 'You know where I'll be if you want me,'
he said.

'I had no idea,' Jerome said, 'that so much junk could fit
into so small a place.' He was on his hands and knees, in the
sitting-room of the Wychgate rectory, surrounded by empty
tea chests and a logjam of books, mantelpiece ornaments,

gramophone records, various heaps of papers and framed photographs.

'The space will be even smaller, where you're going.'

'How do you know? You haven't seen it yet.' Imogen began to pile the heap of books into stacks according to size. There seemed to be an awful lot of old Penguin paperbacks – Chesterton, H. E. Bates, Lawrence.

'Isn't this a bit, ahm, rude, for a clergyman?' she said, handing him a copy of *Lady Chatterley's Lover*.

'A celebration of sexual love? No, I don't think so. Why do people assume that the clergy dislike sex?'

'Just joking.' She was trying to disguise the distress she felt at his determination to go. He was tetchy, irritated by the minutiae of the task of getting his base shifted from one dwelling to another.

'Where you live isn't at all important, you know.' He crammed the books into a case as she handed them over.

'Isn't it?'

'Of course not.' He thrust newspapers on top of the half-full box. He tried not to think of how much he would miss the changing pattern in the fields around the village, of the aconites that still managed to flower in the churchyard, in spite of the PCC's attempts to use herbicide to purify the grasses; of the spring lambs in the field behind the old rectory, where wild daffodils bloomed beneath the lime trees every year, untouched by the sheep that grazed the rest of the grass to a uniform smoothness. And he thought, with regret, how he would miss the new site greening over, healing the scars where the fir plantation had gone, and even how the new houses would look. What would they plant in their gardens? Would there be any Asian families, or even Chinese? He suspected not. 'It's the people you live with that matter, not the place.'

'But neither of us lives with anyone.'

He stopped cramming newspaper. 'Do you imagine I don't think about that? And worry about it? Every bloody day of the bloody week?' He had not intended a display of emotion. 'Oh, for Heaven's sake! Can you do this, I'm *hopeless* with anything practical.' She came and knelt by the case, not taking the newspaper out of his hand, but gently taking hold of both his hands.

'Don't do this, Jerry. Don't go!' He looked at her small hands, felt their roughness, after all that gardening. They were actually browner than his, and more calloused, and his shook; hers were almost steady. 'You don't really know what you're doing, do you?'

'I can't stay. I've got to get out of this place by the end of the month.'

'You could, ahm, move in with me. I'm not exactly short of rooms.' Had he not dreamed of a permanent existence under her roof? This was a cruel temptation. He shook his head.

'That is so sweet,' he said. 'It was sweet the first time you offered too, but, Imogen, can you imagine what people would say?'

'*You* worry about that?'

'No, I suppose I don't, really, but I don't feel I could do it. It's hard to explain exactly why.'

'Jerry, I, ahm, I do need you. I need you quite, ahm badly, as a matter of fact.' She was surprised when he laughed.

'I'm sorry, Imogen, I don't mean to be cynical, but that is one of my own favourite ploys when people I want to help won't respond.' Imogen snatched the newspaper from his hand, threw it on to the floor and began to cram more books into the case with such force that some were bent over and spoiled.

'It does happen to be true,' she whispered. But he hadn't heard above the rustling of paper.

Jerome's plan had been to move as much of his material over to his flat in Stoneford as possible over the few weeks that were left of his incumbency. To save on removal costs, Imogen had agreed to help him pack and to take his stuff in, over frequent journeys, in the back of her new – well, almost new – estate car. Recently, she had got rid of the tiny Ford Fiesta because the remnants of Mrs Crowe's cheap scent were impossible to get rid of and she wanted to wipe the woman right out of her memory. Also, she had wanted a larger vehicle that would accommodate everything from the black Labrador puppy she had purchased, to standard trees collected from distant nurseries. Jerome had already sold his ancient Fiat to raise a little money for his future.

Without another word, she picked up one of the smaller cases and carried it out to the waiting car. Jerome lifted the large case of books, astounded at its weight, and staggered behind her. After toing and froing for a few more journeys, the vehicle was loaded to such an extent that its mud flaps touched the ground. Imogen drove them at a snail's pace, causing a long crocodile of traffic into Stoneford, through the centre of the town to a small, mean street that had originally led to the town gasworks. The rest of the town was built in mellow limestone, but down here, the narrow terrace of houses were red brick, four-square and ugly. Together, they carried his belongings to one of the front doors and piled them outside before he found his key and unlocked the door.

'At least it's a ground-floor flat,' he said. The door opened into a tiny hall with stairs running straight up ahead and a brown painted door to the right. He took a second key and admitted her to his new abode. The room could not have been more than ten-foot square, with a view out to the opposite side of the narrow street. Above the window, black mould had stained the faded wallpaper, where damp had penetrated the thin brickwork. The air in the room was stagnant, heavy with mould spores and the slightly fishy smell of rotting timber. One small sofa occupied the side furthest from the window. Behind this room was a second, once a kitchen, now a tiny cramped bedroom with a small window looking on to a concrete yard that was no more than about twelve-foot square.

'We share a kitchen upstairs,' he said. 'There's a bathroom – well, actually it just has a shower – and lavatory, of course.'

'But you can't possibly live here,' Imogen said. 'It's . . . it's wholly unsuitable.' She was trying not to cry.

'Someone else lived here before me,' Jerome said.

'Only because they couldn't live anywhere better.' The tea chest and few cardboard boxes they had brought was only a small proportion of Jerome's chattels, and yet they seemed to fill the dismal little room. Jerome had not realised, until now, just what a big and rather stupid change he was making. He had not thought out the practical aspect of his move at all. 'Sufficient unto the day' had answered any small, niggling queries coming from the more sensible zone of his mind. Now he realised that not only would he find it almost impossible to achieve the kind of service he felt he needed to give, because of limited space and an almost total absence of funds, but also, his own personal life would become virtually unworkable.

'I have to have somewhere people will want to come to,' he said. 'I suppose I can cheer this place up a bit.' He rubbed some of the grime from the window. 'And there's always the day centre, of course. That's where my real work will be.'

They dumped the last of the boxes on to the floor of the tiny front room and left. As he turned the key in the lock, Jerome tried to tell himself that this was where he should be; at the sharp end, where all the misery was at. But he found it almost impossible to see himself in any sort of context at all, here in the ugliest part of town. He did not even know, really, what to do next.

On the journey home, both he and Imogen were silent. She had been driving, now, for almost a year since her long absence from the wheel, but her technique was erratic and distracted. She earned several angry hoots from drivers who considered themselves more expert but Jerome, who might otherwise have been frightened, sat apathetically staring through the windscreen. As she turned into the drive of Weir House, he said, 'Can I stay for a bit?'

'Oh, I wish you would!'

'You know, Imogen, I've been so engrossed with tying up all my loose ends here,' Jerome said, 'that I have not properly looked at what I'm really going to do next. It is, frankly, rather a mess.'

Later that day, Jerome acted on the kind of impulse that clergymen so often give way to, to the annoyance of their victims, and often to their own embarrassment: he spotted lights on at the Old Stores and, since Graham seemed not to have been in the village for a while, decided to pay him a surprise call.

'I've been visiting our mutual friend, Imogen,' he said, after being admitted into the small kitchen.

'Ah!' Graham composed his features into a half-smile.

'She's been helping me to sort out my move.'

'Really?' Graham seemed to be more noncommittal than usual. 'She seems to be coping remarkably well with everything now.'

'Doesn't she though!' Jerome picked up the bitterness in his tone.

'I thought you and she were, you know, quite close.'

'No one gets close to Imogen.' Jerome felt for the man. Here was a longing similar to his own. 'I thought she was keen on that city type, Rufus, or Rupert, or whatever his bloody silly name is, but I don't think she cares for him either. Except "just as an, ahm, friend".' It was supposed to be a gentle mocking of her mannerism, but it came out as an embittered lampoon.

'I've read your novel,' Jerome said, in an effort to navigate the conversation into more comfortable waters, 'and I have to admit, I rather enjoyed it.'

'Thank you.'

'I didn't recognise any of the characters – was I supposed to have?'

'Not really, although one is based on a relative of mine. A great-aunt.'

'Oh? The lady barrister?'

'Well, she's an academic, in real life, but there are elements of her in my fictitious character, Rose Darley.'

'Really, such as? I say, you don't mind me quizzing about it do you?' Graham shook his head. He was a new enough author to enjoy explaining about what he thought of as his 'art'.

'In *Burnt Acres* Rose has a kink in her character, a blind spot that influences her entire life. Something happened to her, at a relatively tender age, to change her life.'

'But I thought Rose had done rather well. Doesn't she end up a judge?'

'Ah yes, in her *profession*. But what about her relationships?'

'I didn't think she'd had any.'

'Precisely.'

'Tell me a bit more about your aunt. She sounds interesting.'

'Great-aunt. Violet Ball – perhaps you've heard of her?' Jerome shook his head. 'Well, she's pretty famous within her circle. But I don't suppose you've had vast amounts to do with occultism in mediaeval times.' Jerome shook his head again. 'She grew up in this house.'

'She did? Oh, now I think I've an idea who you mean.'

'But she won't come to visit me here. Not for want of being asked. I've begged her to come, but she says she never wants to see Wychgate again. And of course, I'm pretty sure that whatever happened to her, happened here. Something must have cut pretty deep anyway, for her still not to want to come. I mean, she's well into her seventies – can't be far short of eighty, in fact.'

'You wouldn't be able to give me her address, would you?' Graham nodded and went to his desk to find one of his aunt's letters.

The prospect of Jerome's departure from Wychgate filled Imogen with woe. She could hardly bear to think of him rotting in that dismal little flat, and she felt that his move was pointless anyway. He could do far more good, she was sure, if he were sensibly based – at Weir House, for instance – and yet, she could not think how to get him to change his plans. She had never been a good influence on people and the more she tried to do any good for them, it seemed, the more miserable she made them.

Rupert Lilliwhite had been wonderful to her, and was obviously more than fond. But she could not return any sort of feeling for him, even though she was incredibly grateful for his guidance. By allowing him to invest her capital, dividing it between high-risk ventures and solid, low-earning investments, she had watched her nest egg grow until it exceeded the original sum obtained from Hands.

Graham, too, delighted her with his quick wits, his humour and his optimism. He was very attractive, too, she thought, but there was still this icy core in her persona that prevented her from being able to express any deep warmth. He reminded her of Marcus, in some moments – physically, more than in his nature – but if anything, that made her even less able to open up to him. There was also this odd hang-up that had appeared after her thing with Hands. Something about the, well, the *maleness*, in men that made her shrink when they tried to touch her in certain ways. Because of that, she felt guilty for appearing so lukewarm to his advances, even though she still wanted his company and felt cheered whenever he was with her.

But Jerome was something else. He was the only other human with whom she felt truly relaxed. He acknowledged her past and her feelings of guilt – the others seemed to want to gloss over it. He seemed to know almost more intimately than she did herself, the black centre that still, in spite of everything, would not go away and that as long as that dark core was there, her final stages of rehabilitation could not take place. But Jerome seemed unable, or disinclined, to make any physical advances, and she hungered for him – all of him. She knew that she had almost completed rebuilding her life, but there still wanted a support to its central arch, and Jerome, she felt sure, was that keystone.

The telephone interrupted her thoughts.

'Immie? It's Rupert.' After the usual pleasantries, during which Imogen warmed to the voice and felt her own accents converging with his towards the tribal sounds of their class origins, Rupert said, 'Immie, what about your father?' The words came like a glass of ice water, dashed into the conversation.

'What about him?'

'I've been up to Methwold quite a lot, lately. Since your mother, you know . . .'

'I see.'

'And I can't help noticing that he's really not coping terribly well. With Philip abroad, he really has very few people who are close enough to be able to care very much.'

'And *I* should care?'

'Immie, he is your father.'

'Not, ahm, anymore, according to what they said, after . . . after . . .'

'I know you didn't exactly part on good terms, but now that so much time has passed, and you're pretty well OK, might it not be a good idea to restore relations?'

'Might it not be up to, ahm, someone else to make the first move?'

'He's lost an incredible amount of weight, and he's missing out all his usual social functions. Do you realise, he didn't go shooting once this season?'

'Lucky pheasants!'

'Well, I just thought I'd let you know. *I* worry about him, even if you don't.' And after a little more desultory conversation, he rang off, saying, just before he did, 'If you were to pick up the phone, you'd find him in. And I happen to know he'd speak to you.'

It was so terribly unfair of Rupert, Imogen thought, to burden her like this. It was her parents who had thrown her out, not the other way round. Frequently she re-lived the awful moment when Lord Methwold had given her her final dismissal. He had considered the odious Mrs Crowe to be an ally, too insensitive to realise that she had not only been, to some extent, an agent in Imogen's downfall, but had also impeded her recovery. But her father had had tears in his eyes as they parted. She recalled, again, winter afternoons with her brothers, playing 'Snap' or 'Beggar My Neighbour' in their mother's small sitting-room at Methwold, and of slipping off her shoe to feel the caress of the silky Moroccan rug against her bare feet, that lovely, tingly feeling giving a focus to the warmth of those close family afternoons. And she realised how few of those moments there had been in her childhood, and therefore, how precious they were. When they parted, her mother had looked at her as though she had been some kind of dangerous reptile. To all intents and purposes, after Marcus, her mother had considered her dead. An unperson. But her father, she knew, had wept.

She picked up the phone and with a shaky hand, dialled

the number that she had not used in almost a decade, but which she could never have forgotten, even in her blackest moments. The voice that replied sounded tired and flat, but was unmistakable.

'Daddy? Oh, Daddy!'

Chapter Twenty-One

Surprise, decided Jerome, was the best strategy. His first step was to organise what he called, privately, the 'set up'. He managed to wangle a lunch invitation for himself with Michael at Wychgate Manor and, having fixed the date, persuaded Imogen to lend him her car for the day.

Michael and he were back on perfectly friendly speaking terms now, and although the old man was still far from happy, he was at least eating properly. Jerome had persuaded his helper to come back. She had, apparently, lost heart and stopped coming after so many meals had been left uneaten and after her colonel had become so offhand. 'He's such a different gentlemen from before,' she had explained, 'that I hardly like going, but I hate to think of the poor thing so neglected.'

When Michael had, at last, felt able to talk about the felling of the wood, he was still reluctant to provide much detail. Even when Jerome referred to Imogen's revised building plans and her generous gift to the parish, he would simply mutter, 'I'd rather not talk about it.' By snatching at tiny scraps of information, however, and putting these together, Jerome had begun to understand that what had happened concerned not only Michael, but his father and also this mysterious Oxford professor. He had gleaned as much knowledge as he could from Graham Ball and, when he felt his Wychgate contacts could yield no more, had taken a slow, cross-country train to Oxford.

He had written to Professor Ball from his Stoneford address to tell her about a site he knew – he did not let slip that it was Wychgate – where some rushed archaeological work had been carried out. He was not sure of the identity of some of the artifacts, but suspected that they were connected with pagan worship and he wanted to research the subject further. He had pointed out that he happened to be coming to Oxford shortly, and would be delighted if they could meet and discuss.

Her house in Carfax was modest and he had some difficulty tracking it down. When she had opened the door, she had seemed to look right through him, as if she had had a sixth sense with which to weigh him up. She had taken in his civvy clothes – he had abandoned his dog collar for a black shirt, but wore a pale yellow tie, herringbone tweed jacket and grey flannel trousers, which made him look like someone from a gangster film. The weighing-up had taken almost a whole minute before either spoke. She looked considerably younger than Michael, her grey hair cut fashionably short, and brushed back, the dark eyes, though slightly discoloured at the edges of the irises, clear and direct.

'Come on in, Mr Daniels.' Jerome understood that she had been celibate all her life, but there was a sensuousness about her mouth, a softness in her voice and an animal charm that made it hard to understand why she had had neither family nor lovers. 'I've got tea laid on.'

Jerome had realised, as soon as he had seen her, that she would be a challenge. Intelligence shone out of her. She was as assured and stable as Michael was distraught and in disarray. He had to decide, quickly, on what little knowledge he had gained about her, how to tackle this one. The subtle approach, he had decided would not do. He felt that she was brighter than he, and would see through any stupidly transparent tactics.

'I'm afraid I'm here under rather false pretences,' he had said, as she poured out his tea and cut him a generous slice of dark fruit cake.

'That was obvious from the moment you arrived.'

'The fact is, I have a parishioner in distress. It may seem a remote problem, but I think you could help.'

'How?'

'I'm not sure, that's the odd thing about it.'

'May I ask the name of your parishioner – and of your parish, for that matter?'

'You may, but I would much rather tell you a little about the background first.'

She had guessed it was Wychgate within moments. At first she had expressed anger at his interference. Then she had pointed out that it was all history. Happened more than sixty years before. That there was no point at all in going back. A somewhat odd attitude, Jerome had gently pointed out, for someone whose life's work had been devoted to the past.

'It was a childish thing. Nothing more.' Her tone was dismissive, but Jerome had noted that she had put down her teacup untouched, and that she had clasped her hands together on her lap and looked down at them for a while. They were the hands of an old person, with almost transparent skin, dark veins and brown blotches, but they were expressive hands, with slender fingers undistorted by arthritis. By her distant expression, he could tell that she was dreaming a little, of the past.

'And yet, he has never married,' Jerome had said, 'and neither, I believe, have you.' She had displayed her hands, stroking her left third finger to point out the absence of a ring.

'As you see.'

'He is suffering, rather.'

After a while, he had persuaded her to come to Wychgate, and to attempt to talk to Michael. So far, so good, but the next hurdle was likely to prove more difficult. How to get Michael to agree to see her. After rehearsing all kinds of approach in his mind, and imagining a hurt and angry rebuttal at each of them, he had come to the conclusion that only surprise would work. Jerome had driven Imogen's car to his denuded rectory on Friday night, and had left for Oxford at five the following morning, to be able to collect Violet and bring her back to Wychgate in time for lunch.

On the journey, she had chatted about her subject, about Oxford life and about the more interesting of her colleagues.

He told her about his crisis of faith. He had planned simply to gloss over it, merely giving a brief explanation about why his direction was about to change. But she had quizzed him intently, and they had developed a lively discussion, not only about personal faith, but about the state of the Church.

'I, of course, have never believed in the proprietary God,' she said, 'and I stopped having anything to do with church services as soon as I was able. But I did, as a youngster, believe in an afterlife and in the spirit world. In fact, that was really what got me so interested in the more primitive religions of ancient Europe.'

'Wasn't the idea of a "spirit world" a touch unrealistic for such an intelligent young person?' Jerome turned for a second, and wished he could watch her features more closely, instead of having to keep his eyes on the road.

'Perhaps. But I was so in love with all the stories – those wonderful myths – that I longed for them to be true. Also, spiritualism was catching on in those days – all those grieving mothers desperate to communicate with their lost sons after the Great War. I really believed you could make contact with the dead.' She laughed, 'How silly it all seems, looking back.' Then she turned solemn. 'I also learnt that such things, such beliefs can be damaging and dangerous.'

'How so, if they are merely products of imagination?'

'Ah, but Jerome – I may call you so, may I? – the products of imagination can destroy whole worlds.'

'That's not what I meant.'

'No. But whether we really believe, or whether we merely try to focus on things we cannot understand, such thoughts tend to make us turn our backs on reason. Therein lies the peril. Therein lies the kinked logic that legislates to prevent ordinary citizens from being cruel to animals, and yet *protects* by law, the right of certain individuals to cut the throats of terrified sheep or cattle, without previously stunning them. And all that, in the name of God!'

'What, in particular, made you realise that such things as, er, spiritualism can be dangerous?'

'That was a very long time ago.' Violet sat mute, for a mile or more.

'My question seems to have been something of a conversation stopper.'

'How is he – your troubled parishioner?'

'Michael? Better than he was.' She paled a little, at the
sound of his name, looked nearer to her real age, with the
colour ebbing out of her cheeks. 'I'd always known that there
had been some kind of trauma, but I could never understand
what. Michael was always surrounded by question marks.
Why, for instance, is his father not buried by his mother?
I didn't even realise that Elizabeth Pilkington had been his
mother. Why is such a warm, effusive soul – and he *was*
warm – so deeply lonely, without heirs or loved ones? And
why, for heaven's sake, why was he so desperate to have that
awful plantation left alone?'

'I might be able to answer some of those questions,' Violet
said. 'But I'm not going to, until I've seen him.'

'Oh, there is one final point,' Jerome said. 'He doesn't
know you are coming. That's why I was so insistent that
you do not write or contact him.'

'And what if he refuses to see me?'

'Then I hope you'll be *my* guest for lunch, and that you'll
come to have a look at our ancient fragment of woodland,
and the archaeological site – or rather, potential site.'

'I think I'd like to see that anyway.'

'Of course.' Jerome hoped she'd be so locked in talk with
Michael that she would not have time.

Michael, dozing in his study, heard the tyres on the gravel
and frowned with annoyance at an unexpected arrival. He was
expecting Jerome for lunch, on foot as usual, and wondered
who this could be turning up at such an awkward moment.
By the time he had opened the front door, Jerome had leapt
out of Imogen's car to greet him. From the shadows within,
Violet saw his gaunt features, his sunken cheeks, the stoop
and his thin, salt-and-pepper hair.

He looked older than his years, and as thin as a scarecrow
but that was not what moved her. His stance had dignity, and
the smile he offered to Jerome was obviously one of genuine
affection, but underlying the polite greeting was such a depth
of unexpressed sadness that Violet could hardly bear to watch

him. His whole body seemed to emanate a sense of defeat. She couldn't know, but intuition told her that he had dwelled on her all these years, as much as she had on him, probably even more. Looking at it logically, she suspected that the gap, formed by decades of separation, would be uncrossable, but seeing him as yet unnoticed, from the safety of the darkened car interior, her lips formed his name, which she repeated, soundlessly. Michael, Michael, Michael. And the weight of all those solitary years began to lighten and to recede. She remembered running over the meadows in sunshine, the clear water of the stream, its aching coldness on her bare feet, the feel of the sun on her face as she lay in the long grasses. She saw his eyes, clear blue, regarding her through half-closed lashes, his boyish laughter when she caught him observing her. Michael, Michael, Michael. She saw now, those eyes, paler, more clouded, but the same; saw the boy turned man, turned soldier, turned old man, but still the same. Michael!

But misgivings began to crowd in on these images. What would happen next? Could she bear it if he refused to speak to her? What would her presence do to him? This meeting, engineered by the well-meaning cleric, could be more damaging to his poor tortured psyche than all the years of absence. She could not know that his decline into the further limits of old age had accelerated since the felling of the wood, and that he had been really quite chipper for his age, before that. The poor man seemed so broken. And yet he continued to smile, with genuine affection, at Jerome.

'What's all this? A new car?'

'It's Imogen Fitzgerald's. Michael—'

'What are you doing gallivanting about in that instead of walking?' Jerome realised, now the moment had come, that he hardly had the courage to bring the encounter off. Suddenly he hated the hole-in-corner way in which he had tried to bring this whole thing off. If Michael took it the wrong way, he'd interpret it as a dirty trick. And he'd be quite right. It could all turn out to be a cruel mistake. The old man was looking at him, waiting for an answer to his question. Jerome had asked Violet to stay out of sight until he gave a signal, but now the moment had come, he did not know how to start.

'Michael. I want you to . . .' He was unable to find the words he needed. While he dithered, Violet who could not bear to stay concealed a moment longer had begun to emerge.

Michael recognised her in an instant. The initial shock made him feel a little faint but instead of eroding his concentration, this sharpened his focus on her. Jerome and the rest of his surroundings faded and blurred, so that all Michael could see was her face, with the same dark eyes and wistful smile that he had remembered from the meadows of his boyhood; had carried through Sandhurst, into the war, through the perils of the Libya campaign, through fifty years of peace – a sociable but lonely life. The anger of his betrayal still smouldered, but had long since become dulled, a manageable hurt. He should have felt resentment at Jerome's interference, outrage that she should even think of coming here, surprise, perhaps that she would even want to have bothered at this stage in their lives. But all he could do was stare at her, drinking in the extraordinary fact that she was here.

She looked as cool and assured as he had remembered her, year on year. He had not fallen into the trap of harbouring her image as a young girl – or not her face anyway. The lines and greyness of age with which he had altered her features in his mind were so unflattering, compared with the person who now, a little stiff-jointedly, but with as much dignity as anyone could possess, walked towards him. He knew, even in the midst of this sudden shock of her arrival, that he still loved her – not her memory, but her, as she was now. Whatever she may have done to him, whatever influence she may have bowed to, he was ready, right there and then, to embrace her, to hold on to her for what remained of his days. She began to walk towards him, anxious that he was swaying, but not wanting to bring about the rebuttal she half expected. She was first to speak.

'Michael?' All he could do was stare. 'It would appear that I have come to lunch.' She stood in front of him and looked directly into his face. She could still see his beauty, shining through the faded eyes and hollow cheeks. She could sense his love, not the physical urgency of their brief sexual affair but a warmth that radiated, in spite of the years, in spite of the great wrong she had felt for all the time. As if in cinema slow motion, he extended both arms and took her hands in his. His grip was firm. She loved the feel of his hands enclosing hers. He tried to smile, but his lips trembled too much, and his eyes were misty with the beginnings of tears.

At last, he found his tongue and said, in a trembling *pianissimo*, '"Love is not love which alters, when it alteration finds, or bends with the remover to remove."'

'I think I should go,' Jerome said. 'I hadn't really expected to stay to lunch, I do hope you'll both excuse me.' He opened the driver's door. 'I'll be at Weir House, if needed.' Neither seemed to notice him. He reversed out of the gate and drove very slowly up the street.

Though their heads hardly turned, Jerome's departure helped to break the spell. Michael escorted Violet into his house and into the same room where, in a different age, Gerard had discovered the two of them at his piano, the girl demure at the keys, his son blushing and embarrassed, standing by the piano stool. Now, slanting sun shone through the sitting-room window on to Violet's grey hair. Her profile was almost unchanged. He stood by the drinks trolley, uncertain and ill-at-ease. Being with her was too rich a feast to absorb, all at once, and he didn't quite know what to do or say next. He indicated the decanters of sherry and whisky. 'Would you like anything?' She shook her head. He poured himself a whisky and sat, gingerly, beside her on the sofa.

'That sonnet,' Violet said, after some silence. 'Do you know how it goes on?'

'Sonnet?' He wanted to sip his drink, but his hand shook too much to risk lifting the glass. She quoted the second line.

'"O, no! It is an ever-fixed mark, that looks on tempests and is never shaken."'

'Oh, I see. Yes, I think so. "It is the", um, "star to every wandering bark—"'

'No, the next bit.' She recited with a voice held low, but with ringing conviction in the tone. She was used to reading poetry to her students and was good at it. '"Love's not time's fool, though rosy lips and cheeks within his bending sickle's compass come."' But now she caught his look and stopped. He spoke slowly, with equal emphasis on each word.

'I was there. In the wood.' She caught her breath, fighting the surge of *angst* that his words stimulated and composed herself to reply.

'I know. I imagined I could feel your presence. Then, when you wrote, I knew you must have seen us, but I also knew you must have run off. If you had stayed, you would have heard me calling your name.'

'*My* name?'

'I could sense you were close. I had concentrated on you so hard that day. It is still as clear to me now as if it were a day or two ago.' During the next pause, she glanced around the room, wondering whether anything in it would remind her of Gerard. Nothing did. Only Michael was in her sights, in spite of the dozens of teas and tutorials she had taken with his father in this very house. She took his hand. 'Your father was a tortured man, Michael. He missed your mother desperately. Gradually, he began to see me as a replacement for her. He got the two of us muddled in his mind – we must have been so alike.'

'And knowing this, you arranged to meet him, at dead of night, in the middle of the wood – our wood?'

'I thought that if I could, somehow, make spiritual contact with his, with your mother, I could put him in touch. And I knew that the wood had terrific psychical strength. I believed in it then – spiritualism and all that.' She fell silent for a while. 'We were, after all, very young.'

'But what happened in the wood is a fact. I was there! I saw you. I saw him pawing at you, clinging.'

'You could not have seen all, or you would have come to me. You must have run at that moment when he lost his self-control. He must have been wanting me for ages, but I had been too utterly stupid to notice. I adored him, of course, as a child might an uncle, but that night, when he . . .' Violet was struggling, but knew she must tell the full story, 'when he began to . . . to touch me, in that way, I was shocked and frightened – my dearest friend suddenly translated to a monster! But however loathsome his advances were, I could not despise him. All I knew was that, for both our sakes, I had to get away, and that I must never see him again. But *he* ran from me. In fact you must almost have bumped into one another. I called, I searched, but could see no trace of you. Eventually, I walked home.

'Next morning, in daylight, I realised that I was probably being fanciful. I told myself that I had imagined your presence, that it was a ridiculous concept that you could possibly have been there. I wrote to you, each day.' Here, she began, at last, to break down, 'and when . . . and when you did not reply, I began to fear the worst, and then, your letter arrived and I . . . I . . .' She began to weep. Michael stayed quite still, but held on to her hand. Almost sixty years had evaporated. They might have been discussing an incident that had happened a week before. Her weeping subsided, but they stayed hand in hand and silent for several more minutes.

'My God, how cruel that letter must have been,' Michael said, at last. 'And my poor, deranged father. Thinking he could communicate with my mother. It's too ridiculous.'

'He wanted to be with no one else.'

'Until you came along.'

'I was really no more than a surrogate. His love for her translated itself to me.'

Jerome parked the estate car and let himself in through the back door of Weir House. Imogen was in the kitchen, arranging a vase of tall perennials.

'Well?' she asked.

'It's going to be all right. A bit sticky at first – I was quite ready to take the old girl off right away – but you should have seen their faces. It turns out they're still absolutely potty about one another, after all this time.'

'Wonderful.' There was a note of bitterness in her voice that he failed to detect, thinking that she was distracted with her floral art.

'Imogen, I wish you'd seen. I felt so happy for them I could almost cry.' He picked up a fallen stem of golden rod.

'Well, bully for you!' She took the golden rod from him

and pushed it into the vase, knocking two stems of phlox which slowly leaned to the left, pulling the rest of the arrangement askew.

'Damn!' Imogen said, and tried, without success, to straighten the flowers up. 'You're pretty good at making life perfect for everyone else, aren't you?' She yanked the phlox stems out of the water with such vehemence that several other flowers fell out. These she tried to push back but they merely fell out again. 'Oh *sod* it!' she said. With growing rage, she pulled out the whole arrangement and dumped it on the counter, ready to start again, but a heavy piece of greenery fell to the floor, pulling several flowers with it. With a yell of temper and a sudden sweep of her arm, she swept the rest of greenery to the floor. Broken petals and bits of leaf still lay on the kitchen counter, among spilt drops of water and green juice from the flower stem. She was breathing heavily, her eyes dark with anger.

'Imogen, whatever's the matter?'

'You don't know, do you? Mister wonderful bloody Daniels, the great Christian – ooh, sorry, sor*ry* the great *Humanist*. God's gift to mankind,' her voice was rising in pitch and volume, 'befriender of the poor, saviour to the emotionally bankrupt, helper of the hopeless, homeless, bloody, bloody, helpless – you haven't a sodding, clue what's the matter, have you? *Have you*? HAVE YOU?' The vase followed the flowers and shattered on the quarry tiles of the kitchen floor. She burst into tears and slumped across the kitchen counter, howling and sobbing and beating on its surface with her fists. Jerome felt a cold calm descend, as it always did when he was confronted by hysterical behaviour. He stood still, waiting for the storm to subside. He wanted to hold her, and to give comfort, but knew she would simply shake him off. More dear to him, too, was the idea that during an emotional outburst like this, he might be able to lance the hateful wen of guilt that still darkened her life, or might, at least, help her to face it more squarely.

'Actually,' he said, at last, 'I do have a clue.' He waited for the sobbing to reduce a little more. 'You're jealous. It's as simple as that. Wickedly envious, of that pathetic old couple.

You can't bear to see them happy when you think that *you* cannot be.' She was silent now, but still bent over the counter. 'And if you want my opinion, Imogen, I think it's a pretty despicable show of the worst possible emotion.' Her move took him by surprise. She simply sprang at him, her hands shaped into claws, her teeth bared, like a terrier confronting a badger. Still calm, he caught her wrists and enfolded her in his arms. He was stronger, but only just. She did not, as he expected, burst into further tears, but at last, went limp in his arms, and completely silent. Eventually, after he had held her close to him for several minutes, she spoke in a tiny, muffled voice.

'I haven't got anyone.'

'Imogen! That's nonsense.'

'I don't deserve anyone.' The voice was even smaller – hardly a whisper. He had to hold his ear close to her mouth to hear. 'I shouldn't even be alive.' He could have responded with comforting words, but wanted her to express more.

'Why not?'

She did not respond with words, but hummed her little falling cadence: 'Hm. Hm. Hmm.'

'Why Imogen?' He had to work hard, at keeping his voice level and calm. 'Why don't you deserve to be alive?'

'Hm. Hm. Hmm.'

Jerome decided to press her. 'Marcus Fitzgerald. Did he—' She pulled a hand free and placed it, gently, over Jerome's mouth. He took it away again, still holding her very closely. They were silent for a while.

'I killed him,' she whispered, eventually. 'Did you know that?'

'How?'

'After Camilla's party. We gate-crashed it.' A tiny giggle followed, quickly suppressed. 'No one wanted us at parties any more. Marcus said we should crash Camilla's – have one last . . . one last . . .' She fell silent, then, 'Hm. Hm. Hmm.'

'Have one last . . . ?'

'We got thrown out. Walked for miles afterwards – right out to Fulham. Marcus said we'd go with a flourish. We tried walking along the lines.'

'What lines?'

'The white ones, on the motorway. Cars kept hooting but Marcus shouted that they were too chicken to do the decent thing. He ran across then, and on to the flyover. I couldn't get . . . But he ran up and up and up, on the concrete edge thing. I knew he'd fall. I had to find a way to get to him, but I couldn't see how he'd got there. I ran below. I could see him dancing on the edge. Then the police car sirens were going and . . . and . . .' She was silent for a while, then, still in the low whisper. 'You see, if I'd been able to find him, to get to where he was, I'd have gone with him. I should have gone with him. I should. I should.' And at last, the tears flowed again. Jerome held her tightly, stroking the back of her head as she wept, now feeling able to whisper comfort into her unheeding ears. As her tears soaked into his shirt, he felt his own flowing on to her mussed hair. They stayed like that for several minutes, while water from the upset vase dripped on to the floor tiles.   When Jerome felt able to speak again he said, 'Marcus is the lucky one. Not you.' He kept his mouth close to her ear, wanting the feel of her hair on his cheek to stay, warm and damp. 'He's got no problems. You got left behind to face the accusations; to take your punishment.' He stroked her neck, and then held an earlobe, gently rolling it between finger and thumb. He could just feel the hardened centre where her ear had been pierced. 'But, you've paid, now. Paid with interest. You must stop hurting yourself.' He cradled her head in his two hands, turning her face to his gaze. The neck was so slender, the bones so fine and childlike. She seemed surprised to see the redness in his eyes and stared for a full minute. He stared back, watching her haunted expression ease and then turn tender.

'You *do* care,' she whispered, 'you *do!*' Then, after a moment she said, 'will you stay with me? Please?'

'For as long as you want me,' Jerome murmured, and kissed her mouth with a gentleness that belied the dam of passion about to breech within them both.

On Stir Up Sunday, Edmund Keane, the new rector of Wychgate Saint Peters strode in from the vestry and stood before his flock, doing a swift head-count before greeting everyone. Twenty-five. Not bad for such a hateful morning, he thought. He had been rector, now, for almost three months, and numbers were going up, rather than down. In time, the houses on the felled plantation site would be completed and four new families would move into the village. Perhaps there would be young children: little boys who might come home from school to kick a football about the field or, on hot days, to play by the river. Edmund imagined them hunting for sticklebacks, bathing, splashing, filling the air with their excited cries; but he suspected that their mothers would forbid all that, on account of the nitrates in the water.

In the Pilkington family pew Michael, a regular worshipper once more, sat alone, enjoying the warmth from the new oil-fired heating system, installed by the Parochial Church Council, with not a little financial help from Lady Imogen. His heart was bumping with joyful anticipation. He would be travelling to Oxford early next morning, to be with Violet and, nearer to Christmas when the university term ended, she would travel back with him, to Wychgate Manor. He glanced over at the south wall of Saint Peter's church, knowing, with an inner smile, that the knight and his lady still lay side by side in their limestone bed, at peace with one another, and at peace with their consciences.

'"Stir up, O Lord, the wills of your faithful people",' the new rector called out, in a ringing, slightly nasal tenor, '"that richly bearing the fruit of good works, they may by you be richly rewarded."' Michael's prayer, however, was not an appeal for divine succour, and at the end of the Collect, as the congregation uttered their pious 'Amen', he murmured, with a single word, his own thanksgiving for human warmth, human love:

'Violet!'